SAFE IN HIS ARMS

"So where are we, exactly?" He could almost feel her words, as if they were communicating body to body.

"An abandoned mine shaft. It was the closest shelter I could find."

"How did you know it was here?"

"This is my land," he said simply. "I know every inch of it."

Again they lay in silence. He listened to the sound of her breathing. It slowed and then deepened. Sleep would do her good. He closed his own eyes but couldn't stop thinking. He kept seeing her lying there in the snow. *If I hadn't found her* . . . He shivered at the thought. But he had. And now, despite all she'd been through, she'd be all right. He'd make certain of it.

"Michael?" She rolled over to face him, her voice hesitant, her eyes wide. "If someone was out there. In the storm, I mean. Could they . . . could they live through it?"

She suddenly sounded so young and lost, he thought his heart might break. He tightened his arms around her. "Anything is possible, Cara."

"And if they're dead . . . " She trailed off, leaving the question unfinished.

"Then I'll take care of you." He looked deep into her eyes, and before he had time to think better of it, he leaned forward, pressing his lips to hers, the contact sending lightning flashing through him. He pulled back, breathless from the depth of his own emotion, his gaze still locked with hers. "I promise."

THE
PROMISE

DEE DAVIS

LOVE SPELL NEW YORK CITY

To my father,
who taught me how to dream,
and to my mother,
who taught me how to make dreams come true.

A LOVE SPELL BOOK®

January 2002

Published by

Dorchester Publishing Co., Inc.
276 Fifth Avenue
New York, NY 10001

ISBN 0-505-52475-9

The name "Love Spell" and its logo are trademarks of Dorchester Publishing Co., Inc.

Printed in the United States of America.

Visit us on the web at www.dorchesterpub.com.

THE
PROMISE

The woods are lovely, dark and deep.
But I have promises to keep,
And miles to go before I sleep,
And miles to go before I sleep.

—Robert Frost

Prologue

"I don't believe I've ever been this happy." Cara Reynolds hugged herself in the backseat of the car. "It's been an incredible day."

"Well, you're the only daughter we have." Her father's voice was teasing, filled with love. "Besides, you're only going to be sixteen once."

"Probably just as well. I'm not certain I could take this kind of excitement every day. First you give me the new foal, then dinner at the Bristol, and now this." She held up the pendant hanging around her neck. "It's a wonder I'm not spoiled rotten."

"Who says you aren't?" Her father laughed, and Cara thought again how incredibly lucky she was. Not everyone had the family she did: a mother and father who doted not only on her, but on each other. A grandfather who loved them all. She sighed with contentment. Life was practically perfect.

"Do you really like the necklace?" Her mother shot a smile over her shoulder.

Cara caressed the smooth silver, her fingers memorizing

each line. "It's wonderful. It even feels old."

"Over a hundred years." Her father squinted suddenly as a brilliant light appeared over the top of the next hill. Colorado's San Juan Mountains, and the roads through them, were always a bit treacherous. "Come on, fellow, cut your damn brights."

"Jim. There's no need to use profanity." Her mother's voice was gentle but firm.

Cara watched, mesmerized, as the light came closer and closer, its beam filling the car with clear white luminescence, throwing everything into relief. The illumination intensified, and her mother and father were etched in her brain like an overexposed photograph.

There came an odd grinding noise, and distantly Cara heard her father curse again. Then, against the sound of metal on metal and shattering glass, the world spun totally out of control. She was thrown forward and then whipped back again, her head slamming into something hard. Light exploded in her brain, then vanished, pain crescendoing and then dissipating, blackness rushing up to meet her, engulfing her. . . .

Then the world was amazingly quiet. And cold. Something soft and wet was tickling her nose. And her head hurt. Not just run-of-the-mill hurt, but threatening-to-explode hurt. She tried to remember where she was, but her brain could barely function over the pain. With a deep breath, she forced her eyes open.

Snow.

She was lying in the snow.

Which made absolutely no sense at all.

Gritting her teeth, she slowly pulled herself up on her elbows, trying to remember where she was. The ground was bathed in an eerie light. Flickering. *Firelight?* Suddenly everything came back.

There'd been a wreck.

Her vision cleared and she focused on the burning wreckage. A pickup was balanced precariously on two wheels, its frame teetering against something else. She fought against a wave of nausea, narrowing her eyes. *Her parents' car.*

Her brain kicked in, a rush of adrenaline overriding her pain.

Her parents. Oh, God, where were her parents? Choking back a sob, she screamed their names. When her attempts to stand failed, she crawled forward inch by inch, still calling for them, her eyes searching the wreckage, her heart slamming against her ribs, the blood pounding in her brain.

The truck shifted, slamming down on the sedan underneath. She opened her mouth to cry out, but before the sound could leave her body, both cars suddenly exploded, hot flames shooting into the air, the falling snow doing nothing to dampen their fury.

A second explosion quickly followed. Cara dropped to the snow, sobs racking her body. The pain was almost unbearable. This time when the blackness came, she didn't fight its mind-numbing embrace.

Michael Macpherson pulled his sheepskin coat tighter around him. It was cold. Ball-numbing cold. He bit back a laugh, hearing his father's voice in his head. Duncan Macpherson wasn't one to mince words.

Nor was he one to be out in this kind of weather looking for cattle. No, sir, that man preferred to freeze his balls off up in the mountains looking for that elusive mother lode. Or maybe he was holed up somewhere with a bottle of whiskey for company. Michael had to admit that, right at the moment, the idea held a certain appeal. Not that he would trade places with his father.

Duncan had his own share of problems.

Then again, the man also had Rose. Michael's mother was the love of his father's life, and, truth be told, Michael longed for someone like that in his own. Someone to wait up nights for him, fire stoked, supper warming. Someone

Dee Davis

with whom he could share things, with whom he could build a life.

He sighed. His mother always said there was one man for one woman, and that his woman was out there somewhere waiting for him. All he had to do was find her. Not that he was in any hurry. After all, he was only nineteen. For the time being he supposed he was content to wait.

He squinted into the falling snow and tightened his hold on the reins. The storm was worsening, the wind whipping the snow into a frenzied dance bordering on a blizzard. Urging his horse forward, he searched the gloom for lost cattle. Pete should have been out here with him. He could have used the help, but the ranch hand was laid up with a bum knee from an accident in the corral. And Patrick . . .

Hell, who knew where that kid was these days? At the Irish Rose helping his mother and Uncle Owen, no doubt. His brother had no interest in ranching. He'd made that more than clear. Michael reined in his horse, his eyes catching the shadowy mound of a cow under a tumble of rock.

Damn. It looked dead. He swung out of his saddle and dropped to the ground, his long-legged stride taking him quickly to the fallen animal. It was obviously a calf, from the size. The beast was covered in snow, and he bent down to brush it off, his heart heavy. He needed live cattle if he was going to make a go of his homestead, and the harsh Colorado winter seemed determined to take them from him one by one.

His hand touched soft, cold skin and he froze, his eyes widening in surprise. It wasn't a calf at all. It was a woman. He knelt beside her, searching for a pulse, his eyes locked on her pale face. There were streaks of blood on her cheeks, and her hair was crusted with snow and ice.

An ice princess.

She was exquisite! Not a woman—a woman child. And unless he was badly mistaken, she certainly wasn't dead. He wrenched his gaze away from her and glanced up into the blinding fall of snow. One thing was certain: if he didn't get her to shelter fast, neither one of them would be alive much longer.

Cara woke with a start, shivering uncontrollably, with something solid and warm holding her captive. She wriggled against the bonds, not certain whether she was trying to escape or to snuggle closer to the heat. Her head felt as if it might split in two.

"Hush now, be still. I'm trying to get you warm."

The voice was soft, youthful, but very male; its heat radiated through her. She relaxed, allowing herself to settle into his embrace—which in and of itself was unusual. This was a stranger, after all, and she hadn't the slightest idea how she'd gotten here.

Still, all she knew for certain was that her head was pounding and that she was cold, and this man provided solace from one of those two ailments. For the moment that was enough. Her eyes flickered open and she saw firelight dancing on rock walls.

Firelight.

Memory slammed into her: the wreck. Her parents. She jerked free, her heart pounding, determined to go back—to find them. She tried to stand, but the world went topsy-turvy and she collapsed again. Warm arms encircled her, kept her from falling.

"I've got to find them." Her voice came out in a cracked whisper, and she wasn't certain that whoever her savior was would be able to understand her.

"Find who?" Blue eyes moved into her line of vision. Blue eyes and black hair. A face just beginning to hint at the man he would become.

Cara searched those eyes, calmed by what she saw there. "My parents. There was an accident. Everything ex . . . exploded." A vision of the two burning vehicles filled her brain, and tears rolled down her face.

Her companion frowned, one hand absently stroking her

hair, the feeling soothing and somehow right. "I didn't see anything like that."

"Well, I've got to go look. I've got to know for certain . . ." Panic rose inside her, and she tried to push it away. It wouldn't do to lose control, but it was so hard to concentrate. To think.

"You can't." His voice held a note of finality. "There's a blizzard raging outside. You wouldn't get three feet in this weather."

"But they might need me."

"You can't help them now." His eyes were full of compassion, the emotion softening the harsh planes of his face. "And I can't believe they'd want you risking your life against a storm like this." He shifted, pulling her closer into his arms. "We'll look in the morning."

She fought against the blackness that beckoned just at the edge of her consciousness, but it was compelling her to close her eyes, to surrender. The pain in her head was so intense, and she was so tired. So very tired.

Her eyes fluttered closed. "What's your name?" The words came out as a whisper.

"Michael. Michael Macpherson."

Michael. She sighed, letting the darkness carry her away. Michael was the name of an angel.

Michael trimmed the wick on his lantern, trying to save fuel. The fire had burned down to embers, and the lantern was their only source of light—or heat. He reckoned it wasn't too much longer until dawn, though, which meant hopefully they'd be able to make their way back to his ranch.

His horse snorted softly behind him, stamping with impatience, almost as if it had read his mind. But then horses were like that. The woman by the fire moaned and struggled against the confines of his blanket and greatcoat. Golden hair spilled out against the coat's tanned sheepskin hide.

The Promise

The girl was a beauty. Even with the gash on her head.

He'd tried to clean the wound the best he could, and had bandaged it, but it was obvious she needed a doctor. Which presented a problem. Even with the cessation of the storm, they'd be lucky to make the ranch. There wasn't much chance he could get her into Silverthread. There would be too damn much snow.

Hell.

She moaned again and opened her eyes, and the lamplight was reflected in the green of her gaze. Her look of confusion softened as she recognized him. "Michael."

He wasn't certain his name had ever sounded that good. He shook his head, clearing his thoughts, and moved to sit beside her, bringing the meager illumination of the lantern with him. He reached out to brush the hair back from her face. "How are you feeling?"

"Better, I think." She managed a weak grin. "Still cold, though."

He shivered in response.

"Oh, God, I've got your blanket." One hand slid out of her cocoon, confirming the fact. "And your coat. You must be freezing." She tried to sit up, but instead she grimaced and dropped back onto the floor of the cave. "I'm sorry."

He smiled, impressed by her fortitude. She wasn't one to complain. Most ladies he knew would be whining every which way, but not this one. Here she was, apologizing. "Lie still. I'll crawl in beside you. That way we'll both be warm."

She nodded, and he slid underneath both the blanket and coat, and pulled her body back against his. Her warmth seeped into him.

"It's better like this." He couldn't see her face, but he could hear a smile in her voice. Her amusement—or pleasure—regarding their situation made him happy. Perhaps he'd take her mind off whatever had happened to her parents and the fact that for now they could do nothing about it. "Has the storm stopped?" she asked.

"It's dying down. Should be gone by morning."

"And then we can look?" Her voice held a note of determination—and fear.

He understood the feeling. Once, when he was about eleven, his father had been buried in a mine. They'd worked for hours to get him out, each passing moment another step closer to his father's demise. But in the end, they'd won. Duncan had survived. Still, Michael recognized her plight. "And then we'll look," he agreed.

They were quiet for a moment, the only sounds the hissing of the dying fire and the soft movements of his horse. He could feel her breathing. Feel the rise and fall of her body against his own. He supposed in the same way she could feel him. Somehow it made the moment more intimate, as if they were joined—one sustaining the other.

"Cara."

The word filled the night air, jerking him from his reverie, her voice sweet and low. "Cara?" He sounded like a parrot.

"Cara Reynolds. That's my name." Again he heard the smile.

It was a beautiful name. He liked the way it sounded; sort of soft and strong all at the same time. Like the girl herself.

"So where are we, exactly?" He could almost feel her words, as if they were communicating body to body.

"An abandoned mine shaft. A tunnel. It was the closest shelter I could find."

"How did you know it was here?"

"This is my land," he said simply. "I know every inch of it."

Again they lay in silence. He listened to the sound of her breathing. It slowed and then deepened. Sleep would do her good. He closed his own eyes but couldn't stop thinking. He kept seeing her lying there in the snow. *If I hadn't found her . . .* He shivered at the thought.

16

But he had. And now, despite all she'd been through, she'd be all right. He'd make certain of it.

"Michael?" She rolled over to face him, her voice hesitant, her eyes wide. "If someone was out there—in the storm, I mean—could they . . . could they live through it?"

She suddenly sounded so young and lost, he thought his heart might break. He tightened his arms around her. "Anything is possible, Cara."

"And if they're dead . . . ?" She trailed off, leaving the question unfinished.

"Then I'll take care of you." He looked deep into her eyes, and before he had time to think better of it, he leaned forward, pressing his lips to hers, the contact sending lightning flashing through him. He pulled back, breathless from the depth of his emotion, his gaze still locked with hers. "I promise."

Cara woke with a start. The tunnel was filled with half-light. Morning had obviously arrived. She sat up gingerly, her eyes scanning the cave for Michael. She sighed with disappointment; except for a horse, the mine shaft was empty. But a fire burned merrily in a stone firepit. Surely that was evidence that he would be right back. All she had to do was wait.

She explored the injured side of her head carefully, satisfied to note that the bandage felt dry. At least the bleeding had stopped, which was more than she could say for the pounding. Still, all in all, she seemed to have survived.

Guilt racked her. How could she be so casual when her parents might be out there this very moment, injured or worse? She sucked in a ragged breath and fought against the panic that threatened to overwhelm her. Michael would help. He'd promised. She had to hang on to that hope.

Using the side of the cave to brace herself, she pulled to a standing position, still clutching Michael's blanket around her. The world tilted and then slowly, slowly righted itself again.

"Cara?"

Michael. She smiled despite herself and took a wobbly step forward. The voice called her name again, and it was a moment before she registered that it was not Michael's. It was her grandfather's. Joy welled up inside her. Michael had obviously gone for help. Sucking in a fortifying breath, she began to make her way out of the cave.

Somehow, between Michael and her grandfather, everything would be all right.

Michael stood up, carefully capping his canteen. At least the worst was over. The sky was still a hazy white-gray, threatening snow. But the wind was gone, and the air dry. With any luck they'd make it to the ranch before nightfall.

He carefully made his way up the slippery slope of the creek bank. The snow was deceptively thick in places, and he knew that beneath the soft banks there was often ice.

A broken leg out here in this kind of weather would most likely be the death of a man. And he had no intention of cashing in now. Not after last night.

He reached the scattered pile of tailings that marked the entrance to the mine. A small blue spruce stretched its frail limbs from the center of the loose rocks and debris. Michael smiled at the tenacity of the tree. It would probably never make it, he thought, but it sure had courage to try.

A lot like the girl who slept in the tunnel. She had grit, all right. And she was a beauty, too. *One woman for every man.* His mother's voice filled his mind, and he smiled. Maybe, just maybe, she was right. But right now there were more important things to think about. Like survival. He stepped into the mouth of the tunnel.

At first it seemed his eyes were playing tricks on him. Then he thought he was going crazy. But no, the facts were plain as the nose on his face. His gear was right where he'd left it. And the little fire burned cheerily in the stone ring he'd made.

But the blanket by the fire was gone, and with it the girl he'd held through the night. His heart jumped, and he felt panic rip through him. "Cara?" He called her name softly at first, then loud enough that the name echoed off the icy rock walls of the mine.

"Cara?"

Chapter One

San Juan Mountains, Colorado, 1888

Michael Macpherson reined in Roscoe, horse and rider stopping at the top of the rise. Below him the lights of Clune twinkled in the distance, the little ranch resembling a fairyland.

Home.

He sighed and began the descent down the mountain. It had been a long day. But then, that was what ranching life was all about—long days and, in his case, even longer nights. He blew out a breath and then discarded his train of thought. No sense dwelling on what couldn't be. He'd chosen his path in life, and he'd do well to accept it.

Besides, there were people depending on him. His brother, Patrick, and old Pete. His father. Hell, even Owen depended on him some—no other way was the inn's owner going to have prime steer to serve to the hungry miners who swarmed the Irish Rose twenty-four hours a day.

He bit back a smile. All in all, life might be a tad empty, but it was basically good.

The Promise

A gunshot cracked through the stillness of the night, and Michael felt a burning as something struck him.

Son of a bitch!

He wheeled his horse around, simultaneously reaching for his rifle. The movement brought only fiery pain, and his vision blurred, darkness threatening to overtake him. With a shake of his head, he cleared his mind. Passing out would mean death. And just at the moment he wasn't inclined to die.

He moved forward, riding as fast as he could on the downward slope. One stumble and they were as good as dead, but going too slowly would have the same result. A conundrum. He gritted his teeth and reached for his shotgun again. Another bullet whizzed past his ear. He abandoned the effort, slowing for a second, risking a look behind him.

Nothing.

Whoever was shooting was well hidden. He cursed again under his breath, his strength ebbing because of his blood loss. He'd never make it to the ranch. Hell, in just a few more yards he'd be out in the open, a moving target. One that would be hard to miss.

With a quick jerk of the reins he turned Roscoe, and together they moved back up the canyon toward a stand of trees in the distance. If he could just reach the spruce . . . the abandoned mine. Maybe he'd make it.

Another shot rang out, this one farther behind him. Good—he'd managed to gain a lead. With another twist he cut into the pines. *That ought to stop the bastard—at least for a minute or two.* With the dark, he would be nearly invisible in the trees, the rocky tumble of the mountain reaching toward him from the left providing further safety.

He stopped, listening. Everything was quiet, just the soft whisper of the winds in the aspens. He slid to the ground, his head going fuzzy again. He touched his shoulder, unsurprised to find that his shirt was wet with blood.

With a sharp intake of breath, he slapped Roscoe on the hindquarters, sending the horse off into the night. If someone was following him, that ought to provide a nice distraction.

Scrambling farther into the trees, his eyes sought out the scraggly branches of the blue spruce. Despite the odds the little tree had made it. Now over six feet, it still lacked girth, but it had grit. And beyond it lay his sanctuary.

Michael locked his eyes on the tree, fighting the waves of dizziness that threatened to swamp him. All he had to do was make it a few more steps and he'd be safe. He sent a silent prayer to the luckless miner who had started the tunnel, then abandoned it. The tunnel would now provide a haven for him as it had once done for Cara.

The thought of her gave him a sudden surge of strength, and he barreled across the stream and up the rocky embankment to the tree. Leaning against its trunk for a moment, he fought against the pain. *Just a few more steps.*

Rocks below him skittered down the creek bank.

Hell.

He froze in the shadow of the spruce, afraid even to breathe. Any movement now would mean certain death. The night grew quiet. Whoever was down there was waiting, too. Listening. He strained through the dark to try to see his assailant's face, to know who was hunting him. But the dark and the trees provided the killer with the same protection they afforded Michael.

In the distance a horse nickered. *Roscoe.* Michael smiled. Somewhere below him the killer cursed softly, and then Michael heard the welcome sound of horseshoes against rock. The man was leaving, following Roscoe.

Michael waited, letting the tree hold him upright, then finally took a cautious step away from the spruce. The mine was waiting—its black opening yawning darkly against the sharp rocks of the mountainside. His head was starting to spin, and he felt weak all over. He knew that time was running out. He needed shelter, and he needed it now.

With a last burst of energy, he pulled himself up the incline and into the mouth of the cave. The darkness therein swallowed him, and he forced himself to crawl further into its waiting arms, knowing that it was a friend. A sanctuary.

Finally, deep in the tunnel, he allowed himself to slump against a wall, closing his eyes and focusing on his memories. Memories of a night nine years ago—a magical night and a beautiful girl. *Cara.*

In his mind he felt her there with him. Felt her body pressed against his. Felt her healing warmth. And with a sigh he allowed himself to slide into those dreams.

Loralee stood in the soft glow of the candlelight and looked in the mirror. Her straight, lank hair hung in two thin plaits on either side of her head, accentuating the thin angles of her tired face. She scrubbed at the rouge on her cheeks with the back of her hand. Every day she was more a whore and less the girl she'd once been.

Loralee wasn't even her real name. Not that anyone out here knew that. She'd picked it because she'd seen it on a sign pasted to the saloon wall when she'd started working in Del Norte. She'd even made one of the gambling men read the whole poster to her.

It seemed this other Loralee was a traveling singer. She'd come from some far-off place. Nacado . . . something. Anyway, the name sounded musical, and it was a far sight better than Alice. Besides, nobody used their real names in this business. It just wasn't done. With a sigh, she turned from the mirror.

Well, at least there didn't appear to be any more customers tonight. And Duncan, God bless him, had paid her enough to warrant turning out the red lantern in her front window. She wrapped a shawl around her shoulders, crossed to the door, and slid the heavy bar into place. The irony of the situation didn't escape her. She was probably safer alone in her bed than she was with someone in it. And though the bolt was strong, the door wasn't. A good swift kick would probably send the whole wall tumbling down.

She peered out the window at the eerie red glow coming from a dozen or so windows with lanterns identical to hers. Lifting its globe with the edge of her shawl, she blew out her light. A soft whinny drew her attention.

A sorrel horse tied to a post out front tossed its head indignantly. Jack. What the heck was Jack doing here? Duncan had left hours ago. She arched her back, rubbing the hollow at her waist. At least it seemed like hours.

Most likely he was off to the saloons again. He'd been fairly well lit when he had left her place, but it never ceased to amaze her how much a man could drink if he put his mind to it. And if ever a man was in a frame of mind to drink, it was Duncan Macpherson.

The shadows lengthened, and she untied the thin cord that pulled back the tent canvas that passed for her window drapery. Turning her back to it, she headed for the iron bedstead in the corner. Its linen sheets were yellowed with age, the quilt patched and threadbare, but they were clean. She prided herself on that. Her momma had taught her that much.

Cleanliness was next to godliness, and, Lord help her, she could use all the help she could get in that direction. Smiling, she threw her wrapper on the spindly stool that served as a chair and jumped into bed. The tin stove in the corner barely put out enough heat to warm water, let alone an entire room.

Most times it wasn't a problem. Men seemed to generate their own heat. And it was her lot in life to get those fires a-going. Well, most of them. Some, like Duncan, didn't want that kind of fire lit. He mostly came to talk. A bit of female companionship was all he was looking for. Not that she minded. No, indeedy. He paid, same as everyone else.

The Promise

And all she had to do was listen, or pretend to listen.

And Duncan was different, in other ways. He treated her real nice. Not like some of the boys. There were some who liked it rough. Real rough. But they weren't welcome here. She might be at the bottom of the barrel, socially speaking, but she had rules all the same, and she expected her boys to abide by them. Not that she always had a choice. She shivered and settled back into the soft fluff of her pillow, tucking the quilt under her chin.

Yup. She'd take Duncan any day. He might be a bit long in the tooth, but he treated her like a lady. Or how she imagined a lady was treated. And he talked to her about important things. Why, just tonight he told her he'd found silver. Not that that was news, exactly. Everybody around here was always boasting about finding silver, but Duncan had said this was different. There'd been a light in his eyes. She had a feeling he'd found a true strike, sure enough. A big one, too.

The only thing that puzzled her was him talking about the Promise. How could he have found silver there? Everybody knew that mine had played out years ago. Why, Duncan Macpherson ought to know it better than most. The Promise was his mine, after all. His and that "don't get mud on my boots" Owen Prescott.

She placed a hand on the cool silver of the locket between her breasts. Whatever it was he was rambling on about, she'd keep his secret safe. He'd kept hers, after all. She'd ask him about it tomorrow when he came back for Jack. One thing was sure as sunrise with Duncan Macpherson: he would never willingly leave that sorrel behind. He loved that old horse, maybe more than his boys.

Heck, maybe more than his wife. Loralee sighed and snuggled deeper into the covers, sleep starting to overtake her. There was something sad about a man whose best friend was a horse. Yes, indeedy, that was a true tragedy.

* * *

Patrick Macpherson woke with a start. The stillness of the night surrounded him, and after a few moments he relaxed slightly. Moonlight spilled through the window, casting long shadows across the rough log walls. Everything seemed peaceful, but something had awakened him.

With a groan he swung out of bed, cringing when his bare feet hit the cold plank floor. Muttering an oath, he reached for his socks and pulled them on before padding across the room to the doorway. The fire in the main room had burned low, but its embers still cast a faint light across the room.

That, combined with the moonlight, made the room seem abnormally bright after the dim shadows of his bedroom. From his position in the doorway, he could see practically the whole cabin. The big iron stove cast a long black shadow across the floor. The clutter of dirty dinner dishes littered the plank table in the center of the room, testament to the lack of feminine influence at Clune.

His father's cot in the corner was empty, not that that was surprising. Duncan was usually somewhere up in the mountains looking for another strike, or down in town drinking himself into a stupor. Between the two, it seemed there wasn't much time for his sons.

Things had been different when his mother was around. But as Michael always said, there wasn't much sense in crying over spilt milk. Not that that made a lick of sense to Patrick. He hated milk. Now if it had been a shot of whiskey—well, there might have been a good reason to cry. Well, not that he loved whiskey so much, either. Not after last night . . . That was his father's curse.

The door to Michael's room stood ajar. Patrick couldn't shake the feeling that something wasn't right. Unlike his father, his brother was as predictable as a dog in heat. And Michael always, always, slept with his door shut.

Walking cautiously now, he crossed to his brother's room. A quick look inside confirmed what he already suspected: Michael wasn't there. Which meant something was indeed very wrong. A fellow could count on Michael to do pretty much exactly what he said he was going to do. Patrick glanced out the window at the moon, trying to remember what his brother had told him. He'd been heading for the high country to check on the herd, but he'd specifically said he'd be back by nightfall.

If Patrick hadn't spent the wee hours of the previous night playing cards in Owen's saloon, he might have known his brother hadn't come home as expected. Instead he'd stumbled home at midmorning, listened to his brother's endless speech on responsibility, and then collapsed in his bed. It looked like he'd managed to sleep the day away, and a good portion of the night

Damn.

Truth be told, he hadn't meant to waste the night in Silverthread. He really wasn't a gambler, and he sure as hell couldn't hold his liquor. But yesterday had been the anniversary of his mother's disappearance, and, well, he'd just needed something to take the edge off the memory.

Michael wouldn't talk about it. He never talked about it. Truth was, he never talked about anything. Anyway, Patrick had let a moment of self-pity turn into a night of whiskey and gaming, when he should have been here— helping his brother. Which meant he was no better than his father. Somehow that made him feel worse than he already did.

A soft nickering sound filtered in through the window, snapping him out of his reverie. Patrick slid into the shadows, slowly moving to get his Winchester. With an audible click, he cocked the rifle and stepped over to the cabin door. The nicker sounded again, this time followed by the thud of a hoof. Taking a deep breath, Patrick sprang into action, throwing open the door and stepping out into the night air, his gun barrel leading the way.

Cool moonlight washed the dusty ground a pale silver. Patrick froze, his eyes darting back and forth, looking for the source of the noise. A soft snort was accompanied by the whinny of a horse. A hungry one. Patrick relaxed as the roan gelding stomped impatiently.

He'd left his bed for a damn horse? Laying the Winchester across the porch railing, he stepped gingerly off the wood platform onto the rocky ground, wishing belatedly that he'd had the good sense to put his boots on.

"What the hell you doing out of the barn, Roscoe?" Stupid thing to call a horse. Michael had read it in a book somewhere and thought it was a fine name; Patrick thought it was ridiculous.

He hobbled across the ground, the rocks biting into his feet. Reaching the gelding, he grabbed the reins and started to pull the horse toward the stable. "Michael had better have a good reason for not keeping an eye on you." He looked back at the horse and stopped dead in his tracks. Roscoe was still fully outfitted. With a curse, he reached up behind the saddle. Michael's gear was still there, and, more sobering, his rifle was still sheathed in its leather holster.

Patrick absently wiped at a wet splotch on the stirrup and was in the process of cleaning his hand on his leg when he realized what he was doing. Slowly he raised the hand. Moisture glistened black on his fingers in the starlight. The sharp metallic smell of blood filled his nostrils.

"Patrick? That you?"

Patrick looked up as a weathered old cowboy stepped out onto the porch of an equally weathered shanty.

"Whatcha got there?" Pete Reeder slapped a dilapidated Stetson on his head and strode across the yard. Like Patrick, he was clad in long johns. Unlike Patrick, he'd had the sense to put his boots on.

"It's Roscoe." Patrick met the watery blue eyes of Clune's foreman. "Seems he came back without Michael." He held out his bloody hand and nodded toward the stirrup.

Pete examined the stained leather. Looking back at Patrick, he frowned and spat. "Son of a bitch. Ain't no way that horse would leave Michael unless . . ."

Patrick felt a swell of panic rise inside him. "He's not dead, Pete. He's just had an accident. Maybe he sent Roscoe to us. To let us know he was hurt." He couldn't imagine what he'd do if something happened to his brother. Michael was the stable one. Without him, and his desire for a place they could call home, there wouldn't have been a Clune. Hell, there probably wouldn't be a Patrick.

He shivered. "Michael's probably lying out there somewhere right now, hurt and bleeding. Or worse." He grabbed Roscoe's reins and started to swing up into the saddle.

"Whoa there, boy; where do ya think you're going?"

"I'm going to find my brother."

Pete clamped one big hand around Patrick's arm, effectively stopping further motion. "In your drawers?"

Patrick glanced down and flushed. "No. I'll get my pants."

"And your boots."

Patrick shot a look of exasperation at the old man. "And my boots."

Pete stroked the long handles of his mustache, his leathery forehead wrinkled in thought. "Ain't no use going out there now. The moon's a-settin' and you'll be blind as a posthole."

"Maybe. But I've got to do something. I can't leave him out there." Patrick let go of the saddle and moved toward the cabin, Pete following close behind.

"I ain't telling you to leave him. I'm just suggesting we wait a couple more hours until the sun's up. Can't tell a rock from a pit out there right now. You go off into the mountains like that and I'll be searching for two injured men, 'stead of just one."

They stopped on the porch and Patrick looked up at the sky. The moon had almost disappeared, leaving only the last of the stars to light the night. Pete, as always, was

29

right. "Fine, then we'll wait. Two hours. No more."

Pete settled a hand on Patrick's shoulder, his touch comforting. "I know you're worried about your brother. Can't say this sets well with me either, but we're gonna find him. We just gotta hold on for the light."

Patrick looked out toward the mountains that ringed the valley. They were little more than menacing shadows, blending into the dark sky. He wasn't much of a praying man, but he prayed now. Prayed that his brother was safe out there. Prayed that he could hang on until morning.

Prayed that he was still alive.

Chapter Two

San Juan Mountains, Colorado, present day

Cara stood by the edge of the stream staring up at the blue spruce. It called to her mockingly, promising things that could never be. She chewed on the corner of her lip, hesitating, wondering what it was exactly she'd thought to accomplish by coming here.

Drawing in a lungful of crisp mountain air, she let her eyes roam across the narrow valley. The beauty of the mountains was almost unbearable: blues and greens mottled with the oranges and reds of Indian paintbrush and the yellow of coreopsis, the silver and brown of the jagged rocks protruding like broken and forgotten limbs through gentle rolling meadows.

This land was as familiar to her as breathing. And yet, angry and arrogant, she'd run away from it all. A part of her would regret that forever. But she was back now, determined to make a new start. She'd moved into her late grandfather's cabin, established a gallery in the nearby town, and now at last she was ready to try and make peace with her past.

Starting with the tunnel.

With a sigh she crossed the creek, stopping in front of the spruce, memories threatening to overwhelm her. Her parents had been gone nine years, but the night of their death lived on in her mind, teasing her with might-have-beens. She remembered it all: the crash, the fire, the cold snow against her face. And Michael—she remembered Michael.

Only of course she didn't. Like most things good in her life, Michael had been an illusion. The product of a mind tormented by tragedy. Now here she was, standing before an overgrown tree, looking for a doorway to something forever lost.

She skirted the great spruce, making her way through overgrown underbrush and saplings until she was flush against the outcropping of rock that marked the side of the mountain. She frowned at the solid rock before her. Maybe she had the wrong tree. Or maybe she was just coming at it from the wrong angle.

Trying again, she edged her way closer to the tree, ducking under its overhanging branches. Immediately a gloomy hush descended as the tree limbs effectively blocked out light and sound. Holding on to the trunk and keeping her head low, she moved behind the tree. She could see a jumble of fallen rocks at her feet.

With a surge of certainty, she pushed forward through fragrant branches, her vision blocked by the thickness of the tree's pinecone-laden limbs, feeling a lot like Lucy passing through the wardrobe into Narnia. The tree in her memory had certainly been much smaller.

Ducking almost level with the ground, she finally emerged from underneath the spruce. There was a narrow, rock-strewn opening between the tree and the abutting mountainside. She drew in a breath and took a small step forward, waiting for her eyes to adjust to the faint sunlight that filtered through the branches.

Looking up, she could just make out the black gap marking the entrance to the mine. It was barely visible between two large outcroppings of sharp-edged stone, rocky sentries guarding their long-forgotten treasure.

With a smile of triumph, she bounded up the small incline. Standing at the mouth of the cave she felt the years roll away. It hadn't changed much. The entrance still beckoned, its mouth shored up with timbers carefully hauled into place by some long-dead miner.

She stepped inside, squinting to see in the dark gloom of the interior, wishing for a flashlight. The man-made walls were rough-edged and slick with moisture. The air was still and stale, a sharp change after the fragrant mountain breeze. She hadn't been here in years. Not since the last time she'd come back looking for Michael.

She felt a surge of disappointment. The tunnel was empty. She hadn't expected to find anything. Not after all this time. But still, a part of her had hoped . . . She stepped farther inside the tunnel, reining in her emotions. This was supposed to be about closure, after all.

As she recalled, the passageway wasn't deep, only a hundred feet or so. Whoever had dug it had abandoned the shaft almost before he'd started. The lead he'd no doubt been following had petered out before it could point the way to any riches the mountain might hold.

The San Juans were riddled with such mines. Some of them had been successful—mines like the Amethyst, Holy Moses, or the Last Chance. Some of them were legendary—like the fabled Promise. But mainly they were empty holes like this one, carved out of the side of a mountain and then abandoned. They were dreams quashed before even begun. Cara felt a rush of sadness for this shaft's unknown miner and hoped his dreams had found fruition elsewhere.

She stopped about twenty feet into the tunnel, at the

place where the weak light finally played out. Against the wall she could just make out an old lantern. In her mind's eye, she could see Michael holding the very same lamp, its golden glow spreading through the tunnel, illuminating the walls, casting dancing shadows.

She sighed, looking down at the remains of the lantern. It looked far older than nine years; the globe was broken, the metal base rusted with age. Her memories were imagined. Reality bending in on itself, creating something of nothing.

Michael Macpherson was a figment of her imagination. Someone she'd conjured up to help her through the worst ordeal of her life. He wasn't real. Her doctors had told her that. Her grandfather had told her. And now, at last, she believed them. Shaking her head to clear her thoughts, she turned to go. There was nothing for her here. She'd been silly to come.

The faint light from the entrance was almost blinding after the complete darkness of the tunnel. She felt dizzy, and her head spun for a moment, making her almost lose her balance. Reaching for the cold comfort of the rock wall, she leaned against it until the moment passed.

Steady again, she breathed deeply, suddenly needing to be outside in the fresh air. Stories of mine gas and cave-ins crowded into her brain, vying for attention. Shutting the thoughts out, she made her way back to the entrance, and was just about to step into the pine-shadowed sunlight when something behind her, in the depths of the tunnel, shifted.

Rocks rattled against stone as they rolled across the floor. She froze, her heart pounding, waiting for another noise. Curiosity battled with terror. When the mine remained silent, curiosity won and she took a hesitant step back inside.

Squinting into the darkness, she tried to make out the source of the sound, a little voice in her head calmly listing off all the wild animals that could conceivably have made the tunnel their home. It was enough to make her step back toward the entrance again.

Then, just as she turned to leave, something groaned.

She stopped, took a deep breath and swung around again to face the darkness. The groan repeated itself, reaching out from the gloom like a disembodied spirit.

Someone was in pain.

"Hello?" Her voice echoed eerily off the walls. "Is someone there?"

She waited, but there was no answer, nothing at all except the hollow silence. Uncertain now, actually doubting herself, she squinted into the darkness. She *had* heard something, but without any further guidance it would be impossible—and foolhardy, her mind whispered—to try to find the source.

She reached instinctively for the smooth disk of her pendant, the cool feel of its silver casing calming her. Another rustling sound filled the mine shaft and she released the necklace, taking a hesitant step forward. This time the noise was followed by a muffled curse.

She sucked in a breath. "Can you hear me?" Silence. "I want to help, but I can't find you in the dark without a little guidance." She waited, but everything remained quiet. Finally, giving up, she turned to go, moving up the slight slope back toward daylight.

"Wait." The single word echoed through the cavern, somewhere between a plea and a command.

Hairs rose on the back of her neck, but she turned around anyway, caution warring with compassion.

"I'm . . . over . . . here." The voice was louder now, and decidedly male. Compassion won out by a nose.

She stepped over the line of light and moved around a bend into complete darkness. Groping for the wall, she tried to get her bearings. If she remembered correctly, the tunnel went on for forty feet or so, then turned again to go deeper into the mountain before dead-ending into solid rock. Hopefully the owner of the voice wasn't too far ahead.

"Can you still hear me?" She waited, her heart still pounding.

"I'm here." His voice was weak, but clear. "I don't suppose you have a light?"

"No such luck, I'm afraid."

"There's a lantern back there somewhere." His voice filled the darkness, warm and alive, but she could hear the underlying pain.

"I saw it. But it's beyond being useful. The glass is broken."

A sharp curse rang out through the darkness. Concern laced through her. "Are you all right?" She leaned against the wall, all her senses focused on listening.

"I've been better." Was that humor she heard in his voice?

"Can you move?"

There was another groan. "Not without help."

"Hang on, then. I'm coming." She inched forward slowly, keeping one hand out in front of her and the other pressed firmly to the wall.

"Stop." The word was a command. Even in a weakened state, in the dark, this man had presence. "I'm right in front of you."

"How in the world could you possibly know that?" she grumbled, dropping to her knees, both hands stretched in front of her.

"You haven't exactly been quiet." There was the amusement again.

"It wasn't my primary concern." Her hands met solid muscle, and the man groaned. "Oh, God, I'm so sorry," she said. She felt something sticky under her fingers and recoiled. "You're bleeding."

"I know."

"Well, there isn't much I can do for you if I can't see

you." She strove to keep her voice calm, businesslike. "We'll just have to get you into the light."

A resigned sigh echoed through the tunnel. "All right."

"You can lean on me. I'll help you up." She wrapped her arm around his chest and felt his arm drape heavily across her shoulders. "You ready?" He groaned in answer and she felt him nod. "All right, then, on three. One . . . two . . ." She shifted her weight to her inside leg and pushed up with the other one. *"Three."*

He was heavy, and the smell of him enveloped her—raw male mixed with the sick, sweet smell of blood. He groaned again, but managed to pull himself to his feet. They stood for a minute, getting their balance, then slowly began to move forward.

Cara kept her hand against the wall, following it as the path wended its way upward. Finally, turning the bend, they stepped into the weak light of the entrance tunnel. The man stopped, eyeing the opening with concern. "This is far enough."

"But we need to get you to a doctor."

"No doctors." It was too dark to see his expression but she could sense his stubbornness.

Exasperation flooded through her. "Fine." She glared at him. "Look, my house is just down the creek a bit. It's an easy walk." Without a wounded man. No, she had to stay positive. "Do you think you can make it?"

"I can try. But first you'll have to help me stop the bleeding." He motioned to the rapidly spreading stain on his shirt.

"Here?" She tried to keep the panic out of her voice. First aid wasn't her strong suit.

He smiled weakly, the white of his teeth gleaming in the dark. "Don't think I have a choice."

"All right." She nodded, accepting the inevitable. Carefully she lowered him to a sitting position, the strain making her muscles ache. He stretched out his long legs and leaned back against the rock wall. She gingerly pulled his shirt open, exposing a broad expanse of male chest covered by a light dusting of dark hair. The wound lay just to the right of his shoulder. His shirt had fused itself to the skin.

"This is going to hurt." She looked up, trying to see his eyes, but the shadows were too deep.

"Just do it." His voice was taut, and she could feel his muscles bunching in preparation.

Gritting her teeth, she pulled the blood-soaked cloth away with a quick tug. She felt him flinch. "Sorry." His skin was raw and covered with blood, some of it dried and crusty. This wasn't a new wound. "How long have you been here?"

"Don't know, really." He closed his eyes, his voice fading.

"Come on. Stay with me."

He nodded, rallying a bit. "You can use my shirt for a bandage."

She eyed the dirty remnants, shaking her head. "I'll use mine. It's cleaner."

"You'll freeze."

"I'll be fine." She slipped out of the shirt. "I've got a T-shirt on underneath." With a forced breath, she turned back to the task at hand. After ripping the bottom of the shirt into makeshift bandages, she tore a sleeve off to use for padding, then gingerly bound the wound with the strips she had torn.

Satisfied that she had at least stanched the bleeding, she sat back on her heels. He was breathing rapidly and even in the shadows she could see that he was deathly white. Alarmed, she ran a hand across his cheek. His skin was on fire. "You've got a fever. We've got to get you out of here. *Now.*"

"I know." The words were incredibly weak, and she shivered at the thought of trying to get him out of the tunnel and to her house. He wasn't a small man.

She wrapped an arm around him, deliberately keeping

her voice light. "First thing to do is to get you on your feet without reopening your injury."

Together they struggled to their feet, then, precariously balanced, tried a few steps forward. Sweat trickled down between her breasts as she supported his weight. At this rate she'd need a miracle to get him home.

What had been a few easy steps for her was like an obstacle course with a man draped across her shoulders. There was no question of using the rocks to cross the stream. The man remained stoically silent, but she felt his muscles tense as they plunged across the frigid creek.

Icy water soaked through her tennis shoes. "Are you okay?"

The answer was more of a groan than a word, but she was grateful that he was still conscious. They struggled up the rocky embankment on the other side, and she prayed that she had the strength to get him home.

They stopped for a moment at the top of the rise, Cara shifting to more comfortably support his weight. The afternoon sun caught him in its light, and his haggard features were illuminated. His face clearly visible for the first time, Cara found her breath stuttered to a stop, her heart following suit.

She knew this face. She'd memorized it in her dreams.

"Your name?" The words came out on a whisper as she fought for air, for control.

"Michael. Michael Macpherson." His blue eyes snapped open, his gaze colliding with hers. She could see the recognition there. Feel it.

She swallowed, a wave of dizziness washing through her. Her heart rejoiced.

Her mind rebelled: Michael Macpherson didn't exist.

Chapter Three

Patrick stopped at the top of the rise, reining in his black stallion. From this vantage point a man could see most of the valley below. The Rio Grande twisted and turned in the distance, a wide silver band carved into the blues and greens of the surrounding countryside. Nestled into a horseshoe-shaped curve, he could see Clune.

The framing of the new barn shone white against a backdrop of brownish green meadow grass, dwarfing the older structures. The clouds hung low, almost hiding the mountains. Later the sun would burn them off, but for now the somber sky mirrored his thoughts.

He'd been riding since sunrise, impatiently exploring the gulches and hollows of the mountains, but there was no sign of his brother. Rationally he knew it was hopeless. He could look in a thousand places and there'd still be a couple thousand more. It was too easy for a person to get lost up here. Between unpredictable weather and predators, an injured man didn't stand much of a chance.

The sound of hooves against the rocks filtered into his thoughts, pulling his attention away from the valley. With narrowed eyes he watched the approaching horse, trying to identify the rider. It wasn't Pete. He'd be on the other side of the ridge, searching the higher ground. They'd agreed to meet later down on the road.

Patrick laid a hand on his rifle, just in case. The horseman drew closer, raising an arm in greeting. Patrick nodded as he recognized the man, wondering what in the hell Amos Striker was doing this far out of town.

"Mornin', Patrick." Amos reined in his horse, stopping a few feet away.

"Amos." Patrick studied the younger man's face. With his curly blond hair and whisker-free face, he resembled a choirboy more than a gunman, but Patrick knew his looks were deceptive. He couldn't really say why, but there was something about the sheriff he just didn't like. "What brings you out this way so early?"

"Mrs. Hurley. She seems to have lost Arless again."

Patrick smiled despite himself. Lena Hurley was a bear of a woman with a voice to match her stature. Her husband, Arless, periodically took respite from her constant bellowing by up and disappearing. Not content to let her husband roam around on his own, Lena usually waited a few days and then sent for the sheriff. "You think he's up there somewhere?" Patrick nodded toward the peaks behind him.

Amos fingered the brim of his hat. "Well, he's been known to use that line shack of yours. Thought it was worth a look-see."

"Any luck?"

"Nah, he ain't there. Ran into Pete, though. He told me about Michael. Thought maybe you could use some help."

Patrick felt the moment of lightness slip away. He had more important things to think about than Mrs. Hurley's runaway husband. "Much obliged. I've searched the gulches west of Shallow Creek, and Pete is covering the area north of here."

"Fine, I'll head east. There's a couple of places a man

41

could shelter up in Grenard Gulch. First thing I'd do if I were shot is head for shelter, and Grenard is the closest canyon to the road."

Patrick glanced sharply at Amos. "What makes you think Michael was shot?"

Amos frowned, studying the reins in his hand. "Don't know, really. Pete said you boys found blood on Roscoe's saddle. I just figured the most likely thing out here to draw blood is a gunshot. 'Sides, you know as well as I do that we've been having trouble with road agents."

Patrick pushed his hat back, his gaze leveled on the sheriff. "Yeah, but most of that's been up toward Antelope Springs."

Amos grinned, his blue eyes crinkling at the corners. "Well, now, never did know an outlaw who was much interested in boundaries."

"True enough." Patrick swallowed his sense of uneasiness. "Guess we'd best get to it. Right now the most important thing is to find my brother."

"Right. I'll signal with this"—he patted his Winchester—"if I find him."

"Same here. I'll meet you at the turnoff to Clune in a couple of hours."

Amos nodded and wheeled his horse around. Patrick watched as they galloped away, a slow-moving cloud of dust spreading in their wake. With a sigh Patrick turned the stallion, easing him into a smooth canter and heading for the slopes to the south, his eyes scanning the terrain for some sign of his brother.

"I'll tell you, Loralee, I heard you last night and I know he said something about silver."

Loralee grabbed the wad of soggy linen and rubbed it vigorously against a rock in the creek behind the cribs. Corabeth always had her nose in everyone else's business, but, besides being a busybody, she'd been a good friend, and in Loralee's line of work, true friends were a rare thing.

"Loralee, you're not listening to me. I want to know if Duncan really did hit it big."

Loralee turned to look at the girl sitting on the rock, shading her eyes against the early morning sun. Corabeth was a tiny thing, her head crowned with a swirl of henna-dyed curls. At the moment, like Loralee, she was clad in little more than bloomers and a wrapper. There wasn't much sense in getting dressed. The cribs weren't one of those elegant parlor houses where the customers behaved like gentlemen and the whores acted like fancy ladies. No, sir, the cribs were the poor man's version and the niceties were few and far between.

"I don't know, Corabeth. Honestly. Duncan wasn't making a lot of sense last night. He'd been hitting the whiskey pretty hard, and you know as well as I do that he's always bragging about striking it big, but it never amounts to anything." She wrung the water out of the chemise she'd been scrubbing and dropped it into a basket.

"Well, I don't understand why you let the old geezer see you, anyway. He's old enough to be your father." She wrinkled her nose in disgust.

Loralee shuddered. "Believe me, he's nothing like my father." Finished with the wash, she stood and bent to pick up the laundry basket. "He's harmless enough. And he always pays me. Which is more than I can say for some of the men you see. Besides, we get on."

Corabeth followed Loralee back to her door. "Well, I didn't mean nothing by it. Heavens, sugar, it ain't up to me who you see and don't see." Her usually perky mouth settled into a pointed pout.

Loralee smiled. It was just too hard to keep secrets from Corabeth. Surely she could share a little of what Duncan said. There couldn't be any harm in that, could there? Stepping back, she motioned the other girl inside. Corabeth sat down on the bed, bouncing experimentally. Loralee dropped the basket in the corner. She'd hang them out to dry later.

"I still don't see why you do your own wash. The Chinese laundry behind the livery stable does a fine job and it ain't even expensive."

Loralee dropped onto the stool with a sigh. "You know I have to save everything I make. I can't afford to let any of it go for luxuries like laundry."

Her friend reached out to grasp her hand. "I know, honey, and I think it's right nice of you to send all that money to your Mary. But I don't think using a few cents a week for laundry is gonna hurt that child one bit."

Loralee brushed a tired hand through her hair. "You're probably right, but the money's all I got to give her. I know it isn't the same as havin' a mama, but it's the best I can do." She felt her head tighten as the tears threatened. With a groan, she pulled her hand away, automatically reaching up to touch her locket.

Corabeth's eyes settled on the necklace. "I see you got it back."

Loralee nodded. "Got it back last night. Duncan fixed it, good as new. Can't even see where the chain was broke." She held it out in demonstration.

"Mary knows you love her, Loralee." Corabeth's words were gentle.

Loralee bit back her tears, determined to change the subject. "So, do you want to know about the silver, or don't you?"

Corabeth bounced excitedly on the bed, her brown eyes dancing with delight. "Do tell."

"Well, there really isn't that much. Duncan was pretty far gone last night, but he kept rambling on about finding the silver and how it was going to change everything. Honestly, Corabeth, I've never seen him so excited."

"Not even when . . ."

Loralee blushed, surprised that she could still do so. "We don't do that. He just comes to talk."

"Corabeth? You in here, darlin'?" Arless Hurley poked his head in the doorway. "If I have to wait a second more, I swear I'll bust a gut."

"Or something," Corabeth whispered as she rose from the bed. "Why, Arless, you big stud, how'd you ever get away from that monster you call a wife?"

Loralee watched as the two of them sashayed out the door. Walking to the window, she pulled back the drape. Jack was still there. His baleful look made her want to laugh. The horse had definitely seen better days.

"Listen, sweetie," she crooned through the open window, "if Duncan doesn't come get you soon, we'll find you something to eat around here. All right?"

The horse bobbed his head, nodding almost as if he'd understood her. She turned at the sound of a knock, the door shaking beneath an impatient hand. With a sigh she went to open it, mentally preparing herself for another day.

Patrick approached the road. Well, *road* was actually a pretty fancy title for the two muddy ruts that passed as the only wagon trail connecting the ranches scattered along the Rio Grande. Fellow named Mears up around Silverton was supposed to have built a fine road. Word was he actually charged travelers a toll to use it. Maybe one of these days someone would do the same around here.

There was no sign of Pete or Amos, but he was a little early and it was a ways yet to the cutoff to Clune. He was tired down to his bones and the day wasn't yet half gone. There was still no sign of Michael. Nothing. It was as if he'd simply vanished. Of course, people didn't just go disappearing into thin air.

No, he had to face reality. Odds were more than good that his brother was in trouble—or worse. The fact that Roscoe had come back alone didn't bode well. A man couldn't last long out here without a horse. And if Michael weren't badly injured, he'd have made it back by now.

"Patrick? That you, boy?" Pete rode down from the

small ridge he'd just crested, allowing his horse to ride abreast of Patrick's. "Any luck?".

"No. Nothing. I even checked the ranch house again. He's just disappeared."

"Maybe he's laid up somewheres," Pete said, his voice gruff with emotion.

"No. He wouldn't do that. Michael's first thought would be for me and you. He wouldn't want to worry us. If he were able, he'd be back here."

"Maybe. Maybe not. You cain't go losing hope. Ain't been long enough for us to know anything."

Pete was right, but Patrick was finding it mighty hard to hold on to his hope. "Maybe Amos found something."

"Amos?"

"Yeah, I ran into him on Bald Man's Ridge. He said he'd heard about Michael from you and offered to help. I figured we could use all the eyes we could get."

"Guess so." Pete spat tobacco out the side of his mouth, the gesture somehow punctuating his feelings about Amos. "If you ask me, though, I'm still a wonderin' what in tarnation brought our fair-haired sheriff up here this morning."

"He told me he was looking for Arless."

"So he said." They rode on for a bit in silence. Then Pete picked up where he'd left off as if there'd never been any lapse in the conversation at all. "But then again, you ever hear of Arless using the line shack for one of his escapes?"

Patrick looked at the old ranch hand. "No. Not firsthand anyway. But you've got to admit, it's as good a place as any to hole up for a while."

"Maybe."

"So you think Amos was lying?"

Pete shot a stream of tobacco at a bush. Getting him to say what he was thinking could be a painful experience; Patrick had learned that it was best just to wait it out. Pete would talk when he was good and ready. They rode for a while in silence.

"Didn't say that. Just think it bears thinking about."

Patrick slowed as they reached the cutoff. The narrow wagon ruts continued on toward Silverthread. The perpendicular trail to the ranch was barely discernible in the high grass. Off to the left something red showed through the waving weeds. Patrick reined in the stallion and signaled Pete. Whatever it was, it wasn't supposed to be there.

He slid off the horse's back, his heart pounding a rhythm against his chest. Pete stayed in the saddle, his rifle drawn to cover his back. Out here a man simply couldn't take a chance. As he moved forward, the red thing began to take on a shape. A cotton-encased arm extended from a clump of grass, the hand open, beckoning. Pushing through the knee-high plants, he watched for signs of life.

"Michael? Is that you?" Nothing moved except the meadow grass swaying in the wind. He dropped down on his knees beside the body. Black hair spilled out from under the broad brim of a hat. With a shaking hand, he gently rolled the body over, his heart accelerating to a staccato tempo, echoing through his brain.

"Is it Michael?"

Pete's voice sounded far away. Patrick fought to pull in his breath. The bloodied dead man before him was not his brother. But the craggy features were still familiar—achingly familiar. His stomach roiled and he swallowed convulsively, trying to keep the bile down.

"Patrick?" Pete dropped into the grass beside him, pulling him back so that he could see. "Oh, sweet Jesus, it's your father."

Chapter Four

"But they told me . . . They said . . . I mean . . . You're not real." Cara knew she was talking gibberish, but her mind simply couldn't grasp the fact that Michael Macpherson, *her* Michael Macpherson, was walking right beside her.

She shifted, locking her arm around his waist, supporting his weight with her body. Michael groaned as she stumbled. "Believe me, I'm flesh and blood, and right now I feel like it's mainly blood." He sagged backward, his breathing coming in irregular gasps.

Cara tightened her hold, whispering in his ear, "You've got to hold on. I can't do this by myself. Come on, we've gotten this far. Just hang on a little while longer. Please."

His muscles bunched and tightened as he pulled himself upright, but he kept walking. "How . . . much . . . farther?"

"Not much more. Just around the next bend." *Keep him talking*, her mind asserted. *Keep him awake, and keep him talking.* "I looked for you, you know. After you disappeared."

48

The Promise

"I looked for you, too." His voice was rough, colored with pain.

"Then I don't see . . ." She stopped, not knowing how to continue.

"How we missed each other? Me, either. But just at the moment I think there are more important things to deal with."

"You're right. I'm sorry." There was just so much she wanted to ask him. So much she needed to know. But not now. He slumped forward again, his shoulders relaxing. She tightened her grip. "Michael, you've got to stay with me. I can't keep you up here on my own."

He jerked his head upward, pulling himself back to consciousness. "I'm here."

"Good." She stared at the side of his head, concentrating on the way the dark hair curled against his collar, trying to find something of the boy she remembered in the man he'd become. "Just keep talking to me, okay? Tell me what happened to you."

He nodded, shifting a little, leaning into the curve of her body. She could feel the heat from his fever. His shirt was damp with sweat. "I . . . don't know. Sneaked . . . up on me . . . shot me. Lucky to escape."

"Someone shot you?" She tried to make sense of the nonsensical. "Was it a hunter, do you think?"

"Manhunter, maybe." He groaned, tensing with pain as they hit a rough spot.

"You mean you think someone shot you on purpose?"

"Seems likely." His words were a bit disjointed, but if she was following the conversation, he was talking about murder. Or attempted murder.

"My God, Michael, are you saying someone tried to kill you?"

"And did a damn fine job of it." He drew in a ragged breath, and she felt his body slide forward.

"Hang on," she ordered. They stopped and she automatically turned toward him, supporting more of his weight. "We're here."

The warmth of his body surrounded her as he braced himself against her. She closed her eyes, feeling his heart beating beneath her hand. The tangy smell of male enveloped her, and somewhere deep inside, despite the odor of blood and injury, she responded to the memory. She knew this man, knew his scent, knew the feel of his arms. And no matter what anyone had told her, he was real. *Real.*

The feel of something sticky against her fingers pulled her from her thoughts. "Oh, God, you're bleeding again."

He touched the stain on his shirt. "Yeah, I think the walk opened the wound."

"Look, Michael, we've got to call a doctor."

"No." Their eyes met, and she saw his conviction. "But the bullet has to come out now."

She helped him into the house and across the living room, for once thankful that the cabin was small. Reaching the door to the bedroom, she paused, summoning the last of her strength. "We're almost there." She wasn't certain who she was talking to, Michael or herself. She steered him across the room to the bed. With an exhausted sigh he dropped down on it, his eyes closed, his lashes dark against the ashen pallor of his skin.

"Come on, we've made it this far. You've got to stay with me."

His blue eyes flickered open. The pain reflected there made her gasp. With steely determination he struggled to sit up, then leaned back against the pillows. "Have you ever removed a bullet?" He spoke slowly, as if each word were an effort.

"It's not something I list on my résumé," she snapped. He frowned. "I'm sorry. It's just that I haven't dealt with anything like this before." Her voice trembled. What if she lost him?

He reached out, covering her hand with his. "It's all right. I know how. I'll guide you."

She bit her lower lip and nodded. She could do this. A man's life depended on it. *Michael's* life depended on it. If he didn't want a doctor, she was all he had. "Okay. I'm just going to go get some bandages and things."

Pulling her hand away from his, she hurried into the bathroom. Throwing open the doors to the medicine cabinet, she searched among the antacids and cold remedies for something that could treat a gunshot wound. A bubble of laughter rose in her throat. Pepto-Bismol was a poor substitute for anesthesia.

Oh, Lord, she prayed, *help me.*

Clamping down on her rising hysteria, she forced herself to focus on the assortment of containers in front of her. Alcohol, that was important. She picked up the bottle. What else? She grabbed a tube of Neosporin, feeling a lot like a fireman fighting a raging forest fire with a squirt gun. Painkiller. She needed a painkiller. The best she could do was a bottle of Advil, but something was better than nothing.

Reaching for the analgesic, she spied a prescription pill bottle. She picked up the plastic container. Antibiotics. They were probably old—a refill she'd never used. They'd have to do. She grabbed the pills along with the Advil, adding them to the things already in her hand. In her haste she dropped the lot.

The alcohol bottle bounced against the wooden floor, but didn't break. The tube of antibiotic landed near the wall. The pill bottles rolled into a corner. Grabbing a basket of potpourri from the back of the toilet, she dumped its contents onto the floor. Then, on hands and knees, she retrieved the bottles, placing everything into the basket.

Her breath was coming in ragged gasps now, and tears threatened. She had to calm down.

51

Dee Davis

Standing with the basket clutched in one hand, she pushed aside bottles and tubes, discarding the metal box of Band-Aids when she came to it. They would hardly be adequate for the job at hand. Finally, in the back of the cabinet, she found a roll of gauze and some tape. Tossing them in the basket, she turned, her gaze falling to the counter.

A pair of tweezers lay by the sink. She swallowed back a wave of queasiness. She'd need something to pull out the bullet. Throwing them in with the rest, she grabbed a pillowcase and a washcloth from the linen closet and headed for the kitchen.

She needed a knife. Wrenching open a drawer, she surveyed her pitiful collection of cutlery. She'd never been much of a cook, and her array of knives was sadly lacking. Selecting the best of the lot, she threw a paring knife into the basket and grabbed a bottle of water from the counter on her way back to the bedroom.

She stopped in the doorway, trying to compose herself. The situation was dire enough without her panicking. Breathing deeply, she crossed to the bed. His eyes were closed again and beads of sweat dotted his forehead. She placed the basket on the bedside table and sat on the bed beside him. "Michael?" His eyes opened. "You've got to tell me what to do."

He nodded. "Did you get a knife?"

She held up the paring knife. "It's the best I could find."

He reached for it and ran a thumb across the blade, a flicker of laughter passing across his face. "If you want to butter me, this might do, but I don't think it'll actually cut anything."

She flushed. "I don't have anything else."

"You can use mine." He pointed at a small leather pouch hooked to his belt.

With shaking hands she unhooked the flap holding it in place and withdrew a tiny knife. Balancing it in her palm, she examined it more closely. It was beautifully wrought.

52

The Promise

The handle was ivory in color and striated with gray and black. The blade itself was polished brass or some similar metal. It was flat on one side and intricately carved on the other with interlocking circles and curls.

"It's a *sgian dubh*."

"A what?"

"*Sgian dubh*. It's Gaelic."

"Skeen doo." She pronounced the strange words slowly.

"That's it. *Sgian dubh*. It means black knife. This one is very old. It's been in my family for generations. Came from Scotland. But more important, it's sharp enough to dig out the bullet."

She touched the blade experimentally. A thin line of blood appeared on her finger. *Definitely sharp.* "Okay, what do I do first?"

He smiled weakly. "I'd say the best thing to do would be to pull off my shirt. Then you're going to clean the wound with something. Do you have any whiskey?"

Actually it wasn't a bad idea. Maybe after a good stiff drink she could do this. Or better yet, maybe a couple of good stiff drinks. She pulled herself back to the task at hand. "I've got rubbing alcohol. It's better than whiskey. And I brought some Advil. It's not much, but it will help with the pain."

She put the little knife on the table and opened the bottle, shaking out a couple of pills. She glanced up at his face, cringing at the pain she saw etched there. She added a couple more tablets to the pile on her palm. "Here, take these." She held out the medicine, along with the water.

He looked at them with a puzzled expression. "I think I'd rather have the whiskey."

She smiled. "Take them. And this one, too. It's an antibiotic." She added another pill to the pile, fervently hoping it was still potent.

Again he shot her an odd look, his eyebrows rising quizzically. "Antibiotic?" He said it as if it were a foreign word.

53

"You know, for infection." His injury must be affecting him more than he was letting on. He acted as though he'd never heard of an antibiotic. He stared at the pills in her hand, a look of distrust playing over his face. Men were such babies when it came to taking medicine.

"I'll tell you what," she said, placing the tablets in the palm of his hand. "If you take the pills, I'll get you some whiskey. Okay?" She wasn't at all sure letting him drink was the right thing to do, but that was always what they did in Westerns when somebody got shot, and she really doubted the Advil was going to do a lot to deaden the pain.

"Whiskey first."

She met his gaze and was once more surprised at the determination reflected there. This was not a man to argue with, even in his current condition.

She left the room and opened the cabinet where she kept the liquor. Whiskey could mean several things, and, not wanting to waste valuable time, she grabbed a bottle of bourbon and another of Scotch, the thirty-year-old kind. If the guy had to drink his anesthetic, it might as well go down smoothly.

When she walked back into the bedroom he was in the process of trying to peel off his shirt. The look of agony on his face was almost her undoing. Dropping the bottles on the bed, she moved to his side and carefully helped him remove the shirt. The muscles in his back were rigid, taut evidence of a pain more intense than she could imagine.

She slid an arm around his shoulders. "Here, lean back." Once he was propped up against the pillows again, she reached for the bottles. "I wasn't sure what you wanted, bourbon or Scotch—" She cut off the sentence. This wasn't a cocktail party.

He grabbed the Scotch and, after unscrewing the cap, drank deeply.

"The pills." She hated to sound like a taskmaster, but he needed the antibiotics.

With a grimace he swallowed the tablets and took another swig from the bottle, pausing to run a thumb over the ridged glass at the mouth of the container. His brows drew together; then, with a sigh, he lay back against the sheets.

She sat beside him on the bed and carefully began to peel off his bandages. They were stuck in places, and she could feel him tense every time she had to pull at one. Finally there was only the wound. Using the washcloth and some water, she carefully washed away the blood.

She could see the bullet hole now, a perfect little circle, almost as if he'd been hole-punched. The edges were black and the center oozed blood mixed with a greenish liquid. Infection. She could smell it. Swallowing to keep her stomach in line, she leaned back.

"Okay, what now?" Her voice was tight and came out sounding pinched. Her heart was pounding.

"Wash the area out and then make a cross cut to open it up."

She opened the alcohol and poured some onto the washcloth. With a hesitant swipe, she brushed it across the open wound.

"No. Not like that." He took the bottle from her and tipped it over. The liquid ran down his shoulder. His face tightened and she could see the whites of his knuckles as he gripped the bottle. Finally satisfied, he handed it back to her. "Now cut."

Dreading what came next, she picked up the little knife, swabbing it with alcohol. Grimly she bent over his shoulder, concentrating on what she was about to do. Placing one hand so that her fingers splayed out around the wound, she inched the knife downward.

"Do it." His voice rumbled deep in his chest, and she could feel the vibrations with her fingers.

Sucking in a deep breath, she tightened her grip on the knife and cut swiftly across the wound. Placing the alcohol-soaked washcloth across it, she reached for the tweezers.

After blotting away the worst of the blood and sterilizing the tweezers, she began to search for the bullet.

Sweat ran down her face and she used her free hand to wipe it away.

Michael groaned once, but other than that he remained stoically silent, his eyes shut and his mouth drawn tight.

She twisted the tweezers first to the left and then to the right, probing as gently as she could. Finally, just as she was beginning to think there was no bullet, she felt the tweezers hit something solid.

"I think I feel something. Wait." She withdrew the tweezers triumphantly. "I have it." The ball of lead looked more like a metal lump than a bullet. She felt as though she should be dropping it into a metal bowl for posterity or something. "Should I keep it?"

He opened his eyes, meeting her gaze. "No."

With a shrug she dropped it in a nearby waste can, then quickly cleaned the wound. Using the gauze and Neosporin, she formed a pad of sorts, which she bound in place with tape and strips torn from the pillowcase. It was not the best bandage ever made, but certainly one that would do for now.

Michael appeared to have passed out, or at least he was sleeping. She cleaned up some of the mess, leaving most of the medicine on the bedside table, then carefully removed his boots and covered him with a blanket.

Exhausted, Cara crawled up onto the bed, ignoring the fact that she was essentially sleeping with a stranger. Well, maybe not a stranger. She'd slept with him before. It was too much for her tired mind to try to work out, and besides, there was only one bed, and her bedmate was in no condition to take advantage of the situation.

She closed her eyes and allowed her mind to drift, comforted by the fact that she could feel him breathing. It was probably her imagination, but he already seemed less feverish. Just as sleep threatened to overtake her, she felt him move. She turned to look at him, meeting his steady cobalt gaze, shivering at the intensity of his stare.

"Thank you . . . Cara." He briefly caressed her cheek, his touch soft as the gentle kiss of a butterfly. Then his hand dropped and his eyes closed as he slipped back into the healing arms of Morpheus.

"You're welcome." The whispered words were wasted, but her heart sang at the sound of her name. He knew her. He *was* real. The explanations could come later.

She dropped her hand into his, reveling in the feel of his warmth, knowing that life coursed through his veins. By reflex, or intention, his fingers tightened around hers. With a smile she let herself slide into sleep.

Sunlight filtered through the closed curtains, making a cheerful pattern on the quilt. Michael stretched, trying to remember where he was. Dull pain radiated from his shoulder. He frowned as memory flooded back. The gunshot, the mine tunnel—Cara. He turned to look at the pillow next to him. Empty.

She was gone. *Again.*

He wasn't sure how long he'd been here. He remembered Cara removing the bullet, and then things were a little hazy. Mainly he'd slept, but he also had recollections of her lying beside him, warm and alive. He felt his body respond to his thoughts, a sure sign he was on the road to recovery—something he obviously owed to Cara and her medicine.

She'd woken him several times, insisting that he take more of the little tablets. He glanced at the array of medicines on the side table. The bottles were odd, made of a substance he didn't recognize. He touched the big brown one. Hard, yet pliable. Certainly strange, but no doubt there was an explanation. Besides, who was he to argue with success? He wondered briefly what it was she'd given him. Whatever it was, it seemed to be working.

He sat up and rotated his shoulder cautiously. The

wound was tender, but his head was clear, and he was certain the infection was gone. He looked around the room, trying to get his bearings. It had a strange feel. The furnishings were simple, with bright spots of color here and there—definitely a feminine touch.

There were vases of flowers everywhere. And stacks of books. He picked one up from the bedside table. *This Rough Magic.* The title seemed to mirror the situation. Magic was about the only thing he could think of to explain the fact that she'd appeared in the mine tunnel just when he'd needed her most.

He put the book down, shaking his head at the wild turn of his thoughts. There was certainly no such thing as magic—rough or otherwise. He turned his attention back to the room, more than a little curious about the woman who owned it.

The focal point of the room was a magnificent watercolor. He didn't know much about art, but the painting was good, a landscape of a location somewhere in the mountains. The silvery line of a stream marked the edge of a small clearing. He could almost smell the tangy scent of pine and feel the warmth of the sun on his face. The colors were muted, giving the entire scene a dreamy feel. He smiled to himself. He'd actually almost used the word *romantic*.

The center of the canvas was dominated by a huge blue spruce, its massive branches bending low, almost touching the ground. The scene was somehow familiar. He studied it through narrowed eyes and, when understanding came, felt a surprising sense of elation.

It was the mine tunnel.

Just behind the great spruce, in the shadows of its limbs, he could see the opening. And in the mottled browns and blacks of the tunnel he could just make out the image of two figures intertwined. With energy he was surprised he possessed, he got out of the bed and crossed the room to stand in front of the painting. He stared at the couple. The brushstrokes were strong, emotions laid bare. In barely six inches of space the artist had captured both longing and passion. It reached out from the canvas, surrounding him.

In the corner, faint but discernible, was the artist's signature, *Cara Reynolds.* A shiver ran down his spine.

She hadn't forgotten.

A small, tarnished brass plaque at the bottom of the frame caught his attention. He read the words and then, with his heart pounding, read them again. *Lovers' Reunion.* He suddenly felt absurdly happy. Bending closer, he tried to make out the date underneath the title. As he read it, his joy changed to confusion—then the confusion changed to shock. He sat down on the end of the bed with a thud. According to the plaque, the painting had been completed in January of 1993. He sucked in a ragged breath. *Nineteen ninety-three?*

Cara's watercolor had been painted just over a hundred and thirty years after he was born.

Chapter Five

Duncan Macpherson was dead. Loralee bit her lip, surprised at the swell of emotion she felt. She'd certainly cared for the old man, but in her business it didn't pay to make attachments.

"Are you sure?" she asked, fastening the last of the buttons on her bodice.

The burly miner pulled up his pants, popping one suspender into place on his shoulder. "Heard it up at the mine. They found him on the road to Clune. Figure word's spread all over town by now." He pulled the other suspender into place and buttoned his fly with a satisfied grin. "Mighty fine time, Loralee." He reached into his pocket and threw a coin down on the bed. "I'll be back next payday." With a jaunty salute, he strode out the door, slamming it behind him.

Loralee sank to the bed, reaching automatically for the coin. Duncan was dead. She ran a hand through her hair, trying to make sense of it, wondering what had possessed him to head for home without Jack.

Jack.

She rushed to the window, her heart pounding. The swaybacked sorrel was still tied to the post outside. He lifted baleful brown eyes and whinnied softly.

"Jack." She hustled through the door, skidding to a stop beside the horse. There was no way Duncan would leave Jack willingly. No amount of liquor could cause him to forget the beast. So how could Duncan have been found on the road to Clune? Something was dreadfully wrong here. Loralee patted the horse, trying to calm her rising fear. "Wait here, sweetie; I'll be right back." What she needed was help. Two heads were wiser than one, and all that.

She ran up the row to Corabeth's door and pounded on it. There was no answer. Puzzled, she tried to open the door. It rattled but refused to budge. Locked. She pounded again, certain the noise would wake the dead, but there still wasn't an answer. Several tousled heads poked out of doorways along the row. Loralee pasted on a smile, waving with a casualness she didn't feel.

The window to Corabeth's room was shut, the curtain tightly drawn. Corabeth obviously wasn't answering, which meant Loralee was on her own—again. The important thing right now was to deal with Jack. She had to hide the horse—at least until she had a chance to talk to one of Duncan's sons. Until then, the fewer people who saw him outside her crib, the better.

Looking up at the sun, she was surprised to see that the day was already well advanced. She stroked Jack's soft nose and, after making certain no one was paying attention, looped his reins over her arm. "Come on, sweetie; let's get you somewhere safe."

She led the horse down the dusty road and around the corner, away from town, up toward the mines. Jack followed placidly enough, his gait slow and steady.

After a steep climb up the canyon, they stopped at the edge of a rushing stream called Willow Creek, although for the life of her she wasn't certain why. She'd never seen any tree looking remotely like a willow along its rocky banks.

The canyon narrowed here, only wide enough for the rough-hewn logs that, laid side by side, formed a bridge of sorts. Jack took one look at the rickety wooden structure and refused to budge. "It's just a little bit farther. And there's bound to be oats to fill your belly. Come on, sweetie."

Jack curled back his upper lip and refused to move, his stubborn stance worthy of any miner's burro. Loralee wearily pushed a strand of sweat-soaked hair off her face and stared at the woeful-looking horse. "Serve you right if I just left you here." She had better things to do with her time than to try to coerce a washed-out old horse across a pile of shifting lumber.

A crack and roar echoed down the canyon. Jack lifted his head and, with a snort of pure fear, raced across the makeshift bridge. Loralee ran gratefully behind. The sorrel stopped just on the other side, relaxing now that the noise had faded.

"It was only the men at the mine. You should be used to blasting by now. Some miner's horse you are." Jack only shook his head reproachfully. She laughed, letting the tension of the past few hours ebb away.

Around the next bend, a makeshift cabin stood smack-dab against the sheer cliff. Loralee knew from experience that it actually extended cavelike into the rock, a dugout of sorts. Next to the shack was a rickety lean-to, its flimsy boards, whitewashed from exposure, fading into the side of the mountain. The perfect hideaway.

"Come on, Jack. We're almost there." She pulled the horse behind her, leading him by the reins. The door to the shanty opened a crack and the muzzle of a rifle glistened in the sunlight.

"Loralee, that you?"

"It's me, Ginny. I need some help."

The door inched farther open, and a short, sun-weathered figure emerged onto the listing planks that served as a porch.

"What can I do?" The woman pulled a colorful blanket tighter around her shoulders, her question hesitant.

"I need to leave my horse here."

Ginny eyed the sorrel and snorted. "Not much of a horse."

"He belonged to a friend." Loralee felt tears rising.

The woman hopped off the porch, her spry gait belying her wrinkled appearance. "He'll be safe with me."

Loralee handed her the reins. "Thank you, Ginny. Jack's a good horse. Just a little long in the tooth."

Ginny smiled, her slow grin contagious. "We'll have a lot in common then, he and I."

Loralee bit her lip, trying to decide how much to say.

Ginny laid a time-weathered hand on Loralee's arm. "I don't need to know."

Again Loralee felt tears rising. She fumbled in her pocket, reaching for the coins she'd brought. She offered them to Ginny.

The woman folded Loralee's open hand over the coins. "I've no need for your money, girl. Now go quickly, before someone sees you."

She hugged the old woman, who gruffly pushed her away.

"Go on with you."

Loralee turned and hurried down the road. At least Jack was safe. No one ever went to Ginny's. She was Ute, and even a town like Silverthread had its untouchables.

She frowned, making her way across the bridge. She really didn't have much to go on. All she really knew for certain was that Duncan was dead—that and the fact that he'd left Jack behind. It wasn't exactly evidence of anything, but she couldn't shake the feeling that something was very wrong. She rounded another bend and caught sight of the line of cribs. She needed Corabeth. Her friend would know what to do.

* * *

"I don't know what happened. I only know that my father is dead and Michael is missing." Patrick ran a hand through his hair and paced restlessly around the sheriff's office, his mind still reeling from shock. "There's got to be some kind of connection."

Amos leaned back in his chair, his booted feet propped up on his desk. "Best I can tell your father was robbed."

"His pocket watch was gone." Patrick frowned at the sheriff. "But I doubt he had anything else of value on him."

"I've seen men killed for a whole lot less than a watch, Patrick. And everyone knew he carried it. Hell, wouldn't let the damn thing out of his sight."

"My mother gave it to him. It was all he had left." Patrick tried but couldn't keep the bitterness out of his voice.

"Ain't no way around it. Robbery's the most logical explanation."

"Maybe, but that still doesn't explain Michael's absence. And then there's the horses."

Amos sat forward, dropping his feet to the floor, his brows drawn together in consternation. "What are you talking about?"

Patrick sat on the spindle-back chair in front of the desk. "Well, doesn't it seem a little odd to you that my father was found on the road without his horse, and that Roscoe came home as pretty as you please, only without Michael?"

Amos waved a hand in dismissal. "Jack probably wandered off somewhere."

Patrick frowned. "Not a chance. That horse can smell fresh hay five miles away. And the ranch was in view. If Jack was there, he'd be at home in his stall right now filling his belly."

"Maybe the fellow who robbed Duncan took him."

Patrick smiled despite himself. "Only if the thief was addle-brained. Jack isn't exactly prize horseflesh. In fact, sometimes I wonder how he manages to make it from one day to the next." He sobered, his mind returning to grim reality. "Something here doesn't add up, Amos. I can feel it in my bones."

"Look, I know it ain't what you want to hear, but as I see it the facts simply don't support a connection. It's just a lousy coincidence."

Patrick glared at the sheriff. The two events simply had to be connected somehow. In one fell swoop he'd lost an entire family, and he had trouble swallowing the idea that it was only a lousy coincidence. But Amos wasn't listening. He'd already made up his mind, so there was no use in ranting on about it.

"Fine, I'll let it go for now." He stood up, and the sheriff followed suit. "But my brother is still missing, and until he's found I've no intention of letting the matter rest completely."

"Letting what rest?"

Patrick turned as Owen Prescott strode into the spartan office, his face worn and haggard. Patrick breathed a sigh of relief. Owen was his father's best friend—a second father. He'd sort through all of this.

"I came as soon as I heard." He clasped Patrick's hand and pulled him into a quick embrace. "I'm so sorry, son."

Patrick nodded, trying desperately to hold on to his emotions. He suddenly felt like a kid again. Seeing Owen, hearing the sympathy in his voice, somehow lent a cruel reality to the tragic events of the morning. He sucked in a breath and quelled the urge to give in to tears. He was a man, after all, and men didn't cry.

"What aren't you going to let rest, Patrick?"

He struggled to follow the gist of Owen's question, focusing on the concern in the older man's face. "I was just telling Amos that it's reasonable to think that there's some sort of connection between Michael's disappearance and my father's death."

"Amen to that." Pete ambled into the office, perching

himself on the windowsill, his shrewd glance sizing up the others in the room.

Owen looked over at Amos, who was seated again, concentrating on lighting a cigarillo. "Amos, what do you think?" He pulled up a second chair and sat, facing the desk.

The sheriff looked up, the thin cigar dangling from the corner of his mouth, a thin wisp of bluish smoke curling toward the ceiling. Patrick couldn't help but think how discordant the picture was, an angel indulging in a devilish habit.

Amos blew a ring of smoke. "I'm guessing that Duncan's death was part of a highway robbery, nothing more."

Owen frowned and looked at Patrick. "But you have more questions?"

"Damn right I do. I have a little trouble accepting the fact that my father was murdered on the very same night my brother up and disappeared."

Amos narrowed his gaze. "Now there's a thought. Michael getting along with Duncan all right these days?"

Pete let out a string of expletives that would have curled the toes of a threepenny whore.

Patrick felt his hackles rise. He opened his mouth to respond, but Owen beat him to the punch. "Now, Amos, if you think about it, you'll realize there's no way Michael could have killed Duncan." Everyone turned to look at Owen. He smiled reassuringly at Patrick and then leaned back in his chair. "What time was it when you found Roscoe?"

"I don't know, exactly . . . a couple hours before sunup." Patrick glanced over at Pete, who nodded in confirmation.

"Right, so that would indicate that Michael was injured well before dawn."

"You're just speculating that he was hurt. Maybe the blood on the saddle was Duncan's, not Michael's." Amos paused dramatically.

The Promise

For a moment Patrick felt sick to his stomach. Then almost as quickly the feeling was gone. Michael would never kill their father. Never. He looked over at Pete. The old hand was staring intently at Owen, waiting for his reaction.

Owen scratched the side of his jaw absently. "Well, I suppose your theory is possible, but hardly likely. Besides, how would you explain the fact that Duncan's body appeared by the road after Pete and Patrick left to try to find Michael?"

"It was barely daylight when they left. They could've easily missed the body."

"Now, look here." Patrick felt his voice rising. "My brother isn't a killer. He isn't. Besides, there's still the horses. Even if what you're saying is true, and I don't believe it, you can hardly expect Michael to make a getaway on Jack." He glanced frantically over at Pete.

The old man spat out the open window, his grizzled old face shuttered. Whatever he was thinking, he wasn't going to share it now.

Amos stubbed out the cigarillo. "Maybe he dumped Roscoe for a horse nobody would recognize. You boys check your other stock?"

Patrick couldn't believe the turn of the conversation. "No. It never occurred to me to check."

"Well, what do you want to bet you find another horse is missing? I'll bet Michael switched Roscoe for another one. Makes a hell of a lot more sense than that animal finding its way home through the dark mountains."

Patrick bit back a profane retort. "If you're so sure Michael is a murderer, maybe you could give me a reason why?" He glared at the sheriff, his anger threatening to overcome him.

"Sit down, Patrick," Owen said. "There's no harm in listening to what the man has to say."

"Why?" Patrick swung around to glare at Owen.

Dee Davis

"Because even in the wildest conjecture there is often an element of truth."

Patrick sat down, his mind spinning. "There isn't any truth to Striker's conjectures. They're lies. *Lies.*"

"Patrick." There was a note of steel in Owen's voice, and Patrick swallowed back further retort. He respected Owen—loved him even. In a lot of ways he'd been more of a father than Duncan had ever been.

They waited while Amos lit another cheroot, a wisp of smoke making his face momentarily hazy. Amos tilted back his chair, resting it against the wall, his booted feet propped up on the desk. "Word around town is that you all are having money problems."

Patrick shrugged. "We get by."

"Yeah, well, according to Bergstrom over at the bank, you're getting by on very little. And there is the matter of some outstanding loans." Amos smiled, a tight-lipped version that hinted of malice.

Patrick tried to hold on to reason; things were rapidly spiraling out of control. "What the hell does our financial business have to do with Michael's disappearance?" He refused to give voice to Amos's accusation.

"Maybe Michael was tired of living hand-to-mouth. Maybe he saw an easy way out."

"By murdering my father?" Patrick stood up, leaning over the desk, anger consuming him. "That doesn't make sense, Striker."

"Doesn't it?" Amos leaned forward, steepling his fingers, his elbows resting on the arms of his chair.

Owen placed a soothing hand on Patrick's shoulder. He shook it off, dropping back into his chair. Maybe this was a nightmare. Any minute he'd wake up at home, safe in his bed. Pete still sat in silence, but Patrick could tell by the taut line of his shoulders that he, too, was incensed at the accusations. "All right, Amos, if you're so certain Michael did this, you tell me what he had to gain by killing my father."

Amos waited a beat before answering, obviously enjoying the moment. "Silver."

"What?" Patrick sat forward, his attention focused on the man in front of him.

"I said silver. Your father was in town last night—drunk, as usual. He was rambling on about finding silver—the mother lode, to hear him talk."

"That's ridiculous. Hell, my father was always blathering on about finding silver. Except for the Promise, it never amounted to anything."

"Well, maybe this time it was different. Or maybe Michael just believed it was."

Patrick shot a look at Owen, waiting for him to tell the sheriff how crazy all this was. But Owen was silent, a frown creasing his forehead.

"This is insane. Michael was up in the high country all day yesterday."

Amos blew out a smoke ring. "You're certain of that? You actually saw him?"

"Well, no. But he told me he was going up there."

"I see." The sheriff smiled, looking smug.

"Pete, you know he was up there." Patrick met Pete's gaze, begging him to intervene, to say something.

"You saw him, Pete?" Owen turned to look at the ranch hand, his gaze narrowed.

"No. Cain't say that I did. But young Michael's as honest as they come. If he told Patrick he was going into the mountains, then that's where he was."

Amos shrugged. "All right, even if you allow for time in the mountains, he still could have been in Silverthread by nightfall."

"Someone would have seen him." This from Owen, who at last seemed to be getting with the program. Patrick sucked in a breath of relief.

"Not necessarily, and besides, Duncan could have run into him on the mountain. Maybe Michael already knew. Maybe he was waiting for him to come home."

"Ambush his own father? Michael would sooner poke out his own eye." Patrick stood up, his hands clenched in rage. "This is outrageous. And even if it were true, even if my father had found the mother lode and told Michael about it, why would Michael kill him?"

"Well, now, that's the big question, isn't it?" Amos's' mouth curved at the corners in the beginning of a grin. The bastard was enjoying this. "Way I heard it, betrayal isn't exactly an unusual occurrence in your family, is it?"

Patrick sprang over the desk in one smooth leap, his hand closing around the sheriff's collar. "You take that back, you son of a bitch!" He arched his right arm backward, tensing, his fist clenched for the punch.

"Whoa, there, boy. No need to be smacking the sheriff. Ain't his fault any of this happened." Pete planted a beefy hand around Patrick's neck, the gentle pressure enough to force Patrick to release Amos.

"But he . . . I mean, he . . ." Patrick sputtered.

"Easy, Patrick. The sheriff didn't mean any offense. Did you, Striker?" The steel was back in Owen's voice.

"No." Amos rubbed his neck and glared at Patrick, his look belying his words.

"Seems to me we'd all be better off sticking with the facts and not going off making wild accusations." Pete eyed the sheriff.

"It wasn't an accusation. Everyone knows that Patrick's mother ran off and left them for a pile of silver."

Patrick made another move for Amos. Pete tightened his grip and said, "Fact is, we don't know for sure what happened to Rose. Guess we never will."

Amos smiled faintly, as if the situation amused him.

Owen nodded. "And Patrick, you've got to admit that we may never know what happened to your brother either."

"Well, he didn't kill my father." Patrick's words sounded petulant even to his own ears.

"Look, I think the thing for you to do now is go back

to Clune. I'm sure Amos will look into this some more." Owen leveled a look at the sheriff. Amos nodded. "And Patrick, I'll look into it myself. All right?"

Patrick mumbled an agreement under his breath.

"You just go on home. I'll take care of this." Owen looked over at Pete, who had settled back on the windowsill. "You'll stay with him?"

"Reckon I will."

"Good. Have you buried Duncan yet?"

"Up on the ridge, by the river. Did it first thing."

Owen turned back to Patrick. "You go with Pete, and I'll be out to pay my respects in the morning."

Patrick nodded. He trusted Owen, even if he didn't trust the shifty-eyed sheriff as far as he could throw him.

Besides, he had some questions of his own to ask.

Chapter Six

Michael stood in the doorway watching her. Her hair was damp, curling wildly around her shoulders. The satin robe she wore hugged the curves of her small frame, enhancing the smooth porcelain of her skin. He quelled the urge to stride across the room and press her hard against him. It had been a long time since he'd wanted a woman.

She must have sensed his presence, because she turned around, her eyes narrowed in concern. "You shouldn't be up."

He pulled himself from his thoughts and stepped into the room. "I'm fine, only a little sore." He rotated his shoulder in demonstration. "The stuff you gave me really packed a wallop. I feel like I've been sleeping for a week."

She smiled, her wide-eyed gaze meeting his. He felt his stomach do a quick flip. "Not quite two days."

He frowned. That meant he'd been away from Clune for almost three. His brother would be worried, frantic probably. And there was still the issue of who'd shot him. Not that any of that really mattered if the date on the painting

72

in the bedroom was a reality. His mind balked at the idea. It was a mistake. Had to be.

"Michael, are you sure you're all right?" She was standing in front of him, so close that he could smell the sweet scent surrounding her. The word *seductive* ran through his brain.

"I saw the painting."

Her expression changed from concern to puzzlement and finally to embarrassment. A slight flush stained her cheeks. "I painted it years ago, before . . ." Her voice trailed off.

"Are we the figures in the painting, Cara?"

She nodded mutely.

Suddenly the questions he'd intended to ask seemed unimportant. His hand moved of its own accord, gently cupping her chin and lifting her face. She licked her lips nervously, the small pink tip of her tongue fanning the flames already leaping inside him. He had to taste her, just one small sip of those sweet, moist lips.

She closed her eyes as his mouth touched hers, her lips fluttering under his kiss, and he felt the fire grow in intensity. One kiss was not enough. He pulled her closer, wrapping his good arm around her, ignoring the slight pain the movement caused. A tiny moan escaped her lips. With ruthless precision, he used the opportunity to deepen the kiss. Their tongues met, thrusting and retreating, dueling for some unknown prize.

He felt his manhood press against the soft flesh at the apex of her thighs. He could actually feel the warmth of her through the thin satin. Perhaps the prize was not unknown after all. He imagined how tight she'd be, how hot and tight.

With a groan, he moved his mouth, trailing moist kisses down the side of her neck. She threw her head back, allowing him access, her eyes still closed. Pushing back the edge of her wrapper, he kissed the soft alabaster skin of

73

her shoulder, his hand slipping between the satiny sides of the robe.

He felt her nipple tighten as he rolled it lightly between thumb and forefinger, satisfied when she moaned his name. Exchanging lips for hand, he circled the taut bud with the tip of his tongue, enjoying the contrast between her nipple and the silken skin of her breast, his own body throbbing for release. He could feel the fire building, threatening to consume him.

Lifting his head, he found her lips again, his tongue invading the hot, wet sanctity of her mouth. She pressed herself to him and he placed his hand on her bottom, pulling her closer, nestling his shaft tightly against the hot crevice between her thighs.

He tangled his other hand in her spun-gold curls, feeling the fine strands wrap around his fingers, clinging almost with a life of their own. He wondered momentarily what it would feel like to wrap himself in her hair. God, she was magnificent.

Cara tried to think rationally, but it was impossible. This was the stuff of her dreams. She moaned and pressed herself closer, feeling him hard against her, his heat burning through her robe, wanting nothing more than to encase him, to feel him drive deep inside her again and again. Her tongue mimicked her thoughts, and she felt him answer her need with his own.

She ran her hands across the warm skin of his back, feeling the hard muscle encased in sun-bronzed flesh. His beard rasped against her face, and she reveled in the contrast to the velvety touch of his lips. The smell of him surrounded her, teasing her with its potency, hinting of things to come.

His hands cupped her face as he kissed her eyes, her cheeks, her neck. Slowly, surely, he moved downward until she thought she'd scream with need for him. His lips closed again on her breast and she bit her lip to keep from crying out. He nipped and played, enticing the shy bud into rigidity. With each touch and tug, she felt the tightness within her ratcheting up another notch, until she was strung so tightly she thought she would explode.

Her robe hung open now, her body exposed to his hands and lips. She ought to feel like a wanton, but instead she burned with a passion so strong it threatened to engulf her. His teasing hand finally reached the soft curls that guarded her most secret place. Sensation shot through her and she arched against him, a moan escaping from somewhere deep inside of her.

His mouth found hers, and she opened it freely, giving him everything she had. As their kiss grew more frantic his hand grew bolder, and she realized suddenly that she was actually hearing bells.

Bells?

Her mind slammed into gear and she jerked back, gasping for breath. "It's the doorbell." His breathing was labored, too, and the evidence of their passion was taut against the denim of his jeans. He ran a hand through his hair, looking as bemused as she felt. "There's someone at the door." She belted her robe tightly around her waist and tried to smooth back the wild strands of her hair.

They both turned sharply at the sound of a key in the lock. Cara reacted first. "Quick, get in the bedroom."

He stood rooted to the spot, watching the doorway to the mudroom with narrowed eyes. "Who do you think it is?" The words erupted in a staccato burst.

"My housekeeper. She probably just came by to drop off some supplies. Now go." She tried to keep her voice on an even note, but a thread of anxiety slipped in. "She's harmless, but to be safe I think you should stay out of sight. I'll try to get rid of her."

Michael considered her words and finally, with a terse nod, spun on his heel and disappeared into the bedroom, closing the door firmly behind him.

Forcing a smile onto her face, she walked forward, ready to deal with Roberta.

"Cara? Are you in there?"

She came to a full stop, her mind shifting gears, confusion warring with surprise. *It wasn't Roberta; it was Nick Vargas.* But *he* didn't have a key. As if to contradict the fact, the man belonging to the voice stepped out of the mudroom, a key dangling from one finger. She frowned. How the hell had Nick gotten a key to her house?

"There you are, darling." He smiled beguilingly. "Why didn't you answer the door?"

She eyed him warily. He was good-looking, in a smooth sort of way, all blond hair and tanned skin, his face youthful in appearance. One would never guess that he was over forty. "I was in the shower." She waved a hand absently at her robe. "How is it you happen to have a key to my house?"

"I sweet-talked Roberta into letting me borrow hers." The smile broadened, impishly charming, intended no doubt to disarm, but Cara wasn't buying. She'd known Nick most of her life. As a young man he hadn't paid any attention to her. She'd been little more than a child. But now that she'd returned to Colorado as an adult, things had changed.

He'd been pursuing her diligently, offering picnics in the mountains, moonlit hikes, even the pretense of being interested in her paintings. Until today, however, he'd been more of a nuisance than anything else. And despite it all, she'd managed to keep him at arm's length without being rude. But just at the moment he was pushing his luck.

"Why would you need a key, Nick?" She tried to keep her voice neutral, but couldn't stop the tremor of anger that colored her words.

"Why, Cara *mía*, you wound me with your suspicions."

"Don't call me that."

He reached out and twined a rebellious strand of her hair around his finger, tugging slightly so that she was

76

forced to step closer. "Little Cara, always playing hard to get." His eyes raked downward, stripping the robe off with a look.

She pulled her hair free and stepped back, pressing the lapels of her robe together.

"Nick, you haven't told me why you're here."

He leaned against the counter, crossing his long legs, his perfectly creased pants riding up to show argyle socks. Cara sighed and waited.

"I was worried."

"Worried? About what?" She frowned, puzzled by the turn of the conversation.

A loud thud echoed from the bedroom. Nick glanced at the closed door, his golden eyebrows raised in question.

"The cat." Cara plastered on what she hoped was a reassuring smile.

"I didn't know you had a cat."

She racked her brain for a reasonable answer. She had never been a good liar. "She's new—to keep me from getting lonely." She met his gaze, holding hers steady.

He smiled slowly. "You don't need a cat, Cara *mía*. You have me." His tone was teasing, but the humor wasn't reflected in his eyes.

She ignored the remark and the endearment. "I asked you why you were worried."

He shrugged. "I was afraid something had happened to you."

Well, *that* was an understatement. She tried to keep her face pleasantly neutral, sort of a prom-queen-stuck-on-a-float look. "Why would you think something happened to me?"

"Because, *darling*." He paused provocatively, and the word ran down her spine, curling around her, suffocating her. "You stood me up."

"I did?" She eyed him skeptically.

"Yes. You promised to come by the bar." He raised an eyebrow, waiting.

Dee Davis

"Oh, God, Nick, I'm sorry. I forgot all about you." He *had* asked her to come by. They'd been supposed to have lunch. *Yesterday.*

His face darkened, taking on a sardonic look. "And here I thought you might have need of rescue."

She held out a hand. "I didn't mean it like that. You know I'd never stand you up on purpose. Something came up and I forgot all about it. Forgive me, please." She might not be willing to jump into his bed, but he deserved better than a brush-off.

The anger faded, and his lips twisted into an ironic grin. "I hope it was more than the cat that kept you away."

"The cat?"

"Yes, your new pet."

Damn, she really had to bone up on this lying thing. "As a matter a fact, it *was* the cat."

He waited patiently for her explanation, his foot swinging lazily against the cabinet under the counter.

"She's a stray. I found her a couple of days ago out by the trash. She looked so pitiful. Skinny and lonely and, well, as it turns out, sick. She has ear mites. Kept her up all night, poor baby. So I spent a good part of yesterday in Del Norte at the vet." She shot him what she hoped was an apologetic look.

"Ah, Cara, my angel. Always taking care of the misfits." He rose and crossed the space between them. "But now perhaps you can spare some time for me?" His words were a question, his tone was not.

"Of course. Why don't I meet you in town later?"

"But you're here and I'm here; why not now?" He trailed a finger down her cheek. "Besides, as much as I love your company, Cara *mía*, I have some business I'd like to take care of with you."

She didn't want to make a scene, but she'd be damned if she'd continue this conversation in her robe. "Fine. Why don't you make yourself comfortable and I'll get dressed."

"Are you sure you don't want a little help?"

"No, thank you, I can manage. I'll be back in a sec." She fled into the bedroom and leaned against the closed door, her breath coming in short gasps.

"Who the hell is he?" Michael's whispered words made her jump.

"Just an acquaintance."

"He seemed a little more than that to me."

She glared at him. Enough was enough. She was not something for Nick and Michael to throw around like a football. "I think he'd like to be, but he isn't," she said quietly, through clenched teeth.

"I'm sorry." His voice softened and his apology reached all the way to the crystalline depths of his cobalt eyes.

She smiled weakly. "Look, I've got to get dressed or he's going to come in here."

Michael stepped back and waved at the room behind him. "Your room is mine."

Suppressing a laugh, she walked to the dresser and began pulling out clothes with no thought as to what she was grabbing. Then, with garments in hand, she eyed him thoughtfully. "Turn your back." He raised an eyebrow, but didn't budge.

"Unless you want me to go back out there like this, turn your back."

With a rakish grin he shrugged and turned away. She caught her breath at the clean, strong lines of his bare shoulders. The man was a magnet. She simply couldn't quit staring. Even the white of his bandage enhanced his sexuality. With shaking hands, she quickly pulled on a pair of faded cutoffs and a T-shirt.

"You can turn around now."

He spun around, the look of surprise on his face almost comical. "You're not going out there in that."

"You sound like my grandfather."

"Well, I shouldn't wonder, if you insist on entertaining gentleman callers dressed like that."

Gentleman callers? "You were expecting a ball gown?"

"No. I was expecting something that covered more than the robe did." He glared at her, his gaze raking her up and down. Funny; when he did it she felt all hot and squirmy inside, but when Nick did it she wanted nothing more than to slap him silly.

"Cara?" *Nick.*

"I've got to go. This will have to do." She pulled an oversize T-shirt from another drawer. "Here, it wouldn't hurt you to cover up, too." She threw the shirt at him, watching as he snagged it one-handed. With a mock bow, he sent her a crooked smile that for all the world seemed a promise of things to come. She quelled a surge of desire. What had come over her? She waited until he moved out of range of the open door, then walked back into the living room, pulling the door closed behind her.

"There, that's better. Sorry to keep you waiting." She sat on the arm of a chair. Nick traced the curve of her calf with his eyes, and she actually felt herself blush. Maybe shorts hadn't been the best idea. "Can I get you something to drink?"

He was settled on the sofa, one leg crossed casually over the other. He looked as if it were his home, not hers. Today his usual familiarity grated on her nerves.

"I'll take a Scotch, neat."

She was halfway to the cabinet when she remembered the Scotch was in the bedroom—what was left of it. Her heart couldn't stand another whispered conversation with Michael. She obviously was not cut out for subterfuge.

"I'm out."

Nick frowned. "What happened to the bottle I gave you?"

She paused. "It's gone. Gin?"

"Fine."

It didn't sound fine, but frankly she didn't care. She dropped a couple of ice cubes in a glass and mixed the drink, being careful to go light on the gin. No sense in adding fuel to his lust-filled glances. "You said you had business to discuss."

She crossed to the sofa and held out his drink, a cheerful smile firmly in place.

"I want to talk about your paintings." He touched the glass, but rather than taking it he slid his hand down to cover hers. Unless she upended the drink, she had little choice but to join him on the sofa.

"We've been over this, Nick." *Several times.*

"Look. I love the series, and I want them. It's as simple as that." He reached for the drink with his left hand, keeping her fingers entrapped in his right.

"You haven't even seen most of them. You saw *The Promise* once for maybe a second. How could you possibly *love* it?"

"I know what I like, Cara *mía*." He shrugged. There was subtext there, but she'd be damned if she knew what it was.

"Well, I'm flattered. But I've told you, the paintings are no longer mine to sell. They belong to Solais."

He leaned forward, tightening his fingers, a shadow of anger passing across his face. She winced and he loosened his grip, the shadow dissipating almost before it began. "You've already sent them?"

She pulled her hand free, absently rubbing it against her shorts. "No, although I should have. I've gotten most of them crated for shipping, but I need to finish up. I was planning to get into the studio yesterday, but—"

"I know, you were unavoidably detained. Well, you'll simply have to tell them you've changed your mind."

"I can't do that. It's the Solais Gallery, and you know as well as I do that it's a miracle they wanted them in the first place. If I were to back out now, I'd never sell to them again."

"Well, we'll simply have to find a way around that. You can name your price."

81

Dee Davis

"I'm sorry, Nick. I can't. I intend to honor the contract with Solais."

"Damn it, Cara, you're not being reasonable."

"I'll paint you something else."

"But I want *those* paintings, Cara." He grabbed both her wrists in his hands.

She tried to pull away, but his grip was too strong. "Nick, stop it. You're hurting me."

He leaned forward, his glacial eyes boring into hers. "My dear, I simply won't take no for an answer." The icy fury in his stare scared her. He was close enough now that she could smell the gin on his breath.

"I believe the lady said no."

If the situation hadn't been so frightening, it would have been absurd. Michael stood in the bedroom doorway clad in his jeans and her T-shirt. What had served as a nightshirt for her barely fit over his broad shoulders. The cotton clung to his muscles, outlining the hard lines of him and displaying the grossly distorted figure of Tweety bird across his chest.

Nick rose, dragging Cara with him, then froze, obviously completely thrown by the man in the doorway. Cara jerked free and took a step in Michael's direction.

"Who the hell are you?" Nick's normally elegant voice was lost in his anger, his classic good looks marred by the rage etched on his face.

"The cat."

Cara watched as Nick pulled himself together, schooling his face into nonchalance. His gaze went first to Cara, then to Michael, then back to Cara again. "And does the cat have a name?"

Cara opened her mouth to answer, but Michael was faster.

"Michael Macpherson. And I think it's about time that you were going."

Nick's mouth twitched at the corner, the only sign that Michael's words affected him. With a shrug he focused his

82

attention on Cara. "I'm sorry if I upset you, Cara *mía*. I'm afraid I got carried away." He moved to touch her, but Michael moved faster, stepping neatly between them.

"I said it's time for you to go."

Nick was in full control again, cool composure masking any hint of his real feelings. "Very well. We'll talk later."

Cara poked her head around Michael. "I'm not changing my mind, Nick."

"I understand. I shouldn't have overreacted. It's just that I wanted them so badly. Forgive me, darling?" He actually managed to look contrite.

Cara smiled weakly. "Of course." Anything to get him out of here before Michael throttled him.

With a last blistering look at Michael, Nick strode into the mudroom. A few seconds later the door slammed behind him, rattling the windows.

Cara blew out a long breath, her eyes meeting Michael's. "He wouldn't have hurt me. He was just angry about the paintings."

"Maybe not, but I didn't think it was worth taking the chance."

She sank onto the sofa, grateful for its support.

Michael sat in the easy chair, leaning forward, his blue eyes filled with concern. "Are you sure you're all right?"

Cara smiled. "I'm fine. Besides, isn't that supposed to be my line? You're the one who got shot." She leaned back and closed her eyes. "Maybe we should clarify a few things."

"Fine by me. I'll start. Tell me about your paintings, the ones that Nick wants so badly."

Cara opened her eyes, surprised at the turn of the conversation. She'd been expecting him to talk about being shot—not her artwork. "There's not much to tell. Once, when I was a kid, I stumbled on the ruins of an old mine up in the mountains. It was a long way from here. Straight up the canyon, something like five or six miles past the tunnel where I found you. I'm not good at distances.

"Anyway, I managed to climb up to a ridge of sorts, nestled in a valley, and there it was, perched on the top of the mountain, defying nature. There wasn't much left. Fallen timbers and a sink hole. The remnants of a shack of some kind—one window, unbroken, silhouetted against the sky. It seemed so lonely there, sort of lost in time. So I sketched it from various vantage points.

"Then, a few months ago, I came across the sketches and remembered the mine. I tried to find it again. I went to where I thought it was, but I couldn't find it. I guess I'd forgotten the exact location. Whatever had been there was gone. Anyway, for whatever reason, it still called to me. So I painted it. But I never could seem to get it right—to capture the magic. So I painted it again and then again, each time using a different angle and different light, the result being the series of paintings Nick was talking about."

"One of the paintings is called *The Promise*?"

"Yes, that's the only one Nick's actually ever seen."

"So why did you call it that?" His voice was tight, almost tense.

"My grandfather used to talk about a silver mine named the Promise. It was lost, too. Like my mine. Made me think of all the hopes and dreams that died in those mountains." She shrugged. "So I named the painting after it. It just seemed right somehow. Why do you ask?"

"Because"—his gaze met hers, his eyes full of pain—"my father owned the Promise."

Chapter Seven

"I feel like the whole world has turned upside down." Patrick twirled the shot glass with his fingers, swirling the amber liquid inside it.

"Ain't surprisin'." Pete swallowed his whiskey in a single gulp and picked up the bottle for more.

Patrick glanced around Owen's saloon. Dust danced in the sunbeam streaming through the open door. The Irish Rose never closed, and the place was always packed. With the mines working day and night, there was always a steady stream of men either just getting off their shifts or just going on. And it seemed they all wanted a shot to start the job, or a few more to hold them over until they were up the mountain again. Just at the moment Patrick was inclined to agree. He turned back to Pete, fighting the sick feeling in his gut. "Michael didn't kill our father."

"You know that and I know that; it's just that Amos Striker seems to have missed out on the fact."

"Amos Striker's no better than a—"

"True enough, but ain't no good yellin' it out for the

world to hear." Pete jerked his head in the direction of the other patrons in the saloon.

Patrick felt himself go hot, a combination of anger, alcohol, and embarrassment.

Pete lifted his glass, pondering his whiskey for a moment, obviously choosing his words. "On the positive side, Owen promised to ride shotgun on the man. You heard him."

"Yeah, for all the good that'll do." Patrick knew he sounded sullen, but he felt as though he were hamstrung. Everybody was telling him how to think, how to feel.

Pete raised his bushy eyebrows, his steady gaze meeting Patrick's, waiting.

"It's just that it seems to me that Owen could have stood up more for Michael."

Pete contemplated his glass again. "Well, now, Owen likes to sit on the fence until he knows which way the wind's a-blowin'. That's how he's made a success of himself."

"But we're talking about *Michael*."

"Don't make no difference. Patrick, I know you and Owen are close, but you've got to see the truth of it. He ain't got the family loyalty you think he does."

"That's ridiculous, Pete. He and my father have been together almost since they came to this country. He traipsed all over the California goldfields with us, bankrolling my father so that he could discover the next mother lode. Hell, Owen was the one who raised us."

"Rose was the one who raised you. Never forget that, boy."

Patrick felt his face grow hot. "You know I didn't mean any disrespect to Mother. But Owen's always been there for me." He met Pete's steady gaze. "He was there for me after Mother left. Father sure as hell wasn't." He downed the liquor in the shot glass, a shudder rippling across his shoulders. It was still hard to talk about his mother's desertion.

"You see what you want to see." Pete shrugged and filled both their glasses.

"Mornin', boys. Did I hear talk o' the mother lode?" Arless Hurley sidled up to the bar, his cheeks already showing the rosy glow of a bit too much alcohol. "Sorry to hear about yer da, Patrick."

"Thanks, Arless."

Pete signaled the barman, who set a glass in front of the miner. Arless filled it to the rim and swallowed the contents in a single gulp, wiping his mouth with the back of his hand. "Ah, that'll bring a man to his senses, all right." He cocked his head to one side and eyed Patrick speculatively. "Any word on where exactly Duncan found the silver?"

"What do you know about it?"

Arless grinned good-naturedly. "Not much. I heard word 'round town, the night Duncan met his maker. He wasn't being none too quiet about it, if ya take my meanin', but I figured he was just blatherin'. So I didn't give it another thought." He paused and poured another round, obviously enjoying himself.

He leaned forward conspiratorially. "But then this mornin' I found meself in need o' a little female companionship." He burped. "So I headed over to Corabeth's. She don't charge a man his life's savings, like them fancy girls over at Belle's. Why, I remember—"

Pete held up a hand, cutting the man off before he could wander off the subject. "Corabeth, Arless."

"Oh, yes, fine girl. Knows how to make a man feel like a man." He grinned and downed the whiskey.

"What does Corabeth have to do with my father?" Patrick inserted.

"Right, well, ya see, when I got there, Corabeth was full o' the news that Duncan had struck it rich."

"You just said the news was all over town." Patrick shot a disgusted look at the old sot.

"Ah, but Corabeth was certain there was truth to the talk."

"Had she been with my father?" Duncan had taken to spending time at the cribs after Rose had disappeared, but Patrick had no idea if he favored a particular girl.

"No, but she had her information straight from Loralee."

"Loralee?"

"Aye, she and your father were friends, don't ya know." Arless winked and poked Patrick in the ribs. "Seems Duncan was with her the night he died. God rest his soul." He crossed himself, but in his inebriated state he managed only three of the four stations.

"And this Loralee, she works out of a crib?" Patrick felt his spirits rise. If the woman had been with his father, then maybe she'd be able to shed some light on what had really happened.

"Aye, that she does, boy. And I'll be bettin' she knows more than a bit about this claim o' Duncan's."

Pete stroked his mustache thoughtfully. "You been flappin' your gums to anyone else about this, Arless?"

He screwed up his face, concentrating on Pete's question. "Can't say that I did or didn't. I'm afraid my mind ain't what it used to be. The liquor helps me forget about Lena, but unfortunately it ain't particular. So I'm afraid I don't remember much o' anything at all."

He looked so remorseful that Patrick patted him on the shoulder. "Never mind, Arless. Have the rest of the bottle on us."

"Much obliged, boys." He tipped his hat and turned to the bottle, a look of befuddled joy coloring his expression.

Patrick drained the rest of his whiskey, slamming the empty glass down on the bar. "I need to find this girl, Pete."

"I'd say you do. Want me to come along?"

"No, this is something I'd like to handle on my own. I'll meet you back at Clune."

Pete nodded and Patrick turned to go. "Patrick?"

He looked back over his shoulder. Pete was standing

where he'd left him, his eyes narrowed with concern.

"Be careful, son. I don't like the feel of this whole thing. There's more here than we're understanding." He paused and studied the toes of his boots, then looked up again to meet Patrick's gaze. "I don't want to lose you, too."

It was probably the longest speech Pete had ever made. Patrick swallowed over the lump in his throat. "I'll be careful. I promise."

Loralee leaned back against the closed door of her room, grateful to finally be alone. She'd had a busy morning. Not that she wasn't grateful for the money. She needed all she could get to send to Mary.

Of course, her sister, Faye, could more than afford to take care of the child, but Loralee wanted her daughter to know that her mother loved her. It had taken every ounce of self-control she'd had to send her away like that, but the cribs were no place for a child, especially one as lovely as hers. She patted the locket between her breasts. Her baby was safe.

Her sister had done well for herself: a fine, fancy parsonage in Richmond and a handsome young husband to boot. At least, when Corabeth had read her Faye's letters it had sounded that way.

Corabeth.

Loralee frowned. She'd not seen hide nor hair of her friend all day. Of course, it had been a rather hectic morning. First the wild dash to get Jack safely to Ginny's, and then three rambunctious cowboys in town for a good time. She ran a hand tiredly through her hair. It was a wonder she could function at all.

The door rattled as someone pounded on it. Loralee sighed, wishing she'd barred the door.

She drew in a sharp breath and dropped down onto the end of the bed, her heart fluttering in her throat, a sudden thought pushing itself front and center in her brain, making her forget all about the customer at the door. She stared in fascination at the bar hanging beside the door.

When it was in place, the door was locked—from the inside. Otherwise the door was open. There was no other way to lock it. None at all.

All the cribs had bars like hers—including Corabeth's. And Corabeth's door was locked. She couldn't be away. Loralee shivered and rubbed her arms, suddenly certain that something was wrong.

The pounding on the door grew more insistent. Frustration welled inside her. She didn't have time for a randy miner right now. "Go away; I'm not open for business."

Her thoughts returned to Corabeth, her heart pounding against her ribs as fear began to blossom. She struggled to get control of herself. The other girl was probably just taking a day off, getting some much-needed sleep. Her mind accepted the information, but her heart refused to go back to its normal pace.

The pounding on the door stopped, and she looked up in time to see the doorknob turn. She didn't have time for this, but obviously the man on the other side wasn't going to take no for an answer. She sighed and stood up, ready to do what it took to get rid of him. Corabeth needed her. She could feel it.

The door swung open, revealing the man on the boardwalk. He was a stranger, which in and of itself wasn't all that unusual, but he didn't have the look of the men who frequented the cribs. In fact, he really didn't look like the type who needed to hire a woman at all, but it wasn't her place to judge.

He stepped into the room, hat in hand. Well, that was a first. Her empty excuses died on her lips. "Are you Loralee?"

Something in the timber of his voice tugged at her subconscious. She knew that voice. Or at least she thought she did.

"Yeah, but I'm not open for business right now. I've got things need tendin' to."

The man actually blushed, and she bit back a desire to reassure him.

"I didn't come here for . . ." His face turned even more crimson.

She frowned. Now that he was standing in the light from the window, she recognized him, or at least she recognized his features: there was no mistaking that inky black hair. "You're one of Duncan's boys."

The man nodded. "Patrick."

She moved past him, the smell of leather and lye soap filling her nose. Closing the door, she turned around to face him. "I'm so sorry about your father. He was a good man."

His cool green gaze searched her face, looking for answers she couldn't give him. "You were with him last night." It was a statement, not a question.

"I was. And I want to talk to you about it."

He raised his eyebrows, forming a single black arch. "But?"

He must have seen it in her face. "But I need to check on a friend. I think she might be in trouble."

His look changed to concern. "Can I help?"

She nodded gratefully. Duncan's son was a lot like his father: a good man at heart. She led him out the door onto the misshapen boardwalk. "It's just down here." She pounded on the rickety door. "Corabeth? Are you in there?" Silence. "It's me, Loralee." Still no one answered.

"Maybe she's out."

Loralee looked up at the tall man beside her. "That's what I thought, too. But the door's locked." She met his puzzled gaze. "From the inside."

In an instant his expression changed. The confusion was gone. In its place Loralee saw a competence that she knew she could rely on. "How long has it been locked?"

"Most of the day." She looked down at her feet. "I only just realized—about the bar, I mean." She felt guilt welling up inside her.

He touched her arm, the simple gesture absolving her of any wrongdoing. "Is there a back door?"

"No. Corabeth has one of the smaller rooms. There's only the one door."

"All right then, stand back."

She stood aside, watching as he leaned slightly forward, leading with a shoulder. He ran toward the door, ramming into the thin planks of wood. There was a sickly thud as muscle met board. The door cracked off the hinges and fell forward into the room.

The room was ominously quiet.

"Let me go first." He stepped gingerly over the splintered door, reaching back to help her step around it. The room was heavily shadowed, the curtain tightly drawn, the oil lamp unlit.

Loralee pushed past Patrick, her heart thudding in her chest. "Corabeth? Honey, are you in here?"

The bedstead was in the far corner, turned so that the foot faced the window. Corabeth always said she liked to see the sun first thing when she woke. A wash of sunlight from the now permanently open door illuminated the body on the bed.

"Corabeth!" The name came out more a shriek than a word. Loralee swallowed back the bile rising in her throat. She rushed to the side of the bed, almost tripping over an empty bottle, and knelt beside her friend. Corabeth's soft brown eyes were fixed on the ceiling. Her half-clothed body lay askew on the mattress, like a rag doll abandoned and forgotten.

Loralee frantically rubbed one of her friend's cold hands between both of hers, willing her own body's heat into Corabeth's, tears streaming down her face. She anxiously watched Corabeth's face, still holding fast to her hand, waiting for a smile, for some sign that this was nothing more than a twisted prank. But Corabeth didn't move, couldn't move.

Corabeth was dead.

Chapter Eight

"Okay, I'm confused." Cara blew out a breath. "How can your father be the owner of an old mine in the middle of a national forest?"

Michael leaned forward, his eyes narrowed in concentration. Cara had the distinct feeling that whatever he was going to say next, she didn't want to hear. "When did you paint *The Promise*, Cara?"

"A year ago or so." She tried to figure out what exactly this had to do with his father owning the mine.

"I meant what was the date?"

"I'm not sure of the day."

"The year, Cara?" His intensity was beginning to make her nervous.

"Nineteen ninety-eight or ninety-nine, I guess."

He released a deep breath, almost a sigh. "And when did you paint the painting I saw, the one of us?"

This was getting surreal. "I told you."

"The *year*." He reached for her hand.

"Nineteen ninety-three. Right after you disappeared." She tried, but couldn't keep the bitterness out of her voice.

He stroked her hand lightly with his thumb. "When were you born, Cara?"

"Nineteen seventy-six, but I don't see what any of this has to do with—"

"I was born in 1860."

"Excuse me?" She tried to think, to make his words make sense. Surely she'd misunderstood.

"My father discovered the Promise in 1879, the year after I found you in the snow."

"That's impossible." She stared at him, letting the significance of his words wash over her, thinking that any minute he'd suddenly laugh and say it was all a joke. But he didn't. His face was deadly serious, and the look in his eyes told her that he was as overwhelmed as she.

"Two days ago I would have agreed with you, but now . . ." He let go of her hand, leaning back in the chair, a parade of emotions chasing across his face. "Hell, I don't know."

"But you're saying . . ." She broke off, unable to continue the thought. Somehow they'd gone from a miraculous reunion to an episode of *The Twilight Zone*.

"Cara, listen to me." He reached for her hand again, his eyes intense. "The truth is here somewhere. We just have to find it. Tell me what you remember about the morning after your accident."

She nodded, her trust instinctive. "I woke up in that mine tunnel and you were gone. I figured you'd left to find help."

"I was getting water."

She let her mind slip back to that morning in the cave. "It was cold, and my head hurt, and the world was still all wobbly. But I wanted to get up. To . . . to find out what happened."

"Your parents."

She nodded. "They were dead. My grandfather identified the bodies, but they couldn't find me."

"The explosion killed them?"

94

"That—or the car wreck."

"Train car?"

"Automobile," she answered without thinking, her thoughts on her parents.

"Automobile?" If the situation hadn't been so dire, his expression would have been comical. "I've read about them, but I've never seen one. There aren't any in Silver-thread—" He stopped, the impact of his comment hitting home. "In my time."

She knew she ought to be questioning his sanity—or at least his story. But all she could think about was the fact that he hadn't deserted her—at least not by choice. Some-how, if he was to be believed, she had crossed into his world or the other way around. For one night they had occupied the same temporal plane. And then somehow they had been separated again.

By time.

Care swallowed a sob. It was all so insane.

He must have heard her, or felt her pain, or just wanted the connection, because he moved to the sofa and pulled her into his arms. "It'll be all right. We'll figure this out. The most important thing is that you found me again—whatever time we're in. I'd have died without you, Cara. You saved my life."

She nodded against his chest, tears threatening. "Just like you saved mine." She listened to the soft, steady beat of his heart, drawing strength from it.

"I looked everywhere for you, you know." His words were quiet, almost a whisper. "I couldn't understand where you'd gone—I worried about you; I . . . I cared about you."

"I kept telling them you were real, that you'd saved me, that I owed you my life." She rattled on, her tears falling in earnest now. "They thought it was trauma, that the horror of witnessing my parents' deaths caused me to hal-lucinate. Oh, God, Michael, they convinced me that I made you up." She stared up at him, memorizing the curves of

95

his face, trying to understand what was happening to them.

"They who?" His look was at once protective and questioning—angry and concerned. She marveled at his strength. She was sitting here falling apart and *he* was the one who had traveled through time.

"My grandfather, and my doctors." She frowned, remembering. "My grandfather was there when I left the tunnel. I insisted that they look, but you were gone—and the mine was empty." She fought against a sob. "When I woke up in the hospital, they told me that you were a figment of my imagination."

"And you believed them?" His voice was harsh, and she winced at the pain she heard there.

"No. Not at first. As soon as I was well enough I went back there, back to the tunnel. And I waited for you. I came every day, Michael. I was determined to find you, to prove to my grandfather that you were real. But you never came."

"But I did. I searched that damn mountain for you. Had my family out looking, too. They were certain you'd died or gone back to wherever you came from. But I was so sure you were out there somewhere. That you needed me. Then, when it became apparent that my family was right, I stopped searching, but I kept coming back to the tunnel, Cara, on the off chance that you'd be there. That you'd come back."

"But I didn't." Her voice cracked, and the anguish she felt was mirrored in the blue of his eyes.

"You couldn't."

"I wanted to believe in you, Michael. I wanted to so badly. But my grandfather thought I was using you as a crutch. A way to deal with the loss of my parents. He even sent me to a psychiatrist."

He raised a brow in question.

"For my head. To make me see the truth of it. And so,

little by little, I began to accept the fact that I'd made you up."

His hand tightened around hers. "But you didn't."

She smiled at him through her tears. "No. I didn't."

Without a word he pulled her tightly against his chest. She let the warmth of him surround and comfort her. She breathed deeply, letting his scent, so familiar, so foreign, fill her, soothe her.

He was a stranger. He was her angel.

And if they were right, he was lost in her time.

Michael closed his eyes, reveling in the feel of her heartbeat, the soft silkiness of her hair. How many nights had he dreamed about this golden hair and these green eyes? And now she was here, in his arms. He tipped up her chin, looking deep into her eyes. Her face was wet with tears, and her expression was a mixture of awe and fear. With a gentle finger he brushed away the moisture on her cheek, feeling her tremble in response. Carefully, as though he might break her, he pressed his lips against hers.

She opened her mouth, and what had started as a comforting touch ignited into passion born of longing and joy. He circled her lips with his tongue, tasting the salt of her tears. All he wanted to do was hold her—never let her go, to prove to himself that he was alive, no matter the century.

He sighed, pushing away his need. No matter how badly he wanted her, this wasn't the time. He nestled his chin on top of her head. "Cara, we need to talk." He felt her nod, and gently released her. They sat facing each other, still holding hands, as if to be certain neither of them would disappear.

"This all sounds crazy." Cara ran a hand through her hair, her mind in turmoil. On the one hand, she wanted to throw herself into his arms, surrender body and soul. On the other hand she could hear her grandfather's voice warning her that things were not always as they seemed. It was almost more than she could bear.

"I know it does." He looked almost as confused as she felt. "But the reality is that a few days ago I was riding line on Clune, trying to build a life for my family, a real home. And today I discover that somehow I've leaped forward a hundred years and that the people I love are all long dead."

"Family?" Cara felt something tighten around her chest, impeding her breathing. "Are you . . . I mean, do you have a—" She stopped, uncertain how to put her question into words.

Michael smiled. "Do I have a wife?"

She nodded mutely, waiting.

"No, Cara, I don't. I was speaking of my father and brother."

She exhaled in relief, surprised to find that she'd been holding her breath. "What about your mother?"

Cara watched as a parade of emotions washed across his face: anger, hurt, and then finally a cold mask that effectively shut her out. "She's gone."

"Gone?"

"She abandoned us." There was a finality to his answer that made her swallow her curiosity. Whatever his mother had done, it was still painful for him to talk about.

"Okay, so you were riding line," she said, moving them back to the topic at hand.

"Right. I'd been at it all day, checking stock and making sure our fences weren't down. I'd finished with the high pastures, so just after sunset I decided to head back. By the time I got to the main road it was dark. The moon hadn't risen yet, so it was hard to make anything out. I could see lights from Clune—my ranch—in the distance, but it was still a good ways off."

He paused, frowning at the memory. "The shot came from somewhere off to my left. I couldn't see a thing, and I figured it was best to get the hell out of there."

"Why didn't you ride home?"

"There was nothing between me and the ranch but bare ground. I needed cover, and I knew that if I could make the trees I had a chance."

"So you hoped you'd lose your assailant?" She'd never actually used the word *assailant* in conversation before. It made her feel queasy to think that someone had actually been trying to kill him.

"Right, or least keep him well behind me. Unfortunately I hadn't gambled on how badly I was hurt. It was slow going, and I could hear him behind me. I knew it wouldn't be long before he caught up with me. So finally I jumped off Roscoe."

"Roscoe?"

"My horse." He shrugged. "I figured the man trailing me would follow Roscoe back down the mountain, or see that his saddle was empty and assume I was dead."

Cara shivered again.

"I knew I was close to that old tunnel—the one I took you to. The one where you found me . . ." He trailed off, then continued. "If I could just make it there, I was pretty certain that whoever shot me wouldn't be able to find me even if he came back. I waited until I heard him go after Roscoe, then managed to crawl inside. You pretty much know the rest."

She nodded, her teeth worrying the soft inside of her lower lip. "And you don't have any idea who's trying to kill you?"

"None at all. Could have been a road agent. I can't think of any enemies. Truth of it is, there's no way to know—especially now." He grimaced, and again she realized just how difficult this must be for him.

"Your family must be worried sick."

"I'm not certain my father will be sober enough to know I'm missing." Sharp-edged bitterness colored his voice.

"But your brother?"

"He'll think I'm dead."

Dee Davis

"Maybe not. Maybe . . ." She trailed off, wishing she knew what to say.

He shook his head. "It's rough out there, and I was supposed to be back by nightfall. Patrick knows I'd never break my word—unless I had no choice."

"Well, maybe there's some way to get you back." She was surprised how much the thought upset her. She'd just found him. The idea of letting him vanish from her life again was not appealing, but she had to think of his needs first.

"How?" The single word sounded so hopeless it brought tears to her eyes. "Cara, we don't even know for certain how I got here."

She swallowed her emotions. This was not the time. She had to be strong, to think clearly. "Well, we can be fairly sure it has to do with that tunnel where you found me."

"True, but it has to be something more than that. I've been in it numerous times and not a damn thing has happened." There was an edge to his voice, a note of desperation.

She reached for his hand. "We've just got to think it through. The two times something happened, we were together."

"True."

Cara recognized the emotions she saw swirling in the blue depths of his eyes, and she was fairly certain her own reflected his turmoil. She took a deep breath. "Okay, so we know there is some relationship between you and me and the tunnel. Is there anything else?"

"There has to be, but damned if I know what. Maybe it's just coincidence. Maybe those were the only times we were actually in the tunnel at the same time."

Cara shook her head, stroking the smooth silver of her pendant. "No, it has to be more than that, because when you found me I was outside the mine. Remember?"

"You're right." He frowned. "Maybe it's just proximity."

The Promise

"Maybe." A thought occurred to her. "Or maybe it has to do with need."

He shot her a puzzled look. "What do you mean?"

She concentrated on putting her thoughts into words. "When you found me I had just survived the car wreck that killed my parents. I was disoriented and lost in grief. I had no coat and no idea I was in the middle of a blizzard. Without you I wouldn't have survived on that mountain."

He cocked his head to one side, understanding spreading across his face. "And I would definitely have died if you hadn't found me in the tunnel."

"Exactly." She smiled at him as if he were a prize pupil.

"So you're thinking that it's adversity that brings us together?"

She sighed. "I don't know what I'm saying, really. I just know that when I needed you, you were there. And then, after all this time, despite the fact that I no longer—" She stopped, embarrassed at the direction her thoughts had taken her.

"After you no longer believed I existed."

She nodded miserably.

"Cara, it's all right. I'm not sure that I'd have reacted any differently, given the circumstances."

She shot him a tremulous smile, grateful for his support. "Anyway, after all this time, the bottom line is that when you needed me I was there. All I'm saying is that there's definitely a powerful connection between us."

"I can't say I disagree with that." His slow smile made her bones dissolve like a spoonful of sugar in hot tea. She barely knew him, but his power over her hadn't lessened in the nine years since their first encounter. If anything it was stronger, pulling at her like a magnet. She wanted to crawl inside him, to find shelter in his steely strength. She wanted . . . Well, she couldn't put a polite name to *that*. She felt the heat of a blush staining her cheeks.

"What about you?" he asked.

"What about me?"

The smile broadened, telling her he had correctly determined her train of thought. "Surely after all this time
there's someone in your life. Nick?" He sobered, his face
tightening at the thought of her recent guest.

"No, not Nick."

"Well, there must be somebody."

"No. Nothing serious, anyway. It costs too much to give
your heart, Michael. Such promises are made to be broken.
That's a lesson I've learned very well. First with my parents, then with you . . ." She trailed off, embarrassed.

"I'm real, Cara." The fire in his eyes sent a shiver of
desire coursing through her.

"I had no way of knowing that. And it just all hurt so
badly. But gradually, in time, I began to heal, and I threw
myself into my art. Painting was everything for me—emo-
tional involvement at a risk-free level." She shrugged, turning away from him. "Only there's no such thing."

"What happened?" Michael's voice was gentle.

"I got an offer to work in New York with a painter
named Adrian DeBeck. Grandfather wanted me to stay in
Colorado and attend the university. I was young and stupid and certain that I knew what was best for me. He just
wanted me to be nearby. We quarreled." She paused, groping for words. Michael stroked her palm, the gesture at
once soothing and stimulating.

She looked up to meet his eyes and was amazed at the
compassion there. "I walked away without looking back.
And a year later he was dead." She tried to stop the tears,
but they seemed to have a will of their own. "He gave me
everything, and I walked away without even saying thank-
you. Three months after that I found out that Adrian had
been selling my paintings as his own. That he'd . . . that
he'd been using me for months. So in the end, Grandfather
was right."

The sympathy in his eyes was hard to bear. "If we could
only see the future, we'd all handle things differently."

She nodded, wiping angrily at her tears. "I'm okay. I

don't know why I told you all of that. It's just that there isn't anyone in my life. It hurts too much when you lose them."

"Not everyone leaves, Cara." His gaze met hers, his eyes intense.

She looked away, glancing at the clock, trying to ignore the tangled emotions building inside her. "It's late. We've been talking for hours. I shouldn't have let you go this long without a rest and something to eat." She eyed him guiltily, knowing she was babbling.

"And we need to change your bandage. Maybe you could start with a shower." That always made her feel better when she was sick. Not that he was sick, exactly. In fact, at the moment he looked remarkably healthy. *Oh, Lord.* She stood up, fidgeting with the edge of her shirt.

He stood, too, catching her restless fingers between his palms as he pulled her closer. She wanted him so badly she could actually feel it burning in her gut, but she was also aware that her batting average with men was zero. What if she let him down? Or worse, what if he wanted her only for now? She wasn't sure she could give herself to this man without knowing it was forever.

Her brain reiterated all those thoughts as her body melded to his. His heat seared through her, and she thought she might not survive the sheer joy of touching him. She tipped back her head and met the question in his blue gaze.

With an almost superhuman effort, she pushed away, her head prevailing over her mutinous body. She shuddered as they separated, the ache inside shifting from her gut to her heart.

She pasted on what she hoped was a carefree smile and tried to ignore the flash of hurt in his eyes. "Come on; I'll show you how to work the shower."

She turned away, trying to keep her emotions in check.

Michael Macpherson wasn't forever. He couldn't be.

Chapter Nine

"He would have liked it up here." Owen's voice was hushed, almost reverent, as he looked out across the valley.

Patrick followed his gaze. The grave was situated in a tiny meadow at the top of what Michael had always called the Humpback, a high, bumpy cliff hanging out over the river. From here the ranch was visible, spreading out across the valley floor, and—more important, really—the mountains swooped down to the ridge, inviting a person to climb higher, farther, into their waiting purple majesty. His father had always been drawn to the mountains.

"He spent a good part of his life in these mountains, made and lost a fortune here. I thought it only right he be buried here." Patrick looked at the grave marker, his voice filled with sorrow and a trace of bitterness.

"He was a good man, and he wouldn't want you to waste time grieving."

Patrick shrugged. "It's hard, especially when the sheriff seems to believe that my brother murdered my father for some nonexistent silver strike."

"Now, Patrick, you have to admit that from Amos's

104

point of view the facts fit. He's just doing his job." Owen's words were meant to be comforting, but Patrick didn't feel a bit better.

"The only way I'll ever believe Michael murdered anyone is if he tells me so himself." Patrick held the older man's gaze, surprised when he turned away.

"I expect all the talk will come to nothing. With any luck, Michael will come riding in here with some wild story, and the whole thing will be over," Owen said.

His eyes searched the valley floor, almost as if Owen's words could somehow conjure up his brother. "I hope so. But that won't change the fact that my father's dead."

"No. It won't." Owen straightened the brim of his hat and sighed. "I'm sorry I didn't get out here sooner. I meant to, but things just got away from me. Seems there was a little excitement in town yesterday. Some whore decided life wasn't all it was cracked up to be."

"I know, I was there."

Owen frowned. "At the cribs? Jesus, Patrick, how many times have I told you about those places?"

Patrick let out a harsh laugh. "God, Owen, what do you take me for? I lose my father and brother in one fell swoop and then head off to the cribs for a little carnal merry-making? Sounds more like something Amos would do."

"Why would you say that?" Owen asked, his brows drawn together in confusion.

"I don't know. No reason, really. He just seems the type. Speaking of which, any idea where our fair-haired boy was yesterday? I tried to report the death, but he was nowhere to be found."

Owen shook his head. "I've absolutely no idea. The last time I saw him was with you."

Patrick shrugged. "It doesn't really matter. Doc handled things. I just thought he ought to be informed."

"Of the death of a whore? Patrick, who cares if some two-bit floozy uses laudanum to buy herself a ticket straight to hell? I say we're better off without her."

"That's a little harsh, Owen, even for you. I know you don't think much of the profession as a whole, but surely that doesn't mean you wish them all dead?"

"No, of course not. If I sounded harsh, I didn't mean to." He tilted his head to one side, curiosity lighting his face. "You never said what you were doing out by the cribs."

"I was . . . ah . . . just walking, trying to digest the crap Striker was throwing out." He paused, embarrassed to meet Owen's gaze. "You, too, for that matter."

The Englishman sounded apologetic. "I wasn't agreeing or disagreeing with him, Patrick. I was just trying to listen to the facts."

"Well, you're certainly free to believe what you want."

Owen reached over to place a hand on Patrick's shoulder. "I don't believe Michael killed your father, Patrick, and I didn't come out here to fight with you."

Patrick drew in a deep breath and stared at his boot tips. "I know."

"I'm here for you, son. Don't forget that."

Patrick nodded and looked up, his sense of hopelessness overwhelming.

"It's going to be all right. I swear it. You've just got to be patient."

"I know." He strove to display a calm he didn't feel. There was no sense in worrying Owen.

The older man studied him for a bit, then smiled. "I'd best get back to town. You never know when Sam's going to take it in his head to provide drinks for the house."

Patrick smiled wryly. "You know as well as I do that Sam's even tighter than you. If that's possible."

Owen wrapped an arm around Patrick's shoulders. "Walk with me back to the ranch."

"No. I need to think a bit, and this is as good a place as any."

"All right, but I'll come back out in a couple of days to check on you."

"You don't need to do that, Owen. I'll be fine. I'm not a kid anymore."

"I know that. I just worry about you. You're the only family I have left." He pulled Patrick into a brief hug and then let him go. "You know where to find me."

"I do."

Patrick watched Owen make his way down the humpback. Everything was so mixed up, he didn't know which way to turn. Every time he thought he was getting a handle on life, it dealt him another blow. And this time he didn't have anyone to shelter him from it.

Except Owen. Patrick shook his head at the thought. He didn't want to need anyone. It hurt too damn much. But at the same time, he wasn't sure what the hell he was going to do on his own.

If Michael was dead—and somehow he'd actually come to the point where he believed that—then the ranch was his. But what the hell did he want with a ranch? Maybe he'd just give the damn thing to Owen. Or better yet, to Pete.

But at the same time, he couldn't. It was Michael's legacy. Surely he owed it to his brother to keep his dream alive? There were so many questions. What he needed were answers. Patrick ran his hands through his hair, his eye catching on his father's grave.

He walked over to it, looking down at the simple wooden cross. "I don't know what to do." His jaw tightened as he tried to stave off the despair threatening to swallow him whole. "I never figured on standing here, and I sure as hell didn't figure on doing it alone."

He knelt by the grave, running a hand through the loose rocks and dirt that covered his father's body. "Tell me what to do. They're saying Michael killed you. They're saying you struck it rich. I don't know what to believe. I don't know who to believe."

The wind whispered across the silent meadow, swirling bits of dust as it passed across the grave. Patrick blew out a breath and opened his eyes, drinking in the cool colors of the mountains, inhaling the pungent scent of freshly turned earth.

But there were no answers here.

Patrick felt like a buffalo in a china shop. He sat at the table across from Loralee, cattycorner to her friend Ginny, balancing a porcelain cup on his knee. Who'd have thought he'd be having tea with a lady of the line and an Indian squaw in a run-down old shack just outside the red-light district of a mining camp?

But then, who'd have thought his life would have taken any of the turns it had recently?

He lifted the cup to his lips and tried not to slurp the hot liquid.

"Have some cake, Mr. Macpherson."

Jumping at the excuse to put the teacup down, he almost slammed it on the table, stopping himself at the last minute and managing to place it with little more than a clatter, only a small amount of tea sloshing into the saucer. His mother would have laughed.

"Thank you, Miz . . ." He stopped, uncertain how to continue. Womenfolk in these parts, and especially these circumstances, usually didn't have last names, but the moment seemed to call for formality.

"Ginny'll do." The Ute woman smiled at him, and he was surprised at the way it lit up her face. Why, she was almost beautifull. Time—and, no doubt, a rough life—had etched fine lines around her mouth and eyes, but the details seemed only to enhance her appeal. He imagined that she had once been a pretty woman.

He bit into the cake she offered him, allowing the buttery flavor to slide into his mouth and down his throat. It was heaven, pure heaven. He swallowed and blushed under the amused gaze of his two companions. "I, uh, don't get much cake at Clune," he managed by way of explanation.

"Don't imagine you do." Loralee's smile was warm. It had sort of the same effect as the cake, filling him with warmth and goodness, making him want more. *An angel in a hellhole.* The words jumped out at him, and he was surprised at the poetic turn of his thoughts.

"More?" Ginny held out the plate again, meeting his gaze. From the look reflected there, he was certain that she was well aware of the direction his mind had been going. She smiled tolerantly as he took another slice of cake. "Loralee told me about your father and brother. I'm mighty sorry for your loss."

"Did you know my father?"

"Only in passing. But he was a good man."

Patrick nodded, his mouth full of cake.

"Is there any word on your brother?" Loralee leaned forward, her warm brown eyes full of concern.

"Nothing." He felt so hopeless. His brother was never coming back. "I think I'd have heard from him by now—if he was still alive."

"I'm so sorry."

He wanted to reach out and touch her, to let her know how much comfort her words brought him.

Ginny sighed. "Remember, Mr. Macpherson, things are rarely as they seem. One merely has to scratch the surface to see the true reflection."

Patrick frowned. The woman made damn good cake, but she made absolutely no sense. Must be the Ute in her. It seemed they were always speaking in riddles. Pete believed they had a direct line to the Almighty that white men couldn't even fathom. "Call me Patrick."

The older woman nodded, managing to look wise and serene at the same time. Patrick had a sudden longing to tell her all his fears, to unburden himself as if she could wave her hand and somehow make this whole nightmare go away.

But he hadn't come here for absolution, and he certainly hadn't come for tea and cake, no matter how good it was.

He'd come here for answers. "I'm hoping Loralee here can help me get a better understanding of what happened to my father. According to Arless Hurley, she may have been the last person to see him alive." Loralee flinched as if he'd hit her. "Beg pardon, ma'am. I should've qualified that. I didn't mean to imply that you . . . well, that you could have . . ." He hesitated, embarrassed by his blunder.

Ginny reached over and patted Loralee's hand. "Come now, girl; he's not saying you killed the man. Tell him what you know."

Loralee's face brightened. "There's not too much to tell. Duncan had become something of a regular." She ducked her head, her pale cheeks stained with a blush. It was another contradiction in Loralee: at times she seemed so young and innocent, hardly traits one expected in a soiled dove.

Not that he really knew a whole lot about the subject firsthand. That was yet another area of his life he was living vicariously through others. He pulled away from his thoughts, forcing himself to concentrate on the subject at hand. "I need you to try to remember what my father said that last evening." He spoke gently and was rewarded with a nod of approval from Ginny. She leaned back in her chair, subtly withdrawing from the conversation.

"We talked a lot. In fact, you should know that's all we ever did. Your father just needed a friend, I think. He was so devastated when your mama ran out." She paused for a moment, looking at Patrick.

He smiled with what he hoped was encouragement. "Go on."

"Well, that particular night he was in high spirits—"

"You mean he was drunk," Patrick inserted.

"No." She screwed up her eyes in thought. "It was more than that. I mean he was always a little tippled, but this time there was genuine excitement, too. He wasn't making complete sense." She shrugged. "The whiskey, I guess. He kept talking about finding something big."

110

Patrick watched as she struggled to remember, her tiny little teeth worrying the bottom of her lip. "He spoke about finally finding the silver and how surprised you boys would be."

"He talked about Michael and me?"

She smiled. "All the time. He was so proud of the both of you."

"Michael." Patrick mumbled his brother's name under his breath. "My father was proud of Michael."

"He always said that Michael was the glue of the family. That he was determined to keep you together no matter what."

It was true. Michael had spent practically his whole life creating a home for them all, a place they could call their own. In fact, now that Patrick thought about it, Michael had never really shown any interest in things outside the family. Except for the winter he went a little crazy trying to find that girl named Cara.

Loralee leaned forward, her eyes full of concern. "Your father was proud of you, too, Patrick. He always said you were the heart of the family."

For hearing something so simple, Patrick felt absurdly happy. He forced himself to concentrate on the topic at hand. "Did he say anything about where he found this silver?"

Loralee shook her head. "No. I've tried to remember, but it was really just rambling. I do know he wanted to tell y'all."

Patrick smiled at the trace of sweet Southern drawl in her voice. It was almost as lyrical as his mother's Irish lilt had been. "Was he on his way home to do that, then?"

Her face clouded. "No. At least, I don't think so."

Patrick leaned forward, his heart beating loudly in his chest. "What do you mean?"

"Well, maybe it's nothing. But your father loves Jack as much as he loves . . ." She dipped her head in embarrassment.

111

"As much as he loves us," he finished the sentence for her. "It's all right. I think it might be true. Jack and my father were inseparable."

"Well, that's it exactly. If your father had truly been heading back to Clune, then he wouldn't have left Jack in front of my cr . . . house," she amended, color washing across her cheeks again.

"He left Jack with you?" Patrick frowned, trying to find reason where there probably was none.

"Not with me, exactly. I think he was planning to come back. He knew Jack would be safe there."

"Well, that certainly supports what I've said all along. Where is Jack now?"

"I brought him here." She shot a pleading look at Ginny, who immediately intervened.

"Now, don't go thinking Loralee was trying to make off with that horse. She brought him here because she figured he'd be safe from prying eyes."

Patrick ran a hand through his already frazzled hair. "I don't think anyone in their right mind would steal Jack, but you did the right thing. In fact, I think he should probably stay here for now. At least until I can get hold of Amos Striker."

Loralee and Ginny exchanged a look. "What's he got to do with this?"

Patrick considered Ginny's question. "Well, to start with, he's the sheriff."

The woman shrugged slightly, as if to say, So what? "I wouldn't go runnin' my mouth off to the sheriff just yet."

"Well, I can't say that I disagree with your opinion of our erstwhile lawman, but he's still the law around here. And I'd like to point out to him that it's highly unlikely that my father left town alive. Jack's presence proves that."

"Ah, but does it really prove anything? Where your father was killed is far less important than why the man died. And until you know the answer to that question, I'd be careful who I trust."

"I don't trust Striker farther than I can throw him. But he's the law around here. That has to mean something."

"Or nothing." The older woman's face closed, as if she had turned her spirit inward.

Patrick looked askance at Loralee. "Does she know something I don't?"

Ginny opened her eyes, her attention once more focused on Patrick. "Amos Striker is a killer, a cold-blooded killer."

Patrick shrugged. "Most lawmen are."

"But this one murdered my daughter."

Chapter Ten

Michael let the steamy, hot spray beat down on his back. He hadn't experienced much of this new century, but if showers were any indication, he thought he just might like it. Not that he could stay. No one was going to accuse him of being like his mother, he thought bitterly. He wasn't about to desert his family. They depended on him.

He turned, closing his eyes and letting the water slide down his face. A vision of creamy skin and alabaster breasts filled his mind, its alluring presence sending distinct messages to a much lower portion of his anatomy. *Cara.* He groaned. She was everything she'd been nine years ago and more. She was entrancing, and he wanted her—wanted all of her, body and soul.

He leaned back, letting the water pound into him, washing away his need. He couldn't have her. He belonged in another time. He had responsibilities. And unlike his mother, he wasn't going to allow unbridled emotion to let him forget about them.

"Are you going to stay in there all night? I'm starving."

He smiled at the sound of her voice. Just listening to her

talk made him hard. *So much for resolve*. He closed his eyes, pretending that they were just an ordinary couple on an ordinary night. God, how he loved ordinary. He sighed and turned off the spigots and reached for the towel she'd left him. Just two ordinary people—from two different centuries. He ran a hand through his wet hair, trying to gain control of his tangled thoughts.

Maybe ordinary was overrated.

The door squeaked as it swung open. A slender hand crept through the opening with a stack of clothing. "I think these will fit."

He grabbed the clothes, tempted to drag the woman attached to the arm along with them. "I'll be out in a minute."

She mumbled something and closed the door. He stood for a moment dripping on the floor, staring at the space where her hand had been. Lord, how he wanted her.

Cara leaned back against the door, trying to catch her breath. She hadn't even seen him, yet she felt as though she were going to explode. Desire ripped through her like a level-five tornado. He was the most amazing man she'd ever known—or not known, as the case might be.

Desire battled with common sense. He wouldn't stay, couldn't stay. She had to hold on to her emotions. If she lost her heart to Michael and he went back, she'd never survive losing him again. Unfortunately, her body had its own ideas. She ran her hands softly over her breasts, remembering his touch, his searing kisses. She was separated from him by two inches of wood.

Wood with hinges.

With a will of its own her hand reached behind her for the knob. Before she could shift her weight away from the door, it began to swing open. Thrown off balance, she careened backward, colliding with damp, sinewy muscle. *Michael*. She sucked in a breath and attempted to right herself, but he was quicker, encircling her with hard, sun-bronzed arms.

"I've got you." His whispered words tickled her ear, gently lifting the hair framing her face. Desire, hot and insistent, spread through her belly, reaching lower, quivering, waiting.

He bent his head, nuzzling the soft skin of her neck. She shivered in anticipation. With soft, dry kisses, he traced the line of her neck and shoulder, stopping along the way to explore with his tongue. She closed her eyes, allowing sensation to wash over her. His hands massaged her stomach, making slow, languorous circles, inching upward with each pass.

She arched into him, willing his hands to move faster, higher. His lips were at her ear now, causing shivers of pure ecstasy to run up and down her spine as he tugged and licked, exploring every tender crevice. Something deep inside of her began to pulse in response to his tender ministrations.

His hands found her breasts, his strong fingers curving around them, cupping them almost reverently. She arched against him, wanting more than tender touches. His thumbs began to rub and circle relentlessly, until she was rubbing against him like a crazed cat, her body begging for more.

"Tell me what you want, Cara."

She tipped her head back, leaning it against his shoulder. *You. I want you.* She tried to form the words, but his hands were robbing her of speech.

With an earsplitting trill, the phone shattered the silence. Michael jumped back. His face tightened.

"It's all right. It's just the phone." She placed a hand on his arm reassuringly. He relaxed but still looked puzzled. She grabbed the shrieking instrument, unsure whether its shrill interference was a welcome relief or an abhorrent interruption.

"Hello." She put a hand to her breast, trying to still her

heart. Michael leaned against the doorjamb, looking nothing short of magnificent in an old pair of her grandfather's jeans. They hugged his hips, sliding against . . . She sucked in a sharp breath, trying to concentrate on the telephone conversation.

"Cara, darling, are you listening?" There was a pause, and Cara's lust-filled brain finally registered that it was Nick on the other end. A bucket of cold water couldn't have worked better.

"Fine, Nick, I'm fine." At the sound of the name, Michael's lazy grin disappeared. His eyes narrowed as he listened to her end of the conversation.

"Cara, what are you doing? You're not listening to a word I'm saying."

"Yes, I am, Nick, it's just that I was busy." Michael's smile reappeared, and she felt her body tighten in response.

"All right, then, I'll get to the point." Nick's voice was almost petulant. "I wanted to give you a last chance to sell me those paintings."

"Nick, I told you when you were here: I've already sold them. I have absolutely no interest in reneging on the bargain I made."

"Very well, but don't say I didn't give you every chance. I would have paid anything, and I have a feeling you're going to regret your decision."

"I doubt it. Good night."

"Good night, darling. And Cara?"

"Yes, Nick?"

"Enjoy your boy toy." There was a click and the line went dead.

Michael had crossed to her side. "What did he want?"

Cara smiled, not willing to ruin their evening by repeating Nick's snide remarks. "Nothing, really. Just trying to get me to change my mind about the paintings."

Michael nodded, accepting her answer. He picked up the phone's receiver and listened to the hum of the dial tone. "This is a telephone, isn't it?" He held it out to her.

Cara nodded, placing the receiver back in its cradle.

"I read about it. A guy named Bell invented it several years back. I never dreamed it would really amount to anything."

"Oh, it's amounted to something, all right." At the moment she was wishing Alexander Graham Bell had never been born. Out of self-preservation, she scooped up from the floor by the bathroom the madras shirt she'd brought for him to wear, flipping it at him with an underhanded lob. "If we're going out for dinner, I think you'll probably want to get into this."

He caught it and slipped his arms into the sleeves. It was a little tight across the shoulders, but otherwise fit fine. She gulped as he started to button it. Even the simple action of his fingers sliding the buttons through each hole excited her. Oh, Lord, she had it bad.

He sat on the couch and began pulling on his boots. "How long will it take us to get into town?"

"Not long. Maybe fifteen minutes."

He frowned. "On horseback?"

"No, we'll go in my Jeep."

"Jeep?"

She grinned. "A kind of automobile. You're gonna love it." There wasn't a guy alive who didn't love going fast. Not even one from the nineteenth century.

Jeeps were incredible. Not that he was really sure what one was, exactly. He'd heard about combustion engines, but this surpassed his wildest dreams. They'd careened down the mountain in record time. And the road . . . well, the road was amazing, too. No ruts, no mud, just an endless lane of something called asphalt. *Not bad.*

They slowed as they entered the main street of Silverthread, and Michael jerked his head around, staring at the buildings on either side of him. The storefronts were different and the names had all changed, but most of the buildings were the same.

The Promise

The shanties and clapboard were all gone. The bank building was still there, housing something called CompuStore. And across the street, *Bilker's Meat Market* was still carved into the cornerstone of a brick building, although a sign underneath proudly proclaimed *The best bagels in town*. Whatever bagels were.

The dark cliffs of the mountains loomed ominously on either side, narrowing until they almost seemed to touch, framing Silverthread with their rocky crevices. They, at least, had changed very little.

He could hear the soothing rush of Willow Creek behind the buildings on the right. Somehow the noise was comforting. The boardwalks were gone, replaced by sidewalks made of the some material similar to asphalt but smoother. The street was dotted with automobiles, and warm light spilled out from doorways and windows.

They'd passed the new electric plant on the way into town. Now it was nothing more than a dilapidated old building. The mill across the way was almost totally gone, nothing left except a pile of tailings and a section of sluice leaning drunkenly over the stream. He felt a deep sense of loss; everything familiar to him was long gone and forgotten.

The town itself was smaller, certainly, and, of course, modernized. But the myriad of twinkling lights above indicated that the Flats were still the preferred place to live. At least some things never changed.

Everything was different. Everything was the same. Cara pulled the Jeep into a yellow-striped space in front of what had once been an assayer's office. The awning-covered windows now housed an artfully arrayed selection of paintings, each nestled on white velvet and framed in carved gilt. He didn't have to look for the sign. He recognized the work. "This is your gallery."

Cara nodded. "Want to come inside?"

* * *

119

"I have to finish getting these paintings ready for shipping. They're being picked up tomorrow."

He nodded absently, intent on studying a canvas hung in a small alcove on one wall. "Where was this painted?" He kept his voice mild, even though the blood pounded in his ears.

She stopped and turned back, glancing at the painting in front of him. "That's my grandfather's ranch. We passed it on the way in, but it was too dark to see it."

She started to turn away, but he reached out to stop her. "That's Clune."

She froze, staring at the canvas. "Your ranch?"

"Yeah, only it doesn't look like this yet." It was like looking at his dreams coming alive under brush and paint. The barn was there, finished and painted a dark green, just as he'd envisioned it. And the new ranch house, barely more than a plan in his head, sat exactly as he'd intended to build it, nestled in the curve of the creek, shaded by willows and pines.

The old hands' quarters still stood across the way, its walls and roof looking just as dilapidated as they did in his time. Pete's haven. The old man wouldn't hear of any improvements, no matter how much Michael argued that he needed them. He almost expected Pete to be in the painting.

The corral, the outbuildings, all of it. Clune.

"When did your grandfather buy it?"

"I don't know for sure. I think his father bought it, actually, sometime in the twenties. The 1920s," she added sheepishly.

"Do you know whose it was before that?"

"Not really. It belonged to one of the founders of the town, I think. Someone named Preston."

"Prescott?" Michael felt the hair on his arms start to rise.

"Yeah. That's it. The library's named after him." She

chewed her lower lip thoughtfully. "I didn't think he was the original owner, though. I thought it was . . ." She met his gaze. "Oh, my God."

He nodded. "Mine. Do you still own it?"

"Yes, but I lease it to some people who've turned it into a retreat for fishermen. That's why I live up at the cabin."

His head was spinning. How had Owen wound up with his ranch? Had Patrick sold it to him? The boy had never been interested in ranching. Another more sobering thought occurred to him: maybe something had happened to Patrick. His brother and Owen had always been close, especially after his mother left. If anything happened to Patrick, his brother would definitely leave the ranch to Owen.

Not that the saloon keeper would have any particular interest in it. But Owen was a sentimental man. He'd keep it just to remember. Michael ran a hand through his hair, alarm racing through him. What the hell had happened? Unanswered questions rattled around in his brain. Suddenly he felt an overwhelming urge to run, to try to get home.

He felt a hand on his arm and looked down into clear green eyes.

"I know this is hard for you. I wish I knew what to do to help."

Get me the hell out of here. He shook his head, dispelling his panic, and pulled her close, inhaling her soft scent, letting her warmth soothe his soul. Tomorrow he'd find out what he could and then head back to the tunnel. But right now he wanted to be here, with Cara.

"Can I see *The Promise?*"

Cara tipped back her head, trying to focus on his words, not his body. "Of course. It's the only one still not crated." She led the way to the back, a work area separated from the gallery by screens. Her head still reeled with the knowl-

121

edge that her grandfather's ranch—her ranch, now—had actually belonged to Michael.

"We call it the Meadows."

"What?" Michael's breath was warm on her neck as he stopped behind her.

She turned, looking up into the deep blue velvet of his eyes. "The ranch—it's known as the Meadows now."

Michael smiled and brushed a strand of hair back from her face. She resisted the urge to capture his strong fingers in hers. "Clune is Gaelic, Cara. In English it means *meadow*."

"I just can't believe I grew up in your house. That somehow my home is—"

"*My* home. It seems we're attached in more ways than we even imagined." He traced the curve of her lip with his thumb.

She sucked in a breath and tried for a lighter note. "*The Promise* is behind you."

She watched as he turned slowly around, his shoulders tightening as he took in the scene depicted in the painting. She wanted to rub the tension out of his shoulders, to soothe the worry away, but she couldn't find the courage to move. This was so far beyond anything she had ever experienced. And if she felt overwhelmed, she could only imagine what Michael was feeling.

"There's nothing left."

At first she was confused, but then she realized he was talking about the scene in painting. "No. It's almost gone. I'm surprised I even found it."

"Maybe you were supposed to find it. You said you felt drawn to it; maybe it wasn't just a feeling."

A shiver ran up her spine and she suddenly felt chilled. "Is it your father's mine?"

"Yes. This is the upper entrance. There's another one below here." He pointed to the cliff edge. "My father spent most of his life looking for the mother lode. The Promise was supposed to be his dream come true. It assayed out at a hundred ounces of silver per ton. Even for Silverthread that was rich."

She moved to stand beside him, entranced by the painting, lost in his memories. "Why did he name it the Promise?"

A faint smile played at the corners of his mouth. "For my mother. She'd been after him for years to settle down. And he kept promising he would as soon as he hit it big."

"So it was his promise to her." She studied the painting. "What happened?"

"The mine played out. And my mother ran away with the profits."

Cara flinched at the bitterness in his voice.

"She was always the center of our family, my mother. Rose O'Malley. We all adored her. But no one could have loved her like my father did." He reached for her hand, holding it tightly, his eyes still locked on the painting. "My father had two partners: Owen Prescott, an old family friend, and a man named Zachariah Bowen. Zach was a muleskinner."

"Muleskinner?" The name did not conjure a pretty picture.

Michael smiled. "He drove a wagon for one of the freight companies in town. They call them muleskinners because to get down the mountain in one piece the driver had to be pretty handy with his whip, using it to control the team of horses—"

"Or mules," she finished for him.

"Right. Anyway, Zach was young and a hard worker, so my father was glad to have the help. Since the mine was isolated, they did most of the work by hand. It was too expensive to carry the ore out of the mountains, so my father built a crude smelter on-site."

"I don't understand."

"Silver is mixed with loads of other minerals, so the ore often weighs tons. Getting it out of there would have cost almost more than the silver was worth. Especially after the

123

mine played out. Anyway, the idea was to smelt the ore at the mine, and reduce the size of the load to be shipped."

"Wasn't it dangerous to keep the silver at the mine?"

"Safer than a bank, actually. You've been up there. It was hard to find, and even harder to reach. Even Owen never went up there."

"I thought he was a partner."

"Silent partner, mainly. He bankrolled my father. I don't think he ever spent any real time up at the mine." He squeezed her hand, but Cara could see that he didn't really even remember she was there. "Anyway, once the mine played out, it was time to sell the silver."

"Was there a lot?"

"Not really. We'd sold some already. To make ends meet. And to continue working. There was enough left to fill a wagon."

"But the stories make it sound like there was more—a treasure."

"Even when the mine was new there were stories like that." He smiled, caught up in the memories. "And my father didn't help. He loved to spin a story. To hear him tell it, the Promise was going to be the new El Dorado."

"Except silver instead of gold."

"Right. Anyway, there wasn't anything close to a fortune. But there was enough to have been well off for a long time."

"So the last of the ore was smelted?" Cara said, picking up the story again.

"Yes. Each bar stamped with a rose."

"For your mother?"

He nodded. "My father's tribute. It was a surprise. He didn't tell a soul, not even Owen. Just unveiled it there on the mountain for her." He smiled with the memory. "She was so pleased. My father's dreams—our family's dreams—finally coming true. I can still see them standing there, arms locked around one another. It was a magic moment, Cara."

"Then how can you believe . . . ?" She met his eyes, shaken by the pain she saw reflected there.

"I had no choice." He stood there, staring at the painting again, lost in the past, and she thought for a moment that he wasn't going to continue, but then he drew a deep breath, his shoulders tightening. "We crated the silver, and then Zach and I loaded the crates onto the wagon. He was going to drive it down the mountain to the railroad station."

"Where was Owen?" It didn't really matter, but she wanted to reach Michael somehow, to remind him that he wasn't alone with his memories.

His gaze met hers, some of the pain easing from his face. He turned back to the painting. "He was meeting us at the station. Even at the end, he didn't have time to come up the mountain." Cara felt tears well up in her eyes; Michael's voice was so bitter.

"Mother asked Zach if she could ride along as far as Silverthread. She kissed my father, gave me a hug, then hopped up on the wagon and blew kisses at us until they were out of sight." He paused, wiping a hand angrily across his face. "I never saw her again."

Cara waited for more, but the silence hung between them as heavy as a wet blanket. Finally she asked the question, not knowing for sure if she wanted to hear the answer: "What happened?"

"She ran off with Zach Bowen and took the silver with her."

"You're sure?"

"Of course I'm sure." His voice was harsh. "I didn't believe it at first, wouldn't believe it. But the evidence was there. First Owen saw it and then my father. Finally I had no choice but to accept it."

She ran a hand along his cheek. "I know a little about that. What it's like to refuse to believe something and have people keep pounding it into your head, insisting that their version of reality is the truth."

125

He covered her hand, drawing it to his lips for a kiss, his eyes gentle again. "But in your case they were wrong."

"Maybe—"

"No. The evidence was real. She deserted us for a younger man and a wagonload of silver bars." He dropped her hand and shrugged. "It was a long time ago." She watched as the absolute truth of what he'd just said sank in. "A hell of a long time ago."

Cara exhaled slowly, her heart breaking for him. "Can you help me get this into the crate?" She kept her voice matter-of-fact.

Together they eased the painting into its wooden box. When it was finally lodged safely inside, the air in the room seemed to brighten and the somber mood dissipated, as though the painting itself had evoked the memories and accompanying emotions.

"Come on, let's go get something to eat." Maybe discovering pizza would help keep Michael's mind off the past, at least for a while.

"If you liked pizza, just wait until you try Ben and Jerry's chocolate fudge brownie ice cream." Cara swung their joined hands between them, a satisfied smile on her face.

Again he had the feeling that this was life as it was supposed to be, the most pressing issue what to eat for dessert. But he had a life elsewhere, responsibilities, and Cara had a life here. As if to punctuate the thought, Nick Vargas stepped out of a sleek automobile parked by the curb a few feet in front of them.

"Cara, darling." Nick strode toward them, a smile breaking across his face. Michael noticed that it failed to reach his eyes. "How wonderful to see you here." He ran his hungry gaze over Cara. Michael tightened his hold on her hand, feeling suddenly proprietary. "Why don't you and your friend join me for a drink? It'll be my treat. An apology for this afternoon."

126

"It's a lovely thought, Nick. But we can't. I'm determined to introduce Michael to ice cream."

"Introduce?"

Michael jumped in, trying to cover Cara's blunder and avoid further questions. "Yes, Cara tells me that Belle's has particularly good ice cream. Something called Ben and Jerry's?" The irony of the fact that Belle's was a prosperous bordello in his time did not escape him. It seemed the building was predestined for confections of one kind or another.

"Pity. I could have showed Michael the bar."

Michael frowned and looked askance at Cara.

"Nick owns the Blue Spruce. It's the only bar in town." She pointed behind them at a building across the street. Michael felt the hairs on his arms rise. It was the Irish Rose.

Everything was different. Everything was the same.

He suddenly felt as though he had fallen deep into a nightmare and couldn't wake up. As if sensing his feelings, Cara squeezed his hand. "Maybe another time, Nick. But it's late. I think it's ice cream and then home for me."

"All right. I'll let you off this time." Nick smiled at Cara, his expression relaxing. It was almost as if they'd passed some kind of test. "But next time you're in town, the drinks are on me, Cara *mía*." Nick's words caressed her, and Michael fought the urge to slug him.

Perhaps sensing his animosity, the man shifted his icy gaze to Michael, sizing him up. "You said your name's Macpherson, didn't you? I think there used to be a family around here by that name. Any relation?"

"No." No sense in giving the man ammunition against Cara. Besides, it was none of his damn business.

"Hmm . . ." Nick pulled out a silver pocket watch and checked the time. "Well, much as I've enjoyed our little chat, I'm afraid I've got to run. I'm expecting some friends at my bar, and it would be rude not to be there to greet them. I'll call you later darling." He tipped an imaginary

127

hat at Cara and was gone, disappearing into the night.

"Ice cream, then?" Cara tried to be lighthearted and missed by a mile.

Still, it was nice to walk up the street with her. If he ignored the assortment of odd items displayed in the windows, he could almost believe he was walking down the street in his own time. Almost.

"Oh, hell." Cara was looking in the direction of her gallery. "I forgot to sign the manifest. If I do it now, it'll save me a trip into town tomorrow. It'll just take a minute. You don't mind, do you?"

"I'll walk with you."

As they slowly walked back, Michael pulled out the pack of cigarettes he'd bought at the restaurant. He'd always rolled his own, but Cara had explained that now people bought them prerolled. He tapped the end against the packet and lit the cigarette, inhaling deeply. Not bad.

They reached the gallery and Cara unlocked the door. "You'll have to stay outside with that."

He looked down at the cigarette in confusion.

"My rule. No smoking in the building. There are propane heaters in there."

"Propane?" He fumbled with the word.

"It's a fuel, like kerosene. It's used for cooking and heating. Unfortunately it's also a major fire hazard, especially space heaters. One stray spark and kablooey."

The danger of fire was something he understood. Fire had devastated Silverthread on more than one occasion in his day. He drew on his cigarette, oddly comforted. Maybe things weren't that different after all.

"I really ought to have central heat installed," Cara continued, "but it's expensive. So until I can afford it, I just have to be really careful. No cigarettes. I'm always worried I'll burn the place down." She smiled up at him. "I'll be right back."

The door shut and Michael took another pull on the cigarette. Across the street was a theater of some kind, housed in what had been Timberman's Hotel. He walked across the road for a closer look, thinking about Vargas. Something about the man bothered him, a familiarity he couldn't place.

He replayed their conversation, but nothing seemed out of the ordinary. Still, he couldn't shake the idea that there was something he should have picked up on. Whatever it was, it remained stubbornly out of reach. Maybe he just didn't like the man, and, judging from their conversation, the feeling was mutual.

He stubbed the cigarette out against the wall of the theater and was turning to look for Cara when the roar of an explosion split the night. Bright tongues of orange and red shot into the starry sky, eerily illuminating the gallery across the street.

Michael opened his mouth to yell for help, but nothing came out. Flames danced from the windows, licking at the cold mountain air, feeding greedily on the wooden storefront.

His heart in his throat, Michael began to run toward the building.

Cara was still inside.

Chapter Eleven

"I beg your pardon?" Patrick leaned forward in his chair, trying to follow the course of the conversation.

Ginny sat, unruffled, looking more as though she were discussing a list of the day's chores than the death of her child. "I said that Amos Striker killed my girl."

He ran a hand through his hair, looking first at one woman and then at the other. Loralee sat calmly sipping her tea. Obviously Ginny's revelation was not news to her.

"Ginny's daughter lived in Tintown."

Tintown was another mining camp. It had peaked a year or so back, but it was still a lively place, producing a fair amount of silver.

"She was a . . . member of the line," Loralee continued. The telltale blush was back.

Patrick found it entrancing. Hell, he found *her* entrancing. Not that he'd ever really considered the notion of getting involved with a prostitute. No, sirree. Owen would have a conniption fit. Still, the idea was suddenly mighty appealing. He felt his face grow hot, and pushed his thoughts aside. He had no business thinking like that. With a sigh of regret he turned his attention back to Ginny.

"Della was a pretty girl. Smart, too. But people don't have much use for girls with half Indian blood." Ginny's voice held no bitterness and no apology. "She was determined to make it on her own, so she took the only job she could find. At first, I thought she was doing the wrong thing—to give yourself without love . . ."

She paused, her gaze locking with Loralee's. The younger woman touched her hand. With one gesture she conveyed her understanding. Ginny turned back to Patrick. "I came to accept it, though. She was happy. Or she seemed to be. Then she met *him*."

"Striker?"

Ginny nodded. "He was always coming 'round. Even here once. I could see he wasn't no good, but all Della could see were those blue eyes. Figured herself in love with him."

"Why didn't you do something about it?"

"You haven't got kids." It was a statement, not a question.

"No, I don't." He picked at the remainder of his cake, wishing he'd kept his mouth shut.

"Well, let me tell you right now, once they're grown you can't tell them anything."

"So what happened?"

"One week she didn't come home. I got worried. So, I hitched up my mule and headed over to Tintown." She paused and took a sip from her cup, composing herself, the memory obviously still painful. "They told me she'd killed herself. Drank a load of whiskey on top of some fancy patent medicine."

"Laudanum," Loralee added.

Patrick felt a tingle of concern. This was starting to sound familiar. "But you said Amos killed her."

"He did. I just couldn't prove it."

"But I don't see—"

Loralee cut him off with a wave of her hand. "One of

the other girls swore she saw him climbing out the window." She met his gaze, waiting for something.

With startling clarity, it all fell into place. He let out a low whistle. "Her door was locked from the inside, wasn't it?"

The woman nodded.

"But I still don't understand. If someone saw him there, why didn't they arrest him?"

Loralee choked back a bitter laugh. "And just tell me what makes you think anyone would believe a whore over a lawman?"

"I see." He paused, trying to assimilate all the facts. He looked over at Loralee. "You knew about this?"

She shook her head. "Only since this morning. I had no idea when we found . . ." Her eyes filled with tears, making them look even larger.

Patrick hadn't meant to upset her. He was just trying to understand the significance of Ginny's story. "So you're thinking that he's done it again?"

"I'm not thinking it. I'm sure of it." Ginny reached over and patted Loralee's hand.

The girl wiped the tears from her eyes and squared her shoulders. Patrick had to admit she had courage. "Corabeth hated laudanum. She said it made her lose control."

"Well, maybe she changed her mind."

"You don't understand. One of the miners got rough with her once, broke her arm in two places. It was twisted funny and must have hurt something fearsome, but she refused to take anything for it. Not even whiskey. She felt real strongly about it. If she was going to kill herself—and I'm not saying she was—she'd have used a shotgun before drinking that stuff."

"So you think Amos Striker killed her." He was repeating himself, but after everything he'd just heard he was probably entitled to a little repetition.

Both women nodded. Patrick sighed. They'd obviously made up their minds. But even if he accepted their version of the truth, there was still a gaping hole in the story. "Loralee, when we were with Doc, you told him you were with Corabeth early that morning."

"Right, she kept me company while I did my laundry." She frowned, a puzzled expression pulling her brows together.

"That means she died sometime after that. Now, I saw Amos early that morning up in the mountains above Clune."

She looked deflated, turning to Ginny for support.

The Indian woman leaned back in her chair, crossing her arms over her ample bosom. "Was he with you all the time?"

"No, but it's a good ride back to town, and there's the small fact that I spent the better part of the afternoon with him, arguing about who killed my father."

"Seems to me that still leaves plenty of time for him to slip back into town and find Corabeth."

"Maybe, but even if you accept that, there's still no reason why he'd do such a thing."

Loralee nodded in agreement. "I know. That has us stumped, too."

"Who says he has to have a reason?" Ginny grumbled.

"There is one more thing." Loralee chewed on her lower lip, her eyes narrowed in thought.

"Oh?" Patrick sat back, waiting.

"Everybody knows Amos Striker thinks of himself as a ladies' man. He's picky about his women. He's not the type who comes to the cribs. He prefers the women over at Belle's—higher-class whores, so to speak. Frankly, I've always been grateful for that." She ducked her head. "He's not known for being gentle."

Patrick looked over at Ginny. "And Della?"

"She worked in one of them fancy parlor houses. Started out doing their laundry, but she was young and pretty and ambitious." Ginny sighed, lost for a moment in the memory of her daughter.

Dee Davis

"If he does have preferences, then that explains his interest in Della, but not his interest in Corabeth. Maybe they were seeing each other someplace away from the cribs?"

"Patrick, Corabeth was my friend. If she'd been seeing Amos, I'd have known it. Corabeth didn't have any kind of relationship with the sheriff. None at all. I'm certain of it."

"So that would mean that either Amos picked her by chance, or there's something here we're missing. I don't think Amos Striker does anything without a reason." Both women shot him triumphant looks, as if they'd just given him the missing piece of a complicated puzzle. "Look, ladies, even if everything you're saying is true, I don't see what any of it has to do with telling Striker about finding Jack."

Their triumph faded a bit.

"We don't know either." Loralee leaned forward, both hands resting on the table. "But there's got to be a connection somewhere."

"All we're trying to say, Patrick, is that maybe you should think twice about telling the sheriff anything. At least until you've had time to sort this all out and make sure there isn't some kind of link between your pa's death and Corabeth's."

Patrick let out a long breath and held up his hands. "All right. You win. I'll wait."

Ginny beamed at him like a proud parent and held the platter under his nose. "Have some more cake."

Patrick pulled his jacket closer, urging his horse forward. It was colder than a witch's teat out here. He laughed to himself. That was one of Pete's favorite expressions. He wondered why anyone would actually want to feel a witch's teat and, once they did, whether they'd live to tell about it.

Smiling to himself, he tipped back his head and looked

at the stars. They were beautiful, spilling through the night sky with careless abandon. Looking up there, a body would never suspect so much could be wrong with this world.

"Patrick? That you, boy?" Pete's worried voice came out of the shadows off to the left of the road.

"Yeah, Pete, I'm here."

The wrangler materialized out of the dark, guiding his horse alongside Patrick's. "I was getting worried."

"I'm fine. Just wound up staying in town a little longer than I'd planned."

The foreman nodded and they rode for a while in companionable silence, Patrick replaying the conversation at the tea party in his head.

"Pete, you know a Ute woman by the name of Ginny?"

"Don't know her. Heard of her, though." Pete pulled the collar of his frayed coat closer around him.

"Well, I met her today. Turns out she's a friend of Loralee's."

Pete nodded, but made no comment.

"Anyway, she had an interesting story to tell me, one that may relate to the dead woman I found yesterday."

"Corabeth?"

"Mmm-hmm. Seems this Ginny had a daughter. You know about that?"

Pete nodded, his face grim.

Patrick shot him a look.

"It's a small town. Guess everyone knows everyone's business."

"Did you know she was murdered?"

"Heard tell of that, too." This was going to be like pulling teeth.

"So you know she thinks Amos Striker did it?"

"A man would have to be deaf to have missed the fact. It was talk around town for quite a while."

"I didn't know about it." Pete shrugged, and Patrick bristled. "I want to know if you agree with her," he asked.

Dee Davis

"Ain't got nothing to go on. But I wouldn't put anything past him."

Patrick nodded, glad to know Pete shared his assessment of the man. "Seems Loralee thinks that Striker might have had something to do with Corabeth's death, too."

"Wouldn't surprise me none." He turned his head, spitting out into the dark. Patrick wondered if the man slept with tobacco in his mouth. "There are certainly similarities."

"There seems to be one major difference, though."

They rode along in silence, and it took a moment for Patrick to realize that Pete was waiting for him to elaborate. "According to Ginny, Striker had been hanging around her daughter for quite a while. She says the girl fancied herself in love with him. Loralee says that Corabeth and Striker hadn't . . . I mean they didn't know each other—"

"In the biblical sense?" Pete's voice held a hint of laughter.

"Right." Patrick had to get over his inability to talk about sex. The truth was, he didn't have a whole lot of experience, and, well, it was just hard to talk about. But he'd get over it. "The point is that if Corabeth didn't even know Striker, what the hell was he doing with her in the first place? According to Loralee, he's usually not interested in the girls on the line."

"Crib whores ain't his style, true enough." They took the path that snaked off the main road, heading for Clune. "You sure it was Striker and not just suicide?"

"I'm not sure of anything, Pete. But at the moment I'm inclined to believe Ginny and Loralee. Besides, the setup at Corabeth's was the same. Right down to the laudanum."

"So then there's got to be a reason." The lights of Clune shone in the distance as they rode down the crest of the hill.

136

"Loralee and Ginny seem to think it's got something to do with my father's death."

Pete bent his head, a muscle working in his jaw, a sure sign he was thinking it all through. "Don't see how, unless it has something to do with Loralee."

"Loralee?"

"Yup. Arless said it was Loralee."

Patrick's patience was growing thin. "Pete, I've got no idea what you're talking about."

Pete let out an exasperated sigh. "In the Irish Rose, we were talking about Duncan, and Arless said he'd heard about it from Corabeth."

A light went on. "And Corabeth got it from Loralee."

"And here I was thinkin' you were slow." A crooked smile spread across the ranch foreman's face, his teeth shining white in the darkness.

"Very funny." He pulled his jacket tighter, shivering in the brisk night air. "I still don't see why any of that would interest Amos."

"Silver."

"What? You think that Amos killed my father because he claimed to have found silver?"

"Men have been killed for a hell of a lot less. And Striker seemed to think that it was a good enough motive for Michael."

"He did, didn't he?" Patrick frowned. "But then how the hell do Corabeth and Loralee figure into it?"

"If Arless happened to run his mouth in front of the sheriff, then I'd say that would explain a whole lot."

"This is all a pretty big stretch, Pete." He stopped as a shard of fear pierced his gut. "But if there's any truth in this at all, then Loralee could be in real danger." Patrick swung his horse around.

"Whoa, there, boy. Where ya goin'?"

"Back to town. I've got to warn her."

Pete leaned out and grabbed the reins. "Not tonight. Save your heroics for tomorrow. I told you before, it ain't safe out here at night, especially for Macphersons."

Patrick clamped his jaw shut and glared at the older man.

"You told me yourself Striker's gone. Your Loralee will be safe until morning."

"She's not my Loralee." He ran a hand through his hair, wishing he could ask Michael what to do. God, how he needed his brother.

Chapter Twelve

She couldn't breathe.

Cara opened her eyes, then blinked, trying to clear her vision. The room was full of fog, orange fog, and it was choking her. She coughed violently, trying to clear her lungs, struggling to make sense of the swirling haze.

She couldn't move; something heavy was holding her down, partially blocking her vision.

Above her she could see nothing but the fog. Light flickered through it, almost as if it were alive. She fought for another breath. It was hot. Really hot.

She tried to clear her mind, to remember what had happened. Everything was eerily quiet, too quiet. The light continued to dance against the fog. Her brain scrambled to find logic where seemingly there was none. Suddenly it clicked.

Fire. The dancing light was fire. She sucked in a breath, the acrid stench of smoke filling her lungs and stinging her eyes. Oh, God, the fog was smoke.

She tried to stay calm, to hold her panic at bay, but she could feel her heart beating a staccato rhythm against her chest. Closing her eyes, she forced her breathing to stay shallow and even, trying to remember what she was supposed to do.

Stop. Drop. Roll. Stop. Drop. Roll.

The words ran through her brain, a singsong phrase, taunting her with the impossible. Stopping and dropping seemed to be fait accompli, but rolling was out of the question. Unless someone could move whatever it was that was pinning her down. Where the hell was the Bionic Man when she needed him?

Hysteria welled inside her, threatening to take away the small thread of sanity she had left. Digging her fingernails into her palms, she fought to calm herself. She had to think. *Think.*

A sharp popping noise, followed by shattering glass, broke the stillness. The light intensified, and with a low whoosh flames shot out above her head, building quickly until a canopy of fire billowed across the ceiling. Fascinated, she stared as it spread and then almost instantaneously vanished again.

Perversely, the fire itself calmed her as nothing else had, and she forced herself to take inventory of the situation. She could feel her toes. And if she strained, she could even see her left arm. Her fingers wiggled reassuringly.

One of the crates was lying on her arm. Gritting her teeth, she pushed against it as hard as she could. It rose a little and then toppled over, leaving her arm free. She lifted the limb gingerly, flexing the muscles, relieved to see that it wasn't injured.

She pushed her hair out of her eyes, surprised to see her hand come away covered with blood. *Even little head wounds bleed like the dickens,* a voice in her mind soothed. She crinkled her forehead. It didn't hurt. Surely that was a good sign.

The canopy was back. She watched, mesmerized, as the flames writhed above her.

A small explosion somewhere behind her brought her

sharply back to reality. She had to get out of here.

She tried to push against the weight on top of her, her hand recognizing the smooth metal of a filing cabinet. It was warm to the touch, but not hot. *Not yet,* the little voice whispered. She coughed again, grimacing. Her throat was raw from breathing the rancid smoke. At least she was trapped on the floor. There was more air down here.

She tried to look at the filing cabinet, but all she could make out clearly was the tip of her nose, the effort making her cross-eyed. She gave up. The thing must be jammed against something else. If it had landed on her directly, surely it would have crushed her.

Something was braced against her head. When she tried to move she could feel it shift. It was better to hold still. The smoke seemed thicker now. She worked to keep her breathing shallow, her eyes darting back and forth, watching for the fire, waiting for it to find her, devour her.

Fear threatened to do just that. She watched as a burning ember dropped from the ceiling onto the wooden floor. It smoldered but didn't catch, and she felt an absurd rush of relief. She tried to move her right arm, but it was securely pinned at her side. She was trapped. The only thing she could do now was wait, and hope that someone would come.

Michael.

His face filled her mind, and she felt immediately calmer, almost as if he were actually there with her. Surely fate hadn't sent him all the way through time only to let him watch her die.

She shook her head, biting down on her lip, the resulting pain pulling her from her morbid thoughts. This kind of thinking just wouldn't do. She had to hang on. Michael would come. He'd saved her before, and it looked like he was going to have to save her again. All she had to do was hang in there. And that, she could do.

She closed her eyes, blocking out the menacing fire. All she had to do was wait.

Flames shot out between broken shards of glass in the front window. Michael was aware of people in the street, of shouts and cries for help, but all he could focus on was the fire raging inside the gallery.

Cara. He had to get to Cara.

As he ran for the front door, a wave of heat rolled across the sidewalk, enveloping him. Swearing, he backed away, his hands in front of his face. A shrill wail filled the air. He wasn't certain what a modern-day fire wagon would look like, but he recognized a siren when he heard one. He released a breath. Help was on the way.

Turning back to the building, he watched smoke and sparks fill the night sky, obliterating the stars. The wailing was nearer now, and down the street he could see flashing red lights.

With a shattering crash a window exploded, sending bits of glass tinkling down on the street like rain. He whipped around, fear lashing through him. He had to act now. There wasn't time to waste. Sprinting around the corner of the building, he prayed that the gallery had a back door.

The backside of the building glowed with firelight, but the fire had yet to gain a death hold here. A single street-light lit the area around a small ramp leading up to a back door. Sending a chorus of thank-yous heavenward, he ran up the ramp and grabbed the doorknob, relieved to find that it was cool.

He pulled. Nothing happened. The door was locked. Cursing, he rammed a shoulder against the door. It didn't budge. He stepped back, his mind racing. There had to be a way in. A bush next to the ramp waved in the draft from the fire. Something behind it sparkled in the light. *A window.* There was a window. Bending down, he picked up a discarded piece of wood and, swinging it with all the force he could muster, slammed it into the windowpane. Glass flew, and, mindless of the remaining shards, he forced his way through the gaping hole.

142

Dropping to the floor on the other side, he removed his jacket and held it over his face like a shield. The air was heavy with smoke, and he could see flames dancing on the ceiling and walls. "Cara." He called her name, then waited, ears straining for an answer.

"Cara, can you hear me?" *Not now,* his heart pleaded. *Oh, please, not now.* They'd only just found each other. Surely they wouldn't be separated again so soon. Not like this. "Cara!" he screamed, trying to pitch his voice above the roar of the fire.

A small noise separated itself from the bedlam around him. Heart pounding, he ran in the direction of the sound, skidding to a stop in front of a smoldering mound of debris. Cara's desk leaned drunkenly against the wall, a metal cabinet of some kind balanced against the edge. Two empty packing crates lay next to the desk, one upended and the other slanting against the cabinet. The end of a screen protruded from beneath the cabinet, holding it off the floor.

"Cara?" He waited, his heart fluttering in his throat.

"Michael?" Her voice was low but audible.

He grabbed the freestanding crate and tossed it aside. An arm extended from beneath the cabinet. "Cara, honey, can you move your arm?"

Her fingers wiggled and he strained to see her face in the shadows. He moved the other crate and knelt down, his face close to the floor. Her lips lifted in the tiniest of smiles. "I knew you'd come."

He reached for her hand and squeezed it. "Hold still. I'm going to try to move the cabinet."

A sound like thunder filled the air as a section of the ceiling caved in, sending flames shooting down from the floor above. Michael felt a rush of fear. There wasn't much time.

"Hurry," Cara whispered, echoing his thoughts.

He stood up and wrapped his arms around the cabinet. Bracing himself, he sucked in a breath and pulled up, stepping backward as it lifted. Once he was certain it was clear of Cara, he dropped it, the resounding thud shaking the floor.

Kneeling beside her again, he lifted the screen off her. It had probably saved her life. Her face was covered with blood, but a quick examination reassured him that she had only a small cut at her hairline. "Can you move?"

"I think so."

He put a hand behind her to brace her back, and she sat up slowly. He ran his hands along her torso and legs, searching for injury, relieved to find none. The fire was growing hotter, feeding on the gallery in frenzied gluttony. The screen beside them burst into flame.

Michael scooped Cara into his arms, holding her tightly against his chest. "What do you say we get the hell out of here?"

"I'm with you." Her whispered words held a hint of bravado.

He pulled her closer, feeling her hands lock together behind his neck. She was one hell of a lady. Dodging a burning beam, he headed back the way he had come, only to find that the wall was now ablaze, the window completely engulfed. Again fear clutched at his belly. He spun around, frantically searching for another way out.

Suddenly, with a rain of sparks and cinders, part of a wall gave way, and through the smoke and haze he could see the placid night sky.

"Hold your breath; we're going to make a run for it," he yelled, pitching his voice so that he could be heard above the increasing roar of the inferno. She nodded and buried her face in the hollow at the base of his throat. Sucking in a breath full of scalding smoke, he closed his eyes and ran.

The cool night air felt almost frigid after the heat in the gallery. Carefully he let Cara down, reveling in the feel of her body, warm and alive, sliding against his. They stood in the glow of the flames, watching as the arriving firefighters scurried to and fro, trying to contain the blaze.

She clung to him, tears coursing down her soot-streaked face. He wrapped his arms around her in an effort to shield her from the fire's brutal annihilation of her gallery. Stroking her hair and murmuring nonsensical words, he tried to soothe her, to ease her pain, knowing in his head that nothing he could say or do would bring back what she had lost—knowing in his heart that he still had to try.

Cara sat on a cot in front of an ambulance, drinking lukewarm coffee. Michael was nearby, talking with a fireman. He was an amazing man. Watching him wave a hand to emphasize his point, she realized that no one would ever guess he'd just recently popped into this century. He seemed to take everything in stride.

She shivered and snuggled deeper into a borrowed blanket. Her head ached, and it hurt to swallow. But except for the cut on her head, she'd avoided serious injury.

Thanks to Michael. He'd been her angel again.

He glanced in her direction, the smile in his eyes making her stomach turn to jelly. She sucked in a breath and turned to look at the smoldering remains of her gallery. Everything was gone. All her work reduced to cinders and ashes. She felt tears threatening again, but angrily pushed them away. It wouldn't do any good to cry.

This was all her fault.

The man who'd sold her the building had warned her about the space heaters. Even Nick had recommended that she install central heat. But it was expensive, and she'd decided that as long as she was careful, avoiding open flames, she'd be able to make do.

Famous last words.

"Cara, my God, I came as soon as I saw." Nick appeared and sat down on the cot beside her, his face flushed, as if he'd been running. "Are you all right?"

She tried for a smile but missed. "I'm fine. Really."

Dee Davis

"I told you to replace those damn space heaters." There was a note of anger in his voice.

"I know you did. But right now I'm not up to a lecture. Okay?" She closed her eyes, wishing he'd just go away.

"I'm sorry, Cara *mía*. It's just that I heard the fire engines; then I saw the gallery. . . ." His face softened, his anger dissipating. "What were you doing in there?" He gestured to the smoking rubble. "When I last saw you, you were headed to Belle's for ice cream."

"I forgot to sign the manifest."

"The shipment with *The Promise*?"

She nodded her head miserably. Of all she'd lost, the paintings of that mine had been the most precious to her, work that could never be duplicated.

He frowned, then grimaced, the full impact of her words hitting him. "You lost the entire series? Even the ones that had already been crated?"

Cara nodded her head, a tear sliding down the crevice between her nose and cheek.

"Pity." The word hung between them, and Cara wondered if Nick was feeling sorry for her or for himself. "Shall I drive you to the hospital?"

"No." The word came out more sharply than she had intended. "I just want to go home."

"Let me take you, then." He laid a hand on her knee, and she shivered at the contact, pulling away.

"I'll take her home, Vargas." Michael reached the edge of the cot and held out a hand. "Are you ready?"

"Is it okay for us to go?" She took his hand and stood, grateful when he slipped an arm around her for support. "Thanks. I guess I'm still a little wobbly." She leaned against him, feeling his hard body against hers.

He smiled down at her. "No problem. I'd say turnabout is fair play."

"Well, I can see you're in good hands." Nick rose, too, making no effort to conceal the sarcasm in his voice. "You obviously don't need me." He leaned over and kissed Cara

146

lightly on the cheek, sending an angry glance in Michael's direction.

She felt Michael tense, and his arm tightened around her. Nick's eyes met hers and his lips twisted into a semblance of a smile. Then, with a brief nod, he turned and walked away. Cara blew out a breath in relief.

"Where did he come from?" Michael watched through narrowed eyes as Nick disappeared around a corner.

"From the bar, I guess. He heard the sirens."

"You folks all right? We're fixin' to head back to the station." The fireman's teeth gleamed white against his charcoal-stained face.

"We're fine. Thanks for everything." Michael released her and shook hands with the man.

Cara tried to summon the words to show her thanks, but suddenly she wasn't sure that she had anything to be thankful for.

"Any idea what caused this?" Michael's words burned like acid against skin. She swallowed, watching the fireman's face, almost afraid to hear the answer.

"Can't say for sure, but looks like it was a propane heater. Those things are accidents waiting to happen, and when you add paint solvents to the mix, well . . ." He shrugged.

Cara felt sick. It *was* her fault. She clenched her fists, trying to control the agony welling up inside her. Michael and the man were still talking, but the words stopped making sense. They ebbed and flowed around her, but she was no longer listening, her eyes fixed on the charred remains of her building.

Wisps of smoke curled lazily among the broken beams and shattered walls that marked all that was left of the studio. In the span of a few short hours, her life's work had quite literally gone up in smoke.

Michael's strong fingers curled around hers, his touch sending shivers of warmth coursing through her icy heart.

"It's all gone." Her voice quavered, echoing the pain she felt inside.

His hand tightened on hers. "No, Cara, not everything."

She tipped her head up to meet the intensity of his gaze, her belly tightening as he bent his head to brush his lips against hers.

"Let's go home," he whispered.

Michael paced back and forth across Cara's living room floor. What the hell was taking her so long? It seemed that she'd been in there forever. He looked at the closed bathroom door, willing it to open, his body coiled tighter than a rattler ready to strike.

Finally, telling himself that he needed to make sure she was all right, he flung open the door. She was standing in front of the mirror, staring blankly at her naked reflection, tracks from her tears still etched in the black soot on her face, her silver pendant hanging from the fingers of one hand.

"Cara?"

She didn't move. Her other hand gripped the edge of the counter so tightly her knuckles were white. He'd seen this before. One summer when he'd worked at the mine, there'd been a cave-in. Three men were trapped inside and only one had escaped. At first the man had been fine, even making jokes about the incident. Then, a couple of hours later, he'd started shaking, his eyes fixed and staring. The doctor had called it shock.

He took the necklace from her hand, laying it by the sink, and gently loosened Cara's grip on the counter, wrapping his arms around her, pulling her into the curve of his body. Their eyes met in the mirror, and he was relieved to see a spark of life. He rubbed his hands over her, trying to warm her, trying desperately not to think about the bare silken skin beneath his fingers.

"You're cold. We need to get you into the shower."

She nodded, her eyes still locked with his in the mirror.

"Cara, say something. I need to know you're all right."

She tilted her head, regarding their reflection. "Michael?"

"Come on, Cara; you've got to help me."

She nodded, but made no effort to move. He spun them around, away from the mirror, and reached out to turn on the spigots. Water gushed out, and he marveled again at the ability to get hot water with only the turn of a handle.

He urged Cara forward, trying to get her to step into the warm stream of water. But she shook her head and nestled closer to him, evidently unwilling to leave the circle of his arms.

"All right, then we'll have to do this together." Holding her with one arm, he maneuvered them into the stall that held the shower. The water ran over them like gentle fingers, soaking his shirt. She stood still, letting the water run over her, washing away the remnants of the fire. Black water pooled at their feet running down the drain, leaching away until the water ran clear.

Michael took the bar of softly scented soap Cara had and slowly, gently began to massage it onto her. Starting with her shoulders he worked down in slow, soothing circles until she was slippery with lather. Gritting his teeth, he tried not to think about what he was doing, what he was touching. He tried to ignore the single-minded part of his body already swelling with need. A groan emanated from somewhere deep inside him as he tried to forget just how badly he wanted this woman.

Cara sighed with contentment. She had thought she'd never feel warm again, but there was heat spreading inside her, starting in her belly and inching outward. She arched her back, allowing the soothing fingers of water to stroke her.

The water urged the heat onward, and she strained for more, moving her body against the gentle rhythm of the water. Soap slid down her, and the contrast of the water against its slick lather was almost unbearably wonderful. She felt her nipples harden and swallowed a shallow moan.

She ran a hand down her body, lightly touching her breasts and belly, then stopped, puzzled when her hand encountered another hand—one that definitely didn't belong to her. Her eyes flew open and she turned to meet cobalt eyes.

Michael.

Her breath caught and she smiled slowly, feeling the heat build in intensity. He stepped back, frowning, his eyes searching hers. Immediately she shivered, missing the warmth of his body against hers.

She bit her lower lip, suddenly uncertain. Was this a dream?

With a slow, deliberate movement, she raised her hand and ran it along the curve of his jaw, feeling the rough beginnings of his beard. She trailed her fingers across his lips, pleased when she felt his body tremble at her touch. No, he was definitely real.

With both hands she began to unbutton his shirt, her eyes never leaving his. His breathing was harsh and his eyes were still full of questions, but he let her remove his shirt.

Steam from the shower swirled around them, and she reached out to pull him closer. Her soapy skin slid against his, the hair on his chest rasping against her already aroused nipples. With a groan he bent his head, taking possession of her mouth. She traced the line of his lower lip with her tongue, tasting him, teasing him—wanting him.

His hands spread across the small of her back, urging her closer. "Are you sure, Cara?"

The whispered words sent a shiver of desire shooting down her spine to burst into tingling warmth deep inside her. She had wanted this man for nine long years. And suddenly all her worries and fears paled in the blinding light of her need for him.

"Oh, yes, Michael, I'm sure."

She sucked in a ragged breath as he struggled out of his pants. He was magnificent—everything she'd dreamed he'd be. She reached for him, pulling him close, letting the heat from the water beat down on them.

Michael's hands were shaking. He'd never wanted any woman as much as he wanted Cara—*had* wanted her for so many years. But still he hesitated. What did he have to offer her? He was a misfit in her time. And he knew with certainty that he had to go home. So what was he doing? Taking what she had to offer and giving nothing in return?

He shuddered as she wrapped a hand around him, shyly stroking up and down, up and down. Oh, God, she was amazing. He found her lips and kissed her deeply, sucking and stroking with his tongue, mimicking the actions of her hand, longing to bury himself in her throbbing warmth. His hands cupped her bottom. She raised her arms to twine them in his hair, her breasts brushing across his chest.

They gyrated together, following the moves of a spontaneous dance, the feeling of their bodies rubbing together intensified by the pulsing water. He tried to maintain rational thought, but his heart was beating in tandem with hers, and he knew that, at least for this moment, she belonged to him.

And he would give her all that he had to give.

With a groan he bent and took the tip of one rosy breast into his mouth, circling it with his tongue, feeling it tighten at his touch, the fingers of one hand trailing down her belly in slow, sensuous circles. As he sucked vigorously at her breast, his hand moved even lower, and he slid one finger inside, feeling her heat surround him. She cried out as his finger found her soft center, and he smiled, nipping at one taut nipple with his teeth.

Cara's body sang with each stroke of his finger, each tug of his mouth at her breast. The warmth was building inside her until she literally throbbed with desire, wanting him to fill her until she burst.

He shifted, bringing his lips back to hers, kissing and stroking until she thought she would explode. "Please. *Please.*"

He pushed her back against the wall, bracing her body with his, his shaft pulsing against the junction of her thighs. The water was behind them now, a waterfall of sound, the resulting steam twirling around them like fairy lovers.

Keeping his weight against her chest, he cupped his hands under her, lifting her up. With a moan she twined her legs around him, feeling him slide into her. With a gentle rocking motion he began to tease her, sliding in and then out, in and then out, in, out, in, out. . . .

"Now."

The word echoed around them, and with one long thrust he filled her. With driving need she urged him to go deeper, faster, begging for more. She wrapped her arms around him, holding tightly as he held her pinned above the world. Her entire being was concentrated on the exquisite feel of him pounding deeper and deeper, higher and higher, until the world erupted in one amazing explosion of color and light, and she could no longer tell where he ended and she began.

Gradually, softly, she slid down from the precipice until she rested comfortably, her head nestled against his shoulder, a gentle rain washing them tenderly with fine fingers of mist.

Chapter Thirteen

The sun was still hidden behind the gray-white clouds clinging to the mountains. The heavenly curtain diffused the sunrise, giving it an ethereal glow. Loralee sat in the rocker on Ginny's porch, her soft humming a counterpoint to the rhythm of the creaking runners. She breathed deeply, letting the crisp morning air fill and renew her.

It was her favorite time of day, a time of new beginnings. Not that someone like her deserved second chances. She had learned that lesson well. A body had to accept her lot in life. She reached for the silver locket between her breasts, lovingly rubbing her thumb across the carved design. But it was all right to dream—and to remember. Sometimes memories were all she had.

Loralee shook her head, attempting to clear away the past. There was no sense in moping, though. Life was too short. She wrapped her arms around herself, trying to focus on positive things, but all she could see were Corabeth's sightless eyes.

Not for the first time, she wished she'd never left Leadville, but then dreams were powerful things, and she'd been

153

intent on following hers. And, of course, there'd been
Mary. Loralee smiled and rocked, thinking about the tiny
angel who had erupted into her life with a swirl of yellow
curls and a voice that rivaled a preacher at a tent revival.

At least the little girl was safe now.

She shivered and pulled her shawl closer around her
shoulders. The mountain mist swirled across rocky chasms,
taking on an almost ominous cast. For the first time it
occurred to her that she was alone. And with Amos Striker
out there somewhere, alone wasn't good.

Ginny had been up and out before dawn, heading into
town for supplies. Women of ill repute had to shop early
or not at all—it wasn't seemly to mix with proper society—and the Ute were at the bottom of the ladder. Not
that Loralee herself was much better off.

As far as she was concerned, folks didn't come any better than Ginny. Without so much as a whisper of concern,
the woman had insisted Loralee stay with her until things
got sorted out. Yes, indeedy, Ginny was a stand-up gal,
and the color of her skin didn't matter one bit. Why, she
wasn't sure she'd ever met anyone as kind as Ginny.

A picture of Patrick Macpherson flashed into her mind,
his bright green eyes smiling at her. She felt a stirring inside, something she hadn't felt since before . . . She pushed
her hair out of her face, dispelling the image. No sense
letting her imagination run away with her.

The clatter of falling rocks interrupted the still peace of
the morning. Loralee jerked in the direction of the sound,
her heart pounding, her eyes searching the mountainside.

A mule deer stepped out of the shadows, its head lifted,
sniffing for signs of danger. Finally, satisfied that all was
as it should be, the lithe creature walked to the edge of the
stream and bent to drink.

Loralee blew out a breath, holding a hand to her chest
in relief. She was mighty jumpy this morning. She assured
herself once again that there was no reason for anybody

to be after her. She didn't know a thing. Not a dadgummed thing.

But Amos Striker doesn't know that.

Loralee glanced down the road. It was empty. Ginny probably wouldn't be back for another hour or so. There was no sense in getting herself worked into a lather waiting. What she needed was company. As she stood up, the old rocker creaked in protest, the sharp sound sending the deer darting back into the shadows of the mountain.

There might not be any people around, but old Jack was here, and there were certainly lots of men who figured a horse was better company than a woman. What was good for the gander . . .

She grabbed a pail from the corner of the porch and headed out for water. No point in arriving empty-handed. Ginny's spring was off to the side of her house, hidden by a little stand of pines nestled against a rocky buttress of the mountain. Loralee felt her spirits lift as she stepped through the fragrant pines into the quiet clearing.

Kneeling beside the small pool, she stared at her reflection. Distorted by the water she almost looked pretty, her hair catching the first rays of sunlight, drab brown streaked with gold. She dipped her fingers in the water, erasing her image. There was no sense in being vain. She filled her hands with water and drank, relishing the feel of the cool liquid sliding down her throat.

Her thirst quenched, she dipped the bucket into the water, filling it to the brim. A branch snapped behind her, the crack echoing through the still glade. She froze, the bucket still in the water. Holding her breath, she waited for a second sound, afraid to turn around.

Everything was quiet. Slowly she twisted, dragging the dripping bucket with her. Her eyes darted wildly around the clearing, searching for signs of an intruder.

Nothing.

Gradually her heart returned to its normal rhythm. She was way too edgy.

With a shaky laugh, she brushed the dirt off her skirts and headed for Jack's lean-to. The horse was standing in the shelter of the rickety building, watching her with baleful eyes, as if to ask where she'd been.

"Morning, fella. Feeling a bit lonely?" She dumped the water she'd brought into the battered tin pan that served as Jack's trough. The horse bent his head to drink greedily. She stroked his side, not certain who was benefiting most from the contact, her or him.

"I was kinda lonely, too. Thought maybe we could keep each other company for a bit." Jack raised his head, tossing it as if in agreement. Loralee laughed, the sound doing much to dispel her unease. Spying a dusty brush on what passed for a shelf, she took it and began to stroke the old horse. "I've no idea how to do this proper, Jack, but I don't imagine you care much as long as it feels good."

He nickered softly, his lips splitting into an equine grin.

"I thought so." The horse's coat was dappled with patches of winter hair, making him look even more scraggly than usual. "We've got to stick together you and I. There's no one else to look after us now."

She started on the convex curve of his swayback, the brush moving with a slow, steady motion. Jack closed his eyes and blew softly through his nose, the equivalent of horse ecstasy, she supposed. Seemed men were men no matter the species. Just stroke them a little and they went all soft and gooey.

"There now," she crooned, "does that feel better?" She rested her head against his flank, letting the rhythm of the brush lull her, the motion soothing her as much as it did the animal. The sun was filtering through the loose boards of the lean-to, and its warmth seeped into her, adding to the lethargy of the moment.

Suddenly Jack reared his head, his ears laid flat against his skull.

Loralee stepped back, searching the lean-to for a sign of danger, her pleasant mood vanishing as quickly as the mist on the mountains in the hot morning sun. Jack bared his teeth, and Loralee tightened her grip on the brush. It wasn't much of a weapon, but it would have to do.

A jay shot from under the rafters, its shrill call filling the lean-to. Loralee gasped in relief as Jack immediately calmed. "Aren't we a fine pair? Scared to death by a little old jay." She patted the sorrel on the nose. "Well, now that the big, bad bird is gone, what do you say I get you something to eat?"

Jack snorted in agreement, his tail flicking back and forth. He didn't look the slightest bit embarrassed about the bird. Maybe it had been a killer jay. She laughed at her own musings.

"This is what I get for chattin' with a horse." She looped an arm around Jack's neck. "Before long people will start talkin' about crazy Loralee and pulling their children out of my way." Not that they didn't do that already.

"All right then, you stay right here. I'll be right back."

She crossed the dusty swath of ground that passed as Ginny's yard and pulled open the door to the storage shack. It had been an outhouse once, but Ginny had built a new one out over the creek. This building's window had been boarded up, along with the hole, which now served as a kind of shelf. Loralee sucked in a breath and stepped inside. She knew it was probably her imagination, but she would swear the room still stank.

The barrel of oats was in the far corner and she had to step over a couple of boxes to get to it. The top was fastened down with a bent nail. She twisted it and lifted the lid. There was a rusty-looking ladle in the bottom, and she used that to fill the bucket with grain.

Satisfied that she had enough, she dropped the ladle into the barrel just as the outside door slammed shut, smothering the little room in darkness.

Loralee dropped the bucket and the lid, the resulting clatter adding to her terror. She dropped to the floor, crouching in the corner, hoping that the barrel would hide her. Complete blackness surrounded her, feeding her fear. Panic knifed through her.

She tried to breathe slowly, to assure herself that it was just the wind that had closed the door, but try as she might she couldn't move an inch. Over the stench of the closed room, she thought she caught a whiff of something else, something familiar, but for the life of her she couldn't identify it.

She waited, her breath stuck in her throat. The smell got stronger, overpowering the scent of the old outhouse. *Kerosene.* Oh, Lord, it was kerosene! Amos had come to get her! With blind panic, she jumped up, intent on reaching the door, but tripped over something, sprawling across the dirty floor. Without waiting to catch her breath, she scrambled to her knees and began crawling, hands extended, guiding herself through the darkened room.

The kerosene smell grew stronger, and she thought she could smell the first wisp of smoke. She had to find the door. A thin crack of light outlined the opening, and she breathed a sigh of relief at the sight. With trembling hands she felt for the handle, twisting it to open the door.

Nothing happened.

She pushed against it. Again, nothing.

Something was blocking the door from the outside.

A sob welled in her throat and she whispered the word *no*. She could smell smoke more clearly now. She sucked in a breath, determined to get free. She wasn't going down without a fight.

Giving a scream of frustration, she slammed into the door with her whole body. The building shook, but the door refused to budge. She stood back, catching her breath, trying to think what to do.

Suddenly the door flew open, the sunlight blinding her even more than the dark had. Hard arms reached in and encircled her. She tensed, not sure what to expect, her mind too numb to react.

"Are you all right?"

The voice washed over her and her heart sang out with relief. Patrick? Patrick was here!

"Yes, I was . . . trapped. Fire . . . Amos . . . Oh, God." Her words tumbled out without rhyme or reason. She buried her face against his chest, unable to think coherently.

He stroked her hair and back awkwardly, waiting patiently until she found the strength to pull herself together. "I'm all right. Really."

Still clinging to his hand, she allowed him to pull her outside. She gulped the fresh air, grateful for the cool feel of it in her lungs.

"I heard you scream. What happened?"

"I don't know for sure. I went to the shed to get Jack some breakfast." As if to emphasize her point, the horse whinnied from the lean-to. "I was filling the bucket when the door slammed." She squeezed her eyes shut, trying to slow her racing heart.

"It's all right, Loralee. You're safe now."

"What about the fire?" She whispered the question into his chest, not really certain she wanted an answer.

"What fire?"

His response wasn't what she'd expected—his face was a contrast of concern and confusion. "I smelled kerosene and then smoke."

"There wasn't any fire, Loralee."

Now, *she* was confused. "Yes, there was. I'm certain of it. And someone locked me in."

His brows drew together. "No, the door was stuck a little, but it definitely wasn't locked."

She stamped her foot in frustration, her fear turning to anger. "You listen to me, Patrick Macpherson: I know when a door is locked and when it isn't. And I can smell as good as the next person."

Patrick searched her face, and then, finding whatever it was he was looking for, smiled crookedly. "I believe you."

Her heart did a little flip-flop and her anger evaporated. Patrick let her go and walked to the side of the shed, his

Dee Davis

eyes scanning the knee-high grass butting up to the walls.

"What are you looking for?"

"Your fire. If you smelled it, there's got to be some sign of it."

She nodded and followed him as he walked around the little building, staring at the ground. Moving around the corner, he stopped suddenly and she crashed into his back.

"Sorry." He shot her a sheepish grin, then sobered as he knelt for a closer look at something.

"What is it?" She peered over his shoulder. He was staring at the grass.

"The weeds are crushed here. See?" He gestured to a wilted-looking clump.

Bending closer, she could see that the stalks were indeed broken. "But I don't see—"

"Did you walk around here earlier?"

She shook her head, still confused.

"Well, somebody did." He gestured along the wall, and sure enough, she could make out several other places where the grass had been pressed flat. A shudder traced its way up her spine.

Patrick had moved ahead and was standing at the far corner of the shed. She hurried to his side.

"Take a deep breath."

She wrinkled her nose and eyed the converted outhouse. "I'd rather not. I've already had a noseful, believe—"

"Breathe." He cut her off, leaving her nothing to do but obey.

"Kerosene." She smiled triumphantly. "I told you so." She paused, her momentary elation fading. "What happened to the fire?"

"Someone put it out. Look." He pushed aside the tall grass.

Loralee leaned over, her heart beating faster. There was a two-foot expanse of bare earth. Charred bits of kindling and grass littered the ground. Several black stripes ran up the wall, fading into the weather-washed boards. Loralee

160

knelt and placed a trembling hand on the ground, her gaze locking with Patrick's.

He nodded, his expression grim. "It's hot."

Loralee felt a wave of nausea and swallowed, trying to maintain control.

Patrick released the grass, and the evidence disappeared, only the faint scent of kerosene lending credence to her tale.

She swallowed again and stood up, her whole body trembling. "I could have—"

Patrick reached for her hand. "Hush. You're safe now. I won't let anything happen to you, I promise."

Loralee sighed. The words sounded good. But they were just words. Her fingers automatically circled her locket. She had firsthand experience with promises, and she knew that despite the best intentions they meant absolutely nothing.

"Come on; we're getting out of here." Patrick tightened his grip on her hand, propelling her toward the lean-to.

"But Ginny will worry."

"Ginny will be fine. We can get word to her."

"But—"

He stopped, turning her to face him. "I'm not taking any more chances with your life, Loralee." His gaze locked on hers and she shivered at the look in his eyes. Something deep inside her flickered to life, wanting to respond, but before she had time to sort through her jumbled emotions, he moved again, pulling her along behind him to the lean-to. "You ride Jack." Hearing his name, the horse raised his ears and snorted.

Patrick grabbed the saddle and threw it on the sorrel. Still bemused, Loralee tried to focus on what was happening. "Where are you taking me?"

He tightened the cinch, looping the girth into place. "Clune. You'll be safe there."

"But, Patrick . . ." He swung her up onto the horse, then met her gaze, one eyebrow quirked inquiringly. "I don't

want to get you involved in all of this." Her tone sounded
mutinous, even to her own ears.

He gave her an exasperated look. "It seems to me you've
got it backward. It's my family that's gotten you involved.
My father's ramblings seem to be the key to this whole
thing, and until we figure out why, I want you somewhere
safe." He adjusted the stirrup with a jerk, his black brows
drawn into a fierce frown. She found herself thinking this
was not a man to quibble with.

"Fine. Clune it is." She forced her voice to sound light,
but she shivered as the vision of Corabeth's lifeless body
filled her mind. Would she be next?

Chapter Fourteen

Michael sat in an armchair by the window, watching Cara sleep. Even in repose she was beautiful. Moonlight spilled through the window, illuminating the glistening strands of her hair as they fanned out across the pillows. He clenched his fist, filled suddenly with the urge to touch her, to assure himself that she was real.

Making love had been a mistake. Instead of quelling his need for her, the act had intensified his desire. He wanted her now more than ever. And the simple truth was that he couldn't have her. He didn't belong here. He belonged at Clune. He belonged in 1888.

He glanced down, running a hand over the white square of gauze on his chest. He was almost healed. Rotating his shoulder, he was relieved to find that the motion caused him no pain.

It was time.

Patrick and his father would be crazy with worry by now, assuming time was passing more or less the same in both centuries. It was all so complicated. He ran an agitated hand through his hair, the idea of losing Cara again eating at his gut. But there was just no getting around the fact that he had to go back. He had obligations. And he'd be damned before he'd run out on them.

Of course, he could ask her to go with him—but that would mean asking her to give up her way of life for his. And from what he'd seen of the twenty-first century, her life was a hell of a lot easier than his, even with the fire. He sighed with frustration. The simple truth was that he had nothing to offer her but debts and dreams—not exactly an enticing package.

"Michael?"

Startled, he looked up to find her sitting up in bed, tangled curls tumbling over her shoulders, covering her bared breasts. He sucked in a breath, feeling his body quicken with need. She looked like a goddess. Covering her mouth with a slender hand, she stifled a yawn. He smiled. A sleepy goddess.

"How long have you been awake?" She leaned back against her pillows, a soft smile playing about her lips.

"A while. I couldn't sleep."

Her smile slipped away. "Something's wrong." She studied his face, her eyes widening with understanding. "You're thinking about leaving, aren't you?"

He nodded, amazed at how accurately she'd read his mind. He rubbed a tired hand across his face. Maybe he shouldn't be surprised. Mind reading seemed like nothing compared to time travel.

"When?" The word came out as a whisper. She bit her lower lip, and Michael could see intense pain in her eyes.

He groaned and strode across the space between the bed and the chair, bending to scoop her into his arms. Settling onto the bed, he held her close, his breath stirring tendrils of her hair. "Soon."

He started to speak, to try to explain, but she shook her head, then tipped it back in silent invitation. His mouth slanted over hers, feeling the slight tremor of her lips.

He pulled back, his breathing uneven, his eyes searching

hers. With a sad smile she pulled him closer, her lips planting a trail of kisses along his jaw. The heat began to build, spiraling through him with unbelievable force. Oh, God, how he wanted this woman.

He flipped her onto her back, covering her with his body, her softness blending with his hardness, an exact match, a perfect fit. Then with one quick thrust he was inside her, her heat surrounding him, pulsing, alive. Together they moved, establishing a rhythm to a silent orchestra only they could hear.

Their mouths met and he drank deeply, trying to draw her in, to hold some part of her captive in his heart. . . .

A constant memory of what could never be.

Cara woke in a warm cocoon of blankets. The sun streamed in through the window, bouncing across the brightly colored patterns on her quilt. She yawned and stretched, as contented as a cat, her body sated from a night of lovemaking, her brain still fuzzy with sleep. She rolled onto her side, reaching for Michael.

The bed was empty, the pillow indented slightly where his head had been.

She jerked upright, fully awake, her heart pounding as she searched the room for some sign of him. *Oh, God, no. Please, not yet.* Her heart sent the prayer fervently heavenward and she scrambled out of the bed, wrapping the quilt around her.

The empty room silently mocked her.

Soul-rending pain rocked through her.

He was leaving. Had already left, her inner voice brutally reminded her. Sorrow swirled in the depths of her stomach, turning and churning until she felt sick.

"Cara?"

She looked up, her heart refusing to beat. Michael stood in the doorway, a tray in his hands, his eyebrows drawn together in concern. She tried to talk, but her mouth wouldn't move. Suddenly tears were running down her cheeks, and her heart resumed beating with a lurching thud.

"Honey, what's wrong?" He dropped the tray on the bureau, cutlery clanging against crockery. With one swift step he was beside her, his arms pulling her close against him as he lifted her, quilt and all, onto his lap.

"Gone. I thought . . . you'd . . . gone." Between the tears and the huge lump in her throat, she couldn't make the words come out right. She buried her face in the warmth of his bare chest, willing herself to become a part of him.

He stroked her hair, rocking her back and forth, his voice gentle and soothing. "Hush, now, I'm here. You're just reacting to all that's happened. Let it come. That's right, let it come."

She felt his lips on her hair and abandoned any effort at control. With a wrenching sob she pushed closer, obeying him, letting the tears have their way. She cried for all that she had lost: her gallery, her paintings, her youthful innocence, her parents, her grandfather—and she cried for Michael. She cried because he was leaving, and she cried because he could never truly be hers, and she thought that surely her heart would shatter.

All the while he rocked her, whispering nonsensical words of comfort, keeping her safe in the warm circle of his arms.

"Better?" Michael asked.

She nodded mutely.

He relaxed his arms and tipped her tearstained face up to his with a gentle finger. Her green eyes were dark with a mixture of anguish and passion, but her face was calm; the worst of the storm had passed. "I made you breakfast."

She smiled shakily and sat back, the quilt slipping, baring her breasts. He sucked in a breath and forced his hand to remain placidly on her shoulder; the desire to feel her nipple respond to his touch was almost more than he could bear. She made him crazy. With a shaking hand he reached for the corner of the quilt, tucked it securely under her arm, and tried for a casual tone of voice. "Come on; it's probably cold."

He reached for a bowl on the tray and handed it to her. He had to admit the congealed glop in the bottom wasn't very appetizing. Colorful, but not particularly edible. But then, what did he know about modern tastes?

She stirred it with the spoon. "What is it?"

He struggled to remember the name. "Froot . . . something. Loops. Froot Loops. That was it." He smiled at the whimsy of the name.

"Oh?"

"Yeah. The box said it was cereal. I figured I could handle that. I mean all you have to do with cereal is mix it with water and heat it to a boil. Simple enough. I even figured out how to use the contraption you call a stove." He sat back, feeling smug.

She choked on a laugh, obviously trying to swallow it.

"What?"

The laughter escaped despite her efforts, and she almost dropped the bowl. "I'm sorry. I'm not laughing at you." She swallowed. "This is so sweet of you, but you don't cook this kind of cereal." She lifted the spoon and turned it upside down. The rainbow-colored blob hung from the spoon, firmly glued in place. "You eat it right out of the box. With milk."

He looked at the spoon and then at her, his face breaking into a rueful grin. "Patrick's always on me for not reading instructions." He shrugged. "I guess I'm not quite up to twenty-first-century cuisine." The look in her eyes sobered him instantly, and he ran a finger across her cheek, wiping away the last traces of her tears. "I'm sorry."

"For the cereal?" Her gaze met his, and he lost himself in the fathomless depths of her eyes.

"No. For all of this." He shrugged helplessly. "For everything."

She put the bowl down and, with a lithe twist, straddled

him, dropping the quilt, her eyes never leaving his. "Not for everything, I hope." She smiled, a slow, seductive turn of her lips that had his body singing with joy.

With trembling hands he reached for her. "No, not everything."

"Tell me more about your relationship with Nick."

Cara looked across the table at him. "Where did that come from?"

Michael slid a forkful of pancakes into his mouth and licked at the syrup left at the corners of his lips. "This is really good," he mumbled.

She stared at his mouth, imagining that she was the one licking away the sweet, sticky . . . She inhaled sharply. "Surely you have pancakes in 1888?"

He swallowed. "Yeah, sure, Patrick makes them all the time. But they don't taste anywhere near this good."

"God bless Aunt Jemima."

"Who?" He took another mouthful.

She smiled at his obvious ecstasy. "Never mind. You mentioned Nick."

He swallowed and laid his fork on the plate, reaching across to cover her hand with his. "Yeah. I want to know more about him. The timing of that fire is really strange. And I've got the feeling Vargas is at the bottom of it."

"Don't be silly. It was the space heaters. The fireman told us." She leaned forward, searching his eyes for answers. "Are you saying it wasn't my fault?"

He pulled his hand away, running his hand through his hair. "I don't know. I just keep going over it in my head, hearing you talking about no smoking. You said one spark and . . . what was the word?"

"Kablooey."

"Right, kablooey. The point is, you were being careful. Almost overly so, in my opinion." She opened her mouth to protest, but he cut her off with a wave of his hand. "I'm saying that I don't believe anything you did caused the explosion. It just doesn't make sense."

She frowned, letting his words sink in. "But I still—"

"Look, when we left the gallery to go eat, you shut everything down. I remember because I was hungry and you were intent on checking everything twice."

She went over the details in her mind, trying to focus on her actions. She remembered crating *The Promise*. Michael had helped. And then she'd finished the paperwork—except the manifest. And then she'd . . . "Oh, my God. You're right. I *did* turn them off. Michael, I turned off the space heaters."

"Exactly." The smile reflected in his lapis gaze warmed her insides, making her feel she was the most amazing woman on the planet.

"So it's not . . ." She hesitated, unable to finish the sentence.

He shook his head, still smiling. "No. It's not your fault."

She exhaled, the rest of what he was saying sinking in. "And you don't think this was an accident at all."

"Frankly, I don't see how it could be. At the very least, someone had to turn those heaters back on."

The bite of pancake in her mouth suddenly lost its flavor. She swallowed. "And at the very worst?"

"Someone set the fire deliberately."

"But why?"

"I haven't worked that out yet." He frowned. "But I will."

She leaned forward, her mind spinning. "Nick? You think Nick burned down my gallery?"

"I don't know anything for sure, but I think it's a little too coincidental that we saw him five minutes before the explosion and then again right afterward."

Cara shook her head. "That can't be right. Nick can be pushy and even obnoxious, but he'd never hurt me. I mean he—" She cut herself off, wrinkling her nose, smiling in embarrassment.

"Wants you?" Michael raised his eyebrows, his mouth curling into a small grin. "Can't say that I blame him."

Cara's body clenched deep inside, responding primordially to some signal she hadn't even realized he'd sent. She'd never known a man who was so . . . well, manly. His expression sobered and she came back to reality with a crash.

"Did he know about the space heaters?"

"Yes, he did. He was always ragging me about them. Said I was just asking for trouble. But that still doesn't give him a reason to burn down the gallery."

"No, but I'd be willing to bet a bundle it had something to do with your paintings."

"The Promise?"

"Yeah." He rubbed his chin thoughtfully. "I heard him, Cara; he wanted those paintings badly enough to threaten you."

"I told you, I don't think he would actually hurt me. Besides he *wanted* those paintings. That's hardly motivation to destroy them." She winced, the pain of losing her artwork almost physical. "Why would he do something like that?"

"Maybe because you wouldn't sell them to him. I don't know." Michael shoved his chair back and stood, leaning forward, his hands braced on the table, his face hardened with anger. "Truth is, there's only one person who can give us the answer."

"Nick."

"Right. So I'd say it's time we paid him a little visit." He narrowed his eyes, his anger solidifying into granite composure. "Do you have any guns?"

Cara tried to tell herself there was something good in all this.

Michael was still here, his thoughts of returning put on

a back burner. He'd made it perfectly clear that he wasn't going anywhere until he was certain she was safe.

But that was merely postponing the inevitable.

She sighed, sneaking a quick peak at the man sitting beside her. His crash course in driving after the fire might have made *him* confident in his skills, but considering the grinding noises under the hood, *she* was somewhat less enthusiastic. The engine was not responding well to his less-than-gentle manipulation of the gearshift. What in the world had she been thinking when she'd allowed him to drive? She supposed it had been his excitement and her desire to please him which had swayed her.

The steel butt of a revolver jutted out of his jeans—her grandfather's gun. She glanced behind her at the rifle carefully bracketed to her Jeep. It was like riding in a damned arsenal. And she was riding shotgun, literally.

"Turn here." She pointed to an intersection, and Michael swung the Jeep sharply to the left without benefit of braking. The Jeep squealed in protest, but made the turn with all four wheels on the ground.

She sucked in a breath, relieved that they were still upright. "This is it."

He braked, the resulting impact enough to have thrown her through the windshield if she hadn't been wearing a seat belt. For every action there was an equal and opposite reaction—and hers was instantaneous: *she* was driving them home. No amount of testosterone-driven enthusiasm was worth risking her life for.

Michael reached for her shotgun. "You stay here."

"I most certainly will not. It's my gallery that got incinerated, and I want to be there when you find out what happened."

His eyes narrowed, his face turning stubborn. "I don't want you anywhere near him."

She frowned, feeling mutinous. "Look, I'll be perfectly safe. I'll have you and your guns with me." She gave him

171

her most beguiling look, stopping just short of batting her eyelashes.

His lips quirked upward, not a full-fledged smile, but she knew she'd won. "Come on," he said at last. Swinging down from the Jeep, he took off, not waiting to see if she followed.

Nick's house was one of those pretentiously pseudo-Victorian structures, built to look old but with all the modern conveniences. The porch creaked as she walked on it, but it was drowned out by Michael's hammering on the door.

"Vargas, open up!"

Cara reached his side and placed a restraining hand on his elbow. The fury in Michael's face almost made her step back a pace; it had been building since they'd left to come here. She'd been right in her previous estimation: this was not a man to mess around with.

"I don't think anyone is home," she offered quietly.

Her words sank in, and he stopped pounding.

The whole incident was kind of anticlimatic. Not that she was complaining. She hadn't really been looking forward to a showdown.

Michael looked calmer, and she dared a question: "Nick's not here. Now what?"

He reached for the brass doorknob. "We go in."

The house was immaculate, which was unsurprising, really. Vargas was the type to be finicky. The hallway ran the length of the house, with closed doors indicating various rooms opening off the entry. A large staircase sprang from the back of the hall.

Michael stepped into the house, careful to keep Cara behind him. The lady had guts, but he was determined to keep her safe, even if it meant locking her in the closet. He smiled at the picture the thought inspired. Hell, maybe he'd lock himself in there with her.

He opened a door, then peeked into a parlor. It reeked

of some sort of floral scent. He wrinkled his nose and
quickly closed the door.

"We shouldn't be doing this," she said in a hiss from
beside him.

"Doing what?"

"Breaking and entering."

"We didn't break a thing. The door was open."

"Well, we're entering."

"So we are." He couldn't suppress the laughter in his
voice. "Any idea where Nick might keep his secrets?"

"There's a study back this way." She darted around him
to lead the way.

He placed a restraining hand on her shoulder. "Hang
on, sweetheart. I know you're anxious to find out what's
going on, but I think I'd better go first."

She shot a resentful look at him but stopped, allowing
him to pass her. "It's the door on the right."

He opened the door and stepped inside, moving to the
center of the room so that she could follow. It was no
different from any other room in the rest of the house—
which meant it looked more like a museum than a place
somebody lived.

There was a large, ornate desk blocking the wall in front
of the room's only window. On one side of it there was a
large fireplace with two armchairs on either side. The opposite wall was dominated by books—rows and rows of
them. They covered the wall completely, except for an
elaborately carved alcove in the center, used effectively to
showcase a large urn.

"It looks the same as it always does."

"And how is that?" he couldn't resist asking.

"Like an army of maids is standing in the corner waiting
to clean up each speck of dust before it even has time to
land."

He smiled, picturing white-capped women armed with
brushes and brooms. "You take the bookcase and I'll take
the desk."

"What are we looking for?"

He blew out a breath. "I haven't the faintest idea. Something odd or out of place. Something unusual. Something that will tie Vargas to the fire."

She nodded and began to examine the bookshelves. Michael sat in the chair behind the desk and pulled open a drawer. Pads of paper, and odd-looking instruments he assumed were for writing, filled the little compartments of an oblong box. Nothing out of the ordinary here. At least not for someone who lived in the twenty-first century.

He pulled open another drawer and found files, but the contents had nothing to do with Cara or her paintings. *Damn.* He slammed the drawer shut and was reaching for another when he heard an odd scraping noise.

He looked up in time to see Cara, urn lid in hand, disappearing into a gaping hole where the alcove had been. He jumped up, almost tripping over the leg of the desk in his hurry to reach her.

The mechanism clicked shut and the wall was suddenly filled with nothing but books—no alcove, no Cara. Heart pounding, he skidded to a stop, his eyes searching the new shelves for some sign of what had happened. There was nothing to indicate the wall had ever been any different. Just rows and rows of books.

But Cara was gone.

Chapter Fifteen

Patrick watched as Loralee bent and pulled a pan of biscuits out of the stove, the smell of warm bread filling the air, making his mouth water. At least, he thought it was the biscuits. The sight of her soft, round bottom was definitely cause for salivating, too.

"You didn't have to do this, you know." His voice came out more like a croak. Hell, he was acting like a fifteen-year-old boy.

She turned and smiled at him, causing a whole new set of reactions. "I know. But you've helped me out so much, first with Corabeth, then with the fire, and now offering me your home. There aren't many decent men who'd do that for someone like me, Patrick. Heavens, the least I can do is cook you and Pete a nice supper."

"Well, I just don't want you to go to too much trouble."

"No trouble at all." She picked up a bowl and started to stir the potatoes, the action making her breasts push against the cotton of her dress.

He licked his lips and figured he'd best get the hell out of there before his body started to give away his train of

Dee Davis

thought. "Have I got enough time to feed the horses?"

"I reckon there's time." She wiped a strand of hair away from her face with a flour-covered hand, leaving a streak of white across her cheek. He sucked in a breath, his traitorous mind envisioning what it would taste like to lick away the flour. "Let Pete know it's almost ready, will you?"

He nodded and headed for the door, not trusting his voice to perform properly.

"Patrick?"

He steeled himself and turned. Her eyes were as big as saucers and as soft as a deer's. Oh, Lord, what was going on with him?

"Thanks for everything."

"My pleasure." *My pleasure.* What in the world was he thinking? She was a working girl. If nothing else, that meant she had bedroom experience out the wazoo. What could she possibly see in a greenhorn like him? Hell, he'd offered her his protection, not a tumble in the sheets—which was probably the last thing she wanted, anyway.

He stomped out onto the porch and across the yard to the stable. It was a far sight bigger than the one at Ginny's, but still not quite big enough for the ranch's needs. He glanced over at the wood frame standing stark against blue sky. Michael had said that if they were going to make a go of it, they had to invest in their dream. The barn was the first step.

Truth be told, he wasn't sure he wanted to continue without his brother. Clune had always been Michael's. Patrick had just sort of been along for the ride. Without his brother's guiding force, there just might not be a dream anymore.

"I see you been talking to Loralee." Pete ambled up, his eyes on Patrick's pants.

Patrick felt himself go hot all over. "Sheesh, Pete, do you have to point it out to the whole world?"

Pete's eyes crinkled at the corners as his mouth curled

176

into a grin. "Don't need me pointin' it out. You're doin' a fine job all by your lonesome." They walked into the stable to a chorus of whinnies and braying. "Hell, boy, even the horses can see the stick in yer drawers."

"Cut it out, Pete. Besides, even you have to admit that Loralee is a mighty pretty girl."

"Yes, she is. But she's also a—"

"Don't say it."

Pete opened the bin that held the oats and began filling a bucket with grain. "Well, son, I don't mean no disrespect; it's just that I figure you got to call a spade a spade. And I thought you needed remindin'. I don't want you to get hurt—"

"Look, I'm not having feelings for Loralee, if that's what you mean. I just find her attractive. That's all."

"You tryin' to convince me or yourself?" Pete poured some oats in Roscoe's trough. "Get some hay, will you?"

Happy for an end to the present turn of conversation, Patrick forked some hay from an open bale and threw it into a burro's stall. The animal brayed with delight. He continued down the line of stalls, working in tandem with Pete and his bucket of oats.

"You tell anyone else about this morning?"

Patrick frowned, thinking Pete was referring to his preoccupation with Loralee again. He started to retort, but then saw the serious glint in the older man's eyes. "You mean about Amos?"

Pete nodded, squirting a spray of tobacco neatly between his teeth. "Amos, the fire, any of it."

"No. We just came straight here."

"You still thinkin' this has something to do with your father?"

Patrick stopped, leaning against the pitchfork. "Honest to God, I haven't got a clue. It seems like it has to be related, but I can't prove anything. Hell, we don't know for certain it was Amos who set the fire."

Pete nodded, pouring the last of the oats into Jack's

trough. "Well, until we get this all figured out, I think your girl is better off staying out here."

Patrick sighed. "Pete, I told you already, she is not my girl."

The old foreman just shook his head.

Pete grabbed another biscuit, sopped it in gravy, and then popped the whole thing in his mouth. Patrick swallowed a laugh and looked across the table, meeting Loralee's equally mirth-filled gaze. "Pete, you'd think you'd never had one of those before."

The wrangler swallowed and reached for another, grinning. "Them things *you* make ain't biscuits. They're more like river rocks."

"Now look, old man, if it weren't for me, you wouldn't eat at all."

"Well, now, after tasting this, I can't help but wonder if I wouldn't have been better off." He smiled congenially and reached for the mashed potatoes.

Loralee beamed at them both, and for the first time in a long time Patrick actually felt like the ranch was home. He slurped up a mouthful of stew, wondering just what the woman did to get the rabbit so tender. His always came out stringy and tough—it took practically a whole meal to chew one bite.

The door shook as someone pounded on it. The mood was shattered in an instant. Loralee jumped up, panic flashing across her face. Patrick reached for his rifle, glad to see that Pete was doing the same.

"Hey, what's a fella got to do to get some grub around here?" At the sound of Arless's voice, everybody relaxed. The door burst open and the red-faced Arless staggered into the room. "I could smell that stew all the way from the road. 'Bout time you took some cooking lessons, Patrick, me boy."

He came to a full stop upon spying Loralee, then ripped his tattered hat from his head. "Why, Miss Loralee, I should have knowed right off those heavenly smells weren't caused by anything Patrick concocted."

Pete indicated the empty chair. "Have a seat, Arless; there's plenty to go around."

He straddled the chair backward, then, at a look from both Pete and Patrick, stood up and turned the chair around, sitting on it properly. "Don't mind if I do." He heaped his plate with stew and potatoes, took three biscuits, and dug in with a sigh. "Now, this is eating."

"What brings you out this way, Arless? Besides free food," Patrick added dryly.

"Figured I'd best head for home. Lena don't tolerate my being gone for long."

Arless and Lena lived up the valley a piece near Slumgullion Pass. Arless often spent the night at Clune en route one way or the other.

"To hear the sheriff tell it, she's already on the warpath." Pete's gaze met Patrick's, a question in the older man's eyes.

"Could be. Danged woman won't let me alone." Arless shot them a black-toothed smile and lifted another biscuit. "Me, I ain't in no hurry."

"Well, you know you're always welcome here," Patrick said. The words were halfhearted, though, as his body and his senses were being assailed by the sweet floral fragrance Loralee favored.

"Coffee?" She smiled down at him.

He nodded and she bent over his shoulder to pour the hot liquid into his cup, her nearness making him almost numb with desire. He managed to refrain from pulling her into his lap, instead mumbling a thanks to her breasts as they brushed past.

She moved away and he sat back, relieved that the sensual onslaught was over. He was just congratulating himself on handling it all with some amount of dignity when he realized Arless and Pete had stopped eating, their know-it-all eyes twinkling with laughter.

"Ready for a little dessert, boy?" Pete asked, winking.

Heat washed across Patrick's face. A quick glance at the stove assured him that Loralee had her back turned. He glared at his two dinner partners.

"Who wants pie?" Loralee carried the plate over to the table and watched as three pairs of hungry eyes devoured the dessert before she even had a chance to cut it. She'd forgotten how much men could eat. It was amazing. Why, she'd made two dozen biscuits and there wasn't one left.

She had to admit that it made a body feel good to have her cooking appreciated. And truth be told, that wasn't the only thing making her body feel good. Every time she got within three feet of Patrick Macpherson, her palms started to sweat and she felt tingly all over. She sucked in a breath, swallowing her thoughts. No good ever came of feelings like that . . . no good at all.

She focused on the pie, cutting it into hefty slabs and placing them on four tin plates.

"Patrick, why don't you and Loralee take your pie out on the porch? Me and Arless have some business to discuss."

Arless looked up from pouring a flask of whiskey into his coffee. "We do?"

Pete shot him a look. "We do."

He frowned, then grinned. "Oh, right."

Pete made a shooing motion toward the door. "Out. Sunset won't last forever."

Loralee tightened her grip on the plate, of two minds. *Go . . . Stay . . . Go.* Her feet seemed to have made their own decision, and she started for the door. Patrick jumped up, managing to knock over his chair, hot color staining his face.

Good, at least she wasn't alone in her embarrassment. They arrived at the door at the same time and got stuck trying to pass through. She sucked in a breath as his hard body pressed against hers. Lord, she was behaving like an untried schoolgirl, and that was hardly the case, to say the least.

Finally they managed to get out of the house and settle on the porch. Loralee sat on the top step and Patrick sat across from her, his long legs straddling the railing.

"I think we were set up." Patrick's emerald eyes met hers, then darted away, and she felt a sudden burst of warmth somewhere deep inside.

"Yes, but with such a lack of subtlety." They laughed and then ate in companionable silence. The sun hung orange-red at the crest of the mountains, almost as if it were riding their peaks. Loralee knew that in just a few minutes it would dismount, dropping below the horizon, leaving behind pale streamers of pink and orange. And even those would soon slip away. Sunset came fast in the mountains.

"Why'd you become a—" Patrick blurted, then stopped.

"Whore?" She filled in the word, glancing over at him. His face was burning.

"I'm sorry. I shouldn't have asked you that. It's just that sometimes you seem so innocent, I forget that you . . . that you . . . Aw, hell."

She reached up and patted his knee. "It's all right. It's an honest question." She sighed. "I ran away from home when I was thirteen. My daddy drank. And when he was through sleeping with Mama, he started turning on us."

"Us?"

"Me and my sister, Faye." She set her plate and fork down on the step and leaned back, looking out at the mountains, remembering. "I woke up one morning, stiff and bruised, and figured I'd had about enough. So I packed up my stuff and left."

"What about your sister?"

"I tried to get her to come, but she was afraid. In the end I just left her."

"Where'd you go?"

"Here and there to begin with. I took odd jobs: washing,

cleaning, sweeping up, whatever I could find. I worked mostly for a place to lay my head and a bite to eat. I wound up in Saint Louis, cooking for the girls at a fancy bordello." Patrick sat down beside her on the step, his presence comforting somehow. "I worked there for almost five months. The money was good and my bed was clean. Then one night a drunken customer mistook me for one of the girls. I fought like a hellcat at first, then finally decided it wasn't like I had anything to lose."

She laughed and was surprised at how bitter it sounded. "The next morning he was gone and I had twenty-five dollars. Well, it didn't take too much ciphering to figure out that was more than I made in a week of cooking. And all I had to do was what my pa had already forced me to do." She shrugged philosophically. "Only problem was, I wasn't one of the girls. Word got out, and I found myself out of a job right quick. So I nosed around and tried to find a place in another parlor house."

"In Saint Louis?"

"Yes, at first. Only, see, there's rules to everything, even whoring, and none of the fancy houses wanted a scrawny kid like me. About the only place I was accepted was on the streets—and that was too risky. I headed west on the first stage out of town.

"Followed the miners mostly. Started out in Del Norte in a dance hall. That's when I changed my name. Saw it on a flyer. Loralee. Thought it sounded real pretty. Anyway, before long I was making my way. Never had the looks for the fancy places, but I did all right for myself. Finally wound up in Leadville." She stopped the memories crowding in faster than she could put them into words. She reached for her locket, comforted by the cool silver.

"Who gave you that locket, Loralee?"

She brought herself back, focusing on Patrick. He had such a strong, handsome face. She could see bits of Duncan in him. She chewed the side of her lip, trying to decide how much to share with him, then finally let the soft light in his eyes decide for her. This was a good man.

"My husband."

Patrick couldn't have been more surprised if she'd up and told him she was really a man. She smiled and squeezed his hand reassuringly. He tried to stop the wave of jealousy that washed through him.

"I met him in Leadville. Handsomest man you ever did see. Tall like you, but thinner, with a real wiry build. He was a charmer. But real kind to all the girls. He moved around a lot. Always after big money, I guess. Anyway, he always brung us presents when he got back. He never treated us like working girls. Always had respect for us." She stopped and looked up into his eyes. "Like you." Her whispered words reduced his muscles to jelly.

She turned away again, fixing her gaze on the shadows in the barnyard. "He always seemed to wind up with me, and we started spending more and more time together. He even took me out in a rented buggy once."

The happiness that the memory brought was reflected in Loralee's face and made Patrick want to buy her a fleet of buggies. She leaned back and sighed. "We spent a whole summer like that. I'd never been with anyone like him before. He made me feel special, like I was the only woman in the world. I quit seeing other men. Didn't seem right. Then I found out I was pregnant."

Patrick felt her confusion and pain as if it were happening right there on the porch. He smoothed the soft curls hanging over her shoulder, his hand aching to touch more than just her hair. But that would be foolhardy, he reminded himself fiercely. He dropped his hand to his side.

"At first I wasn't sure I should tell him. I mean, I was a whore. And, well, I knew it was his baby, but there wasn't a dadgummed thing I could do to prove it. Finally I decided I had to." She tipped up her head to look at him. "It was the right thing to do."

183

He nodded, too full of conflicting emotions to string to-gether any words.

"Well, he was so proud you'd have thought he was the only man ever to make a baby. Started talking about how we had to get married and give our child a home. A home. Can you imagine me with a real home? After all the things I'd done?" She managed to sound outraged and wistful all at the same time.

He whispered "Yes," but didn't think she heard him.

"At first I said no. I mean, I couldn't very well go and marry him. It would have spoiled his reputation. But he just laughed and said he hadn't any reputation to spoil. And he told me he loved me more than he'd ever loved any living thing. Well, I couldn't resist that long. We got married. And me with a belly already swelling.

"We took a room in town and lived like fancy folks. But the money soon ran low and he said he'd have to go off and find us some more. I wanted to go back to work. Cooking or something. Women do it all the time, but he wouldn't hear of it. I guess in his mind he'd made me respectable, and he didn't want me to go and mess it up.

"The night before he left, he gave me this locket. Said it was a reminder that we belonged together. And that he'd be back to get me just as soon as he could." She ran her hand along the filigreed chain. "He fastened it around my neck and kissed me." She ran a finger across her lips, so lost in memory that Patrick doubted she'd even realized she'd done it.

"I remember his exact words. 'Loralee, darlin',' he said, 'this locket is forever. It's a symbol of my promise to you. No matter what happens, it will keep you safe. Always.' And then he kissed me again. Then he was gone." She exhaled, her eyes still fixed on the deepening shadows of the yard.

"Three months later Mary was born. Girls I'd worked with, they helped me, gave me a place to stay. And we waited, Mary and I. He wrote every week. Always promising that we'd be together, that we'd be a family. His last letter said he'd struck it rich, and that he'd wire us the money to meet him. I waited and waited. I never heard from him again."

"What happened?"

"I never knew. But I know in my heart that he's dead." She said it with finality.

"Oh, God, Loralee, I'm sorry."

She patted his shoulder, as if he were the one who needed comforting. "It's all right. It was a while ago. I've had time to make my peace with it."

"What happened to Mary?"

Her face tightened. "We tried to make it on our own for a while, but no one wants a woman with a child. So I moved on." She opened her mouth to continue, then closed it as if deciding to skip over part of the story. Patrick wondered what she wasn't telling him.

"I wound up here and found a place in the cribs and went back to whoring, but the cribs weren't any place for a little girl. Mary was two, and I didn't want her to have the same kind of life I did. So I swallowed my pride and wrote to my sister."

"Faye?"

"Yup. She'd done real well for herself. Married a preacher man. I figured it was the best possible kind of home for Mary. So I sent her to Virginia."

"Have you seen her?"

"No. Folks write for me sometimes, but I don't want her to be ashamed of her mama. So I've tried to let her go. I know my sister is telling folks Mary's hers. She can't have children of her own."

A tear slipped down her nose and cheek. Patrick reached out to wipe it away. "Loralee, anyone should be proud to have you for a mother."

She gave him a watery smile. "Well, I made my try for a better life, but I guess I just wasn't meant to be anything but a whore. And I can't say that my life has been all that

bad. I mean, I had a wonderful husband and a beautiful daughter. Most folks never even have that much. Maybe I was just being greedy to want more." She ducked her head.

Patrick tipped her head up with a finger, his eyes searching hers. "You're being no such thing. Everybody has a right to find their own way, Loralee, no matter what happens to them. And I can't believe your husband would want you to quit living just because he's gone."

He wasn't certain if he was saying the words for her or for himself, but either way he knew they were true.

And living was just what they were going to do.

Chapter Sixteen

Michael frantically scanned the bookcase, trying to find some clue as to how to open it. He was supposed to protect Cara, not lose her through a trick door.

With a hissing swish the books started to revolve again, and then Cara stood in front of him, a sheepish expression on her face. "How's that for unusual?" She asked.

Michael grabbed her, holding her close. "Don't ever do that to me again. I thought I'd lost you."

She pushed back, her eyes meeting his. "I'm sorry; I had no idea the thing was going to do that. I just lifted the lid on the urn and whoosh, I was revolving."

"How did you get back?" His pulse still hammered in his ears.

"Elementary, my dear Watson; I just put the lid back." She grinned and reached for it again.

He intercepted her arm, taking a firm grasp of her hand. "Hold it. If we're going to do this, we're doing it together." He stepped into the recess with her. "Ready?"

She nodded, looking as if this was a great adventure. Maybe in her world secret passages were a common thing,

Dee Davis

but in his time they usually spelled trouble. He lifted the lid, and the wall groaned and spun slowly, revolving until they were standing in another room.

He moved out of the alcove, dragging Cara with him, the lid still in his hand. The room was small, lit by a narrow window, and, in contrast to the rest of the house, it was in shambles. A large map was tacked over a ramshackle desk, littered with files, books, and more maps.

Large velvet drapes hung haphazardly across an adjacent wall as if they'd been hung in great haste. He walked over to the map, squinting in the poor light, trying to see what it depicted. A brass bar hung above it, and brightly colored stick pins dotted the paper contours of mountains.

Cara reached around him and clicked a knob at the end of the bar. The map was flooded with bright light—definitely an improvement over kerosene lanterns. Hell, it was even brighter than the new electric lights they'd installed in Silverthread. "Does any of it look familiar?"

She studied the map, biting on her bottom lip, a habit he was beginning to recognize. "Maybe. See these grids?" She pointed at a series of overlapping boxes outlined with different colors.

Each box was marked with a name: Dealers Best. Homespun Dreams. The Big Bonanza. "Mining claims."

She nodded. "And from the looks of the topography, I'd say it's the area just north of Silverthread."

He looked at it, struggling to find something he recognized. Some claims had been marked with a colored pin and others had been crossed out with a large X. He dropped his gaze to the desk. The maps there were older. Some of them dated back to before his time, each of them marked similarly to the one on the wall.

The books were all about lost mines, legend and fact mixed indiscriminately, it seemed. And the files were marked with coordinates; they held notes on topography, the names of mountains, gulches, and streams carefully recorded. "I'd say he's looking for something."

The Promise

"The Promise."

Her hushed voice came from behind him and Michael pivoted, startled to realize she'd moved from his side. She had drawn back the velvet curtain and stood transfixed. Light from the window streamed across the little room, illuminating a wall covered with paintings—Cara's paintings of the mine.

And right in the center, surrounded by its companions, hung *The Promise*.

"They're here." Cara whispered, her mind scrambling to make sense out of what was rapidly becoming an insane situation.

"The son of a bitch stole them," Michael said.

She turned to look at him, tears filling her eyes. "At least they're not gone. When I saw the crates burning, I thought . . ." In two strides he was standing behind her, his arms wrapped around her, giving her needed strength. How was she ever going to live without him?

"They're safe, Cara. And we'll get them back, but right now I think we ought to get out of here. I wouldn't like for Nick to find us here in his little hidey-hole."

He started to pull her away, but she placed a hand on his arm, still staring at the paintings. "Wait a minute." There was something here, something more than stolen paintings. She just needed to figure it out. She took a step back, her gaze sweeping across the wall of paintings. Next she studied them each in turn, finally ending with *The Promise*.

There was logic here. She gasped as the light finally clicked on in her brain. "They're in order, Michael. He's put them in order."

She turned to look at him. He was frowning at the paintings, obviously struggling to follow her train of thought.

"I painted them randomly, as the light changed or the spirit moved me. But these are hung in specific order. As if they were a map. See, he's grouped them using the sun,

189

east to west. Michael, he's trying to find the Promise."

"You're saying he stole your paintings to use them as a map?"

"Yup. I know it sounds crazy, but you have to remember that the Promise has been considered a lost mine for at least ninety years. I found it totally by accident. And if the light hadn't been just right, I'm not sure I'd have seen it at all."

"But even if I accept that as true, why in the world would Nick be going to such extremes to find an old, abandoned mine? The Promise played out years ago—in my day. Hell, just under a hundred and fifteen years ago, now."

She cringed at the confusion and bitterness playing across his face. "It doesn't make sense, Cara," he said.

"I know. But Nick is a deliberate man. So there is a reason. We're just not seeing it."

Michael stared up at the paintings. "You never actually told me about Nick Vargas."

"I guess we kind of got sidetracked." She focused on Nick, letting her mind pull together what she knew about him. "Nick's dad owned the bar before he did, and to hear Nick tell it, he practically grew up there, hanging on the words of the old-timers—men who'd lived through Silverthread's glory days. That's where he got his interest in history."

She reached for a thin book on the desk. "This is his. *Silverthread Boom to Bust*. It chronicles Silverthread's history." She flipped open the book to a photograph of a tin-starred lawman, his angelic countenance at odds with his steely-eyed gaze.

She shivered, closing the book and dropping it back on the desk. "Anyway, I don't think his life was a good one. His father drank, and I think he slapped Nick around some. But I don't know for sure. It was all a long time ago, most of it before I was even born. Nick talked about it some, but only a little."

Michael frowned, his mind obviously working on the puzzle. "None of that ties him directly to the mine, yet he seems to be obsessed with it. Why?"

She crossed to the desk, randomly picking up one of the books and leafing through it to the index. Turning to the P's she ran her finger down the list until she found the entry she wanted. Flipping back to the referenced page, she scanned the paragraph about the mine, feeling Michael's breath on her cheek as he looked over her shoulder.

"What does it say?"

"Not a lot. A version of the story about your mother. With the added caveat that neither Zach nor Rose was ever seen again."

Michael's eyes hardened. "Best for all, I'd say."

Cara reached for his hand. "This book is right, Michael. Anything could have happened to them." She read further. "It goes on to say that the silver was never recovered and is considered by some a lost treasure. Could that be what Nick was looking for? The silver?"

Michael blew out a breath. "You said it yourself: Nick is a deliberate man. He'd have to have something more than a legend to go on. Besides, there's no silver at the mine. My mother and Zach took it with them. The reason it was never found was that they spent it." His last words came out harsh, bitter.

Cara wanted to hold him—to make him see that not everyone was as callous as his mother had been, but now was not the time.

"I think we should go. Vargas could be back any minute."

She nodded and put the book back on the table, but knocked a map onto the floor as she did. Reaching down to pick it up, she noticed a slip of paper stuck between the back of the desk and the wall.

"Wait a minute; there's something down here." She slid her hand behind the desk and came up with a tattered newspaper article.

Gooseflesh broke out along her arms as she read aloud the faded print:

MACPHERSON KILLED IN GUNFIGHT

Silverthread, Colorado. Patrick Macpherson was shot and killed yesterday in gunfire exchanged at his ranch, Clune. Macpherson, 21, was fleeing Sheriff Amos Striker at the time. Striker was attributed with firing the fatal shot. Macpherson stood accused of murdering two Silverthread prostitutes.

A lifetime resident of the valley, Macpherson surprised everyone with his duplicity. Owen Prescott, a close family friend, attributed the change to the recent death of Patrick's father, Duncan, and the disappearance of his brother, Michael.

Duncan Macpherson was found stabbed to death along the road to Clune several days before his son was killed. Sheriff Striker suspected that Macpherson's older brother Michael might have killed his father in an argument over a silver strike. However, in light of recent events, suspicion has now turned to Patrick. "I don't believe any of this," Prescott said. "It's all so tragic."

Instability seemed to run in the family. Duncan was a reputed drunk and womanizer, and Macpherson's mother, Rose, ran away with her lover years back, reportedly taking a small fortune in silver. Although this latest transgression fits the family profile, it comes as a surprise to those who knew Macpherson.

"Guess you just can't ever tell about folks," Amos Striker said. "It's a sad day . . ."

Cara stopped, frustrated. "That's all there is. The rest has been torn away." She knelt by the desk, squinting into the gloom, hoping for the rest of the article. "There's nothing here."

Michael leaned down and grabbed the article from her hand, his eyes darting across the page. "This can't be right." The pain in his voice threatened to undo Cara. He looked terrified, and she wanted to do something, anything, to erase his fear. "If this is right, then everyone in my family was murdered. Patrick . . . my father . . ." He crumpled the article in his hand. "This is a lie."

"We don't know anything for certain, Michael. We don't even have the whole article."

He rounded on her, his blue eyes turning black with anger, his fingers digging into her shoulders. "My brother wouldn't kill anyone."

She bit her lip, trying not to cry out in pain. He wasn't even seeing her. He would never intentionally hurt her. He was blinded by rage. As if he'd read her thoughts, his grip loosened and he gently massaged the skin he'd been gripping so ardently.

"There's no way Patrick would kill a woman—any woman." His words were softer now, deceptively calm. He waved the wadded-up article in punctuation of his words. "These charges aren't true."

Cara tugged on his arm. "This isn't the place to talk about this, Michael. We need to get out of here. We need to get *you* out of here. Take the article. Nick won't miss it in all this mess. Come on."

Grabbing the urn's lid from off of the desk, she pulled him into the alcove and slammed it into place. The mechanism whirred and scraped, and slowly they returned to the immaculate library.

Michael moved slowly, his mind no doubt numbed by the things they'd discovered. She had to get him out of here. She had to get him home—to 1888.

And to save his family, she had to do it as quickly as possible.

* * *

Michael paced back and forth across the rug, his emotions in knots. He was marooned in the twenty-first century, and because of it, his brother and father were dead. While he'd been cavorting like a stud in heat, someone had murdered his father and then set his brother up to take a fall. He was supposed to have protected them.

"Michael?" Cara's touch on his arm pulled him out of his reverie. "There's no sense in blaming yourself. It wasn't your fault you were shot . . . that you came here. In fact, I'll bet it was related somehow to all of this."

"Maybe so. But how. Damn it, how? And where does Nick Vargas fit into it all?"

"I don't know." She stared down at the crumpled newspaper article, her eyes narrowed in thought. "And I'm not sure it matters right now."

"How can you say it doesn't matter?" He knew he sounded harsh, knew that he was hurting her, but his pain was so deep, so emasculating . . .

She held out the article, as if somehow it contained all the answers. "Michael, what was the date when you were shot?"

He forced himself to concentrate on her question. She was only trying to help. "I told you before—1888."

"No, I don't mean the year; I mean the day." She was still staring at the article in her hand.

"May twenty-first."

"This was written on May twenty-seventh." She pointed to the heading at the top of the page.

"So?" He struggled to pull himself out of his lethargy, to think clearly. But it was hard—damn hard.

"So today's the twenty-fifth." She stared at him, waiting for the impact of her words to reach him.

His stomach roiled, and in an instant he sprang back to life, hope blossoming. "You're saying that if time passes the same here and there, then Patrick isn't dead yet."

"Exactly."

The Promise

He pondered the enormity of the thought. "So if I can get back, I can save him."

Cara's gaze met his. "It's worth a try."

Hope collided with despair. He had to go. There wasn't a choice. Patrick's life hung in the balance. But he couldn't imagine what it would be like never to hold Cara again. "You realize what you're saying." There was so much between them but no time for words.

She nodded, tears filling her eyes. "You have to save Patrick. Nothing else is as important as that."

He pulled her to him with a groan, burying his face in her hair, glorying in the softness of her skin, the smell of her perfume—trying to memorize the way she felt in his arms—knowing that without her, he would never be the same.

"You realize that we have no idea if this is even possible." Michael's voice was tight, his body tense.

"I know, but we'll never know for certain unless we try." Cara wanted to scream or explode or do something to stop him. But she couldn't. His pain was her own, and she had to send him back. It was the only way. No matter what she lost in the process, she was determined to help him.

They walked on in silence, and Cara forced her thoughts to the practical, running through everything they'd discovered in the last few hours, trying to make the pieces fit. There were just so many unanswered questions. Halfway to the mine tunnel, her overloaded brain suddenly pushed a thought front and center. She stopped dead in her tracks. "It's the pendant."

Michael stopped, too. "What are you talking about?"

"The pendant is the key."

He frowned down at her. "You think this whole thing was caused by a necklace?"

"No, but I think it's part of the equation."

"Why?" He raised an eyebrow skeptically.

"Because I had it on when you found me. And again when I found you."

"So it's a special pendant?"

"Yeah, it belonged to my great-grandmother. My mother gave it to me on my sixteenth birthday."

Understanding flashed in his eyes. "The night your parents died."

She nodded miserably.

"Oh, sweetheart, I'm so sorry." He pulled her into his arms. "No wonder it means so much to you."

She nestled there for a moment; then, swallowing her pain, she pushed back so that she could see his eyes. "It's the only thing I have of my mother's—of her family. When my great-grandmother, Faye, died, my mother went to Virginia to sell her house. In the attic she found a trunk. It belonged to a woman named Alice Camden. Inside she found the pendant—and a packet of letters from Silverthread."

She leaned into him, her voice muffled against his chest. "The letters were all addressed to my grandmother, Mary. They were short letters, without much news really. References here and there to life in Silverthread, but mainly they were filled with words of love. Words from a mother to a daughter."

"So Alice was really your great-grandmother?"

"Yeah. Faye was her sister. Anyway, Mom went to Silverthread, trying to find out about her, but there was nothing. It was almost like she'd never existed at all. Except that we had her pendant. So you see, it was a big deal when she gave it to me. It represented all we had of our true heritage." She bit her lip, trying not to cry. This wasn't the time.

"It's a lovely story, Cara, but it could just be coincidence."

Her gaze met his. "There's more. When they couldn't find you, when they told me I'd imagined you, I couldn't stand it. I'd lost everything: my parents, my old life, and then you." She exhaled on a sigh, feeling his arms tighten around her. "I thought I was going to die, too, for a while. And then slowly, surely, I healed. But I couldn't bring myself to wear the necklace. It symbolized all I had lost. I gave it to my grandfather and told him to sell it."

"But he didn't."

"No, he didn't. He kept it in a drawer by his bed. One more thing he was right about." She fought to keep the pain from her voice. "It was silly to blame an inanimate object for all my troubles."

"But easier." As always, Michael understood without the words even being spoken.

She drew in a deep breath. "Anyway, I found it when I was going through his things. I still couldn't bear to look at it, but I took it with me to the cabin. Then, a few days ago, I saw it in my jewelry box and put it on. I can't explain why I did; it just felt right."

She reached up and laid a hand on his cheek. "It was the day I found you. I just didn't make the connection until now. It's the pendant, Michael. Alice's pendant."

"You think it's what pulled me through time?"

"I do. That and the connection between us. First I needed you, and then you needed me. Or maybe it was me who needed you the second time, too. I don't know. It's confusing."

He brushed his lips against hers, even the slight contact making her ache for him. "I would have died if you hadn't found me in the tunnel."

"I know," she whispered. "But I would have died in the fire if you hadn't pulled me out." She shook her head. "Anyway, it's not important who saved whom. What's important is that you need the pendant to get back, and I don't have it." She tried to keep a brave face, but the hopelessness of the situation overwhelmed her and she felt tears threatening. "I must have lost it."

"Shh." He placed a finger over her lips. "It's okay. The necklace is safe. It's in the bathroom cabinet. I took it from you after the fire. You were a little shaken up."

Dee Davis

She nodded, pushing aside memories of him coming to her that night, consoling her. She could remember them later, when she was alone. "We need the pendant, Michael."

"So, let's go get it." He was already turning back.

"No." The word came out harsher than she'd intended. He would be leaving her soon. She needed time to think, time to figure out how to keep her feelings in check. He swung around to look at her and she forced a smile. "It'll be faster if I go back for it on my own," she added.

He pulled her to him and kissed her hard, and she wondered if he could sense her turmoil. "I'll wait for you at the tunnel," was all he said.

Cara reached the porch that wrapped around her house in record time. Taking the three steps in one stride, she inserted her key and swung open the door, bursting through the little mudroom almost before the door had closed behind her.

"Cara, darling. I was wondering when you'd show up."

She froze, her eyes riveted on the gun in Nick Vargas's lean hand.

Chapter Seventeen

Moonlight sifted through the gauzy curtain, spilling out across the bed. Patrick turned away from it, pounding his pillow into submission and wondering if sleep was ever going to come. His mind was a tangle of thoughts. Michael. His father. Amos. Loralee.

He closed his eyes, concentrating on the oblivion of sleep. Nothing. With a sigh he turned onto his back, linking his hands behind his head. Shadows on the ceiling made shifting lacy patterns of light and dark. He watched as they kaleidoscoped across the wooden planks, intricate lines leading into and away from each other.

He couldn't shake the feeling that somehow the events of the last few days were like those shadows—overlapping, connecting. If only he could find the key. Michael had disappeared first. He still couldn't bring himself to think of his brother as dead. Was there something in his disappearance that had triggered the entire chain of events?

It just didn't make any sense. Michael hadn't known Loralee, and, as far as Patrick knew, he'd never had a run-in with Amos Striker. His father had babbled on about

199

Dee Davis

some silver, but that, in and of itself, didn't really mean anything, despite what Pete said. Duncan was always claiming he'd just struck it rich. No one ever believed him. And even if they did, who the hell would kill a man for a strike? A producing claim maybe, but a strike? It just didn't make any sense.

And now to complicate things, he himself had gone and fallen for a crib whore. One who was still grieving for her dead husband. Oh, yeah, things were just peachy.

In his mind's eye he pictured Loralee's sweet face, her small pink tongue darting out to moisten her ripe, red lips. He smothered a groan and rolled over, pulling the pillow with him. Now, to top it all off, he'd gone and gotten himself excited. *Great*. Just what he needed to help him drift off to sleep.

Loralee sat up in bed, tired of fighting off dreams of Amos Striker's leering face. She pushed the hair out of her eyes and got out of bed, crossing to the window and pulling the curtain back. Light flooded the room. Its presence was calming. She was safe. Outside, a slight breeze ruffled the silver-washed grass, bending the blades in unison, almost as if they were dancing a reel, following the commands of an unseen caller.

She wondered what it would feel like to dance with Patrick, his strong hands guiding her through the intricate steps. She pushed the thought away. It was highly unlikely that they'd ever be attending a dance together. The Macphersons were well thought of in these parts. She rubbed her arms, a sudden chill chasing down her spine. No, they'd never be able to dance together.

Her thoughts turned to Mary. She wondered if her baby even remembered her. She'd heard somewhere that babies had no memory. The thought brought tears to her eyes, and she wondered what her life might have been like if— She bit back the thought. There was no sense in wasting time on "what-ifs."

She turned from the window, no nearer to sleep than she'd been ten minutes ago. Maybe some pie would help. She made her way to the door of Michael's room, relieved that she hadn't made any noise. The last thing she wanted to do was wake everyone up.

She moved cautiously into the darkened outer room, jumping when a wheezing snore erupted from a dark corner. The noise repeated itself, and she relaxed, smiling. Arless.

A slice of moonlight cut across the floor, and she realized the front door was open. Since the door locked from the inside, that meant someone had gone out. And since Pete was sleeping in his quarters and Arless was snoring in the corner, that meant Patrick.

Her heart fluttered at the thought, but she clamped down on the feelings. She'd had experience trying to cross over from her appointed place in life. It didn't work. And she wasn't about to go and set herself up for that kind of heartache again.

Still, it couldn't hurt to talk to the man. After all, they were both awake. Without so much as a by-your-leave, her traitorous feet took steps toward the open door.

He was sitting on the steps, his head buried in his hands. The slump of his shoulders made his state of mind apparent. So much had happened to him in such a short time. It would be hard for anyone to bear—and Duncan had always said that Patrick was "real sensitive."

He was a tall young man—just past the bloom of boyhood, really—and there was something compelling about him, something that reached out to her.

She shook her head. There was no sense in turning camaraderie into fantasy.

"Loralee? Is that you?"

Startled, she stepped back a pace, stopping herself when she realized he'd turned to look at her. "I . . . I didn't mean to bother you. I was just . . ." She tried again. "I couldn't

201

Dee Davis

sleep." She shrugged helplessly, hoping she didn't sound as foolish as she felt.

"It's all right. I couldn't sleep, either." He patted the space on the step next to him.

She frowned, telling herself the thing to do was go back inside before she was in over her head. But the next thing she knew, she was settling in beside Patrick as though she'd been doing it all her life.

"You thinking about Amos?" he asked.

"Some. I can't help wondering if he's out there somewhere, waiting for me."

Patrick nodded, his big hand reaching for hers, enclosing it in warmth. "You're safe here. I won't let that son of a bitch get anywhere near you. I swear."

She placed a finger across his lips, absorbing the jolt of electricity that sparked between them. "Don't make promises you can't keep."

He ran the back of his hand along her cheek, his eyes searching. He paused for a moment, as if considering something momentous. Then he said, "I can take care of you, Loralee. If you'll let me."

Oh, God, how she wanted to abandon herself to him. But another part of her, the part that was still thinking with her head, warned that nothing good could come of it. Nothing at all.

She sat back and pasted on a cheerful smile. "Tell me about your family."

Patrick frowned, uncertain what had just happened. One minute there were sparks flying between them; the next she was asking him his life history. He sighed and leaned back against the post, realizing he really didn't know the slightest thing about women.

"I guess you could say we started out as vagabonds. My father was always certain there was a fortune to be had just over the next hill. That's why he came to America in the first place."

202

"From Scotland?"

He glanced over at her to see if she was truly interested. She was watching him with doe eyes, and he fought the desire to pull her over and kiss her until neither of them could breathe. "Yes. The Macpherson's have a place—sort of like a ranch, I guess—called Crannog Mhor."

"Cran what?" She tried to say the name but failed.

"Crannog Mhor. It means 'lake dwelling.' To hear my father talk about it, it must be the most beautiful place in the world. It's real remote. Up in a mountain valley somewhere."

"That would explain why he liked it here."

"I never thought about it one way or the other, but I imagine you're right."

"So what made him leave, if he loved it so much?"

"Well, like I said, part was the adventure of it. That, and the fact that he was the fourth son. His brother Calum was set to inherit." Patrick shrugged. "And there were two more in line after that. So he set off for America."

"And landed in New York. He told me a little of it."

"Yeah. That's where he hooked up with Owen. They were just boys, really. Younger than me now. But they hit it off. Complemented each other, really. I mean, Father always had his dreams, but not really any focus—and Owen, he's always been the practical one. Their friendship just seemed a natural thing. And Owen, well, he's always been there for all of us. Many was the time when the money he made put a roof over our heads and food in our mouths."

"You're close to Owen, then?"

He nodded. "Since my mother left us, Owen has been more a father to me than my own. For a while he was the only one I could talk to. Michael was too angry. And Father was too drunk." Bitterness rose in him, sour like bile.

"But he wasn't always like that."

Patrick smiled, remembering. "Oh, no. Once upon a time Duncan Macpherson was a charmer. His smile could light a room, and he could make you believe anything was possible."

"Was New York where Duncan met your mother?"

Patrick smiled. "Yup. According to my father, she was the prettiest girl in the city. And I reckon it's a mighty big city."

"Her name was Rose?"

"Just like the flower. Heck, she even smelled like roses." He inhaled deeply, remembering the sweet scent that had marked his mother. "She was just off the boat herself, from Ireland, waiting tables at a place called Paddy's. That's who I'm named for."

"A bar?"

"No, the man who ran the place. My mother always said he was an angel."

"And that's where your father fell in love with your mother?"

"To hear him tell it, it was a magical thing. One look and he knew she was the woman for him. Owen says it wasn't quite as magical as my father would have us believe. According to his version of the story, it took quite a bit of wooing on my father's part."

"What did your mother say?"

Patrick fought a wave of sadness. He'd loved his mother more than anyone in the world. "She always said that Duncan Macpherson was the finest gentleman in the whole world, and that she was the lucky one. I really believed she loved him, Loralee."

She squeezed his hand. "I imagine that she really did."

They sat together in the moonlight, listening to the whisper of the wind in the pines, and Patrick thought, just for a moment, that maybe she really had. Maybe she'd loved them all. His heart contracted in anguish. But if she'd loved them, then how could she have ever left them—left *him*?

"Were you born in New York?" Loralee asked, breaking the silence.

"No. Michael was. But tempers started flaring between

the north and south. Owen and my father decided they didn't want to fight a war they had no stomach for, so they hightailed it out to the goldfields."

"California?" She shifted slightly, her hand still warm in his.

"Mm-hmm. I was born in a shanty in some long forgotten boomtown. We kicked around California for a while, until the gold got scarce and folks started talking about Colorado."

"Silver." She said the word almost with reverence.

"Except of course we never seemed to be able to find any."

"Until the Promise."

"Yeah, fat lot of good it did us." He was surprised at the bitterness in his voice.

She looked up at him, her wide eyes filled with concern. "I'm sorry. I didn't mean to dredge up old memories."

"It's all right. They seem to have a way of coming up all by themselves anyway." Which brought them full circle.

If the Promise hadn't failed, maybe his mother would still be around. And if she were still here, then his father wouldn't have become a drunk. And he and Loralee would certainly never have hooked up. And then she wouldn't be in danger.

He blew out a sigh. Yup, everything always seemed to lead back to the Promise.

Chapter Eighteen

Michael reached the clearing and began methodically searching the far bank of Shallow Creek for the blue spruce. It wasn't particularly easy. There were plenty of other trees mixed in among the aspens. And the course of the stream was different than it had been in his time.

The changes seemed to mock him, pointing out with painful clarity the precariousness of his situation. Lost in time. It sounded like the name of a dime novel, not reality.

He blew out a breath and tried to concentrate on his search. One spruce in particular kept catching his eye. It towered above the others, its limbs fanning down to the ground. Something about the rocks jutting out beside it rang a bell. The little scraggly tree of his memory had filled out majestically.

He started to cross the creek, then stopped short, his mind filled with a picture of Cara disappearing into the gallery minutes before it exploded. He let out a string of words fit for the crustiest miner. He was a fool. Letting her go back to the house alone had been a mistake—especially with Nick Vargas out there.

He spun around and headed back toward the cabin. Hopefully he was just making a mountain out of a molehill. She'd come bursting through the brush any minute. Fifteen minutes later, he wasn't as sure. Cursing himself, he increased his pace, fear lancing through him. *Oh, God,* he prayed, *let her be all right.*

"What are you doing here?" Cara tried to keep the tremor out of her voice, but succeeded only partially.

Nick smiled, a slow, lazy smile that never reached his eyes. "I think you already know that."

Cara felt the hairs on her arms rise. "You took my paintings." She was amazed at how calm her voice sounded. It wasn't every day she had a gun pointed at her.

He sounded amused. "Well, I did try to buy them. I told you that honest heart of yours would get you in trouble. Where's the boy toy?"

"He's not here."

"This gets better and better, Cara *mía*. How delightful to have you all to myself." There was a caress in his voice that sent shivers of dread down her spine. He frowned. "Of course I'll still have to deal with Mr. Macpherson." He spat the name out as though it were a curse. "But first I'll have the pleasure of dealing with you." The lecherous look was back. "Come here, darling." He motioned her forward with the gun.

It took everything she had to hold her ground. "I'm not coming anywhere near you."

"Ah, but that's where you're wrong, darling." He was across the room before she could blink, his free hand closing around her wrist. She would never have guessed he was capable of moving so quickly. He pulled her close, the barrel of his gun digging into her ribs, his warm breath fanning her face.

"Back off, Nick." She gritted her teeth and tried to wrench her wrist free.

"I hardly think you're in a position to be giving me or-

Dee Davis

ders." He twisted her arm behind her, pulling her even closer, her hand pinned against her back. He traced the tip of the gun along one breast, then used the barrel to work one of the buttons of her shirt free. "I've been waiting for this a long time."

A scream split the air.

Michael broke into a full run, leaping over the fence into the yard. His brain clicked into gear just as he was starting to bound onto the porch. No sense in tipping his hand. He swerved to the side, bending low to the ground.

The Jeep was parked at the side of the house. He moved to its far side, inching the door slowly open. The rifle was still hanging against the back window. Reaching for it, he prayed that whoever was inside wasn't looking out the window.

His hand closed around the stock, and he lifted the gun carefully out of the brackets. He had to admit that it felt good to have it in his hand. There was definitely something equalizing about carrying a weapon, no matter what century a man was in.

He slid along the side of the house, ducking under the window. Slowly, slowly, he inched his way up until he could see into the room. He choked back a cry of rage. Vargas had Cara trapped, his gun at her. . . . He clenched a fist. The bastard would pay.

He ducked back down and slipped around the corner to the rear of the house. The bedroom window was cracked open slightly. He heaved a sigh of relief and shoved it higher. He tossed the rifle onto the bed and threw a leg over the sill. Dropping to the floor, he retrieved the gun and edged forward toward the open door.

Cara closed her eyes, trying to think what to do. Nick's hand was firmly holding her captive, threatening to snap her wrist each time she tried to rebel against him. She squirmed as the hand with the gun dipped lower, tracing

208

a path against the bare skin of her abdomen.

"You didn't realize a weapon could be used with love, did you, Cara?"

She heard the slide of her zipper and sucked in her stomach as cold, hard steel rubbed against her skin. "What you're doing has nothing whatsoever to do with love, Nick."

"You disappoint me, Cara. I thought you were more adventurous." He kissed her, forcing her mouth open and drilling into her with his tongue.

Cara gagged and tried to wrench her head away. Yanking her free arm from between them, she dug her nails into his skin. He jerked back, a queer smile lighting his face, a trail of blood along his cheek. She sucked in a ragged breath, realizing he didn't seem to mind.

"So the lady likes it rough." He jammed the gun upward, digging into her flesh. "Do you realize, darling, that if I were to pull the trigger now, you would be shattered inside and out?" He waited, watching her, wanting a reaction.

She bit her lip and met his gaze head-on, trying to keep her emotions in check. She'd be damned if she'd add to his pleasure.

He frowned and moved the gun muzzle up to the tender skin under her chin. "But then, we don't want things to go too quickly, do we? After all, we're still waiting for your man of the hour." He pushed the pistol into her neck, pressing it against her larynx. Then he slid around so that he was behind her, her body pressed against him, her arm trapped between them.

"Let her go, Vargas."

"Ah, Macpherson. Right on time," Nick jeered. "I've been expecting you."

"I said to let her go."

Cara had never seen him look so angry. He held her grandfather's rifle pointed at them, his stance stiff and unyielding. His eyes were narrowed into thin slits of cobalt, and if the old adage that looks could kill was true, then Nick Vargas was already a dead man.

Nick's gun bit into her throat. "I hardly think you have the upper hand here, Macpherson. If you don't want to see Cara's brains splattered about this charming living room, I suggest you drop the Rambo imitation and the gun."

Cara wanted to laugh at the absurdity of the situation. Michael didn't even know who Rambo was. She heard the click of the safety being removed and held her breath.

Michael dropped the rifle, but kept his tense stance, looking a lot like a snake about to strike. "All right, I've dropped it; now let her go."

"Well, now, that would be a mistake, wouldn't it? Just the edge you need." Nick's voice was even and pleasant, as if they were all at a dinner party. "Kick it over here."

Michael kicked the shotgun and it spun away to the left.

Nick watched the weapon slide across the wooden floor. "Not very good at following orders, but it will have to do. I know who you are, Macpherson."

Cara sucked in a breath and watched as Michael stiffened. How could Nick possibly know?

"Did you think I wouldn't recognize the name? I had your family thoroughly investigated, but obviously the buffoon missed a branch. According to him, the only related Macphersons left are in some godforsaken lake valley in Scotland."

"Crannog Mhor."

"Whatever." Nick waved the gun, and Cara took the opportunity to suck in a deep breath, relieved. He didn't know Michael was from the past. He thought he was a relative of the Promise's past owner—which he was. "Obviously he was wrong. You're here. But never mind. I still have no intention of sharing my find with you."

"Find?" The word popped out before Cara could stop herself.

Nick slammed the gun back into place at her neck.

"Why, yes, Cara. Treasure beyond my wildest dreams."

"What treasure?" Michael spat the words.

"Remember, Mr. Macpherson, curiosity killed the *cat*." Nick's eyes narrowed, his voice malevolent. "But then, I suppose there's no harm in telling. Dead cats tell no tales, after all." He tightened his hold on Cara, his breath hot against her temple.

"It all began with the fact that little boys are great listeners, and doddering old men love to talk. One in particular." Nick sneered. "My grandfather. He spent his days in the bar. And I spent my days at his feet. *Listening.*

"It seems *his* father, a cowboy named Amos, was obsessed with finding the silver from a lost mine. A fortune to hear him tell it. Anyway, my grandfather inherited the obsession. Sadly, he died before he could find it." Nick's voice held no remorse. "So the quest passed to me, along with his wordly goods. And, until recently, I was cursed with his bad luck." Nick sighed. "You see, there's been the little problem of finding the mine."

"The Promise."

"A star for the boy toy."

Michael frowned. "That's why you wanted Cara's paintings!"

"They were really just insurance." Nick relaxed his hold, and Cara tried to struggle free. "Do hold still, darling." He twisted his hand, turning her wrist until she thought it would snap. An involuntary moan slipped between her clenched teeth. Michael's look turned murderous.

"Insurance against what?" Michael said in a growl.

"Perhaps I should have said backup. You see, Cara here is the real prize." Michael took a step forward. "I'd stop, if I were you." Michael held his ground. "Now, I know you have the hots for our little girl. Truth be told, so do I." He placed a kiss on the top of her head. "But she is oh, so much more important than that. You see, Cara can take me to the Promise."

"There's nothing to take you to, Vargas. There is no silver. It was stolen long ago."

"That's what you'd like me to believe, isn't it? But I think your appearance here is testament to the fact that there's something up there. And Cara here is going to show me to it."

"She doesn't remember where the mine is," Michael said. "Only I do."

"Rubbish. But a good try, Macpherson. Unfortunately, the truth is you have absolutely no value at all. "So . . ." He slowly pointed the gun at Michael.

Cara reacted instantaneously. She slammed her free hand into Nick's arm and bent back her leg, driving her foot into his groin with all the force she could muster. He grunted in pain and relaxed his grip. She wrenched free just as a shot rang out.

She ran for the rifle as Michael dove for Vargas, Nick's bullet ricocheting harmlessly off a wall. Circling Nick's gun hand with steely fingers, Michael shoved him backward. They struggled and the gun went off again, the bullet embedding itself in the ceiling. Cara scooped up the rifle, but realized that the two men were too entangled for her to get a clear shot.

They continued to wrestle, each, from Cara's vantage point, seeming to hold his own.

Then somehow, Nick managed to twist their arms around so that the gun was between them, pointed at Michael. Cara froze, watching as an unholy smile lit the man's face.

"Michael!" She screamed his name in warning. He reacted instantly, managing to turn Vargas's hand just as the gun went off. The sound reverberated through the room. The two men both went still. Gripping the rifle, she inched forward, her heart beating a frantic cadence in her ears.

One of the bodies moved, disentangling itself from the other. "Michael?" Her voice came out as a croak. She seemed to be incapable of saying anything but his name.

Dropping the gun, she threw herself at the man standing before her.

His arms locked around her, and she heard him murmuring her name over and over. She breathed his scent, feeling the press of tears now that the danger had passed. They stood locked together for a moment—an eternity—content to simply feel the other breathe.

Finally she tipped back her head, meeting his blue gaze. Blood streaked his cheek, and she reached to wipe it away with gentle fingers.

"Is he dead?" she asked.

"I think so." Michael pulled away and walked toward the body. Nick lay facedown, his blood staining the floor.

Suddenly she felt sick. "Don't touch him. Let's just get out of here. Please." She felt the world start to spin. Michael caught her just as her knees gave way, swinging her into his arms. He started for the door, and she remembered their mission. "The pendant."

He nodded and deposited her gently near the door to the mudroom. "Stay here."

She leaned against the wall and smiled weakly. "Don't worry."

He dashed into the bathroom and was back in an instant, handing her the necklace. "Shouldn't we call the sheriff?" He jerked his head toward Nick's body.

"Not now. There isn't time. It's already nearing sunset. And if we're right about time being the same, then tomorrow is the day."

Michael's face tightened. "All right. Let's go."

"It's not working." Cara was exhausted, driven only by her overriding need to help him get back to his brother.

Michael looked as tired as she felt. "I've walked in and out of this blasted tunnel in every conceivable way. I don't know what else to do." He sank down on a rock in the entrance, staring off at the orange rays of the sinking sun.

There wasn't much time left, and they didn't even have

213

a flashlight. She rubbed her arm. It ached where Nick had twisted it, but, thank God, nothing was broken. "We've just got to try again. It has to work." She reached for the pendant, surprised when it wasn't there. "Michael. The necklace . . . it's not here."

"What?"

"It's not here!" She met his gaze, then dropped to the ground, frantically searching for the pendant. A sparkle beneath a rock caught her eye. She smiled and reached for it, surprised to see how much her hand trembled. She grabbed the chain, but somehow, between her shaking hand and the finely wrought silver, she managed to drop it again.

It clattered against the floor of the tunnel and rolled deeper into the mine. Cara watched it disappear, but her tired body was slow to respond.

Michael moved faster, heading into the tunnel after the necklace. "Cara. Come here." The words were sharp, and pulled her immediately out of her lethargy. She stepped into the faint light of the tunnel. Michael was standing with the pendant in his hand. It had evidently split in the fall.

Heartbroken, she met his gaze. "I broke it?" She'd meant the words as a statement, but they came out a plea. What had she done?

"No." His whispered words were almost reverent. "It's a locket, Cara. The fall must have triggered the mechanism holding it closed."

"A locket?" She felt stupid. All she seemed to be able to do was mumble questions.

"Yes." He extended his hand, and even in the growing shadows she could see that the broken pieces were in fact the two halves of a locket, still joined by a slender hinge.

"Is anything in it?" She held her breath, not knowing what to expect. She'd never even realized the pendant was a locket.

"Yes." Again his tone bordered on amazement.

"What?" She snapped the word out impatiently. God, she needed sleep.

"Well, there are two locks of hair. And a note."

"There's a note?" She was back to repeating. She swallowed and tried to pull her brain on-line. "What does it say?"

"I don't know. It looks like a code of some kind. But Cara, I recognize the handwriting."

The hairs on the back of her neck stood at attention as a chill splintered down her spine. "Whose writing is it?"

"My father's."

She opened her mouth to speak, but before she could even formulate the thought, a strong arm wrapped around her throat and she felt the cold metal of a gun against her back. "I'll take that, Macpherson."

Nick?

She twisted her head around, trying to see him, and wished she hadn't. His face was caked with dried blood, distorting his features. His mouth was swollen and twisted, making him seem almost inhuman.

Michael took a step forward, his hand clenched in anger.

"Oh, please. Let's not go through this again." Nick shifted the gun to Cara's head. "Give me the locket or it's all over for your lovely girlfriend."

Michael held out the necklace. Keeping the gun firmly against her temple, Nick released his hold on her throat and reached for it. "The paper, too. What do you take me for, a fool?"

Michael's mouth tightened into a grim line, but he held out the note. Nick snatched it and, with a hard shove, sent her sprawling toward Michael. Everything after that happened in an instant.

Michael snarled and dove forward just as Nick fired. The gun went off a second time. There was a loud rumble and then the entire earth seemed to move. Rocks and debris from the tunnel rained down on Cara.

She huddled on the floor, trying ineffectually to cover

her head, surprised to hear someone screaming. It was a moment before she realized the blood-curdling sound came from her own throat.

A solid chunk of rock crashed against the back of her head, sending shards of white light dancing through her brain. She struggled to hold onto consciousness, but felt the encroaching blackness taking control. As her vision dimmed and the darkness enveloped her, she called out.

"*Michael!*"

Chapter Nineteen

Loralee yawned and curled closer into the warmth of the comforter. She couldn't remember the last time she'd slept in a comfortable bed—alone. It was downright sinful. A girl could get used to it. She stretched contentedly, then let her eyes slowly flicker open.

Flecks of sunlight filtered through the faded curtains, dappling the bedclothes in soft light. *Heaven.* With a blissful sigh, she threw back the covers and sat up, marveling at the fact that the day was hers. Totally hers. *Unless Amos Striker arrives.* She shivered, her mind conjuring a picture of Corabeth. Not for the first time, she was grateful that Mary was safe with her sister.

She slid out of the bed, crossing over to the dresser in the corner. A small mirror was the room's only adornment. She pulled her long hair over her shoulder and began to braid it, then twirled the finished product into a ring around her head. A halo. She smiled at the thought and fastened her hairpins into place. She looked almost passable. With a quick smile at the face in the mirror, she reached for her dress, skipping the corset in favor of breathing room. It was slightly immodest, but it wasn't as if she had a reputation to ruin.

Loralee laughed. That thought was oddly freeing. Finishing the last of her buttons, she peeked under the bed, searching for her shoes, her mind turning to that evening— with Patrick. The man had no idea how charming he was—a real innocent. And that was a rarity in her line of work, to be sure. Men like Patrick Macpherson simply didn't frequent the cribs. Loralee struggled into her boots, wishing she had a buttonhook.

Still, she'd done right to ignore Patrick's obvious interest—a fancy feat of willpower, if she did say so herself. The boy was taken with her; she could tell. But she couldn't give in to her desire for him. Patrick wasn't a one-night kind of man, and if she let him . . . Her hand drifted across her gingham-clad breast, then down across her abdomen, her eyes drifting shut as her imagination took control.

Oh, Lord.

She forced her eyes wide open. Yes, sirree, she was better off on her own. A man like Patrick Macpherson was the worst thing for her. If she ever had a taste of him, she'd only want more. And a good, kind man like him would never be happy with a whore like her. There was no sense in setting herself up for a fall. No sense at all.

A rap on the door brought Patrick to hazy consciousness. He opened one eye, the last of a very provocative dream bursting like a soap bubble. "Go away." He sighed and reached for a pillow. Maybe if he covered his head, the knocking would stop and he could find his way back to dreamland and Loralee. *Loralee.* He smiled, wrapping his arms around his pillow.

The knocking continued, and Patrick threw his pillow at the door. "Patrick," Arless asked through it. "You seen Loralee? She promised me breakfast this morning."

"She's sleeping in Michael's room, Arless; just hang on

to your drawers. I'm sure she'll be there directly." He snuggled back down into his bed, closing his eyes, picturing the woman's perfectly formed behind. It was so soft. So sweet.

"Patrick?" Arless called again.

"I told you—" Lord, couldn't a man be left to his own fantasies?

"But she ain't in there."

He sat up, no longer tired. Ignoring his pants, he grabbed his rifle. If Loralee was in trouble, there was no time for niceties. Hopping on one foot, trying to pull on a boot, he reached for the door, almost toppling over when Arless yanked it open.

"False alarm." The Irishman's grin broadened when he saw Patrick's relative state of undress. "She was just in the privy."

Loralee's face appeared in the space above Arless's shoulder, her angelic smile belying the wicked twinkle in her eye. "Mornin', Patrick. I see you're up and dressed." She disappeared, but he could hear giggling.

"What are you staring at, Arless?" He scowled at the man. "Haven't you seen a man in his underwear before?"

"Sure have, Patrick. Just never seen anyone turn that color afore. And you ain't even been drinkin'." Arless backed away from the door, leaving it standing open.

Patrick reached for his pants, his dignity hanging by a thread. "Would somebody please shut the damn door?"

Fifteen minutes later he emerged from the bedroom, boots in hand. Loralee was dropping batter onto the griddle, the picture of domestic tranquillity. His heart quickened at the sight. *Ah, sweet Loralee. A whore,* the little voice in his head sternly reminded. And he wasn't surprised at all that the voice sounded an awful lot like Owen's.

"Glad to see you're finally up and dressed." She shot him a crooked smile, then turned back to her cooking.

Arless was sitting at the table, lost in his own kind of bliss. "She's making griddle cakes."

219

Patrick pulled on his boots and straddled a chair. "I kinda figured that."

The other man inhaled deeply and sighed.

"Arless, doesn't Lena cook for you?"

"Not like this she don't." He gestured to a sizzling pan of sausage.

Patrick's mouth watered. "Well, it does smell good." He was rewarded with another of Loralee's smiles. "Where's Pete?"

"Said he was going to feed the stock." Arless's eyes never left the stove.

Patrick was enjoying the view himself, although he was far more interested in the cook than in the fare. Loralee expertly flipped the griddle cakes. "If one of you boys will go get him, I think breakfast is about ready."

Arless stood up. "I'll go. Might as well do something to earn my keep."

He ambled toward the door, shooting a last loving look in the direction of the food. "Don't you go eatin' it all while I'm gone, Patrick."

"Don't worry, Arless; I'll leave some for you."

Satisfied, the man opened the door and went outside.

A shot rang out, its report echoing through the house.

Patrick jumped out of his chair, already reaching for his rifle. "Get down."

Loralee dropped to the floor, her face ashen. "What is it?"

"Probably nothing. Stay here. I'll go see." Crouching below window height, he ran across the room, slowing as he reached the open door. Carefully he edged into the doorway, his gaze darting around the barnyard, trying to locate the source of the noise.

"Arless? You out there?" He waited, holding his breath, silence permeating the air. When nothing moved, he took a cautious step out onto the porch, the floor creaking beneath him. A low moan broke the stillness.

"Stay back, Loralee," he called over his shoulder, his

gaze moving along the ground in front of him, trying to locate the source of the cry. A crimson-stained mound about halfway between the porch and the corral shifted: Arless. The old miner lay in the grass, clutching his middle, his shirt red with blood.

Patrick had just started to step off the porch when Pete burst from the confines of the stable, his Colt drawn, motioning for Patrick to stay put. Reaching Arless, he knelt beside him, one hand assessing the damage while the other held the gun ready.

It was quiet again—almost too quiet. A shiver of dread ran up Patrick's spine. Pete slowly stood, pulling Arless with him. The other man was deadweight, and it took Pete a minute to find his balance.

Patrick scanned the trees that surrounded the place, but if anyone was out there, he was well hidden. Pete took a step forward, Arless draped against him, but another shot rang out. Pete's eyes widened and he dropped Arless and fell backward. Patrick had never felt so helpless.

"Loralee, get out here." She was beside him in an instant. "Can you shoot this thing?" He held out the rifle.

"I can manage." She took the gun.

He nodded, relieved she wasn't the swoon-in-a-crisis type. "All right. Here's what we're going to do. I'm going out there—"

"No." Her hand shot out and she clamped her fingers around his arm.

He ignored her panic, keeping his voice low and soothing. "I want you to cover me. I've got to try to get Pete and Arless back to the house. We can't do anything to help them out there."

She released his arm. "All right. But how will I know where to shoot?"

"You won't. Just fire into the brush in several places. Hopefully that'll scare whoever's out there enough to buy me some time." Loralee squared her shoulders, lifting the rifle, so Patrick added, "Don't fire unless he does. There's a small chance he's gone. And we don't want to waste ammo." They were likely going to need all the bullets they could get.

"Patrick?" she asked. He met her frightened gaze. "Be careful."

He grinned with a courage he didn't feel. "All right. I'm going." He crouched as low as he could and scrambled across the yard, running in zigzags toward Pete and Arless. Bullets shattered the dust at his feet. Answering shots rang out from the porch.

Reaching the fallen men, he dropped to his knees. Arless was on his back, sightless eyes staring at the clouds above him, his gut torn open from one of the shots. Pete was facedown in the dirt.

Patrick shifted, flinching as another shot rang out. He couldn't tell if it came from their assailant or Loralee. A deep red wound already stained the back of Pete's thigh. Gingerly Patrick rolled him over, relieved to see the even rise and fall of the man's chest.

"Pete, can you hear me?" The foreman wasn't a small man. Without his help, Patrick wasn't sure he could manage getting him back.

The older man groaned and opened his eyes. "What the hell happened?"

"Sniper."

Pete nodded. "Arless?"

"Dead."

Pete closed his eyes, regret tightening his face. "Damn it to hell."

As if in echo of his sentiment, another shot stirred the dust of the yard, this one only a few feet away. Answering gunfire echoed from the porch. *God bless her.* "Come on, old man. It's now or never. You got to help me get you to the house."

Patrick struggled to his feet, Pete pushing up beside him with a groan. Wrapping his arm around the ranch hand's waist, Patrick braced himself, and the two of them began to stagger back toward the porch. Pete groaned as another bullet grazed his arm, blood burgeoning across his sleeve. He sank, deadweight against Patrick.

"Come on, just three more steps. You can do it."

Gritting his teeth, Pete rallied, and together they made it across the last few feet of ground and up the steps, bullets flying all around them. Loralee lowered the rifle, her face pinched with fear. Grabbing Pete from the other side, she helped Patrick get him in the house. Behind them, a bullet ricocheted onto the porch, imbedding itself in the floor where they'd been standing.

"How many do you think there are?" Pete was propped up against the back wall, his arm extended while Loralee cleaned it. She was attempting to maintain her calm, concentrating on Pete's injury and not the situation.

"I don't know. Maybe only one." Patrick was crouched under the window, his back to them, watching the barnyard.

She dipped a rag in a basin, then carefully sponged away more of Pete's blood. "Do you think it's Amos?"

"Maybe. Hell, probably," Patrick answered without looking back at them. "Who the heck else could it be?"

"Well, whoever the son of a bitch is, he has us pinned." Pete grimaced as she probed his wounds.

"I'm sorry." She glanced up at his face and saw that his eyes were closed. Wringing the rag out, she dipped it in the now red water.

"How's Pete?" Patrick asked.

"I ain't dead, ya know. I can speak for myself."

"I know. I meant your injuries," Patrick clarified.

Pete shifted, trying to find a comfortable place to sit. "The arm's not bad. The bullet passed clean through."

"And the leg?"

"Not so good. I think the bullet's lodged next to the bone."

Loralee bit back an exclamation. What they didn't need

right now was a hysterical female. She placed a compress against both sides of Pete's thigh and bound his arm with a strip of linen torn from a sheet. "There, that ought to help with the bleeding."

"Much obliged, ma'am." Pete tried for a smile, but the look was sickly. "See anything out there?"

Loralee glanced over at Patrick. Tension tightened the lines of his shoulders. "Not a damn thing," he said.

"Can't we just crawl out a window or something?" She hated the tremor in her voice.

Patrick crossed the room in a crouch, settling in beside them. "Wouldn't do us any good. There's just these two." He indicated the windows fronting the porch. "And the ones in the bedrooms. They all face the same way. Michael's idea. He thought it would help keep the house warm."

"But surely there's some way out of this?" She saw the two men exchange a look and her fear increased, threatening to explode into full-blown panic.

"No easy one, Miss Loralee," Pete said. "Unless he gets tired and heads for home."

"Or help arrives." She knew she was clutching at straws. "What about your friend, Owen?" She might not like the man, but she'd happily cook him meals for a week if he'd get them out of this.

"No. He's not going to just drop by. He doesn't know anything about this. I didn't have time to tell him. I was so intent on getting you out here." Patrick met her gaze, his face clouded with guilt. "Loralee, I'm so sorry."

"Oh, fiddlesticks, there's no way you could have known Amos would do this. You did what you thought was right." She reached over and squeezed his arm. "Right now you have to help me do something about Pete's leg. I don't know much about this sort of thing, but I do know the bullet ought to come out."

Pete groaned. "I think I'd rather we just leave it be."

She rolled up her sleeves. "Well, Mr. Reeder, I don't think I'm giving you a choice."

"See anything?"

Patrick felt her come up behind him, her soft scent filling his nose. What had he done? He had promised she'd be safe, and now look at the mess they were in. "Nothing. How's Pete?"

"He's asleep. He drained what was left of Arless's whiskey."

"You get the bullet?"

"Yes, but I don't know what kind of damage I did to his leg. It was real deep."

He reached out and squeezed her shoulder. "I'm sure you did just fine."

She held out a plate. "I brought you something to eat. It's cold, but I figured it was better than nothing."

He looked down at the griddle cakes, the food making him think of Arless. His stomach turned. He took the plate, but set it down beside him. "Thanks, I'll eat in a bit. You go on and tend to Pete."

He stared out the window, trying to decide what to do. Maybe he could make it to the stable. And then, with a little luck, he could outride the gunfire and go for help. The problem was that he'd be leaving Loralee and Pete unprotected. The ranch foreman wasn't any good to anybody right now, and Loralee had spirit, but she couldn't hold off a sniper.

The fact was, he couldn't leave them. They'd be sitting ducks for whomever was out there shooting at them.

The yard looked painfully normal. From here he couldn't even see Arless's body. He looked at the sun, trying to figure out how long they'd been pinned in here. Maybe the sniper had given up. Suddenly he couldn't stand it anymore. He had to know.

"Throw me that blanket, Loralee."

She grabbed one of the blankets she'd wrapped around

Pete, lobbing it to him from across the room. The glass in the window above him shattered, the sound of a gunshot reverberating through the room. The blanket hit the floor with a soft thud. It could just as easily have been one of them.

"Well, that wasn't what I had in mind, but it answered my question just the same."

"He's still out there." Her voice trembled.

"Yup. And he's closer."

Chapter Twenty

It was dark—so dark Cara couldn't even see her hand in front of her face. She sat up, disoriented, trying to remember what had happened. Her head hurt. She probed her scalp gingerly, relieved to find only a small lump. She rubbed her throat, surprised at how tender it was.

Nick.

Memory came crashing in, her mind replaying the moment when he'd shoved her forward, the sound of his shots reverberating off the walls. A cave-in. She drew in a breath, choking on the dust that filled the tunnel. Nick had caused a cave-in.

"Michael?"

The silence echoed back at her, mocking her with its emptiness. She swallowed, wondering if the sudden dryness in her throat was caused by the dust or her rising fear.

"Michael? Can you hear me?"

The tunnel remained silent. She closed her mouth, forcing herself to breathe through her nose. The dark was overwhelming, pressing in on her, threatening to consume what little courage she had left. She had to find Michael. He was

Dee Davis

here somewhere. All she had to do was to stay calm and search. She stared into the darkness, trying to see something, anything.

There was no light at all, nothing to distinguish a wall from a shadow, the front of the tunnel from the back. She forced herself to picture the tunnel. In her mind's eye she saw the entrance and, using her memory, traced a path all the way to the rear. She could do this. She just had to rely on her sense of touch.

Rocking up onto her knees, she crawled forward, one hand extended in front of her, sweeping through the endless blackness, searching for him. After only a few feet, her hand met rock—solid, impenetrable rock.

Standing, she stretched her arms out to both sides and swung them slowly up and down. Nothing. Feeling again for the wall in front of her, she moved along it until she felt the junction of wall meeting wall.

A corner.

Progress.

There were only a couple of corners. She ought to be able to orient herself. She ran a hand along the two adjacent walls. One was smooth in comparison to the other. She sucked in a breath, almost choking on the dust. She had found the slide. Following the path of the cave-in, her trembling fingers searched for a hole, some portal for escape. A stone wobbled under her touch.

With a pounding heart, she carefully tried to pry it away from the blockage. It fell heavily into her hands, but the resulting hail of loose stones filled its place almost immediately. Reaching higher, she grabbed another protruding rock and yanked it free. Again, stones and dirt rained down on her. A rumble filled the tunnel, and she dropped to the floor, covering her head with her hands as large chunks of the ceiling crashed to the floor around her.

She scrambled away, tripping, falling to her knees, gulping for breath, the dust again filling her lungs. Reaching out, she tried to find the wall, afraid that somehow in her

228

panic she had disoriented herself. Her hand groped through the dark, closing around something cold and pliant. She jerked back, recoiling as her senses registered the feel of a human hand.

"Michael?" she called.

Nothing moved, and another thought entered her head.

"Nick? Is that you, Nick?"

Again, nothing.

Fighting her fear, she stretched her hand out again, steeling herself for the feel of cold flesh. Slowly she closed her fingers over the hand's digits, noting that there was no reaction, not even a quiver of movement. The skin was cold and soft. She released a breath she hadn't even realized she'd been holding. It was not Michael's work-worn hand but Nick's I-never-work-when-I-can-pay-someone-else-to-do-it hand.

She sent a prayer heavenward.

She followed the hand until she felt the adjoining wrist and arm. Tracing her way up his arm, she felt the solid barrier of rock before she'd even reached the elbow. He'd been crushed. She shuddered with revulsion, tears filling her eyes. Not even Nick deserved to die like that.

A harsh hacking sound filtered through her terror-numbed mind. She whirled around. "Michael? Is that you?" The coughing grew louder as she groped her way through the darkness toward the sound. "Michael?"

"I'm here, Cara."

Her tears began to fall in earnest, the dam threatening to break. She struggled for control, stumbling as she ran forward, rocks rattling around as she did.

"Hang on, sweetheart. I'm going to light a match."

A soft light flared in front of her, illuminating a small circle around him. Nothing had ever looked so beautiful. She threw herself at him, mindful of nothing but her overriding need to feel his arms around her. Surely now that they were together everything would be all right.

"Hey, easy now." He laughed as she burrowed close,

the sound of his voice music to her ears. "I'm not going anywhere."

She winced at the truth in his words. If what she suspected was right, neither of them would ever go anywhere again. The match fizzled out and blackness surrounded them once more. He pulled her closer, wrapping his arms around her.

She buried her face in his chest, his warm breath fanning across her hair, her arms circling his waist. He pulled her onto his lap, cradling her. She sighed and leaned into him, content for the moment just to feel his even breathing.

"Are you all right?" She shifted, tipping her head up toward him.

"I think so. Just a knock on the head. How about you?"

"Same." She felt his hand gently search her skull, stopping when it found the lump.

"That's a pretty good knot."

"It's nothing, really." She smiled in the darkness.

He felt for her face and ran his palm along the line of her cheek, bending his head to find her lips. The kiss was like an explosion, passion fueled by a wild mixture of fear and relief. She clung to him, her body melding with his, her lips opening to his touch, drawing him deeper, closer. Despite her exhaustion, her need for him crescendoed into hot, burning desire.

She pressed against him, willing his body to become one with hers, wanting only to be closer. He ran his hand across her breast and she winced as his fingers came in contact with torn flesh. He pulled back, his voice tightening with concern. "You're hurt."

"I don't think so." She blinked in the sudden flare of light as he lit another match, surprised to see that his hands were shaking. "I feel fine." She tried to settle back against him, her thoughts still centered on her need for him.

"I'll be the judge of that." He pushed her back and held the flame between them. With his other hand he pulled back the torn material of her blouse. "There's a cut here."

He ran a gentle finger along the soft peak and she jerked a little at the contact. He audibly released a breath. "It's all right. It's just a scratch."

"I told you."

"Damn." He pulled away, dropping the stub of the match as it burned his thumb, plunging them into darkness in an instant. He found her hand and linked his fingers with hers, gently pulling her forward until she was once again nestled against him. Somehow, like this, the whole thing seemed less frightening.

She settled closer into the curve of his body and drew in a breath for courage, a vision of Nick filling her brain. "I . . . I found Nick."

His arm tightened around her as he waited for her to say more.

"He's dead." She shivered at the thought of the lifeless hand.

"Well, I can't say that I'm sorry. What happened?"

"He was . . ." She swallowed, trying to find the words. "Buried . . . in the cave-in. All I found . . . was his hand." The tears started again. She was nothing more than a blubbering baby. "I thought . . . Oh, God, Michael . . . I thought it was you."

He pulled her close, rocking her soothingly in his arms. "I'm here, Cara. I'm fine. It's going to be all right, sweetheart, I promise. Somehow it's going to be all right."

She tried to nod, to rally, to let him know she was okay, but the tears just kept coming. Reaction, that was all it was. Reaction. She'd just let them come and *then* she'd pull it all together.

But right now, this minute, she just wanted him to hold her. She'd be strong in little while, she solemnly promised herself—in just a little while.

Michael felt Cara stir in her sleep and reached to smooth a wayward curl from her face, stunned to realize just how much she'd come to mean to him. He didn't know when it happened, but somewhere along the way she'd become a part of him.

He sighed, pushing his feelings away. Now wasn't the time.

Time.

He groaned at the irony of the thought. Unless he'd missed something, their time was running out. He leaned over the small lantern, adjusting the wick so that it would continue to burn slowly. The little light was the one good thing he'd found in his search of the tunnel.

He turned again to survey the space around him. The light faded to black long before the rubble from the cave-in began, but even though he couldn't see the wall, it taunted him with its impenetrability.

There was no way out.

The flame in the lantern flickered, and Cara moaned in her sleep. He blew out a breath and ran a hand through his hair, wondering how fate could possibly have allowed them to survive all that they had, only to leave them trapped here until the air ran out.

He cast a glance upward. It seemed that somebody up there had a vicious sense of humor. He swallowed bitter laughter. And Patrick. What of his brother? Was he still alive? Clenching a fist, Michael swung at the air.

He had never felt so helpless.

He was the one who was supposed to take care of everyone. Fine job he was doing. His father was dead and Patrick was . . . well, if not already dead, then certainly on his way.

And Cara . . . His eyes dropped to her sleeping form. Oh, dear God, what had he done to Cara? He'd sent her right into the arms of that sniveling excuse for a human, Vargas. And then he'd managed to rescue her only after the bastard . . . He felt bile rise in his throat as the scene between Cara and Nick replayed itself in his mind.

At least the son of a bitch was dead, though not because

of anything Michael himself had done. He sighed. Some protector he'd turned out to be.

"Where'd you get the light?" Cara's eyes flickered open, and she smiled up at him.

"I found it by the wall."

She nodded sleepily. "So what's the prognosis?" She sat up and yawned delicately, stretching her body so that her arms were above her head, her breasts thrusting upward as she arched back.

His body tightened in response. Hell, all she had to do was move and he found himself getting excited. He squatted down beside her, the warmth of her smile easing the pain in his gut. He strove to keep his voice light. "We're stuck here, I'm afraid."

She met his gaze unflinchingly. "Forever?"

He nodded, unable to say the words.

"I see." She nibbled at her lower lip.

"I'm sorry, Cara."

She frowned up at him, the delicate arches of her eyebrows flattening. "For what?"

He shook his head and shrugged. "Everything."

She reached out, laying a gentle hand on his cheek. "This isn't your fault, Michael."

He covered her hand with his, still holding her gaze. "Of course it is. If I hadn't gotten shot, then none of this would have happened."

She laughed, the light tinkle echoing through the shadows. "Right. You purposely got shot so that you could travel a hundred years through time and screw up my life. I'm sorry you were shot. I'm sorry your father was killed. But I'm not sorry I found you again."

He studied her face, trying to understand. She turned her palm, capturing his fingers and pulling his hand to her lips. With a soft, slow movement, she kissed it, the gesture sending shivers of desire shooting through him.

With a groan he pulled her into his arms, crushing her to him, wanting nothing more than to pull her deep within him and hold her there, safe and secure. He covered her face with kisses, touching each crevice and plane with his lips, memorizing the feel of her as her heart beat in syncopation with his.

He ran his hands along the curve of her neck and shoulder, smoothing her shirt across the swell of her breast. She sighed and pushed against his hand, demanding that he take her. He bent his head, circling her nipple through the fabric with his tongue, waves of passion threatening to up-end him.

God, he wanted this woman, wanted her on a level far beyond the physical. It was almost as if she were a newly discovered part of him, and without her he would never be whole again. He groaned and lay down against the rubble-strewn floor, pulling her with him, nestling her atop the length of his body, his tongue exploring the soft hollows of her ear.

He found the zipper of her jeans and, with a gentle tug, exposed the filmy lace of her underwear. His hand slipped beneath it. Her mouth found his and her tongue playfully traced the line of his teeth. He gently slid a finger between the soft folds of her skin, feeling the heat of her envelop him. He lightly flicked the tiny nub of her desire and felt her bite down on his lip in response.

She sat up, the motion taking his finger deeper, and shrugged out of her shirt, the soft yellow light of the lantern washing her bare breasts in its pale glow. "Make love to me, Michael." She pressed against his finger and tightened herself around it, then leaned down, her hair curling around them, her fingers fumbling open the buttons of his shirt. Finally, with a moan, she pressed herself against him, rubbing her nipples against the hair-roughened skin of his chest.

He stroked her, gently rubbing the center of her passion until she moaned his name and pressed her mouth to his, her tongue mimicking the rhythm of his finger. Twining his other hand through her hair, he drank greedily from her lips and pulled her up, inching her forward. He replaced his finger with his tongue, never breaking the rhythm.

She writhed above him, her breath coming in short gasps that made his blood burn. Her warmth was almost overpowering, and she breathed his name, melting into him.

With a sensuous smile she slid downward, her hand freeing his hardened shaft from the confines of his jeans, firmly kneading him, stroking up and down. She moved lower, her lips replacing her hand, the sweet heat of her mouth surrounding him, driving him wild.

With a groan he pulled away and they rolled apart, both clumsy in their need, tearing off the rest of their clothing, making a crude bed of their discards. Finally, skin to skin, he took possession of her mouth again, his tongue thrusting deep, the fire of his need raging out of control.

She sat up, straddling him, and with a shy smile she leaned forward, placing her hands on his shoulders, her eyes locked on his. With shaking hands he cupped her buttocks and raised her gently, groaning as she slowly slid down, impaling herself on him. Then, just when he thought he couldn't hold on for another minute, she was moving up again, and he fought to keep from pulling her back into place.

They continued the languorous dance—in and out, up and down—until the pleasure had almost become pain. With a cry he wrapped his hands around her waist, bringing her down around him until he was sheathed to the hilt.

She bent and kissed him then, her breasts pressing against his chest, and together they found a rhythm that carried them higher and higher, until the world disappeared. He cried out her name as fragments of light and color twirled around him like a kaleidoscope gone wild. Locking his arms around her, feeling her body quiver around his, he knew that the moment was absolutely perfect.

* * *

Cara opened her eyes, her gaze fixing on the hypnotic dance of the flame in the little lantern. She smiled as the memory of their lovemaking swept her away again, allowing her to lose herself in their passion. She wondered idly if it would always be like this between them.

The thought brought reality crashing in. There wasn't going to be a future. She bit her lip to keep the tears at bay. Michael shifted in his sleep, one leg thrown possessively across her thighs, a hard-muscled arm wrapped securely around her waist. His hair fell forward into his eyes, and she resisted the urge to straighten it. With a sigh she closed her eyes, the lantern's golden flame still burning in her mind. How wonderful light was. How comforting.

How wrong.

She sat up, her heart beating faster, her eyes searching the lantern for signs of age. She'd seen this lantern when she'd rescued Michael. But it had been older, rusted.

And broken.

She touched it. The smooth metal base was practically unblemished by age, the glass of the globe unmarred. She searched the shadows surrounding the soft ring of light. Nothing was visible beyond its glow. She frowned. Before falling asleep they'd moved back, deeper into the recesses of the tunnel, afraid that the ceiling near the cave-in was too unstable.

Was it possible? Her heart was in her throat, hope poking a timid head into the cavern of her mind.

"Michael?"

He sat up immediately, his face wary.

"Where did you say you found this lantern?"

He relaxed and his expression changed from startled to confused as he tried to follow the gist of her conversation. "By the wall, in the front of the tunnel. Why?"

She ignored his question, too full of her own. "Did you see the cave-in? By lantern light, I mean?"

He shot her a look that clearly said he thought she'd taken leave of her senses. "No, I didn't. I stumbled over the thing and decided to bring it back to where you were sleeping before lighting it. I didn't want to waste a match, and I was afraid it might go out while I was walking."

"So you didn't see the cave-in."

"Cara, I just said no. What's this all about?"

"I saw this lantern, Michael, after you'd been shot. It was broken. Remember, I told you." She held her breath, waiting for him to comment, but he only stared at her uncomprehendingly. She released the breath and tried again. "It was old. Really old."

His eyes widened as the import of what she was saying sank in. "A hundred years old?"

She smiled. "I think so. The lantern I saw was the same, I'm sure of it. Only my lantern was rusted and the globe had been shattered."

"So if the lantern is new again, then—" He broke off, the beginnings of a smile lighting his face.

"Then maybe, just maybe, the locket has worked its magic."

The smile faded as he drew his brows together in thought. "But Nick had the necklace. It must have been buried in the rockslide."

"Maybe it doesn't matter. I mean, if this lantern is any indication, then maybe the locket did its stuff."

His brow cleared and the smile burgeoned in full. "And if the cave-in occurred in your time, then—"

In her excitement, she interrupted him. "Maybe there wasn't one in your time. Which means that—"

"I might be home."

Her face fell, the moment of elation evaporating as the meaning of his words became clear. If he was home that would mean that she, too, had taken the trip to the nineteenth century.

But without the locket, it was a one-way ticket.

Chapter Twenty-one

"Cara? Honey, are you all right?"

Cara forced herself to focus on Michael's face, pushing her panic down. If she was going to be trapped in another time, so be it. She'd learned a long time ago that she had no control over her life. And nothing happening now was changing her opinion. She squared her shoulders. Their immediate concern had to be getting Michael to his brother. "I'm fine." She'd face the enormity of what she was doing later, when she had the luxury. Glancing to the shifting shadows beyond the lamplight, she drew in a fortifying breath. "Let's get out of here."

Michael squeezed her shoulder, then bent to pick up the lantern and moved toward the front of the tunnel. She started to follow, but noticed the pack of matches at her feet. *"Waste not, want not"* and all that. She scooped them up and stuffed them in her pocket, then quickened her pace, following the pale glow of Michael's lamp.

Rounding the last bend of the tunnel, she skidded to a stop. Sunlight was filtering in through the cave's opening, a truly awesome thing to behold. It played off the rock

walls, making them glitter. Michael was already heading
outside, his mind obviously centered on the task of finding
his brother. She started to follow just as he stepped out
into the sunshine.

One second she saw his silhouette outlined by the sun,
the next he disappeared and everything went a deep, impenetrable black. Fear stung her throat as she swallowed
a scream. Choking back a sob, she forced herself to walk
forward, hands extended. In only a few short steps, her
worst nightmare was confirmed; her hands touched the
sharp-edged roughness of the cave-in. Michael was gone.

She sank to her knees, trying to think. She'd watched
him walk out of the tunnel. The sunlight had been blinding. One minute he was there, and the next—gone. When
he'd left the cave, he must have sealed the passage to his
own time. Which meant she had been left on her own—
with no way out. As if to underscore the thought, a small
stream of rocks trickled down from the ceiling.

"Cara?" a voice called.

She jerked her head up. "Michael? I'm here." She could
hear his voice from the other side of the rocks. Then suddenly he was back, and the mine was filled with light again.
She flung herself into his arms, content for the moment
just to feel his heart beating next to hers.

"What happened?" he asked. "You disappeared."

She sucked in a breath. "I don't know." She paused,
trying to force the words out. "One minute you were there,
the next you were gone."

He massaged her back with one strong hand, the other
reaching under her chin, tipping her head up. "You were
still in your time?"

She closed her eyes and drew in a calming breath, ex-
haling slowly. "Trapped."

He frowned at the entrance, shining as it was now with
its false offer of freedom. "But I got out."

"Michael, maybe we're meant to stay where we belong."
She tried but couldn't keep the hopelessness from her voice.

"I can't go through those rocks. I can't go back to your time with you."

"I won't accept that." His eyes flashed with anger.

She shook her head, shaking off her self-pity. "You may not have a choice."

He frowned, considering what she'd said. "There's always a choice, Cara. I won't leave you here to die."

"So . . . what? You'll stay here and die with me? You'll let Patrick die, too?" She tried but couldn't keep the bitterness out of her voice.

"You're making this all too cut and dried. There has to be a way out."

"Maybe. I don't know." She ran a hand through her hair, trying to fight against the feeling of inevitability. "But the fact remains that you got out and I couldn't."

He shook his head, trying to puzzle it out. "It doesn't make sense. Why can I leave this tunnel and not you?"

"Maybe you're the time traveler, not me."

He sat down beside her, staring out at the sunlight. "But you can see the sunlight, can't you? You can touch the lantern. They're both in my time."

He held the lamp out and she ran a finger along the base, a tiny flicker of hope blossoming within her. Then it died. "But those things are only in the tunnel."

He blew out a breath. "Well, maybe it has something to do with the locket."

She felt hope die. "Great. It's buried under ten tons of twenty-first-century rock."

He wrapped an arm around her. "Okay, it's not that then. Cara, we're not giving up that easily."

"But I don't see how—"

"We'll try going out together." She opened her mouth to argue, but he covered her lips with a finger. "If that doesn't work, we'll figure out something else. I'm not leaving you."

"But your brother . . ." How could she expect him to choose?

The Promise

He met her gaze, his eyes reflecting an emotion she suddenly found herself wanting desperately to identify. "I'm *not* going to leave you." He grabbed her hand, his fingers wrapping securely around hers. "Ready?"

She nodded and allowed him to pull her slowly forward. She concentrated on the swaying green of the spruce tree outside. The warmth from Michael's hand radiated up her arm, infusing her with courage. One step at a time.

She stepped again and a wrenching pain seared up her arm. She jerked back, rocks scraping her. It was almost as if she were pulling her arm out of the debris. Black descended again, but this time the accompanying fear was duller, more resolute. Some part of her had already known that this wouldn't work.

"Michael? Can you hear me?"

It happened as it had before. One moment it was dark; the next, the cavern was filled with light, the change occurring so quickly it made her dizzy. Michael swept her into his arms, the force of his embrace lifting her off the ground. He cradled her against his chest. "We're going again. Hold on tight." His voice was strained with anxiety.

"I can't."

He gave her a piercing look; then he spoke. "Yes, you can." His tone brooked no argument. "You just have to hold on to me, I won't let anything happen to you. Believe in this, Cara. You have to believe. Believe in *me*. I think you're holding yourself back."

Suddenly, part of her knew he was right. She tried to push her doubts aside, wrapping her arms around his neck, comforted by the smell and feel of him.

"Are you ready?" he asked at last. She nodded, afraid to say anything, feeling his muscles tighten and bunch as he prepared to run.

The dark was almost overpowering this time. She could feel it all around her. The stones scraped her arms and legs, the weight of all the rock crushing down on her. She tried to focus her thoughts on Michael, to hold tightly to him, but she could no longer feel him, only the darkness. It ebbed and flowed around her. It was cold, so cold. She tried to fight, to hold on, to find Michael, but there was nothing but the icy darkness and the crushing weight of the rock. She knew she was dying, was certain of it somewhere deep inside, and with a soft sigh she let go, floating off into the waiting arms of the darkness.

"Cara, sweetheart, can you hear me?" Her hands felt like ice. Michael rubbed them between his own, willing her to open her eyes and look at him. Her breathing was shallow, but right now any movement was a positive sign.

He closed his eyes, for a moment reliving the absolute terror of their exit from the tunnel. He'd actually felt her being ripped from his arms. He'd tightened his grip, his muscles twisting with pain as he'd struggled to maintain his hold.

He shook his head. He'd taken a huge risk, literally dragging her into his time, but she had made it! Opening his eyes, he studied her face. Even asleep she was beautiful. His heart rate increased as he thought again how close he had come to losing her. Nothing was as important as keeping Cara with him. Nothing.

She moaned, the small sound seeming to reverberate off of his soul. With a flicker, her eyes opened and she looked up at him. "Michael? Where are we?"

He helped her sit up, keeping an arm around her. "Judging from the size of that spruce, I'd say we're back in my time."

Fear flickered across her face, but almost as quickly it was gone. She smiled hesitantly. "As long as we're out of that tunnel, I'm happy to be anywhere."

He ran a gentle hand along the line of her jaw, suddenly contrite for the danger he'd put her in. "I thought for a minute there I was going to lose you."

She shivered, lost in memory, then squared her shoulders and met his gaze. "But you didn't."

"I'm sorry about all this." He waved a hand in the direction of the spruce, the little tree signifying everything.

"We've covered that before. And don't be sorry. You saved me. Right now that's all that matters—that and finding your brother." She met his gaze squarely. "When the time comes, I'll find my way home."

Michael winced. He couldn't, wouldn't, think about losing Cara again. Not now. Maybe not ever. He'd have to find a way to convince her to stay. But first he had to make things right. He had to save his brother. "There's a line shack not far from here. I can leave you there until I find Patrick."

Her eyes narrowed and her lips tightened. "No way, Michael," she said. "Until we resolve this, whatever we do, we do it together." Cara crossed her arms and squinted at him angrily, looking like a bizarre cross between an avenging angel and a street urchin. She stood up, wiping her hands against her jeans, all business. "What do we do first?"

He held up his hands in surrender, but a sense of pride welled up inside him, and something else, something powerful and possessive. This was the most amazing woman he had ever known. And he'd be damned if he'd let her willingly walk out of his life. He forced himself to focus on her question. There'd be time to examine his fragile new emotions later. "Can you handle a gun?"

"Like a pro. My grandfather taught me to shoot about the same time he taught me to ride." She smiled up at him, determination glinting in her eyes. "But, Michael, where are we going to get weapons?"

"There'll be some in the line shack. We'll go there, and then we'll head to Clune."

"Can you see anything?" Loralee poked her nose above the windowsill, searching the yard for some sign of their tormentor.

"Stay low." Patrick glanced over at her, then returned his gaze to the ranch yard.

Dee Davis

"I can't stand much more of this." Loralee kept her voice in a whisper. Pete was sleeping and there was no sense waking him. "It's like torture, Patrick. Waiting and waiting. If we're such sitting ducks, why doesn't he just kill us?"

Patrick reached over and covered her hand with his, the contact comforting. "I don't know. Maybe he just wants to pick us off one by one."

Loralee squared her shoulders, determined not to give in to her fear. This was by far the worst spot she'd been in over the years, but that didn't mean she hadn't seen her share of trouble. And she'd survived it all. She would survive this.

"There's got to be something we can do," she said, glancing over her shoulder at Pete. "He's got a fever, Patrick. I don't know how much longer he can hold out."

Patrick ran a hand through his hair, leaving it sticking up every which way. "I've been over it and over it, Loralee. There's just nothing to do but try to wait this sniper out. Maybe he'll make a mistake."

She stared out at the tall grass waving in the breeze, trying to find her courage. "You could make a run for it."

"I'm not leaving you alone."

"If leaving me alone saves our lives, it'd be more than worth it, don't you think? If you do get out, then you'd be able to bring back help. And I can hold the fort until you're gone." She gave him a determined smile.

"No. Even if I could get out alive—and I doubt I could—I'm not about to leave you and Pete undefended."

"Patrick, I've been taking care of myself as long as I can remember. I reckon I can handle it just a little bit longer."

He ran the back of his hand along her cheek. "You're as brave as they come, but you're no match for whoever's out there. Hell, neither am I. That son of bitch is holding all the cards."

"Don't mean nothing." They both turned to look at Pete, who had struggled to a sitting position.

His face was ashen, and Loralee marveled at his inner strength. A lesser man would be dead right now. Or at least unconscious. "Pete, you shouldn't be up. You need rest."

"If we don't do something real soon, I'll be doin' nothin' but restin'. Figure now's as good a time as any to formulate us a plan." From Pete, it was a speech. Loralee crawled over to his side and dipped a square of linen in the pan of water. She reached to wipe it across his brow, but he pushed her hand away, his gaze never leaving Patrick. "So what you thinkin' of doin'?"

Patrick crossed the room, staying low, settling on the floor beside them. "Okay, Pete. If you cover me, I might make it to the barn. From there I could try to ride for Silverthread."

Pete closed his eyes, scrunching up his face in thought. "Might work."

"Yeah, and it might not."

"It's worth a try." Loralee looked from one man to the other. "You said yourself that sooner or later he's going to get us if we stay pinned like this. Seems to me a little chance is better than no chance at all."

"Girl's got a head on her." Pete nodded with approval, and Loralee felt pleased at the praise.

"I still don't like it. If I get shot, how are you all going to manage?"

"If you don't try, we're gonna be in the same kettle. It's just a matter of time." Pete leaned back, all the words exhausting him.

Loralee met Patrick's gaze, her own steady. She'd played poker before. She wasn't half bad at it actually. And she knew it was time to call the hand. "Pete's right, and you know it."

Patrick looked from one to the other and then out the window, his eyes narrowed. "All right. I'll do it, but not until it gets dark. It'll be safer then."

245

Dee Davis

Loralee blew out a breath and raised her damp cloth again, this time successfully wiping Pete's brow. "You get some sleep now," she said to him. "You'll need your strength later."

The old man looked across the room at Patrick. "More likely we'll need a miracle."

Chapter Twenty-two

Michael scanned the scene below him, searching for signs of life. The ranch yard was peaceful, almost serene, but in his estimation it was too quiet. There was nothing to indicate any activity at all. No horses in the corral, no smoke from the chimney, no gear lying about. Nothing.

The place looked deserted, the skeleton of the new barn casting long shadows across the house and stable, giving the buildings an almost sinister look. It had stopped him from going right to the front door. He shook his head, clearing his vision. Maybe it was just his mood.

"Can you tell anything?" Cara lay next to him, her voice lowered to a whisper.

The ridge was sparsely dotted with trees, but the little clump of aspens provided cover. They were tucked in among the tall meadow grass, so there was no way they could be seen. But from this vantage point, they could see the entire ranch. "No, but it just doesn't feel right."

"Well, it looks calm enough."

"Looks can be deceiving."

Dee Davis

"True." She narrowed her eyes, studying the scene below. "So what is it that seems off?"

Michael focused on the ranch, trying to identify what was bothering him. The late-afternoon sun shone on the front of the cabin, its rays sparkling off the windows. He blinked slowly and refocused on the house. Nothing changed.

He narrowed his eyes, trying to find the inconsistency. He knew it was there. He just had to find it. It was amazing, really, how the light reflected off the windows. They looked like rainbow-hued jewels, colors winking in the sun. He sucked in a breath, his mind finally identifying the anomaly. The window to the left of the door wasn't twinkling. Granted the porch provided some protection, but the glass ought to be reflecting at least a little of the sunlight.

It wasn't.

"There." He poked Cara and pointed toward the house. "The window glass is gone."

She frowned and squinted at the cabin. "How can you tell from this far away?"

He moved his head so that his mouth was just above her ear. "Look at the other ones."

She studied them, and he watched as understanding washed across her face. "Okay, so what do you think it means?"

"I don't know for sure. Someone either shot it or knocked the glass out." He clenched a fist, his gut churning at the thought of what might lie inside the house.

"So you think we're too late?" Her whispered words held a trace of fear.

"No point jumping to conclusions. There might not even be anyone in there. Still, things just feel strange. And I don't like the look of that shattered window."

Cara nodded, her eyes still turned toward the ranch. Suddenly her hand closed around his wrist, her other arm extended, pointing at something. "Michael?"

He jerked his head around, his eyes locked on the area

248

she pointed to. The grass in the yard between the cabin and the corral rippled in the slight breeze. "What? I don't see anything."

"Over there, by the big rock." She gestured, her chin and hand both jerking upward in an almost synchronized movement. "That spot of white. I think it's a—"

"Body." He finished her thought, a band of steel tightening around his chest. White and blue showed through the waving grass.

Cara's hand tightened on his arm. "Can you make out who it is?"

Michael stared at the inert form lying in the yard, but the distance was too great. "No." He pulled out of her grasp, sliding back from the edge, his brain racing. It couldn't be Patrick. Could it? "I've got to get down there." He scrambled to his feet.

He turned to go, halting only when he felt Cara's touch on his shoulder. "Michael, you can't just go running down there. You don't have any idea what you're going to find. Whoever did that"—she gestured toward the ranch and the body—"might still be there. You could be walking into a trap."

She was right. This wasn't the time for rash decisions. "All right."

She sighed and dropped her hand. "So what do you want to do?"

He tried to clear his mind of the awful images his imagination was dredging up, to concentrate instead on what to do next. They had to get closer, to get a better feel for the situation without anyone knowing they were there. His gaze fell on a stand of pine trees just below the ridge. Large boulders, the remnants of a long-ago landslide, dotted the slope between the aspens and the pines. "There." He pointed at the trees below them. "We go there."

She followed the line of his hand and stared at the trees. "And how exactly do you propose we get from here to there without being seen?"

"Those rocks will provide cover. And once we're in place, we should be close enough to make out the—" He stopped, rage and anguish mixing inside him, filling him with hopelessness.

"Michael, it's not Patrick. We have to believe that."

He looked down into her eyes, trying to let her steady gaze comfort him, but the reality was too grim. "Well, somebody's dead down there, and I'm pretty damn certain it isn't Amos Striker. And if it isn't him . . ." He stopped, trying not to think the worst.

"My grandfather always said to believe the best even when the worst is staring you in the face."

"Sounds reasonable." He tried to let her words buoy him, but his doubts continued to suck at him, pulling him deeper into the quagmire of fear. If the newspaper article was right, he'd already lost a father, and now it looked as though he was too late to save his brother. He shook his head, trying to shift his thoughts away from the macabre image of Patrick sprawled across the yard. "What else did your grandfather say?"

"That it's best to face your fears head-on." She struggled to smile, but managed only a lopsided grimace. He blessed her for the effort.

"All right, then." He turned back to Clune. "Let's go." He started down the hill, his mind fervently praying that the body wasn't his brother's.

"How's he doing?" Patrick knelt beside Pete and Loralee, his gaze meeting hers.

"Not good." She ran a gentle hand along the old man's cheek.

Sweat beaded out across Pete's forehead and he moaned, his shoulders twitching in agitation. Patrick reached out to still him and was shocked as heat seared his hand. "He's burning up."

"I know. And it's just getting worse. I'm real worried."

"How long has he been asleep?"

250

"For at least an hour. I haven't been able to wake him up." She bit her lower lip, her face reflecting his fears. "Patrick, I don't think he can wait until sunset."

"All right, I'll go now. I didn't want to do this, or at least wanted Pete to . . . Never mind. You cover me. His Colt at the ready, he moved to the closed door and placed a hand on the doorknob. He watched as Loralee crawled across the floor to the window. She stopped about halfway, jerking up a hand, sucking on her palm. "You all right?"

"Fine. I just cut my hand a little." She tore a ruffle from her sleeve and tied it around her hand. "There's glass everywhere." She scooted the last few feet and settled in below the window, raising the Winchester so that the butt rested on her shoulder, the muzzle propped on the windowsill.

"You ready?"

"I think so." Her eyes darted over to him and he read a thousand things in their luminous depths, none of them making it any easier to pull open the door, but then Pete moaned and he knew it was time. Sucking in a breath, he yanked the door open, stepping into the opening just as a rifle blast filled the air.

A bullet smashed into the transom a couple of inches from his head, and before he could even react, a second one splintered the wood of the doorjamb. He jumped back, swinging the door shut with enough force that the remaining window glass shook in its frame. The door clicked shut just as a third bullet hit it with a thwack.

He dropped down and scrambled to the window, already hearing the crack of the Winchester as Loralee tried to return fire. "Hang on. You're not going to hit anything, and we need to preserve the bullets."

Loralee lowered the gun. "I just wish I could see him."

"I know, but he's not going to show himself now. Not when he's got us right where he wants us." He peered surreptitiously out the window, too, searching the barnyard for signs of the intruder. Loralee slid down to the floor, her eyes closed, holding her injured hand in her lap. "You okay?" he asked her.

Her eyes fluttered open, and she held it out for him to see. The makeshift bandage was red with blood, but it wasn't too soaked.

"It's just a cut," she said.

"I promised I'd take care of you, Loralee, and now . . . well, it looks like I may not be able to keep that promise." He ran a hand down her cheek, and she covered his fingers with hers, a spark of lightning shooting up his arm at the contact.

"It's all right, Patrick. Promises aren't all they're cracked up to be anyway." She pulled her hand away, her eyes shifting to the window. "We're not going to get out of here, are we?"

She already knew their chances. He could see it in her eyes. Sugarcoating things wasn't going to help one iota. Now was a time for honesty if ever there was one. "No, angel, I don't expect that we will."

"What the hell?" Michael stared at the house, listening as the last of the shots died away. One minute a man had been outlined in the doorway, and the next, all hell had broken loose, bullets flying everywhere. Everything had happened so quickly there hadn't been time to react.

"Was that—" Cara stirred beside him, her eyes wide, her breathing audible.

"Patrick." Michael finished for her, his eyes still riveted on the ranch house. A gun barrel flashed in the setting sunlight as it was withdrawn from the window. That meant there were at least two people inside. Patrick and Pete? His eyes jerked back to the body in the yard, recognition dawning. Arless Hurley.

"Is he one of ours?" Cara's voice was soft, reverent.

"Yeah. A friend." Michael ground his teeth together, his

eyes locked on Arless's body. "Amos Striker has a lot to answer for."

Cara laid a soothing hand on his arm. "The shooting came from there." She jerked her head in the direction of the stable.

Michael frowned, turning to view the building. "Where?"

She nodded. "Up there." She pointed to the loft.

"You're sure?"

"Positive. When the shooting started, the door up there swung open a little wider, and I swear I saw the barrel of a gun."

He studied the upper story of the stable, visualizing the inside. It was nothing but a crude storage platform for hay. It ran along the west side of the stable, opening out onto the stalls below. There was a door in the wall they used to get hay bales in and out. At the moment that door stood about halfway open.

He looked up at the shadowy opening. He had to admit it was an ideal setup. A man could pretty much hit anything that moved in the ranch yard from that vantage point. Anyone pinned in the house wouldn't have a prayer of escaping as long as the assailant didn't run out of ammunition. All he had to do was wait. Sooner or later they'd have to make a break for it. And when they did . . .

"I'm going to try to get to the back of the barn."

Cara looked up at him, her eyes wide. "You're going *in* there?"

"I don't see any other way. Besides, the odds are in my favor. He won't be expecting me. With a little luck I'll manage to sneak up on him, and good-bye, Amos Striker." He smiled at her, hoping he sounded more confident than he felt.

"But what if he sees you and picks you off before you get the chance to surprise him?"

"Well, my sweet little crack shot, that's where you come in."

Dee Davis

Her eyebrows arched upward. "And . . . ?"

"You need to create a diversion. Keep his attention focused on the ranch yard."

She nodded, her hand tightening around her rifle. "I think I can manage that."

"Listen to me, Cara: draw his fire if you can, but don't take any chances."

"I'll handle it." She tipped back her head, her eyes lit with determination.

He leaned forward and gave her a hard kiss, the contact making him long to pull her closer, lose himself in her sweetness. He ruthlessly pushed the thoughts aside.

It was time for Amos Striker to pay for his sins.

Cara watched and waited. Surely Michael had had enough time to get into place, but there was no signal. She strained her ears, listening for his whistle.

Nothing.

She fingered the trigger of her rifle. It had sounded easy in principle, but now she wondered if she was truly up to the task. The little door was only a couple hundred feet away. She'd certainly hit smaller targets, from a longer distances, but there'd never been as much at stake.

She shook her head and worked to bolster her confidence. This was a piece of cake, a walk in the park. Oh, God, who was she kidding? This was a life-and-death situation. She steadied her arm and gave one last survey of the area. Everything was so quiet. So peaceful. A stand of pines just behind the corral danced in the wind. The breeze was picking up, and she could feel its cool touch against her face and hands. It would change the bullet's trajectory slightly.

Her mind had automatically started to make the adjustments when her eyes froze, sending a frantic signal to her brain. A sparkle in the trees grabbed her attention. More than a sparkle, really—a bright flash.

Light against metal. Sunlight bouncing off a gun barrel.

Her blood ran cold.

There was someone out there. Someone else.

There were *two* of them.

She frantically tried to assimilate the information, to decide what to do. If she shot at the barn, she'd alert the other man to her presence, most likely drawing his fire. But if she stayed quiet, the other man was far more likely to notice Michael. And even if Michael successfully got Amos, he'd have no way of knowing about the second man.

Her stomach churned. Of course, there were the people in the house, but she had no idea what condition they were in. Besides, they'd be sitting ducks if they so much as opened the door.

She closed her eyes, willing herself to make a decision—the right decision.

Grabbing the rifle, she sprang to her feet, using the tall pines for cover. She had to get to Michael. If she hurried, maybe she could stop him in time. Warn him. Then they could rethink their position.

She sprinted to the edge of the trees, her heart beating a staccato rhythm high in her throat, keeping her eyes on the stand of pines. From this angle she ought to be protected from view. *Ought to be.* That was the operative phrase.

She sucked in a breath and then blew it out forcefully. It was now or never. Tightening her hold on the Winchester, she began to run.

Chapter Twenty-three

The contrast between the light of day and the shadows of the barn was dramatic. Cara stopped, waiting for her eyes to adjust, the pungent smell of hay and animals filling her nose. It seemed that barns smelled like barns in any century. The thought was somehow reassuring. She combed the shadows looking for some sign of Michael, but in the gloom it was hard to see anything. The gunman inside would suffer the same problem.

Something hard rammed into her back. She spun around, heart pounding, rifle at the ready. A pair of baleful brown eyes met hers, and she relaxed, biting back a nervous laugh. A dilapidated-looking old horse hung his head over the wooden crossbar of his stall, butting against her for attention.

She pushed him away, turning back to the stable, searching the darkness for a sign of Michael or the gunman. Nothing moved. Everything was quiet except for the soft sound of horses shifting in their stalls.

She took a hesitant step forward, followed by another,

careful to stay low and silent, certain her tympanic heartbeat could be heard from every corner of the barn. A soft
noise filtered though the silence, so faint she almost
thought she'd imagined it. She froze, her back pressed
against the hard post of a stall, her eyes straining into the
gloom. There, in the darkness, a shadow moved, stepping
forward into a weak shaft of sunlight coming from the loft.
Michael?

She released a breath she hadn't realized she'd been
holding, and started for the front of the barn, her heart
resuming a more modulated rhythm. Michael had stepped
into the shadows again, but she could see him now that
she knew where to look. He was examining a ladder that
led to the loft. She picked up her pace, not daring to call
out to him.

The old horse evidently had other plans; he gave a loud
neigh. Michael turned to look toward the stall just as another shape detached itself from the shadows above. Cara's
heart caught in her throat. The shadow took on human
form. A man with a gun—a gun pointed at Michael's back.

Reacting on instinct, she pulled her rifle into position
and fired. The sound was deafening. It took her a second
to realize a second shot had been fired—not hers. Out of
the corner of her eye, she saw Michael drop to the ground.
Rage and adrenaline pumped through her. She lifted her
rifle again, intent on killing the son of a bitch who'd started
all this.

The man spun, looking for who'd shot at him. She
inched forward. He crouched, peering into the dark—still
looking for her. Then, suddenly, Michael moved. The gunman pivoted, bringing his rifle to bear.

Cara stepped out into the open, her eyes narrowed, her
weapon already sighted. "Wrong way, you bastard."

He spun back and she fired.

The impact knocked him off his feet, throwing him
backward off of the loft. His hat flew off, out the doors
to the outside and his body landed with an audible thud

in the center of the barn. Still enraged, she pumped another bullet into him, watching as he jerked once and was still.

"That was for Michael." Her whispered words swirled through the air and faded into silence. Her rage vanished as quickly as it had come, instantly replaced by fear. *Michael*. Was he all right? She tried to turn, but her legs had turned to butter. With a squeak of protest, she slid to the ground still clutching her rifle.

"Cara?" Michael's voice was like an infusion of energy. She struggled to her feet as he reached her side, obviously unharmed. Relief almost made her collapse again, and she leaned against her Winchester for support.

Michael's arms closed around her and she buried her face in the familiar warmth of his chest, trying to get control of her roiling emotions. They stood for a moment, locked together in silent communion. Then Michael pushed her back, holding her at arm's length, his eyes smoldering. "What in hell are you doing in here?"

Cara felt a flash of resentment. "Saving your ass. If I'm not mistaken, that *gentleman*"—she gestured toward the body in the doorway—"was about to blow you away."

The anger faded from his eyes and, with a groan, he pulled her to him, his mouth closing over hers. The kiss was quick and hard yet thorough, then Michael hugged her tightly against him. She stared over his shoulder at the fallen man, clarity returning. "There's someone *else* out there."

"Where?" Michael pulled back, instantly alert.

"In the stand of pines by the corral. I saw his gun barrel. I came to warn you."

"You're sure?"

"Positive."

"All right. I'll check it out. You"—he tipped her head back so that he could see her eyes—"stay here."

"Can you see what's happening?" Loralee peered out the window, trying to see what had caused all the commotion.

"It's hard to tell," Patrick said, his eyes narrowed against the setting sun. "I think there's something on the ground by the barn door, but I can't say for certain."

"I can't see anything either, but I definitely heard gunshots." She chewed on her lower lip nervously.

Patrick tightened his grip on the rifle. He'd taken it from Loralee, in case he had a chance to shoot back. "Me, too. From the direction of the barn."

"Any possibility help has arrived?" She turned to look at him, hope surfacing, swelling through her.

"Maybe. But I'd feel a hell of a lot better if I knew exactly who was in there doing the shooting." He scooted toward the door.

"All right. Give me back the rifle. I'll cover you."

He paused, and their eyes locked, something hanging between them that she wasn't ready to recognize, let alone accept. With a faint smile he tossed her the rifle and drew his Colt.

He inched the door open. Loralee held her breath, waiting for the resulting gunfire.

Nothing happened.

He opened the door wider, this time sticking his hat out. Again nothing.

He swung the door all the way open and stepped out onto the porch. Loralee bit her lip, keeping her rifle trained on the barn.

Silence. The porch creaked under Patrick's weight. Loralee's heart almost stopped.

"It seems to be clear." He moved toward the window, stepping into her line of vision. "I'm going to try the barn. Wish me luck."

"You won't need it," she said with false bravado.

Brave words. She hoped they proved true.

Cara leaned back against a stall, eyes closed, drained of all emotion and energy. The strain of the last few days was taking its toll. Here she was in another time, facing killers, and she had no idea what would come next.

Somewhere deep inside, she was worried for Michael, but her body had had enough. She couldn't even find the energy to lift a hand and scratch the old horse. He'd obviously accepted the fact, bless him, and he stood guard, his head hanging out over the stall just above her, protecting her in his own equine way. She felt absurdly grateful.

"Move an inch and you're dead." The voice came from the shadows of the stall to her right.

Cara felt a bubble of hysteria rising in her throat. She couldn't move an inch even if he had ordered it.

"Drop the rifle and raise your hands."

She tried to force herself to let go of the rifle clutched in her right hand. *No go.* The hand had taken a vacation along with the rest of her body. She struggled for her voice, surprised when it came out sounding fairly normal. "I can't move." The horse nickered in agreement, bending his neck to nuzzle her head.

The voice disentangled itself from the shadows, taking the form of a fierce green-eyed man. Cara winced as the horse nipped at her ear. "Cut it out." She slapped at the sorrel, delighted to see that her mobility had returned.

The man was eyeing her as though she had flown in on a flying saucer. Which actually wasn't too far from reality, when she thought about it. She realized she ought to be afraid, but found that she simply didn't have the energy.

Dropping her rifle, she looked up into the man's face, surprised to find she recognized it—at least parts of it. The dark hair fell forward in a familiar way, and the jut of the chin reminded her of another that was just as stubborn. This man was a stranger, yet she knew him. "Patrick." The word came out as a sigh. She recognized the relief in her voice, and was pleased to note that she still had some emotion left.

"Who the hell are you?" The green eyes flashed with anger, and she recognized the twist of his mouth.

Now, *there* was a good question. Let's see, she was Michael's lover who just happened to be from the future. And she was someone who, in a brilliant imitation of television's *The Rifleman*, had had the very great pleasure of pumping a nineteenth-century sheriff full of lead. Not to mention the fact that she was practically Rasputin—surviving a fire, an assault, and a cave-in.

She leaned back against the stall again, ignoring the sorrel's nudges. Oh, yes, she'd almost forgotten, she was also the newest paramour of an over-the-hill equine. She decided on simplicity. "Cara. I'm Cara."

The rifle lowered, and Patrick's look of anger changed to one of disbelief. "Michael's Cara?"

She'd have bowed if she could have, or curtsied, but instead she tipped her head. "One and the same."

"But . . ." Patrick looked totally confused.

She took pity on him. It wasn't his fault she'd just been through more crises than a *Die Hard* movie. It wasn't fair to take it out on him. "I came with your brother."

Instantly, hope flared in his eyes. It was eerie how much he reminded her of Michael. "He's alive?"

"Yes." She struggled to stand, relieved when he reached out to help her. Once she was no longer leaning against the stable, she felt better. "He's out looking for the other man."

"What other man?" Patrick asked, supporting her as they walked.

"There were two of them. Amos over there." She motioned toward the booted feet of the dead man. "And someone else."

Patrick went for the body, and Cara followed. She steeled herself to take a look.

"Did Michael kill him?"

Cara wrenched her gaze away. "No, I did."

"You?"

She felt a surge of indignation, the emotion refreshing her. "Yes, *me*. He was trying to kill Michael."

Patrick nudged the body with his toe, and Cara was relieved that it didn't move. Then Michael's brother said, "This isn't Amos Striker."

It was Cara's turn to be confused. "What?"

"You said this was Striker. It's not. I've never seen this man in my life."

Cara sucked in a breath, one hand clutching at Patrick's arm. "If this isn't Amos Striker, then he's probably out there right now—with Michael."

Patrick placed both hands on her shoulders, the intensity of his gaze feeding her panic. "Which way did he go?" he asked.

"Toward the stand of pines behind the corral."

"How long ago?"

"I don't know. Not long. Maybe a quarter of an hour."

"All right, you stay here. I'm going after him."

Cara ran back to the horse's stall, surprised at how quickly she could move. Grabbing her rifle, she sprinted after Patrick, catching him at the edge of the corral. "I'm coming with you."

After everything they'd been through, she wasn't about to let Amos Striker win.

Chapter Twenty-four

Michael stood in the shelter of the towering pines, holding back a curse. Striker, if he'd ever actually been here, was long gone. He'd probably hit the trail as soon as he heard shooting in the barn, realizing that reinforcements had arrived. He blew out a breath and knelt in the pine needles beside a small sapling.

From here the vantage point was perfect. He could see the ranch house and the barn. He studied the area, searching for signs that Amos had been here, something to prove Cara's belief that there had indeed been a second shooter.

There were indentations in the soft ground, and some of the needles had been disturbed, but that didn't necessarily mean anything. He shifted, his eyes scanning the ground. With a sharp intake of breath, he stopped his gaze on a spot at the foot of a large pine.

Cigarette butts.

His mind's eye obediently hauled out an image of Amos Striker, a thin cigar clamped firmly in his mouth. Cara was right: the son of a bitch had been here. Michael scooped up the remains of the cigarillos, glancing up at the sky. It was almost dusk. There was not much sense in trying to track Striker tonight.

What he needed to do now was find Patrick, see if he was okay. See if the two of them could make sense of what was happening. A fresh wave of grief washed through him. If the things he'd learned in Cara's time were right, his father was dead, and by God, the least he could do was bring the man who'd killed him to justice. He dropped the cigarillo butts into his shirt pocket. Unless he missed his guess, he knew exactly where he'd find the bastard.

A twig snapped somewhere off to his right, and he pulled his gun, pivoting in the direction of the sound.

"Wait. Don't shoot." Patrick stepped into the shelter of the pines, his hands held up in placation. "It's me."

Michael lowered the gun and stood up, anger and relief rocketing through him. "Patrick, what the hell are you doing? I damn near shot you."

Patrick lowered his hands, the expression on his face mirroring Michael's feelings exactly. "Me? I should be asking you that. You're the one who's been missing for days. What the hell do you think *you're* doing?"

"Rescuing you."

Patrick frowned, his eyes narrowing. He was evidently put off by such a description. Michael had forgotten how resentful his brother could be about being protected. "And just what made you think I needed rescuing?"

"You didn't look to be doing so good from where I was standing, little brother."

"Well, maybe I could have used a little help." Patrick shifted, many emotions playing across his face. "Father's dead." The words hung between them. "And then I thought you were dead, too . . ." He trailed off, anguish playing across his face.

Michael closed the distance between them in two strides, pulling his brother into a bear hug, grateful for the warm, solid, nineteenth-century feel of his own flesh and blood.

"Michael?" *Cara.*

He released Patrick, his eyes finding her as she burst through the brush. Uncertainty dominated her expression, her eyes wide, her teeth pulling at her lower lip. He was home. But she . . . she was marooned here in a time that was far less civilized than the one she knew. He felt a flash of guilt. But before he could think of the right words to say, her strained look vanished, replaced by one of determination. Cara was a fighter.

"Did you find any sign of Amos?" Her question broke the silence, bringing all three of them firmly back to the present—and the issue of Amos Striker.

Patrick's face hardened. "Was he here? Cara said there was a second shooter."

Michael raised an eyebrow at the two of them. Obviously there'd been introductions, and there would come a time for explanations—explanations that would likely make no sense—but this wasn't the place. He pulled his thoughts back to Patrick's question, reaching into his shirt pocket for the cigarette butts.

"He was here."

Patrick eyed the tobacco remains. "Should we go after him?"

Michael shook his head. "It'll be dark soon. Best if we wait until the morning. He won't get far tonight."

"You sound like Pete." Patrick grimaced. "Son of a . . ." He paused, shooting an embarrassed look at Cara. "I forgot Pete." He turned his gaze to Michael. "He was shot."

"Is he all right?" Fresh concern washed through Michael. Amos Striker's sins were racking up, and Michael fully intended to see him pay.

"He's alive, but he's in bad shape. Loralee's with him."

"Loralee?"

"She's ah . . . well, she's a . . ." His brother stumbled over the words, a dark red flush appearing on his tan skin. "She's a friend. She's been helping me with Father's death."

"A friend?"

Dee Davis

"Not like that." The blush deepened. "She knew Father. Was with him right before he was killed. It all started when Amos tried to tell us that you killed Father." Patrick frowned at the memory. "Owen said he was just doing his job, but I didn't believe him. Not after Loralee told me about Corabeth, and then Amos tried to kill her, and I was protecting her . . . Ah, hell . . ."

Michael leveled a look at his brother. "Looks like I'm not the only one with some explaining to do."

Loralee stood on the porch, her hand raised to shade her eyes from the last of the setting sun. It would be dark in just a little while, and she hadn't seen hide nor hair of Patrick since he'd headed for the barn more than an hour ago. There was only so much a girl could handle, and frankly, she was at the end of her rope.

She glanced over her shoulder through the open door of the house. Pete was settled on the cot in the corner, sleeping. His fever was down a little, but she still didn't like his color. With a sigh, she focused her attention back on the barnyard. *Best just get on with it.* Bolstering her courage, she stepped down onto the rocky ground, the grass brushing against her dress.

She held her rifle ready. At least it evened the odds a bit. Besides, everything was quiet. Most likely Patrick had gone out the back of the barn. There hadn't been any more shots, so the odds were that he was fine. Just thoughtless—leaving her waiting like this without so much as a word.

But then, that was what she got for depending on a man. It seemed that she still hadn't learned her lesson. And it was such a simple one. Men couldn't be trusted. They'd leave you crying every time. She grimaced, wondering when and why it was exactly that she'd come to care about Patrick Macpherson, anyway. He was just a pup, still wet behind the ears. There wasn't any room in her life for personal involvement. She was a working girl, pure and simple, and didn't need anybody to take care of her. She was doing just fine on her own.

She started for the barn, the tall grass waving in the wind, all about her. Reaching the building, she looked in and caught a glimpse of color. Her stomach clenched and her heart started to pound. There was a body here—a man sprawled on the ground in the center of the hay.

She gripped the rifle tighter and edged up to it, nudging it gingerly with her toe. Dead. He was dead. And he wasn't Patrick. She released her breath in a whoosh, and pulled her skirts back to step around him, intent on finding Patrick. But the dead man's features were burned into her brain, and she stopped short, realizing she recognized him.

Even death couldn't remove the cruel twist of his mouth and the harsh angle of his jaw. Joe Ingersoll. The man was probably wanted in a dozen counties. She couldn't say she was sorry he was dead. Word had it he had roughed up several of the girls over in Tintown.

She wondered what he was doing here, then dismissed the thought. His kind could always be bought, and Amos Striker wasn't the kind to do his dirty work alone. Loralee resisted the urge to kick the body, and instead stepped over it. Jack gave a baleful whinny, but aside from him, the place was empty.

She frowned and stepped back into the barnyard, scanning the area for signs of life. There was nothing here but the dead. Arless's body lay sprawled off to the left, looking for all the world as if he'd just stopped for a nap. Tears filled her eyes, as the old miner's voice filled her head—talk of griddle cakes and butter.

Arless Hurley had been a good man. Maybe not a sober one, but a damn fine one just the same. The least she could do was show him some respect. She stepped back over Joe and grabbed an old blanket hanging from a peg in the stable, then went outside and walked over to her friend's body.

His eyes stared sightlessly up at the twilit sky. She bent

267

Dee Davis

to gently close them, swallowing back tears. Then, with reverent hands, she flipped out the blanket, letting it drift slowly downward to cover the battered body.

Kneeling beside him, she lowered her head, searching for the right words. "Lord, you know I ain't exactly on your list of holy folks, but I got an honest heart and this here was a good man. So you be sure and open those pearly gates for Arless. He's on his way. And if you got any whiskey, you better hide it, 'cause I suspect he'll be ready for more than a drop when he gets there."

She paused and studied the wool-covered mound, the pain of the moment nearly undoing her. "Godspeed, Arless." She crossed herself, surprised that she remembered how. It had been a long time since she'd been in a church.

She stood up and surveyed the surrounding countryside, her eyes searching for a sign of Patrick—or any of the other shooters. A slight movement from beyond the corral caught her attention, and she let out a cry of joy when she recognized the tall figure emerging from a stand of pines.

There were two others with him. One man, bigger than Patrick, walked beside him, their dark heads bent together, obviously deep in conversation. The other figure was smaller, a woman. One dressed like a man.

She frowned, watching as the group drew closer, trying to puzzle out who the newcomers might be. Finally she shrugged. It didn't really matter. Whoever they were, Patrick seemed happy to see them. She glanced down at Arless, then into the barn at Joe Ingersoll's body, shivering.

Lord knew she could use some friendly faces right about now.

Cara hung back a little as they walked toward the house, wanting to give the brothers time together. Their resemblance was uncanny. The two dark heads bent together in conversation were almost identical. There was no chance anyone could possibly miss the fact that they were brothers. She felt a little pang of jealousy. An only child, she herself had never experienced the bond that siblings had, but, looking at the two of them, she knew it must be something special.

Now that the immediate danger was gone, Cara again felt terribly drained, as if all the emotion had simply been sucked out of her. Drained and alone.

She swallowed back the beginnings of tears. Now was definitely not the time for a meltdown. Amos Striker was out there somewhere and they had to find him—to eliminate the threat to Michael. Then her job would be done and she could go back to where she belonged.

If she could find her way.

As if he'd read her thoughts, Michael slowed his pace and waited until she caught up. Looping a casual arm around her shoulders, he resumed his conversation with his brother.

She could see the ranch house illuminated in the last fading rays of the sun. It looked so much smaller than it did in her time, but still the lines were familiar, comforting in some intrinsic kind of way. Perhaps home was home no matter the time. She shook her head at her own silly musings.

She was a hell of a long way from the Meadows. This was Clune, and she was in 1888.

"Cara?" Patrick's voice pulled her out of her troubled thoughts, and she was surprised to see that they'd arrived in the barnyard. "This is Loralee."

Cara looked over to see a smiling brunette, and she tried to find the energy to return the gesture. Before she'd managed to move a single facial muscle, though, she froze, her eyes locked on the necklace around the other woman's neck.

The silver was intricately carved, flowers engraved across its face. Cara gasped, her heart stuttering to a stop.

Loralee was wearing her great-grandmother's locket.

Chapter Twenty-five

"I don't believe any of this. People simply do not go traveling through time. It's impossible." Patrick paced in front of the porch steps, his frown underscoring his disbelief.

Cara leaned back against the wall of the house, trying to think of something that would persuade them of the truth. Something that didn't sound like a Jules Verne story. She sighed, realizing that Jules Verne was probably alive and writing somewhere at this very moment.

"I know it's hard to believe, Patrick. I probably wouldn't have believed it myself if it hadn't happened to me, but it's the truth." Michael was leaning against a porch pillar, his relaxed position contrasting with the tense line of his shoulders.

"What I don't understand is the part about you and me being related." Loralee looked over at Cara, her eyes filled with a mixture of wonder, disbelief, and, strangely, hope.

"It's the truth. The locket proves it. My mother gave it to me on my sixteenth birthday. She inherited it from her mother—your Mary."

Loralee's eyes widened and she wrapped her arms

around herself. "So you said. But my Mary doesn't have it. *I do.* And she's just a little girl."

"I know. But someday you'll give it to her." Although, who was to say how things would play out now? In coming here, Cara had changed everything. Who knew what she would find had changed when she went back. Maybe there was a happy ending for Loralee, too. She smiled at the younger woman, pushing away her negative thoughts. "And then she'll pass it on to my mother and then to me."

"And then you'll come here and . . ." Loralee's eyebrows drew together in confusion. "It just don't make sense."

"None of it does." Michael's words were firm, his expression grim. "But the fact is that it's all true. Nine years ago I found Cara in the snow."

"And if he hadn't been there, I would have died," Cara said, picking up the story. "But once the crisis passed and my grandfather came for me, we got separated again."

"Until I got shot." Michael moved to stand by her.

"And then she rescued you," Loralee finished with a faint smile. Patrick shot her a look. "Well, I like that part." She stuck her chin out. "A woman saving a man. Seems to me there's something kinda nice about that. And I also like what she said about the fact that in her time, women and men are treated as equals."

Patrick shrugged. "It doesn't make any sense to me."

"Patrick. We've been over this and over this." Michael ran a hand through his hair in frustration. "And nothing I can say is going to make it easier to accept. You'll just have to take my word about what happened. The important thing now is to deal with Amos Striker."

A loud groan issued from somewhere inside the house, followed by a string of extremely colorful oaths, some of which Cara had never heard before. Loralee stood up, wiping her hands on her skirt. Suddenly she said, "Before we take on Amos Striker, sounds to me like we'd better see to Pete."

* * *

"I don't want any more." The old rancher closed his mouth with a click, his teeth locking firmly together. "Tastes like horse piss."

"It's willow bark tea," Loralee said. "Ginny says it helps with fever."

"That Ute woman? I ain't drinking no Indian tree potion."

"Come on, Pete, you don't mean to tell me that after all you've been through you're going to balk at a little tea?" Patrick lifted the grumbling man's shoulders, and Loralee held the cup up to his lips. He grimaced but opened his mouth and obediently drank the stuff.

"So what the hell happened out there?" he asked after a moment, looking first at Michael and then at Patrick.

"We're not really sure. Cara killed the man in the barn. She thought it was the sheriff." Michael sighed and shrugged.

"It wasn't?" Pete's brows pulled together in consternation.

Patrick shook his head, remembering the dead man's face. "Nope. It was some guy I've never seen before."

"I recognized him," Loralee added. "His name's Joe Ingersoll."

Pete stroked his mustache. "Bad *hombre*. Do anything for money." He looked over at Cara. "You telling me this little thing brought down Ingersoll?"

Cara's head shot up, her eyes flashing. "Why is it no one can believe I shot the man?"

Michael held up a hand. "Easy, honey. I saw you." He turned back to the old man. "Trust me, Pete, she's a whole lot tougher than she looks."

Pete grinned. "Just what you need, boy." He sobered. "Any sign of Striker at all?"

Michael reached into his pocket and pulled out the cigarillo butts. "Only these. Found them under one of the pine trees where Cara said she saw a rifle barrel."

Pete lifted his head for a look. "So he *was* out there."

"Someone was. Probably him. And I figure he hightailed it once he saw that Ingersoll was dead." Michael dropped the butts onto the table.

"Amos never was one to go against the odds," Pete agreed.

"You mean he's a coward?" Cara asked. She gave them all questioning looks.

"Yellow as they come," Pete grunted, then looked up at Loralee, who was refilling his cup. "Any chance I could get some whiskey?"

She shook her head. "More tea."

"Hell." He jerked as a coughing fit shook his entire body.

"I think it's time we got you to bed." She gave him a fierce look.

"I ain't going." Pete crossed his bony arms across his chest, wincing a little with the movement. "I want to talk to Michael some more."

"Later. Right now you need some sleep." Loralee's voice was gentle. Pete tried to look mutinous, but the effect was ruined when he yawned. "Patrick, you and Michael help me get him to his room."

Patrick reached down to help his brother lift the old man.

"Watch it, boy. I ain't no bale of hay."

Patrick grinned, adjusting his grip. "Sorry, Pete." Obviously the willow bark tea was working. The foreman was as cantankerous as an old mule, and their mother had always said that when a sick person started to complain, he was bound to be getting better.

"Come on, old man; let's get you out of here." Michael winked at Patrick and they started to move toward the door, careful not to jar him.

"Who you calling old? I reckon I can whup your skinny behind any time I've a mind to."

Patrick smiled as they passed through the door into the cool night air. Yes, sir, Pete was going to be just fine.

273

*   *   *

"Do you think he's still out there?"

Michael surveyed the dark perimeter of the ranch from the porch and considered Patrick's question. After depositing Pete in bed, they'd come outside to talk. "Striker? I'd be surprised if he was. He probably liked the odds better before Ingersoll got shot."

"So you figure he's high-tailed it out of here?" Patrick sounded hopeful.

"Not entirely. Whatever's going on here, it's not over."

Patrick frowned into the darkness. "There's got to be something more we're missing, maybe something to do with that Vargas fellow."

Michael had explained about Nick and his preoccupation with the Promise, but even going over it with his brother had failed to clarify anything. "It's all got to be tied together somehow," he agreed. "But I'll be damned if I can see exactly how."

"Well, whatever it is, Striker thought Loralee and Corabeth knew about it. That's why he killed Corabeth and why he tried to kill Loralee. And Father."

"Makes sense. And then when you rescued Loralee, you became a threat, too."

Patrick nodded. "We'd have been dead if you hadn't gotten here today."

Michael looked over at his brother, aware how much it cost Patrick to admit that. The boy had been mollycoddled all his life—first by their mother, and then by Owen. And Michael supposed that in some ways, he'd spoiled his brother, too.

And done him a disservice. The boy was chomping at the bit to prove himself, to make a difference.

"I imagine you'd have found a way out if I hadn't arrived in time," he said.

Patrick grinned, and the look reminded Michael of his mother. "Maybe. But I'm glad you came all the same."

The Promise

Michael reached down for a rock and lobbed it out into the darkness. "Where'd you bury him?"

Patrick jerked his head toward the Humpback. "Up there. Seemed the right thing to do."

Michael swallowed back his pain. "What'd you do with his things?"

"There wasn't anything left. That's what made everyone think it was a robbery at first."

"What about his pocket watch?" It was the only thing of real value Duncan had carried. A gift from their mother. Even after she ran off, he'd refused to be parted from it.

"The watch, too."

Suddenly an image filled Michael's head. Vargas on the street corner, checking his watch. "Son of a bitch."

"What?" Patrick dropped his foot and turned to face his brother.

"Vargas had Father's pocket watch. I saw him with it. It just didn't register completely until now."

"But how . . ." Patrick's voice trailed off uncertainly.

"His *grandfather*." Michael paused, the understanding hitting him even before he could complete his thought. "Nick said his grandfather left him all his possessions. The watch must have been part of it."

"But where did Nick's grandfather get it?" Patrick looked blank. "Surely he wouldn't have been old enough to know Father?"

"No, but Vargas said his great-grandfather was a cowboy named Amos."

Patrick's eyes widened. "Amos Striker?"

"It fits. Striker worked the Wason ranch before he came here. That makes him a cowboy. And now that I think about it, there's a likeness between Vargas and Striker. That's why Vargas seemed so familiar."

The two of them stood silently for a moment, each lost in his own thoughts, silhouetted in the deepening gloom. Patrick was the first to break the silence. "There's little chance of proving he has Father's watch."

275

Dee Davis

"But we know now. That's what really matters. The thing to figure out is why he killed him."

"So we're back where we started." Patrick sighed.

"The locket." Michael hit his head with the heel of his hand. "Hell, I forgot about the locket. Father left a message in Cara's locket. Vargas took it before I could get a good look; then we lost it in the cave-in."

"But Loralee's locket," Patrick said triumphantly, "is the same as Cara's."

"Exactly." He grabbed his brother's arm impatiently. "What do you say we find out what's inside that locket?"

"Michael says you're an artist." Loralee shot a look at Cara from under her lashes as she measured coffee into the coffeepot.

"A painter," Cara said, nodding shyly.

"I ain't never met an artist before. But I saw an exhibit once when I was in St. Louis. They were French paintings. The prettiest things I ever did see. You paint like that?"

"Well, I'm not sure what you saw. But I love to paint. Maybe I can paint you someday."

Loralee felt herself blush. "Don't know why you'd want to go and do that. Ain't nothing worth painting about me."

"Sure there is. You're beautiful, Loralee." Cara was eyeing her as if sizing her up, her head tilted. "Besides, you're family."

"Your great-grandmother." Loralee tried to say it calmly, but her voice trembled with—what? Fear? Elation? Awe? There really weren't words for a situation like this. "I reckon it's going to take a little getting used to."

Still, it explained a lot of things. Like why Cara was the spitting image of Mary, and why Loralee herself felt such a strong bond for the girl. *Girl.* Heavens, she was already thinking like a granny. *Great*-granny. And here she was, younger than her own great-grandchild. The thought was sobering.

Loralee thought about her own granny, the only bright spot in an otherwise nightmarish childhood. Granny Shaw had been from Ireland, an imp of a woman with dark hair and laughing eyes. She'd always said there were things in this world a body simply couldn't believe with the eyes alone. *"Listen with yer heart, girl,"* she always said. *"That's where ye'll be finding the real answers."*

Loralee closed her eyes and concentrated on her feelings, shutting out her doubts. As quickly as it had come, her confusion vanished like so much smoke in the wind, and she knew in her heart that the things Cara was saying were true.

For the first time in a long time, Loralee didn't feel alone. Tears pricked at the corners of her eyes as she opened them. Cara was watching her, her sea green gaze reflecting her own fears. Without a word Loralee raised her arms, and the two women embraced. This might not be a normal family reunion, but it felt mighty good all the same.

"I can't read the first letter. Something W, then T3." Patrick held the scrap of paper up to the candlelight.

Loralee's locket lay open on the table, the entire group's concentration centered on the note. Cara still couldn't believe she hadn't thought about the note when she first saw the locket. Too much to process, no doubt. And it didn't really matter; Michael had remembered.

Patrick blew out a frustrated breath. "I can't tell for sure. See what you think." He passed the paper to Michael, who also held it up to the light.

Cara leaned forward, staring at the paper, willing it to yield answers. "Maybe it's directions of some kind."

Michael frowned. "Could be. That would mean the missing letter is either an S or an N."

"Right." Patrick reached for the note. "But what in hell is T3?"

"Tunnel number." Michael looked up, exchanging a look with his brother.

Dee Davis

"So these are directions to a mining tunnel?" Cara asked incredulously, not certain exactly what the information meant.

"Not just any mining tunnel—one in the Promise. The main shaft goes laterally into the mountain with other tunnels branching off to either side—"

"The north and south sides." Patrick interrupted his brother. "The slant is then either to the west or the east."

Cara nodded in understanding. "So the directions are for the third tunnel on either the south or north sides with a westward slant."

Michael shot her a quick smile. "Exactly. With this, we can narrow it down to two tunnels."

"But what good does it do to know where, if we don't know what and, more important, why?" Loralee asked.

"Patrick and I think it must have something to do with Father's ramblings."

"About the silver?" Loralee leaned forward, her elbows propped on the table, her eyes on the paper in Patrick's hand.

"Right."

Cara frowned as something nagged at her brain. She tried to focus on it, but whatever it was, it remained just on the edge of her subconscious. Reluctantly she let it go and focused again on the conversation.

"That and the fact that Vargas may have been related to Striker."

"The great-grandfather!" Cara realized, thinking back to Nick's confession. "His name was Amos!"

"Exactly." Patrick smiled. "So, somehow this is all related."

"What's most important is that Striker knows how." Michael's face hardened in the glow of the candlelight.

"And killed our Father because of it." Patrick's face tightened, too.

Cara was grateful suddenly that they were on her side. Their anger was a force to be reckoned with. "So you think

278

that Amos is on his way to the Promise now?"

"Maybe. If there's really something up there, he'd want to get to it before everything blows sky high."

Patrick grimaced. "And Striker doesn't seem the type to abandon something he obviously believes is worth killing for."

"Duncan was awfully excited about the silver," Loralee put in.

Suddenly a little thought pushed its way into the forefront of Cara's brain. She sucked in a breath.

"He said *the* silver, not silver. Right?"

"What?" Three heads turned to focus on her.

"When you all talk about it, you say *silver*, as though it's not specific. But whenever Loralee talks about what your father said, she always refers to *the* silver. Specific silver." She groaned with frustration as three pairs of eyes looked equally blank. "Don't you see? Nick had books about 'the lost silver.' That's what he was looking for. *The* silver."

She watched as the impact of her words sank in, satisfied to see comprehension dawning. Michael was the first to understand. "You think Amos found the silver from the Promise?"

"I think it's possible."

"So then what? My father found it, too?"

"It would make sense. That would explain his excitement."

Michael ran a hand through his hair. "But if he found it, he would have told Owen. They were partners." He looked over at his brother.

Patrick frowned. "He tried. Or at least that's what Sam said. But Owen was out, so Father got drunk instead."

"And came to see me," Loralee added.

"That must be when he put the note in the locket," Cara said, her mind trying to put it all together.

"It's possible." Loralee scrunched up her forehead in thought. "In fact, it makes sense. Duncan had my locket

279

with him. I'd broken the chain, and he said he'd fix it for me. Never let anyone have it before. But I trusted him." She looked up to meet Patrick's gaze.

"Our father was a wily old goat, Loralee. I wouldn't put it past him to slip the coordinates into the locket and expect to retrieve them later. Especially if he thought there might be trouble."

"Look, this is crazy." Michael held up a hand. "Father couldn't have found the silver from the Promise. We're ignoring the fact that my mother ran off with it. She and that son-of-a-bitch muleskinner." He spat out the word as if it tasted vile.

"His name was Zachariah Bowen, and he didn't run off with anyone." Loralee's voice was tight with anger. "My Zach never ran off with anybody."

"Your Zach?" There was a note of incredulity in Michael's voice.

Loralee squared her shoulders and lifted her chin. "Zach Bowen was my husband."

Chapter Twenty-six

There was complete silence around the table. Cara studied each of the faces. Loralee looked angry enough to spit nails. Michael looked equally angry, but his anger was tinged with amazement. Patrick simply looked sick to his stomach. Cara couldn't empathize with the emotions around the table, but she was astute enough to know that with one sentence Loralee had managed to change everything.

"Did my father know?" Patrick's question was almost a whisper.

Loralee nodded. "That's how we came to be friends."

"I see." His mouth tightened into a thin line, hurt radiating from his eyes.

Loralee placed a hand on his arm. "I'm sorry I didn't tell you, Patrick. I tried that night on the porch, but somehow I just couldn't." She stared at her hand, looking miserable.

"Zach never mentioned the fact that he was married." Michael's words were clipped, harsh.

Dee Davis

Loralee's chin went up again. "That was because of me. I didn't want him telling folks."

"Why the hell not?" Michael barked. Loralee cringed, and Cara put a gentle hand on Michael's knee. He glanced over at her and some of the frustration in his face faded away. "I mean, it seems odd that you wouldn't want anyone to know," he continued in a gentler tone.

"It was for him, not me. I didn't think folks would cotton to him being married to a . . ."

"Working girl?" Patrick finished for her.

"A whore, yes." Somehow, coming from Loralee's mouth, the term sounded almost dignified. "I didn't want folks looking down on him. I'd already quit working, but you know how gossip travels from camp to camp. He was going to send for me and Mary when he had enough money. Then we were going to try to start over, someplace far from here." Tears welled in her soft brown eyes. "We were going to make a go of it."

"But he decided to run off with my mother instead."

She glared at Michael. "He didn't run off with your mother. I don't know what happened, but there's no way he would have done something like that."

Michael's voice softened. "I understand the way you feel. In fact, I admire your loyalty. But face it, Loralee, you aren't the first wife to be jilted by her husband."

"You don't understand." She rubbed at her eyes, wiping away the tears. "When I found out I was pregnant with Mary, I knew it was his. I hadn't been working, but just being with him." She sucked in a deep breath. "But I still wanted to get rid of the baby. There's ways to do that, you know. There's always some gal around who has a potion or a doctor willing to take care of things for a price. Anyway, I was certain it was the right thing to do. I cared about Zach, but there wasn't any future in it. It wasn't proper, and besides, he didn't seem like the marrying kind."

Patrick's eyes were now filled only with concern. "But you did marry him," he said.

"It was like I told you the other night: Zach wouldn't have it any other way."

"You knew about this?" Michael shot Patrick an accusing look.

"Only that she'd been married."

Cara reached out to pat Loralee. "Go on."

She responded with a watery smile. "Well, Zach was tickled pink about the baby. More than any man I've ever seen." She smiled to herself, lost in her thoughts. "He used to lie with his head on my stomach and talk to her. Tell her silly stories and dreams. About what our life would be like, the places we'd go, the things we'd do. Oh, he had grand plans for us all."

"I still—" Michael started, but Cara waved him to silence.

Loralee sighed. "He was pretty persuasive, Zach Bowen. Finally I was so worn down I said yes." She hugged her middle, rocking back and forth. "And for a while we were real happy. Then the money ran out. He headed here to try to make more. He wrote every week."

Patrick's look had changed to a thoughtful expression. "You told me the last letter you had from him was about silver."

"Right, he said he'd struck it rich and that as soon as it was all mined, he'd be wiring the money for me and Mary to come and join him."

"And you never heard from him again?"

She lowered her head, staring at her hands on the table. "No."

"Further support for the theory that he ran away with the silver and our mother." Michael rubbed a weary hand across his face.

"Look, Michael, I can't give you any proof. But I know for certain, in here"—she pointed to her heart—"that my Zach never ran off with your ma."

283

"I'm not trying to hurt you, Loralee, but I don't think you're facing facts."

"You don't have any children, do you?"

Michael looked surprised. "No."

"Well, if you did, you'd know that even if Zach had decided to leave me for your ma, he could never have left Mary. I'm telling you, if my husband were alive, he'd have contacted me. If not because he loved me—and he did— then because he loved our child."

"Our mother left us." The pain in Michael's face made Cara ache with the need to comfort him.

"Maybe she didn't." Patrick met his brother's gaze with a steely-eyed certainty.

Michael ran a hand through his hair. "This is insane. Now you want me to believe that my mother and that mule—Loralee's husband—are dead?"

"It's not impossible, Michael." Cara spoke tentatively, unsure of his reaction.

"The hell it's—"

"Hear me out." She covered his hand with hers. "What if there was an accident? You said yourself the roads are bad. And you said yourself how dangerous a muleskinner's job could be. A single flick of the whip often controls the fate of a wagon, right?"

Patrick nodded enthusiastically. "Hell, yeah. I've seen muleskinners practically make a curve on two wheels and still wind up with cargo and driver in one piece."

Cara met Michael's gaze. "The point is, maybe Zach and Rose didn't make it down the mountain. Maybe someone found them and the silver."

A faint glimmer of hope dawned in Michael's eyes.

"Maybe they had a little help meeting their maker." Patrick's voice was sharp.

"Amos Striker." Loralee said the name as if it were poison.

"But what about the stagecoach? The stationmaster told

us they'd boarded the stage at Antelope Springs." Michael looked at his brother.

"Maybe it was a setup." The two men turned to look at Cara. "Well, it's possible. Say Amos did find them and . . ."

"And killed them," Patrick finished for her.

"Right. Well, it would follow that if anyone found them, there would be questions about the ore. He would have arranged for it to look like they ran away. It wouldn't have taken much."

Loralee leaned forward, caught up in the idea. "And he would have hidden the silver. There's no way people wouldn't notice if it turned up around here all at once."

Cara nodded. "So all he had to do was stash the loot somewhere."

"But he wouldn't have hidden it in the Promise. We were still living up there."

Cara met Michael's skeptical gaze. "Maybe he moved it there later. I mean, you have to admit there's a certain touch of brilliance to hiding it right under your noses."

Patrick half nodded.

Michael wasn't so easy to convince. "What about the bodies?"

"Hell, Michael, you know as well as I do that a body doesn't last long out here. Between the wild animals and the weather there usually isn't much left." Patrick waved his hands, emphasizing his words.

Loralee winced and Cara laid a soothing hand on her arm.

Michael drew in a long breath. "So what you're all trying to say is that Amos Striker either intentionally or accidentally came across the silver, disposed of Zach and our mother, and eventually hid the silver in a tunnel at the Promise."

Cara nodded, taking up the story. "And your father found the stash. But before he could tell either of you, Amos figured it out and murdered him—"

Dee Davis

"Mistaking you for Father and almost killing you in the process," Patrick added.

"But somehow Amos managed to lose the treasure," Cara concluded.

"Which is where this tale starts to get fanciful." Michael's tone conveyed his skepticism.

"Not necessarily." Cara chewed on her lower lip, thinking about the twenty-first-century part of the story. "We know the silver was still lost in my time. Nick confirmed it. That's what he was looking for. It all fits."

"So . . . what? My father moved it?"

"It seems possible."

Their gazes collided, and he sighed. "The only man with all the answers is Amos Striker. We find him, we'll find the truth. I'll set out first thing in the morning."

Patrick opened his mouth to argue, but Michael stopped him with an I'm-older-than-you look. "You need to head for Silverthread. Someone's got to talk to Owen. If the silver is up in the mountains still, part of it belongs to him. He deserves to know what's going on."

Patrick reluctantly nodded in agreement. "All right. But as soon as I talk to him, I'm coming up there."

"I'm counting on it."

"I'm coming with you." Cara met Michael's gaze, lifting her chin defiantly.

"No. I want you to stay here where it's safe." Michael held her gaze, the message in his eyes perfectly clear.

Cara ground her teeth, feeling anger surge through her veins. "In the middle of nowhere, a hundred years before I was born?" "I said I was in this to the end, and I meant it. Have you forgotten who it was who shot Joe Ingersoll?"

Michael glared at her, but she glared back. Eventually he gave in. "Fine."

"I'll ride into town with Patrick," Loralee said. "Pete needs to see the doctor."

Michael pushed away from the table. "Then it's a plan. We'll all leave at first light."

* * *

"I need to talk to you." Michael stood in the doorway, his hand resting against the doorframe, his stance deceptively casual.

Cara looked up from the shirt she was mending, her stomach churning at the look in his eyes. "About Striker?"

"No, Cara. About us. About what happens after all of this is over."

She stared down at the needle, willing her fingers to stop shaking. "Maybe this isn't the right time."

He sat on the bed beside her, taking the sewing out of her hands. "There will never be a *right* time, sweetheart. And I've always been a man to speak my mind."

She nodded, still unable to look at him, her heart thudding against her chest.

He gently cupped her face in his hands, forcing her to meet his gaze. "I love you, Cara." His eyes reflected his words, and her breath caught in her throat. "I think maybe I always have. Since that night I found you in the snow. But I didn't know for certain until this morning, when I almost lost you in the tunnel."

"Michael, I—"

"Wait." He laid a finger against her lips. "Let me finish. I know that you are afraid. Hell, I know better than anyone how you're feeling. Like a fish out of water. But I can make it better. I can make a life for us here. I know I can— if you'll just give me the chance."

She swallowed tears, fighting for control. "I can't Michael. I don't belong here."

"How do you know that?" His eyes searched hers for answers she knew she couldn't give.

"I don't know, I just do." She stood up, walking to the window, trying to sort through her thoughts.

"Are you saying you don't love me?"

"No." She swung around, her eyes meeting his, begging him to understand. "I care about you. I do. It's just . . . that isn't always enough."

"What the hell is that supposed to mean?" The words exploded from him, full of pain and anger.

"I can't afford to love anyone. Don't you understand? Every time I believe in someone, every time I love them, I wind up getting hurt. I loved my parents, I loved my grandfather . . . Adrian, young and stupid as I was. But they all left me. Even you left me, Michael."

"Adrian was a fool. And your family didn't leave you on purpose, Cara. They died. And I certainly had no control over our situation."

"That's just the point, isn't it? None of us has any control. Anything you love can be wiped out in an instant without the slightest bit of warning. And when it happens, your heart is ripped out and torn to shreds." She pushed her fist against her chest, physically trying to hold in her emotions, to protect her heart. "Don't you see, Michael? I can't go through that again. I just can't."

"Cara, you're not making sense." His face was a wash of emotion, pain and frustration warring with compassion and love. "None of us knows what's going to happen from one moment to the next. That's part of life. You can't just sequester yourself from caring."

"I can try." She paused, searching for the right words, trying to make him understand. "You make me feel things I haven't felt in years, and it scares the hell out of me. Every day that goes by I care a little more. I know that. But I don't think I could survive the pain of losing you, Michael—not if we get any closer. And the truth is, one way or the other, whether it's today or tomorrow, I *will* lose you."

"But isn't some time together better than no time at all?"

"No." She had to force herself to say it, but she managed to keep her gaze steady. "I'll stay until we've seen this through. Until I know that you'll be okay, but then I have to try and find my way home."

"What if you're home now, Cara?" His words were soft, the expression in his eyes breaking her heart.

The Promise

"This can't be my home, Michael. I'd always looking over my shoulder, waiting for the other shoe to drop. Waiting to wake up and find you gone again."

"So for peace of mind you're willing to give up all that's between us?" His fists were clenched at his sides, his fury washing over her.

"I *have* to." She deliberately turned away, fighting her tears, and cringed as the door slammed behind her.

This was the only way. She didn't belong here. Didn't belong with him. No matter what her heart said, she had to listen to reason and logic. She and Michael were from different worlds, and no matter how much she wanted him, she was better off letting him go.

Loralee stood at the window looking out at the moon, her thoughts filled with a jumble of emotions. Memories of Zach and their days together danced through her head. She could still hear his laughter, see the crooked slant of his smile. She'd loved him with all her heart. But when he'd abandoned her, she'd shoved those feelings so deep inside, she'd never thought to see them again. Now here they were, crowding into her heart, reminding her all over again of everything she'd lost.

Tears filled her eyes, joy warring with grief. She'd meant what she'd told Michael: Zach *had* loved her. And he'd loved their child. And part of her truly believed that he'd never have deserted them willingly. Yet another part of her, the contrary part, believed the story about him and Rose. She had even secretly hoped it was true. Because even if it meant he'd up and left her, it also meant that he was still alive.

She sighed, watching the grass waving in the silver moonlight. But if this new story was to be believed, he was dead. He'd loved her, but he was dead.

It was almost as if he'd disappeared all over again. She looked up at the star-filled night and wondered if she'd ever be able to let him go completely. He was so much a part of her, a part of Mary. In truth, one of the reasons she'd sent her daughter away was because seeing her every day had been too painful a reminder.

Shame washed through her, and Loralee tightened her fingers around the soft cotton of the curtains. She loved Mary with her whole heart, but what kind of mother could she possibly be? What kind of life did she have to offer?

Loralee turned resolutely from the window, putting the moonlight firmly behind her. Moonlight was for dreamers, like Duncan—or Patrick. He was more like his father than he knew. He had the same charming manner. And she suspected that, like his father, when Patrick loved a woman, it would be forever.

She wondered, just for a moment, what it would be like to be that woman—but then she pushed the thought away. She'd already lost one man. Truthfully, she didn't know if she could stand to lose another. She sat down on the cot and leaned back against the wall, closing her eyes. A picture of Zach filled her head, his crooked grin a reflection of the love in his dark eyes. But then, without so much as a by-your-leave, he faded away, his brown eyes turning green, his face turning into Patrick's. It was then that Loralee realized it was too late to decide not to care about Patrick Macpherson. Her heart had always had a mind of its own.

Loralee smothered a sob, burying her face in the pillow. There was no sense waking the rest of the household with her tears.

Patrick sat on the edge of the bed, listening to Loralee's soft crying through the thin walls. He wanted to go to her, to hold her—to somehow make her believe everything was going to be all right. For the first time in his life he wanted to make things right for someone else, and the thought amazed him.

And shamed him.

The Promise

Before his mother died, life had been one long picnic. Someone had always been there to clean up his messes and make sure he had what he needed. His mother and father, Michael, and even Owen had all treated him like a little king. Whatever Patrick wanted, Patrick got.

But then, when his mother disappeared, his kingdom had collapsed—everyone lost in their own grief. Owen had tried to insulate things, to preserve Patrick's fairy-tale existence, but there was too much gone.

He stared out the window at the pale silver of the moon. He'd been angry at them all. Angry because his mother had run out on them. Angry because his father and Michael hadn't stopped her—even angry with Owen, because he'd tried to pretend that nothing had changed. But the truth was, he'd been angriest at himself. Angry for not being enough to make her want to stay.

He sighed, looking again at the wall. All was quiet now. Maybe Loralee was sleeping. Or maybe she was lost in her memories, too. He pictured her sweet face and wondered what it would feel like to hold her in his arms, to be the kind of man she deserved.

He grimaced, knowing that she'd had more men than he could possibly imagine, and that, in many ways, he was no different from any of them. What did he have to offer? He had nothing to call his own. Nothing that wasn't Michael's or Owen's.

He was a shadow man, existing on memories and anger . . . on resentment for what had been and could never be again. And now . . . now it seemed that even that had all been a lie. His mother hadn't run away at all. She was simply dead.

The words brought bitter tears to his eyes.

Dead.

Because they'd all been so quick to believe the worst, they'd betrayed her far more by their distrust than she ever could have ever betrayed them.

Patrick stood up, crossing to the window, the moonlight

washing over him, soothing him. His mother had been his whole world. And maybe, he admitted, that had been the problem. Maybe he needed to find himself, to figure out who the hell Patrick Macpherson really was. Only then would he be able to love someone else. Only then would he have something to offer.

He closed his eyes and wondered if Loralee would be willing to wait.

Michael stood in the doorway, watching Cara sleep. She was absolutely the most beautiful woman he'd ever seen. He let his eyes trail downward, taking in the soft curve of her shoulder and the sweet swell of her breasts, and he felt himself growing hard despite all that lay between them.

God, how he wanted this woman.

He crossed to the bed, sitting down beside her, tracing the curve of her face. Her eyes flickered open, regarding him with a sleep-clouded gaze. "Michael." His name came out like a sigh, and he shivered as the sound caressed him.

"I'm sorry." He blew out a breath. "I shouldn't have walked away."

"No." She shook her head. "It was my fault. I just can't tell you what you want to hear."

"I know." He stroked her soft skin, needing her more than he could have believed possible.

"Nothing's changed, Michael." She met his gaze, her eyes searching for confirmation.

"I know that, too." He sighed, letting his hand fall to his side.

"Stay with me, then." She reached for him, her need reflected in her eyes, and his heart began to hammer in his chest as the desire burning in his loins spread upward and inward, filling him with need.

Hands shaking, he pulled off his clothes. Her body was warm against his as she helped with the buttons. Reaching back with one hand, he cupped her neck, twisting around, pulling her with him, satisfied when the maneuver placed her firmly beneath him. She arched her back so that her breasts pressed against his chest, her nipples tracing lines of fire upon him each time she moved.

With a groan he took possession of her mouth, his tongue thrusting deep into her warmth. She met his passion stroke for stroke, and when her hand closed around his aching manhood, her rhythm matched that of their dueling tongues. Balancing on the precipice, he held tight, wanting more than quick release.

He rolled onto his back, taking her with him, their mouths still locked in a mind-numbing kiss. His fingers closed on her nipples and he rubbed and teased until she cried out for more. Replacing his fingers with his mouth, he suckled at first one nipple and then the other, his mouth relishing the feel of her body responding to his. He tugged lightly with his teeth, and she ground her hips against him, writhing with need.

"Now, Michael, please."

The entreaty was all he needed. Rolling over again so that she was nestled in the warmth of the covers, he lifted his body, bracing himself on his elbows, his eyes locked on hers. With one smooth stroke he drove deep inside her, her body surrounding him with throbbing heat.

Her legs moved farther apart as she shifted, pulling him deeper, her arms locking around his shoulders. He lowered his head for a reverent kiss and then, feeling her tighten around him with impatience, he began to move, his thrusts meeting hers, body against body, until he truly couldn't tell where he left off and she began.

And in the moment just before the world erupted with light, he knew that somehow he'd find a way to convince her to stay. They belonged together—now and always—and he wasn't about to let her go without a fight.

Chapter Twenty-seven

The first trace of fuchsia had inched its way over the tops of the mountains, the color reflecting off of the bottoms of the clouds as if a celestial spotlight lit each one. Cara sat on the porch steps, hugging her middle to ward off the early-morning chill, her attention riveted on the magnificent display above her, watching as the deep pink slowly faded into orange-tinged gold. She longed for a paintbrush, wanting to capture the magic.

"Penny for your thoughts."

Cara started at the sound of a voice, glancing up to see Loralee emerge from the doorway. She smiled at her great-grandmother, the concept somehow seeming less foreign now that she'd had a little time to get used to it. "I was wishing I could paint the sunrise." She patted the plank next to her, and Loralee dropped down beside her.

"It'd be nice to capture its beauty. Hold onto it for the hard times." Loralee closed her eyes, the sun illuminating her face. "This is my favorite time of day."

"Mine, too." Cara studied her. She'd always imagined that ladies of the evening were a harsh lot, but Loralee's soft features had a special glow about them. Almost as if the sunshine emanated from inside her. Goodness—that was what it was. Pure and simple goodness.

"Are you going to stay here? When this is over, I mean?"

Cara bit her lip, considering the question. "I don't think so."

Loralee opened her eyes and smiled gently. "There's a connection between you and Michael, Cara. Anyone can see it."

"I care about Michael, but . . . I've had firsthand experience with losing people I love, and I'm not willing to risk that kind of hurt again. We're playing with time, for God's sake. Who's to say that the decision to stay or go is even mine to make?"

"I think you have to make up your mind what it is you really want." Loralee closed her hand meaningfully over the silver locket hanging between her breasts. "And when you do, I suspect the decision will be yours. No matter where you come from, the future has yet to be decided."

Cara sighed. "It's all so complicated."

"I reckon everything in life is complicated."

"True enough." Cara decided turnabout was fair play. "How about you? Will you stay?"

"There's reasons I might want to stay here."

Cara had seen the way Patrick and Loralee looked at each other, but she was uncertain what it all meant. "But there are complications," she said sympathetically.

Loralee nodded, without bothering to deny anything. "Not the least of them being my daughter."

"But surely after everything you've been through, you deserve a happy ending."

Loralee looped her arms around her legs, resting her chin on her knees. "I honestly don't know if I believe in happy endings." For the first time, Cara thought she heard a trace of bitterness in her great-grandmother's voice.

"Sometimes happiness is only a heartbeat away. You

just have to look inside yourself to find it." Cara smiled. "My mother used to say that."

"Your mother was a wise woman," Loralee said, and stood up, all traces of bitterness gone. "I suppose things will work out one way or another—for both of us."

"I hope so, Loralee. I truly hope so."

Michael swung up into the saddle, his hand automatically closing around the butt of the Winchester tucked safely into the leather holster on his saddle. It felt right.

He looked over at Cara, who was leaning forward checking her horse's bridle. She sat her mount with the ease of someone comfortable with horses. In fact, if he ignored her strange leather shoes, she almost looked as though she belonged here. Truth was, he wanted her to belong here, wanted it more than he had ever wanted anything, but the fact was, she didn't. And she'd made it perfectly clear last night that she wasn't going to stay.

"Maybe he won't even be up there."

Michael pulled his attention from Cara and focused on his brother. "It's possible, but I've got a feeling he's there. If we're right about the silver, he's not likely to go far without it."

"I suppose you're right." Patrick brushed absently at a stray piece of Roscoe's mane. "I wish you'd let me come with you. I don't like the idea of your going up there alone."

"I can handle it." Michael smiled and looked over at Cara. "Besides, I've got a sharpshooter with me, remember?" She met his gaze and smiled in return. His heart did a little somersault, and suddenly the day seemed to grow brighter.

"I still want to go with you."

Michael recognized Patrick's mutinous look. "I know, but we've been over this. Someone's got to tell Owen. He deserves to know. It's half his silver."

"A third." Patrick's words were soft, but certain, the lines of his face hard. "A third belonged to Zach, and no matter what really happened, his share should go to Loralee."

"I've got no problem with that."

Patrick relaxed. "Best you get on, then. I'll follow you as soon as I find Owen."

Michael looked over at Cara. "You ready?"

"As I'll ever be."

He turned Roscoe with a slight movement of the reins. "All right, then—"

"Wait." Loralee came running out of the house, a leather satchel in her hands. "I've packed some food." She held up the bag. "Can't let you all go off without something."

Michael took the satchel and secured it on the back of his saddle. "We'll be glad to have this, Loralee. Thank you."

She tipped her head up and smiled at him, then turned to Cara, holding out something in her hand. "Take this. It's as much yours as mine, and it seems to have brought us both luck. I like the idea that it'll be there if you need it."

Cara took the proffered object and fastened it around her neck. *The locket.* Michael felt a shiver of dread. It was possible that the locket had the power to send Cara back. He tried to push the thought away, to postpone the inevitable.

"I'll take good care of it, Loralee." Cara's voice was low, choked with emotion.

"You just take good care of yourself." The two women clasped hands, their eyes fixed on each other.

"I will."

Michael pulled his attention away from Cara and Loralee, glancing up at the sun, which was already beginning to climb in the sky. It was time to go. He looked down at his brother, meeting his solemn gaze. "Watch out for yourself."

"It's not me riding into danger," Patrick complained.

"You keep your eyes open. I'd just as soon not have to bury you twice."

Michael rubbed his injured shoulder. "My sentiments exactly. So you get your ass to Silverthread and then up to the Promise. I'm counting on you to watch my back."

Patrick nodded, the trace of a grin relieving the tension on his face. He raised a hand in farewell. "Good hunting."

Patrick kept a tight rein on the horses, trying to keep the wagon from bouncing too much on the rutted street. Loralee was in back, Pete's head on her lap. His face was still pale, but his fever seemed to have broken. Arless's body was back there, too, underneath a blanket, silent testimony to everything that had happened.

The noise of the town was almost deafening. Men lined the streets, about half of them staggering home for a few winks before their next shifts started, the other half heading for the saloons, ready for some action now that their shifts were over.

None of the more respectable people of Silverthread were to be seen on Gin Avenue, as it had most suitably been named. All told, there were about thirty-five drinking establishments along the street—and that wasn't even counting the tents that consisted of nothing more than a whiskey barrel with a plank that served as a bar.

But that was where Doc kept his office—closer to the action, no doubt. Although lots of injuries occurred up at the mines, a more impressive number happened right here in the middle of all the taverns, drink tending to make men a little less cautious and oftentimes a hell of a lot more foolish.

The occasional catcall or whistle marked their passing, but for the most part their group might as well have been invisible; people in Silverthread tended to mind their own business. Patrick pulled the wagon to a halt in front of Doc's office and jumped down. "How's he doing?" he asked, shooting a worried look at the old ranch hand.

"Better, I think. Although the bouncing broke open the wounds. He's bleeding again." Loralee kept her eyes on Pete. She and Patrick had hardly spoken since Michael and Cara left. Each had been lost in their own thoughts.

"Quit talkin' about me as if I was dead already. I ain't." Pete opened his eyes and struggled to a sitting position. "Course, if you take me in there"—he jerked his head at the office behind him—"my chances of kicking the bucket before my time go up considerably."

"You hush now, Pete." Loralee ran a soothing hand across the old man's cheek. "Doc needs to see to that leg of yours, and no backtalk is going to change my mind."

Pete frowned, and Patrick bit back a smile. "Come on, old man; let's get this over with."

"I ain't old. And I don't need no help." Pete scooted off the wagon, but almost toppled over when he tried to stand on his injured leg.

Patrick quickly flanked him, an arm going around his waist for support.

The foreman grinned weakly. "Well, maybe a little help wouldn't be out of line."

Doc Whatley appeared on his other side, lending more support. "Looks like you ran into a little trouble, Pete." They started to walk slowly toward the office door.

"Nothing I couldn't handle. Just didn't want to worry these young folks none." Despite his brave words, Pete's breath was coming in little gasps. "Arless is back there."

"He need help?" Doc shot a concerned look back at the wagon.

Patrick shook his head, his eyes meeting the doctor's.

"Well, why don't you let me have a look at you first, Pete; then we'll see to Arless." They managed to get him into the office and up onto an examining table, Pete grumbling the whole time. "You all wait out there, and I'll see what I can do for him," Doc said, motioning to the waiting area Patrick and Loralee had just come through.

"You go on and find Owen, Patrick. I'll be fine. If Doc

gives me any trouble, I'll just wallop him." Pete grinned and then lay back, closing his eyes.

"He'll be fine." Doc nodded at them, then turned to his patient.

"Come on." Loralee pulled Patrick into the waiting room. "I'll stay here and watch out for him. You need to tell Owen what's going on. Michael and Cara are counting on you."

Patrick nodded, his gaze meeting hers. "Thank you, Loralee—for everything." There really wasn't anything else to say, or if there was, he hadn't earned any right to say it.

She smiled up at him, her eyes a little sad. "I think you have it backward, Patrick." She leaned up and kissed him on the cheek. "It's me who should be thanking you."

He stood for a moment lost in the soft warmth of her eyes. Then, with a deep breath, he turned to go. There was no sense thinking of things that couldn't be. He'd covered that territory last night, and nothing had changed. Besides, he had a killer to find.

Patrick walked along the boardwalk, thinking about Amos Striker. It was still hard to believe that Striker had killed his mother and Zach. There was just something about the story that didn't ring true. Oh, Striker was capable of killing people, all right; the last few days had more than proved that.

But something just didn't feel right. For one thing, it was a hell of a coincidence that Striker would come across Zach and his mother and the silver by chance. It wasn't impossible, certainly, but it all seemed highly unlikely. The Promise was isolated, high up in the mountains above Clune.

The owners had been careful never to let on the exact location. His father hadn't wanted anyone to be able to find it. They'd even filed their claim over in Del Norte, changing details here and there, so that anyone who did manage to find the papers wouldn't actually be able to find the mine.

It had been Owen's idea, but Duncan had liked the plan, too. Most likely his father thought the whole thing a grand adventure. It hadn't been wealth that called to his father; it had been excitement. Duncan Macpherson liked living on the edge.

Patrick frowned, turning his thoughts back to Striker. The sheriff wasn't a bright man, just a devious one, and the elaborate scenario they'd come up with last night required something more than being devious. So either they were dead wrong about Rose and Zach and the silver, or there was someone else involved. Someone who was calling the shots, and using Amos Striker as muscle . . . or a fall guy.

Patrick pushed through the swinging doors of the Irish Rose, the cacophony of voices, laughter, and tinny piano assaulting his ears. Patrons in various stages of inebriation lined the big mahogany bar and clustered at the tables scattered about the room. Sam was behind the bar, busy with the raucous miners. The barman raised an arm to Patrick in salute, but his attention was quickly drawn back to patrons demanding more liquor.

Patrick headed for the back and Owen's office, his mind still puzzling over the problem of Amos Striker. If someone else was behind everything that had happened, it was likely someone they knew.

Who the hell could it be?

"Loralee." Ginny burst through the doctor's door, her dark eyes filled with relief. "Oh, honey, I thought . . . Well, there's been all kinds of talk. And when you just up and disappeared . . ."

Loralee hugged the older woman, fighting to keep from bursting into tears. "I've been at Clune with Patrick." Then she pulled away and whispered, "Amos Striker tried to kill me."

Dee Davis

"You all right?" The older woman eyed her worriedly.

"I'm fine. It's Pete who's in trouble. Amos Striker shot him. He followed us to Clune and pinned us in the house. If it hadn't been for Michael, we'd be dead for sure. Like Arless."

"Michael's alive?"

"He is, and he brought—" She broke off, not knowing exactly what to say.

"Don't matter—you can tell me later. Where's Patrick?" Ginny asked, her dark eyes intense.

Loralee frowned. "He's gone to find Owen. To tell him what's happened."

Ginny grabbed her by the shoulders. "You got to find him. Now. Before he finds Owen."

"Why? I don't understand." She met the older woman's gaze, and something in her eyes made Loralee shiver.

"Because Owen Prescott's telling folks that Patrick is the one who killed Corabeth. He's the one who sent Amos Striker out to Clune."

Chapter Twenty-eight

Cara drew her horse to a stop, her eyes glued to the steep rise of red-brown rock ahead. It was almost as if a giant hand had thrust it up, splintering the earth, shattering its symmetry. The face of the cliff was sheer and inaccessible, ascending a thousand feet straight into the air.

She sucked in a breath as her eyes found what she was seeking. There, jutting from the craggy stone, about a hundred feet down from the upper rim, was a dark blotch against sunlit rock.

The Promise.

In her time it hadn't been much more than a gaping hole surrounded by fallen timbers, easily mistaken for shadow. But now, in this time, it was whole, the shoring intact, marking the entrance to what had recently been a working mine. It filled her with a sense of awe, a sobering symbol of man's desire to conquer nature.

Heavy cables bowed away from the mountain's rocky walls, extending through the bright spring air, dropping gracefully down to the narrow canyon floor. At the bottom of the gorge, straddling the rushing waters of Shallow

Creek, was another building, its rough log walls extending into the opposite slope of mountain. It was built on wooden scaffolding with two chutes jutting out of one side. A rutted path ran underneath the structure, paralleling the stream.

The cables disappeared inside an opening in one side of the building. She frowned, then suddenly smiled as she realized what she was seeing. What appeared to be four cables were actually two. One set going in, the other going out. She was looking at some kind of tram station.

"Amazing, isn't it?" Michael was staring up at the mine, his hands resting on his saddle horn. "I never get tired of seeing it."

"It's awe-inspiring." She followed his gaze up to the entrance high above them. "How in the world did they get up there?"

Michael smiled. "You mean *we*."

The enormity of it all hit her like a sledgehammer. This mine was part Michael's. He'd helped his father find it, build it. "Of course, I meant you—and your father," she added.

He pointed to the top of the cliff. "There's another entrance up there. It's what you first painted. That's where Father found the first vein."

"So you can reach it from the back side of the mountain. If that's an easier way in, then why—"

"I didn't say it was easier." He shifted in his saddle. "We sank a shaft about one hundred feet straight down into the mountain. From there we dug the main tunnel. In addition, there are probably another dozen or so smaller tunnels and drifts."

"Drifts?" She frowned.

"Tunnels without a second opening."

"Dead ends?" Her knowledge of mining was minimal.

"Right. There are three levels in the mine, each connected to a shaft. But the main work was done on the first level."

"That's the level your dad indicated in his note?"

"I think so."

She shaded her eyes with a hand and looked again at the timbers jutting out from the side of the mountain. "So how do we get there?"

Again Michael smiled, his eyes crinkling at the corners in a way that made her stomach tighten. "We fly."

Cara eyed him dubiously. "Beg your pardon?"

"I said, we fly. Come on; I'll show you."

They dismounted; then he led them up the incline and through a small door in the building at the base of the gorge. It took her a minute to adjust to the gloom. The floor was dusty—the building was probably the winter home for a menagerie of animals. One side of the cable hung suspended over their heads, above the plank platform. On the other side the cable ran across the openings for the two chutes.

"It's a turning station."

Cara looked at Michael. "A what?"

"A turning station. The ore comes down the mountain in one of these cars." He tapped the side of a shallow, rectangular bucket, its handles attached to the cable with what looked like a pulley, the pulley in turn attached to the cable. Several of the cars stood in a row just to the left of the platform—ready for takeoff, no doubt. "Once it gets here, it follows the cable there"—he pointed at the wires above the openings in the floor—"and the ore is dumped down the chutes into a waiting wagon."

"I thought the cables meant a tram of some kind, but I don't see how—"

He cut her off with the wave of a hand. "It's also used to get supplies"—he paused for effect—"and men"—he grinned like a mischievous little boy—"up to the mine."

Understanding washed through her with the force of a tidal wave. "Oh, no, I'm not going up there." She pointed through the opening in the opposite wall at the distant

305

mine, then eyed the narrow metal box with something bordering on panic. "Not in that."

"It's fun. I've done it a million times. And besides, it's faster than climbing up the back of the mountain."

She looked up at the cable, trying to judge its strength. When the hell would someone invent reinforced steel, anyway? The wire above her head looked strong enough, but when she imagined riding it across the gulch, she wasn't as certain. "How exactly do you propose we do that? There isn't an engine."

Michael laughed. "We don't need one. The thing works by gravity. As a loaded tram car comes down, it pulls the one here back to the top."

"Well, we've got a problem, then. There's no one up there to fill a car and send it down," she announced triumphantly.

"My father rigged it so that we always leave a full one at the top."

"Great." She blew out a breath and tried to look enthusiastic. "Of course," she added, "it has been a while since you were up here, and between your dad and Amos Striker there's every chance the loaded car has been used and not replaced." She tried to keep the pleading note out of her voice, but she had absolutely no desire to emulate Peter Pan.

Michael turned his back, examining a gizmo that ran out of a window on one side of the door. "Of course, we have a backup system."

"Oh?" A sense of inevitability hit her.

"Yeah, there's a horse winch, too."

"A horse winch?" She knew she sounded like a parrot.

"Yeah." He gestured out the window. "It's out there. Sort of a horse-drawn pulley."

She schooled her features into what she hoped was her calm, sensible look. "But the horses are tired."

Michael actually laughed. "Don't worry, sweetheart. I'm fairly certain we won't need the horses."

She frowned at him and turned away, walking to the far edge of the platform. The opening here was large, taking up almost the entire side of the building. And what little wallboard there was looked as though it would disintegrate with a small tap. The first ore bucket in line sat only a few feet from the edge, ready to leap out into the air.

Her stomach dropped. The whole thing reminded her of a rinky-dink version of the aerial tram at Disney World, and she'd refused to ride that, too.

She looked down at the rushing water. The noise from the stream below was deafening—perfect white noise. She grinned, thinking of how much people paid to emulate a sound like that.

"I . . . go . . . ng . . . ut . . . ide," she heard. Swinging around, she looked at Michael. His mouth was moving, but she couldn't understand the words. She pointed at her ear.

He, in turn, pointed at the door. "I'm going outside for a minute," he yelled.

She signaled "okay," then wondered if he even knew what she meant. Shrugging, she turned back to the view from the open wall. It was magnificent. She looked down again. Compared to the top of the run, they were fairly close to the ground here, probably only a couple of hundred feet or so. Still, the rocks below looked deadly, and the rushing stream did nothing to alleviate her fears.

She'd just have to tell him she couldn't do it, simple as that. Behind her the door banged. "Michael." She turned around ready to confess. The words died on her lips.

The man in the doorway wasn't Michael. But she knew who he was—his resemblance to Nick was uncanny. Fear danced its way along her spine.

Amos.

A slow, delighted smile spread across his face. "Well, well, what do we have here?" He took a step toward her, and she took a step back. He took another step and she immediately moved back again, as if they were locked into some kind of strange dance. He moved forward again, this time into a pool of light slanting down from the opening behind her. Her eyes still locked on him, she realized it was her move. She opened her mouth, but nothing came out.

"Cat got your tongue?"

She licked her lips and stepped back, only to realize she'd run out of floor.

Amos's lips thinned as his smile grew broader. "And just where do you think you're going, darlin'?" he drawled.

She felt the skin on the back of her neck crawl. She slid sideways behind the last tram car. She could feel the wind through the opening at her back, but even so, she felt more secure with the hunk of metal between her and the sheriff.

"Come here, angel." He gestured with a finger. "I won't hurt you."

Like hell. How stupid did he think she was? *Stupid enough to wind up alone in the middle of another century with a murderer,* her mind suggested. She watched as he took another step toward her. *Help.* She needed help. She opened her mouth, praying for a voice. "Michael?" Her call came out a muted squeak.

Amos was at the corner of the ore bucket now. She inched back until her heels rocked out over the edge of the platform. Startled, she reached for the ore car, gripping the edge with both hands.

"I wouldn't bother calling him, darlin'. I think he's past hearing you." He patted a Colt stuck in the waist of his pants.

Michael's gun.

Cara sucked in a ragged breath and shoved hard against the bucket, but it didn't move.

Amos laughed. "Only goes one way, I'm afraid, and it'd be a shame to see a gal as pretty as you go over the edge." He nudged the bucket with his knee and it lurched forward, resting against her legs. Then, with a booted foot, he rocked it slowly so that it rubbed provocatively against her. "Think of that as a little warm-up, darlin'." His mouth still curled into a smile, but his eyes were like shards of ice. She felt their frigid touch as his gaze moved down her body.

There was a flicker of movement behind Amos, and with a war cry that made William Wallace seem tame, a bloodied Michael surged through the door, leaping at the sheriff. He tackled him from behind and the two men rolled onto the floor, locked together, struggling for the gun that had fallen nearby.

Cara watched in fascinated horror as they fought, her numb brain trying to get her to act. She'd always hated heroines in the movies who stood and watched as the hero battled the bad guys. In theory, it had seemed easy to do something to help. In practice, it turned out she was totally incapable of movement.

The men flipped over, Amos on top. With a triumphant grin he reached for the gun, but Michael was fast and slammed one fist into the man's jaw. Thrown off balance, the two of them tumbled backward, ramming into the tram car. It swung forward, moving along the cable. Cara's brain sent out a frantic message to move, but it was too late.

She grabbed the rim of the bucket just as she felt her feet slide off the end of the platform. The car slid effortlessly into the air, taking her with it. She felt her arms jerk like a ski rope after takeoff and wondered briefly if arms could actually be pulled out of their sockets.

Holding on for dear life, she forced herself to look down and immediately wished she hadn't. Her feet dangled high above the narrow gorge. The rocks looked even more sinister from up here than they had from the platform. She bit her lip, willing all her strength into her arms. Surely all those pull-ups in sixth grade had been good for something.

The bucket's forward momentum died, and it swung back and forth, almost as if it were trying to shake her off. She gritted her teeth and tightened her grip. She'd be damned if she'd let an overgrown tin pail be the death of her.

From her dangling vantage point, she could still see the two men struggling. Amos had managed to get the Colt, and she watched with mounting terror as he knocked Michael to the ground.

She closed her eyes, and the sharp report of a gun sounded.

"Michael!" She screamed his name, then fought to hang on to the undulating tram car.

Chapter Twenty-nine

Cara forced herself to open her eyes, her fear for Michael momentarily distracting her from the searing pain in her arms. Michael still lay, unmoving, but Striker now teetered on the edge of the platform, his arms windmilling wildly. Then the sheriff fell, his body tumbling down onto the rocks far below. The water swept him away.

Cara shuddered, tightening her grip. Her eyes locked on Michael—willing him to move, willing him to be alive. After a moment she was rewarded. He struggled to his feet, and she exhaled slowly, relief filling her. But it was short lived.

A movement to Michael's left caught her attention, a shadow cautiously detaching itself from the wall. Her heart stopped. A man carrying a smoking rifle stepped into the light. The two men stood for a second, looking at each other, then embraced.

Cara blew out a breath. A friend. The man was a friend. A minute later, he was pointing at the ore car with his rifle, and Michael was rushing to the edge of the platform, his face tight with worry. "Hang on, sweetheart," he yelled.

She bit back the desire to laugh. What exactly did he think she was going to do, let go?

The bucket rocked and bucked as Michael swung out onto the cable. Hand over hand, he made his way toward her. The little tram car was rocking furiously now, and she closed her eyes, swallowing back nausea. Her arms were beginning to weaken, and she realized she couldn't feel the fingers of her left hand.

"I'm almost there. Just a few more feet."

She opened her eyes, and her gaze met Michael's. She attempted a smile, but knew she'd failed miserably when the little muscle in his jaw started to jump. He was working to keep his face calm. He reached the edge of the bucket, but he was at the far end—almost three feet away. In this position it seemed like a million miles.

"Cara, sweetheart, you're going to have to inch your way around to this side of the bucket. Do you think you can do that?"

She gritted her teeth and, with a nod, forced the fingers of her left hand to move. For an agonizing second her entire weight was supported by her right arm, and then she felt her left hand close again around the lip of the ore car. Inch by agonizing inch, she moved along the bucket, stopping only when the swinging got too wild. Her eyes remained locked on Michael's as she tried to ignore the searing pain in her arms.

At last, after what seemed an eternity, she reached Michael's side of the ore car. He was close enough to touch—not that she dared give in to the desire.

"Good girl."

She felt absurdly pleased with the compliment. No one could say she wasn't a trooper. Feeling light-headed and a little giddy, she wondered briefly if she was going to lose consciousness. She felt her eyes closing, darkness creeping around the edge of her vision.

The Promise

"Cara, don't give up. We're almost there."

She forced her eyes back open, her gaze again locking with his. "What do I do now?" Her voice came out as a cracked whisper, and she wasn't sure he could hear her over the roar of the water below.

"I want you to swing up and grab me around the neck. Do you think you can do that?"

She looked down at the stream beneath her and thought briefly about an act she'd seen once in a circus. They'd had a net.

"I'll catch you; don't worry."

Taking a deep breath, she rocked the car, swinging back and forth, getting used to the motion; then when the bucket arched upward and she was more or less level with Michael, she let go with her left hand, reaching for him as she let go with her right.

Alley-oop . . .

She was flying. For one glorious second she was free, the horrible pressure on her arms relieved. Then, with a satisfying thunk, she collided with Michael, his arm circling her waist. They hung for a moment like that, suspended over the canyon. Then she twisted, locking first one arm and then the other around his neck, gripping her left wrist with her right hand.

"You all right?" he asked with a grunt, both hands back on the cable.

Again she felt the urge to laugh. *What a ridiculous question.* But she didn't have any further time to worry about it. Michael started to move back across the wire, his muscles straining with their combined weight.

Again, their progress seemed agonizingly slow. She saw the worried face of the shadow man. He was standing at the opening, hands out, ready to help. *About damn time somebody came to help us!*

They reached the platform, and the mystery man reached up to grab her legs. She slid into his arms, her whole body suddenly feeling like rubber. The stranger's

313

Dee Davis

arms were replaced by Michael's as he dropped down onto the platform. She nestled against him, drawing comfort from his nearness. She felt his lips moving against her temple and pressed closer, unsure whether she had the strength to stand on her own.

"That was a near miss." The voice was cultured, with the trace of a British accent, which seemed somehow out of place in the Wild West. And she knew now just how wild the West could be.

Michael was answering. She could feel the vibrations of his words through his shirt. It was strangely comforting. "It would have been a hell of a lot closer if you hadn't come along."

"Well." Cara could hear the pleasure in the other man's voice. "My timing has always been impeccable. I should like to hear what exactly the two of you were doing up here with"—he paused, and Cara imagined he was looking down at where Amos's body had been washed away— "riffraff like that."

She smiled into Michael's shirt. He sounded so pompously English. "But," he went on, "I should think the first thing to do is get this young lady a cup of coffee. Hardly civilized to go on with explanations and leave the poor thing hanging onto you for dear life."

Cara was beginning to like this man. She pulled away from Michael, relieved to find that her feet were capable of supporting her. She winced as she straightened her arms. "Take me to the coffee." Her voice had even returned to some semblance of normality. She took a shaky step forward, linking arms with both men.

"My kind of girl," the Englishman said, patting her hand paternally.

"Mine, too, Owen, mine, too," Michael added, his hand covering hers with a gentle squeeze as he led them across the platform toward the beckoning doorway.

Owen. She turned the name over in her mind, matching it to the man. So this was Owen Prescott. They moved

314

toward the door, Michael laughing at something Owen said. It was good to hear the sound.

Maybe the nightmare was finally over.

Owen's office was empty, and from the looks of it had been empty for a day or so. Patrick leaned back in Owen's chair and ran a finger through the light coat of dust that covered everything. Owen was nothing if not fastidious. There could be only one reason everything was this dusty.

Owen was gone.

Patrick frowned, wondering why Owen would have left with everything in such turmoil. Granted, he didn't know about Striker's duplicity, or about Michael's return. Still, he knew what Striker had been saying, and he knew how much pain Patrick was in. It wasn't like Owen to desert him. He'd always been there when Patrick needed him. He was the one person in this world Patrick knew he could count on.

It had been Owen who'd told him about his mother and Zach. He'd been out to the ranch even before Michael and his father had come down off the mountain. Why, it had been Owen who'd figured out about the stagecoach.

Patrick drew in a sharp breath. *Owen!* Oh, God, it couldn't be. Not Owen! But the very things that had comforted him at the time, mocked him now. Owen had been there, always there. Patrick's heart rebelled at the direction his thoughts were taking, but the evidence continued to mount. His father had found something in the mountains. Something involving silver. And he'd come to town to tell Owen. His friend. His confidant.

His murderer.

It all fit. And yet he still couldn't make himself believe. Why would Owen have done it? The silver had already been partially his. Patrick frowned, pushing the horrible notion away. There had to be another explanation, someone else who was behind everything. It couldn't be Owen. It just couldn't.

Dee Davis

"Patrick?" Loralee's soft voice pulled him from the horror of his thoughts.

"Is Pete all right?"

She nodded, her hands clenched at her sides. "Doc says he's gonna be fine. Ginny is with him."

"Is there something else?"

She nodded again, shifting her weight nervously from one foot to the other, her eyes darting around the office. "Where's Owen?"

"He's not here."

She relaxed a little. "There's something you've got to know."

Patrick walked over to her, his hands reaching for hers. "Whatever it is, just say it."

She drew in a deep breath. "Ginny overheard Owen talking to the sheriff yesterday morning. She was working at the hotel. She cooks there to bring in some extra money. Anyway, he—Owen, I mean—was telling the sheriff that he believed *you* were responsible for Corabeth's death."

"Me?" The word exploded from his mouth, his fears resurfacing in full force.

"Yes. And there's more. He told Amos that he'd best get on out to Clune and arrest you, before you hurt someone else. He told the sheriff I was missing and that he thought maybe you'd taken it into your head to kill me, too."

"My God. You don't believe . . ." He trailed off, his eyes locking with hers.

"Of course not." Her hands tightened around his. "But don't you see, if Owen is saying things like that, then that means—"

"He's behind all of this," he cut her off. His heart plummeted. He'd placed his faith in the wrong person, and because of it, he'd failed to see who the real enemy was.

"But I don't understand why, Patrick." Loralee looked up at him, confusion playing across her beautiful face.

"I don't either, but I intend to find out." He spun

316

around, intent on finding something in the office that explained what the hell was going on. Once again, his whole world had turned upside down, but this time he wasn't going to just hide from it. *No, sir.* He was going to face it head-on.

He yanked open a drawer on one side of Owen's desk. It was full of ledgers, neatly organized by date. He pulled one out and quickly discarded it, already reaching for another. Account books for the Irish Rose. Frustrated, he slammed the drawer shut and pulled open the bottom one.

It was less tidy than the other. Patrick's eyes locked on a black rectangular object, the gold embossing hauntingly familiar. Reaching for it with a shaking hand, his fingers closed around the cool ebony union case, confirming what his eyes already knew.

"What is it?" He felt the soft whisper of Loralee's breath against his shoulder as she bent over to see what he held in his hand.

Slowly he opened the little case, his heart pounding as horrifying thoughts poured through his head. His eyes focused on the image in the frame. The woman in the picture smiled up at him, and he felt tears pricking the backs of his eyes.

Loralee's grip on his shoulder tightened. "Patrick, what's wrong? Who is that?"

Wrenching his gaze away from the daguerreotype, he looked up at her.

"It's my mother."

"Rose?" Loralee looked up at Patrick and then back at the smiling face in the union case. The woman was pretty, in an elfin sort of way. Dark hair and flawless pale skin. The eyes were Patrick's—emerald green. Irish eyes. It seemed Patrick resembled his mother even more than he did his father.

"My mother," Patrick repeated in confirmation, his face locked into a mask of disbelief.

"Patrick?" She reached out and laid a hand on his shoulder. "I don't understand."

He sighed and ran a hand through his hair, his voice full of anxiety. "This belonged to my mother. There used to be a picture of my father here." He pointed to the inside of the lid of the case. Sure enough, there were little yellowed bits in the corners, as if something had been torn out. "They had their pictures made right after they were married. There was a photographer. . . ." He paused, lost in his own thoughts.

"Where?" Loralee urged gently.

"Some fair out by the seashore. My mother said it was a remembrance of a perfect day. She always carried it with her." He turned the case over. "See? There's a pin here. She wore it fastened to the inside of her shirtwaist. So that she wouldn't lose it." He looked up at her, his eyes full of pain. "She'd never willingly let anyone have this, Loralee, never."

"Of course not." She knew the words were inadequate, but she wanted so much to comfort him.

Sparks shot from his eyes. "It was Owen, Loralee. It was all Owen. He killed my mother. That's the only way he could possibly have this."

She met his gaze, her anger echoing his. If what Patrick was saying was true, then Owen had likely killed Zach, too. "But why?"

Patrick stood up, tucking the union case into his shirt pocket. "I don't know for certain."

Loralee met his gaze, understanding dawning. "You think he's gone for the silver?"

"I'd bet my life on it."

A new thought occurred to her, terror rising in its wake. "But Michael and Cara—"

He nodded grimly. "Are riding right for him."

Chapter Thirty

"So Amos Striker was behind the whole thing." Owen sipped his coffee thoughtfully.

"It seems the most logical explanation." Michael methodically broke off pieces of a stick, throwing them into the fire.

Cara leaned back against a rock, allowing the conversation to flow around her, watching Michael's surrogate father. They'd filled Owen in on almost everything—at least, everything relevant to Amos and the missing silver. The rest, Loralee and Zach, and the fact that half the story had taken place a little over a hundred and ten years in the future, would only have provided needless confusion.

"The question, my boy, is *why* did he do it?" Owen tilted his head quizzically, and Cara forced her wandering mind back to the conversation.

"Greed, most likely. I guess we'll never know for sure."

Owen looked up at the mine. "And you think Duncan rehid the silver?"

Michael followed his gaze. "It sure seems that way."

Dee Davis

"Crafty old bugger." Owen's eyes narrowed, and Cara could have sworn she saw a flicker of something less than congenial in them, but before she had time to examine the thought, the look was gone.

Michael dumped the grounds from his coffee into the fire and put his cup down on a rock. "You never said what brought you up here, Owen."

"Oh, curiosity mainly." He stretched his legs, leaning back against a rock. "I had business in Tintown and expected it to take somewhat longer than it did. When I finished early, I felt the need of a little"—he paused, sipping the last of his coffee—"holiday. And so here I am."

"Well, I, for one, am delighted you showed up when you did." Cara smiled at him and gathered the tin coffee cups. She pulled herself to her feet, surprised to find that she was feeling almost normal. "I'll just wash these out." She walked to the stream and bent to rinse them. The cold water felt good against her bruised hands.

"Owen." Cara could hear Michael's voice clearly even though he was behind her. "There's one thing I haven't told you. There's a note—from my father. I think it's directions of some kind."

"To the silver?" There was a new note of enthusiasm in Owen's voice, not that she could blame him. It was his silver, after all, or at least a third of it was.

"I think so."

"Well, my boy, where is it?"

Cara cocked her head to listen. There was something in Owen's voice that bothered her. In fact, now that she thought about it, there was more than that. Something about his reaction to the whole thing was off.

"The note? I don't have it."

"Where is it?" There was a chord of urgency in the older man's voice.

"Patrick has it."

Owen coughed, but Cara would have sworn it started

out as a curse. "Really? I assumed, of course, since you're up here, that you'd have it."

"Well." She could hear the smile in Michael's voice. "I do have it. Sort of."

She realized he was teasing Owen. Michael had memorized the short note, just to make sure Amos couldn't get his hands on it. She waited for him to enlighten his friend.

"It's in here." She turned around in time to see him pointing at his head, a boyish grin on his face.

"Well, why didn't you say so? Let's get up there." Owen's face was positively jubilant. Again Cara had the feeling there was something false about it. She pushed the thought aside. Her adventures were making her cynical. This was Owen, after all. Michael's Owen.

"Hang on. Cara's not in any shape to go up there. We're better off waiting for Patrick to catch up."

"But we don't know when he'll be here." Owen sounded petulant. He glanced over at Cara, looking apologetic. "Forgive me, my dear, I wasn't thinking."

She stacked the clean cups in front of Owen's rucksack. "It's all right. Besides, I'm fine. If you all want to go up there, I'm game." She paused, looking across the stream at the turning station. "As long as we take the ground route."

Michael frowned at her, his eyes exploring her from head to toe. "Are you sure you're all right?"

"I'm fine, really. After everything we've been through, a little acrobatics over Shallow Creek is a drop in the bucket." She winced at her own bad pun.

"Very funny."

Owen stood up. "It's decided then. We head for the mine, using ground transportation, of course." He smiled over at Cara conspiratorially. "I never much cared for those ore buckets myself."

They were well on their way over the mountain before Cara realized what it was that had been bothering her. At no time during their discussion of Amos and the silver had

Owen asked about Michael's mother. Granted, it probably wasn't as big an issue for him as it was for her sons, but according to Michael, he'd been close to her.

Surely he should have at least asked about her. Didn't he want to know what had really happened to Rose?

Cara's first thought was that it was amazingly dark. In her time, the historical society had worked frantically to try to make the mining museum in Silverthread accurate—to the point of countless arguments about the lighting. In the end they'd settled on lighting so low it was sometimes impossible to see the mine exhibits clearly. Accuracy over practicality. She blinked against the dark. Compared to the Promise, the museum was brighter than a floodlit ballpark.

They stood at the bottom of the mineshaft in the main tunnel of the first level. Cara looked at the candle in her hand. It barely illuminated her arm, let alone the cavernous dark. She shivered, remembering the ceiling collapse in the other mine.

The Promise was easily four or five times bigger than the tunnel where she'd met Michael, and a heck of a lot darker. Peering into blackness, she imagined she could see the light from the opening she knew was far ahead—the one leading to the tramway. Granted, it wasn't much of an escape route—unless you counted the high wire—but it was better than being trapped in all this darkness.

The candleholder was interesting. It was a wrought-iron affair with a hook just below the candle, and a long, pointed stake coming off of the hook that allowed a miner to thrust the holder into the wall. The hook formed a handle for carrying or a convenient way to hang the candle from any protrusion. It was efficient, if somewhat lacking in luminary capability.

Michael was lighting candles in similar holders for himself and Owen. She looked back up the black hole they'd descended. The tail end of the rickety ladder was just visible. Again she marveled at the courage and tenacity of nineteenth-century miners.

Owen and Michael had stopped a little way down the tunnel, conferring about something. She hurried to catch up.

". . . but without a level number, the directions could be for any one of six tunnels, and that's assuming Duncan got his directions right," Owen was saying, waving a hand in exasperation.

"Calm down." Michael's voice was patient. "I'm pretty certain he was referring to this level. Most of the silver was found here, and besides, it'd be quite a chore to lower all those bars down a shaft with a mucker's bucket."

"Yes, but you're assuming Amos's hiding place was on this level." The Englishman's features looked sharper, almost sinister in the flickering light.

"Well, basically I'm assuming a hell of a lot. But all I know to do is start looking. Come on, Owen, have a little faith in my father." Michael patted the man on the back and turned to Cara. "How are you holding up?"

She smiled at the concern in his voice. "Fine. I'm a little sore, but all in all I'd say I'm up for a treasure hunt."

He bent and lightly pressed his lips to hers. "That's my girl."

It was absurd how such a simple phrase could bring so much joy. "Where do we start?"

They'd been walking as they talked, and now Michael came to a halt in front of a narrow fissure in the tunnel wall. "Here."

"In there?" Cara was incredulous. "Nobody could squeeze through that."

Owen held his candle closer to the opening. "The shadows make it look smaller than it is." Sure enough, the small crack enlarged as if by magic. It was still tiny by doorway standards, but it did look passable—barely.

"Are you sure this is the right tunnel?" She eyed the crack skeptically.

Dee Davis

"It's a drift, actually, but I'm fairly certain this is the right one. Northwest tunnel three should be just up there." Michael motioned ahead with his candle.

"How can you be sure?" Owen still sounded frustrated.

"You forget that I helped to dig most of these tunnels. It's been a while, but I still remember where most of them are."

Owen nodded, seemingly satisfied. "Well, no time like the present, I always say." He started toward the fissure.

"Wait." Owen stopped, turning back at the note of authority in Michael's voice. "I think it would be better if you let me go in there. It's a tight fit, but I'm used to it."

"So you want us to just stand here and wait?" The idea obviously didn't excite Owen.

It pleased Cara no end. She'd had about all the adventuring she could take. Frankly, she was beginning to think any amount of silver wasn't worth all this effort.

"Why don't you and Cara go on and check out the other tunnel? It's just up there." He met Cara's annoyed look and smiled. "It's a lot wider."

"Right." Owen started off in the direction of the other tunnel, calling over his shoulder, "We'll meet back here."

Cara held her ground. "If I have to go into one of these things, I'd rather go with you."

Michael placed a hand on her shoulder. "This isn't an easy tunnel. It widens out pretty quickly, but the first fifty feet are narrow and low. If I remember right, there are places where you have to crawl."

She shuddered, memories of the cave-in flashing in her head. "Well, if it's so tricky, maybe you shouldn't go either."

"I'm a prospector's brat, remember? I've been crawling around mines since I was a kid."

"Well"—she looked him up and down pointedly—"I'd say you're a little bigger now." He shot her an I'm-going-to-do-what-I-want-no-matter-what-you-say smile. *So much for arguing.* She blew out a breath. "All right. But I'm

324

staying right here in case you need me."

He grinned, his mind already on the fissure. The man was actually enjoying himself. "I'll be back."

"Yeah, you and Arnold Schwarzenegger," she mumbled. He looked at her blankly, dropped a kiss on her cheek, then disappeared into the hole. She stood for a minute waiting patiently. "Michael?" No answer. The rock seemed to absorb all sound. She turned back the way they had come. It was dark. Really dark. Looking the other way, she could just make out the light from Owen's candle.

She glanced again at the fissure where Michael had disappeared, then turned her gaze up to the rocks above her. Several small stones broke free and clattered to the ground at her feet.

She turned back toward the bobbing light heading down the tunnel, her mind made up.

"Owen," she called. "Wait for me."

"So, how much farther back do you think this goes?" Cara peered into the darkness. Somehow she'd wound up in the lead. It wasn't exactly her first choice, but at least she wasn't alone.

"I'm honestly not sure. I never spent much time at the mine. I was more the money man; Duncan was the spelunker. Mind your head. It gets low here."

She ducked, wondering how he knew to warn her of the tunnel's obstacles when he'd just admitted he'd not spent much time here. She shrugged mentally—probably just amazing eyesight. "Do you think Michael's found anything yet?"

"No, there hasn't been enough time. That's an incredibly narrow passageway. It will take him a while just to get into the wider part of the drift."

Again, he seemed incredibly knowledgeable. She blew out a breath, her eyes searching for a glint of silver, even as her mind churned. She was overreacting. She knew it. Amos Striker was dead. The worst was behind them. Still, she'd feel better when they'd found the damn stuff and were safely out of this mine.

She'd never thought of herself as claustrophobic, but she was beginning to change her mind. She stopped, holding up her candle. "I don't think this thing is ever going to end."

"It's not much farther." His voice echoed out of the dark behind his candle.

"I thought you'd never been here." Again she felt the niggle of concern.

"I haven't," he said quickly. "It's just that the tunnel is narrowing here."

She looked up, holding her candle high. Sure enough, the rock walls were closer together and the ceiling was more rounded. Owen stabbed his candleholder into a soft place in the wall, the glow illuminating a circle of stone. Cara tried to follow suit with hers, but had trouble pushing it into the rock.

"Here, like this." Owen took it from her and, after examining the wall, shoved it into a muddy-looking patch.

The combined light almost made the cavern bearable. She thought she could just make out the back of the tunnel. "Now what?"

Owen shrugged. "We search."

Cara took a step toward the back wall, her eyes sweeping across the shadowy ground. "I'm not sure exactly what we're looking for."

"A stack of silver bars. I imagine the crates have long since rotted away." His disembodied voice echoed across the emptiness as he stepped out of the light. "Each bar is marked with a rose."

"That's right; I'd forgotten about the rose. The rose for Michael's mother." She bent down to reach behind a fallen rock, her blood suddenly running cold. Only Rose and Duncan and Michael had known about the imprint. It had been a last-minute addition. Owen hadn't known——couldn't have known, unless . . .

She slowly stood up, her heart pounding. "I'm not finding anything. Maybe it's not here."

"We haven't searched all the way to the end of the tunnel. Let's keep looking." He was still out of range of the light, his voice echoing sinisterly. "Cara?"

"I'm here, Owen, just not finding anything." She tried but couldn't keep the fear from her voice, the truth now blindingly obvious. Owen Prescott wasn't a friend. He was the enemy.

Michael struggled to move forward and keep his candle alight. It was slow going, but if he remembered correctly he was almost through the hard part. Of course he had to get out again, but he'd made it this far, and he figured he could make it back. And with any luck at all, there'd be a payoff at the end of the drift.

He wasn't really a material man, but the thought of being able to provide a good life for Cara—if she stayed—appealed to him. The silver would go a long way toward making Clune the kind of place she would be proud of. And maybe, if it was all it could be, she'd be content to stay here in this time—with him.

He pushed thoughts of Cara away and worked to inch a few feet farther along.

"I'm afraid, my dear, we've run out of time."

Owen seemed to materialize out of nowhere, his voice trailing along the edge of Cara's ear, sending shivers up her spine. She jumped back, holding a hand to her chest. "Owen, you startled me!" He smiled, but it failed to reach his eyes. They reminded her of marbles, beautiful but lifeless. She took a step backward. Something was very wrong.

"I'm afraid I've made a serious blunder." He moved with a speed that amazed her, his hands closing around her throat. "I've let my secret slip, and you are entirely too clever to have missed it." She tried to struggle, but he was larger and his grip tightened, cutting off her oxygen. "I'm sorry, darling; it couldn't be avoided. She simply knows too much. Forgive me."

Cara thought at first that he was talking to her. But it came with sudden clarity that he wasn't. Her vision began to darken, and she could no longer draw a breath. He was crazy, her beleaguered brain pounded out. *Crazy.* She reached inside for strength. Thinking of Michael, she twisted against the murderous hands, the movement allowing her a tiny breath.

"Bitch!" She had no idea who the word was meant for, and frankly she didn't care. Her time was running out. Her flailing arms hit something—something cold, metallic: the candleholder. Her fingers closed around it, even as bright points of light began to dance before her eyes. With a last burst of energy, she brought the iron stake down with all the force she could muster.

Owen screamed as the sharp metal glanced off his cheek and dug into his shoulder. His grip loosened and she jerked free, thrusting the now-extinguished candle and holder in front of her, point out. It was deathly quiet. She stepped into the shadows, her eyes scanning the area for Owen. It was as if he had disappeared. She rocked from right foot to left foot, crouched in the dark, waiting.

Suddenly something rattled in front of her.

"Stay back," she called. Her voice cracked as she spoke, coming out as barely more than a whisper.

"There's no escape, my dear. Michael can't hear you, and I'm much stronger than you are. It may take time, but I'll find you. And when I do . . ." His voice trailed off, and she shivered at the implication.

She swallowed nervously, waiting. The other candle suddenly blew out and all was impenetrably dark. She had matches in her pocket, but any light now would only give away her position.

She bit back a scream. Owen was right about one thing: Michael would never hear her. But Owen would. *Owen would.* She took another step, unsure of whether she was going backward or forward. It was like the cave-in, only this time the cold darkness was embodied in flesh and blood. *Owen.* And he wanted to kill her.

"Checkmate," a soft voice whispered in her ear just as a hand closed on her elbow. She swung blindly with her candleholder and ran, maniacal laughter echoing after her. One minute she was on solid ground and the next she was falling, like Alice down the rabbit hole. She'd have closed her eyes, but it wouldn't have done any good.

With a peculiar lurch, it almost seemed that her descent slowed, and then she crashed to the rocky floor, wondering idly why a mine would smell like roses.

Chapter Thirty-one

Michael squeezed himself out of the last few feet of the fissure and back into the main tunnel. He'd obviously been a lot smaller the last time he'd worked his way in there. He should have realized there'd be no way to easily get the silver into and out of that crack. Although, in a perverse kind of way, it was exactly what he would have expected his father to do.

He wiped the dust from his hands on his jeans and looked around. The passage was dark—no sign of Cara and Owen. Maybe they'd had more luck. He set off in the direction they'd gone. If he remembered correctly, the north tunnel wasn't more than a few hundred feet ahead.

He looked down at the length of iron in his hand. The candle was burning low. He stopped and reached into his pocket. Never one to take chances, he lit the new candle and pushed it onto the stub of the old one. The new wick flickered briefly in an unseen draft and then burned brightly, casting a cheerful glow on the cold damp walls he passed. He wished it echoed his feelings, but he couldn't seem to shake the apprehension that had settled over him like an icy blanket of snow.

A scream broke the dark silence of the tunnel—a woman's scream.

Cara!

Michael willed his feet to run, to move, but his terrified brain refused to release the brakes. The sound died almost as quickly as it had begun. One minute it was sending shivers of dread down his spine, the next it was gone, as if swallowed by the dark. Despite the chill of the tunnel, sweat beaded across his forehead. He wiped a hand across it, trying to make sense of what he'd heard.

A light appeared in the tunnel, not far from where he seemed permanently rooted to the spot. "Michael, is that you?" The light swung upward, and he recognized the voice as Owen's.

He tried to form a coherent sentence, but Cara's scream echoed over and over in his head. As the light began to move toward him, he finally found his voice. "Owen, what happened?"

"It's Cara," came the answering reply.

His heart was beating so loudly it almost drowned out the words.

"I'm afraid she's had a fall." Owen materialized out of the dark, sliding to a stop in front of him. Blood darkened a cut along the side of his face, and another darker stain spread across the torn shoulder of his shirt. *More blood,* Michael's brain assessed.

"Is she . . ." He hesitated, afraid to finish the sentence.

"I'm afraid I don't know. We were in northwest three and there was a bit of a cave-in. We fell backward and . . ." He paused, ineffectually dabbing at his blood-stained face with his handkerchief. His eyes met Michael's, and the look there made Michael's stomach contract in fear. "I'm sorry, my boy, I tried to grab her, but . . ." His eyes were full of regret—tragic regret.

331

"Michael?"

He spun around at the sound of his brother's voice. "Patrick? Is that you?" The light at the far end of the tunnel was faint, but his brother's voice carried through the tunnel as if he were only a few feet away.

"Hang on, I'm coming! Is *Owen* with you?"

The name came out with a strange emphasis, and the hair on Michael's neck rose. "Yes, he's here!" he called. He glanced back at Owen, surprised to see the man flinch. He tried to make sense of it all, but found that all he could think of was the sound of Cara's scream and the pain etched on Owen's face. He'd seen that look when Owen had come to tell him about his mother.

"Michael?" Evidently the sound carried only one way. Patrick's light moved closer, bobbing up and down as though his brother was running.

"Don't move." Owen's words were not a question, but a command. Michael's brain cleared in an instant. "Turn around." The words were issued in a staccato bark Michael hardly recognized.

"Owen? What's this all about?" he asked, trying to keep his voice calm, but every inch of him was screaming for Cara. Slowly, he turned around.

Owen had a derringer pointed directly at his heart. His father's friend's eyes were narrowed and his face was shuttered with a cold mask Michael had never seen. "Throw your pistol over here," he said. He gestured with his gun.

Michael slowly drew his six-shooter from his jeans and threw it on the ground. "I don't understand."

Owen picked up the Colt, pocketing his tiny derringer, and smiled ruefully. "And I'd hoped you never would, but I think your brother has nosed his way into the answers."

"What answers, Owen?" *Keep him talking,* Michael's brain urged.

The Englishman laughed, and Michael shivered at the hatred and anger in the sound. "Ah, dear boy, 'tis your mother who should be answering these questions, not I."

Owen's eyes glittered in the candlelight, the blood on his face giving him a sinister look.

"My mother? What in hell does she have to do with this?" Michael felt a growing chill of understanding.

"Michael?" Patrick skidded to a stop as he came into the light, his eyes moving quickly from his brother to Owen. "Where's Cara?" His voice was low and intense, his attention focused completely on Owen.

"At the bottom of a very long hole, I'm afraid. Such a lovely girl. Rather like your mother. Stubborn to the end. Always ready to believe the worst." Owen's voice had lost the edge of rationality.

"What! Where is she?" Michael's voice echoed through the tunnel.

Owen waved the gun. "I told you, Michael, she fell down. Way down." His laughter held the echo of a madman.

Patrick tried to inch around Michael, his gun drawn.

"Drop it." Owen's lucidity was back with frightening clarity.

Patrick stopped, but didn't drop the gun. Michael heard its hammer click into place.

Owen stood his ground, Michael's Colt pointed not at Patrick, but still at Michael. "Shoot me if you dare, boy." There was a condescending note in his voice, almost as if he wanted Patrick to shoot. "But"—he waved his other hand in the air in a theatrical gesture—"I'll kill your brother, even if you do manage to shoot me." Again he let out his tortured laugh.

Patrick met Michael's eyes and he shrugged, disengaging the hammer and dropping the gun.

"Kick it over here," Owen barked.

Michael reached over with a booted foot and kicked the gun. It landed to the right of Owen in the shadows of the tunnel.

"That's not exactly at my feet," Owen said with a snarl, "but it will have to do. Now, move over there by the wall."

He gestured to the left side of the tunnel, away from the gun.

Michael met Patrick's gaze and tried desperately to read the message there.

"I said now!" Owen cocked his pistol, the sound echoing through the stillness of the tunnel.

Oh, God, she was destined to spend eternity in the dark. First the cave-in and now . . . Cara paused, trying to remember exactly what had happened. The rabbit hole. She sighed. At least Alice had been able to see. She'd had the white rabbit and the little glass table. Cara had, well, inky blackness and . . . roses.

She sniffed deeply, but the smell evaporated almost before she was certain it *was* roses. She shifted uncomfortably, realizing she was lying on a bed of rocks—sharp ones. Sitting up, she took hesitant inventory of her body, relieved when all parts reported in. Her ankle felt a little iffy, but for the moment, at least, there seemed no real pain. As long as she was seated, she was fine.

A sharp jabbing in her left hip stopped when she shifted to the right. Reaching across with her hand, she located the source of her discomfort—the candleholder. Wrought iron did not make a comfortable seat cushion, especially if it had a sharp point. There was no way to see the thing, but she recognized the feel of it, remembered the satisfying feel of it sinking into Owen Prescott's flesh.

She hoped it had hurt like hell.

For a moment she pictured Michael, and her heart twisted with agony, but then her mind stepped in with a public-service announcement about people stuck at the bottom of deep, dark rabbit holes. A picture of a long-forgotten episode of *All My Children* flashed in her mind.

Natalie at the bottom of a well.

That had ended happily, hadn't it? Oh, God, she didn't remember. She never watched regularly, and Natalie was off the show now. Had she died in the well? Cara forced back a swelling of hysteria. She wasn't Natalie, and Owen certainly wasn't Janet. *No,* whispered a perverse voice in her mind, *Owen is much worse.*

She struggled to gain control and was relieved when all the images, television and otherwise, disappeared and she was alone in the deep darkness, clutching a twisted piece of wrought iron. *Used for lighting,* her still-functioning brain pointed out. She frowned, the information failing to have significant impact.

Lighting, her brain repeated. She slapped a hand to her forehead and felt for the hooked end of the candleholder, finally getting the message. With a shaking hand she touched the candle. Wax had never felt so good.

Drawing the matches from her pocket, she lit one, relieved when the pale white light of her candle was finally casting a feeble circle into the darkness.

Let there be light.

There wasn't a white rabbit or a glass table. She'd known they wouldn't be there, but she was devastated nevertheless. Most likely because it meant that this wasn't a dream. And because it meant that there wasn't a sister at the top of the well. Only a madman and Michael.

Michael. God, she hoped he wouldn't fall into Owen's trap. The saloonkeeper was insane. She shook her head to clear it of the image of him. No use in borrowing problems she didn't have. Her main concern had to be getting out of here. And that was damn tough enough.

Her language was going to hell. So much for her parochial-school upbringing, but then again, the nuns hadn't covered what to do when one was pushed down a mine shaft. Probably even Sister Inez would allow for a few curse words in this situation.

She shook her head hard. She had to stay in control. No time for hysteria.

She struggled upright, wincing as she put weight on her right foot. It was not broken, at least, but it hurt, a lot. She focused on the flickering candlelight. Holding it away

335

from her body, she surveyed the shaft. Only about half of it was illuminated by her candle, and that part was frustratingly round, curling in an almost perfect semicircle without an opening to mar the arc. *Damn.*

She limped forward, holding her candle high so that the other half of the shaft was illuminated. The light glanced off ivory, and two black eyeholes stared back at her. She bit back a scream and tightened her grip on the candle. The bony hollows sat above a skeletal grin.

Her heart lurched and descended a moment for a conference with her stomach. Cara could only stare at the remains—all that was left of a person. Her cellmate, so to speak. Cellmate*s.* Her stomach twisted again as she spotted a second skull. This one looked somehow gentler than the first, smaller. Perhaps it was the skull of a woman or child.

Her stomach heaved, then settled, her mind screaming at her to find a way to escape. She circled the cavern looking for an exit. There wasn't any. What had once been a tunnel to the left was now nothing more than a pile of shale and rubble, the pair of skeletons marking the heap with frightening punctuation. There was no exit except up. This was the end of the line.

The smiling skulls seemed to mock her, and she turned away to avoid their knowing gazes. A glint of something caught her eye as she turned, and she bent with the candle to see what it was. A band of gold encircled the smaller skeleton's bony finger. Cara fought with her stomach, heart, and brain before she found the strength to reach for it. With a deeply drawn breath and a mumbled apology, she snatched the ring away.

The gold was smooth from years of wear, the faint pattern of etched flowers almost faded from the band. A wedding ring. She held it up into the soft glow of the candlelight. *R. O., D. M., 1858.* Initials. A date. Her sluggish mind processed the information.

D. M.—*Duncan Macpherson?* Her mind clicked. *R. O.*—

Rose O'Malley! Oh, God. Now she knew what had happened.

She looked at the remains of Michael's mother and what had to be Zach, then took a deep, but not particularly cleansing breath. What did one say to the dead? She sank to the ground, leaning back against a wall, her right hand still clenched around Rose's wedding ring, her head inches from Zach's skull. She ran her left hand over the cool silver of Loralee's locket, tears filling her eyes. So many dreams . . .

Michael grabbed Patrick's elbow, recognizing his brother's need to fight. But that would only get them both killed. "We need to find Cara," he whispered, and his brother nodded in mute acceptance. They moved to the wall of the tunnel.

"I see you both remember how to follow orders." Owen sounded smug, almost relieved.

Michael had to bite his tongue to keep from responding. Patrick had no such self-restraint. "You killed our mother." The words were harsh, pain-filled.

Owen narrowed his eyes. "No," he said angrily. A mad look filled his eyes, and he shook his head. "She killed herself."

"Why?" Patrick asked. "Because she loved Father more than you?"

"She loved *me*." The words were clipped, explosive.

Michael was beginning to follow Patrick's intent. "She never loved anyone but our father," he added. "You know that, Owen."

He threw the words out, trying for distraction. What he got was rage—a rage so fierce and out of control, he felt his brother flinch.

"She loved me," Owen said again.

"No." The word was salvation, the two brothers finally understanding what had happened so many years before, but Patrick spewed it almost as if it were an obscenity.

"She always loved me. That's why I did it," Owen retaliated.

"Did what?" *Keep him talking*, Michael's brain demanded. Patrick was face-forward against the tunnel. Michael had opted for a less conciliatory stance, his back to the rock wall.

"Killed her."

Michael felt sick inside. "*You* killed her, Owen?"

"I had to."

The man in front of him shrank some, and Michael swallowed back bile. "Why?"

"She wouldn't come with me." Owen sounded like a three-year-old who hadn't gotten his way.

"When you offered her the silver?" Patrick asked, his back still to the saloonkeeper.

Owen leveled the gun, his chest heaving in and out. "I offered her more than the damn silver. I offered her my life." He waited for some reaction, and when he got none, he continued. "Duncan led her on. Year after year he promised her the moon, but never, *never* did he deliver."

Michael couldn't argue about his father's faults, but the fact was, his mother had loved his father despite those flaws. They hadn't mattered. Which made him think of Cara. *Was she still alive?* His mind fastened on the idea—she had to be alive.

"She turned you down. All of it. She turned you down," Patrick hissed.

Owen's face twisted with anger. "I did it all for her, and she had the audacity to say no. No one says no to Owen Prescott, no one."

"What about Zach?"

Owen waved his gun. "Oh, he was simple enough. I used my rifle. The man was dead before he knew what happened."

Michael took a step forward.

Owen pointed the gun at his head. "Move back."

Michael obliged him. "But surely you didn't expect my

338

mother to fall into your arms after you murdered her friend?"

Owen looked surprised. "He wasn't her friend. He was a no account muleskinner. Beneath her notice. It never occurred to me that he might *matter* to her."

Michael was stunned.

"But he was a husband and a father," Patrick put in.

Owen shrugged, obviously not comprehending the relevance of Patrick's statement. "He was nobody. And if he did have a wife, she was nobody as well."

"So you proposed to do what?" Michael asked. "Take my mother away from all the murder and mayhem?" The sarcasm was wasted.

"Of course," Owen said. "She deserved better."

"And you were the one to give it to her?" Patrick's jaw tightened, his hand moving between his body and the wall.

"I was the only one who could give it to her," Owen snarled.

Michael grimaced. "But she didn't *want* you."

Owen's face flushed with fury. "No. She only wanted your father. The stupid woman couldn't see what was right in front of her eyes. She called me a murderer and a traitor. Me! Who'd loved her since New York . . ." He broke off.

"So you killed her." Patrick's voice was calm but firm.

Owen cocked his head, looked at them both. "I killed her." The pronouncement was absolute.

Michael needed to know. It was probably perverse, but he needed to know. "So then you took the silver?"

"Well, after I'd killed them I couldn't exactly leave it lying around, could I? And I couldn't just sell it. Thanks to your father it was readily identifiable." Owen sounded almost disdainful.

"The rose."

"Yes." The Englishman sighed. "It's a pity you two had to figure this out. I had hoped to avoid the unpleasantness." He cocked the trigger on his gun.

"So, what? You hid the silver?" Patrick asked.

Dee Davis

"Right here. Under your father's nose. I used the lower level. One of the tunnels we'd abandoned. I hid it in some old machinery."

"But father found it. That's why you killed him."

"The drunken bastard. Always nosing around. I should have melted the damn stuff and sold it off."

"Why didn't you?"

"I got lazy." Owen shrugged. "Truth is, it was more work than it was worth. I didn't need the money, and I never thought anyone would find it. Besides, I liked knowing it was here, right under everyone's nose."

"But when Father found it, he moved it," Michael prompted.

"The stupid ass."

"But if you didn't need it, why go to all this trouble?" Patrick frowned. "Why not let someone else find it and cart it away?"

"Because sooner or later the story was going to come out. You were already starting to ask questions, Patrick. And Michael was a wildcard. I didn't know if he was alive or dead. I have Striker to thank for that."

"So you killed him," Michael said, trying to make sense where there obviously was none.

Owen shrugged. "It was kill him or kill you, and he'd outgrown his usefulness. I had to tie up my loose ends."

"Like us?" The pain in Patrick's voice was almost palpable.

Owen sighed. "As I said, I was trying to avoid this."

"But now, just like this, it's over? Your loyalty to our family—*to me*—was all a lie?"

"I loved you in my own fashion, I suppose." Owen waved the gun in Patrick's direction. "Michael, too, for that matter. But in the end, you're both like your mother. You'd rather be with your father than me. The old bastard didn't deserve what he had."

"More than you, Owen." Patrick's words were whispered, his voice tight with emotion. "More than you."

"Spoken just like a good son," Owen sneered. "Which brings us full circle, I'm afraid."

Michael started to move, to lunge forward, but he caught his brother's eye and froze. "Wait," Patrick mouthed, his gaze darting downward significantly. Michael followed his eyes, sucking in a startled breath. Patrick had a second gun concealed between the wall and his body.

"One more move like that and my Rose is a mother without children." Owen shot into the air to prove his point and rocks rained down around their heads.

Patrick seized the moment. He swung around, gun blazing.

Owen fired in response, but it was too late; the shot went wild, and he dropped to his knees, clutching his chest, his eyes locked on Patrick, his expression one of disbelief. One minute he was frozen; the next he collapsed, twitched once and was still.

Patrick let out a long breath, somewhere between a moan and a sigh. "He never really understood."

Michael laid a hand on his brother's shoulder. "Understood what?"

"That it is all about family. Always about family." Patrick lifted his head, tears making his eyes seem bright in the flickering darkness, the gun dangling from one hand. "We take care of our own, Michael, and it was my turn."

Michael squeezed his shoulder, realizing his brother was no longer a boy. Somewhere in all that had happened, Patrick had found his way. He'd grown into a man.

"Patrick?" Loralee's frightened scream reached them just before she ran into the circle of light. She skidded to a halt, her eyes wide as she took in the two of them standing over Owen's body. "I heard gunshots. I couldn't wait outside where you told me. I thought . . . I thought . . ."

"We're all right."

"Is he dead?" Her eyes searched Patrick's face, and he nodded.

"Did he . . . ?"

Again Patrick nodded. "My mother—and Zach."

"Then I'm glad the bastard is dead." Loralee pulled in a shaky breath, searching the darkness. "Where's Cara?"

"I don't know." Michael felt as if the words were wrenched from him.

Patrick grabbed his shoulders. "Where were she and Owen before this started?"

Michael drew in a deep breath, forcing control. She might still be alive. She might still need him. And he'd promised he'd be there. "That way." He pointed into the darkness, moved in that direction. "In tunnel northwest-three."

Chapter Thirty-two

Owen Prescott.

Cara leaned back against the wall, anger washing through her. *God damn him.* The man had destroyed two marriages, and now he was intent on destroying her life and Michael's.

She glanced over at her two companions, wondering if they had found peace. She touched the silver of her locket, Loralee's locket, and thought of the love it embodied, of Loralee, Zach, and Mary.

Her hand tightened around the ring, a symbol for Duncan and Rose's love, and suddenly she knew that love was the magic. It was the one thing that Owen Prescott couldn't destroy. No matter how many lies he told or how many lives he took, the love would live on.

Forever.

Which made her realize Loralee was right. The future was an unwritten page, and the only thing standing in Cara's way was her own fear. It had kept her locked inside herself, unwilling to give love—to give life—a chance. It had trapped her in that time tunnel, almost taken her life.

Michael's love had carried her safely out of the dark, but now it was up to her to take herself the rest of the way. The decision was hers, and it had been all along. She had to believe in Michael, to believe in their love. In the end if she'd let it, love would truly conquer all.

Suddenly, in the darkness of the cavern, in the flickering light of her candle, with two skeletal witnesses who'd long ago joined the ranks of the angels, Cara realized that no matter what tomorrow brought—past, present, or future— her place was with Michael.

Always and forever.

She stumbled to her feet, her heart pounding, praying that her epiphany hadn't come too late, that her fears hadn't contributed to Owen winning the day. With trembling hands, she felt along the rough-hewn walls of the shaft, trying to find handholds, a way to climb out.

She had to reach Michael, to stop Owen from hurting him. She pushed up off of the floor of the mine shaft, her fingers jammed into a crevice, her other hand groping for purchase. She managed to climb a foot or so before her hand met nothing but roughly shorn rock. Nothing to hang on to, she tried to cling to the wall, but her arms were too tired and she couldn't support herself.

With a cry of frustration, she let go, dropping back to the floor, the grinning skeletons a testament to her failure. She fought for control, but her nerves were shot. Michael was up there somewhere, alone with a madman. And there was nothing she could do.

Nothing at all.

If she got out of this, she would never again refuse the opportunity to have Michael's love—for however long it was granted her. Now all she could do was wait.

"Cara?" A voice filtered down through the dark, and Cara's grief-numbed brain struggled to respond. It called again, its tone insistent, urgent.

Cara blinked, trying to focus, her brain finally clicking

into gear. Michael? The voice belonged to Michael! Adrenaline surged on the wings of hope, and she scrambled to her feet. She winced as her weight fell on her injured ankle, but her eyes locked on the light shining from the top of the shaft. "I'm here. Michael, I'm here."

"Are you hurt?" The concern in his voice carried down to her, washing through her, rejuvenating.

"I'm fine. It's just . . . Is Owen there?"

"He's dead." The words drifted down to her and she felt a rush of relief.

"Cara?" Michael's voice was gentle. "I'm going for the rope. I'll be right back. Hang on, sweetheart."

The light disappeared again, this time completely. She settled back onto the floor of the shaft, leaning back against the hard wall.

Owen Prescott was dead. It was finally over.

"Just a few more feet," Michael called.

Cara could see his face now. It was strained from the effort of pulling her out, but it had never looked so wonderful. With one last tug she was up and over, his arms pulling her onto the rocky floor of the tunnel. She rolled onto her back, gasping for breath, and smiled up at the three pairs of eyes staring down at her—Loralee, Patrick, and Michael, all present and accounted for.

She sat up slowly and began to fumble with the knotted rope around her waist, her hands shaking too badly to accomplish much of anything. Michael knelt beside her, his hands covering hers. "I'll do it."

With something approaching reverence, he untied the knot and slid the rope away, his hands leaving a trail of fire where they touched. With a groan, he pulled her forward, settling her on his lap, his lips taking possession of hers. She opened her mouth, drinking in the taste of him, knowing she would never be able to get enough.

"Mm-hmm." Patrick cleared his throat loudly. "Not to interrupt, but I think we ought to think about getting out of here." As if in echo of the sentiment, the mine walls began to rumble ominously, the noise crescendoing and then dying away. "All the shooting has made things a bit unstable." Patrick pointed at a timber that had cracked. Dirt was trickling from the ceiling.

Cara scrambled to her feet, reaching into the pocket of her jeans. "Wait a minute. You need to see this." She handed Rose's ring to Michael. He stood up and held it to the light.

"My God, was this . . . ?" He looked down into the dark shaft.

"Yes, I . . . I took it off her finger. I figured she'd want you to have it." What had seemed right in the dark of the mine shaft suddenly felt wrong in the flickering light of his candle.

But her fear was short-lived. Michael handed the ring to his brother and pulled Cara into his arms. "You did the right thing. She can rest now."

"Is she alone down there?" Loralee's question was low, almost unintelligible.

Cara broke away from Michael and reached for her great-grandmother's hand. "No. Zach was there, too. At least, I think it's your husband."

Loralee nodded. "Is he . . . I mean, was he . . ."

Cara tightened her fingers around Loralee's. "I think he's at peace, too. I have a feeling he knows about Mary and you. About how much you loved him." Again she ducked her head in embarrassment. There just weren't any words.

The mine shook again, this time sending down a shower of rocks and pebbles. The timber cracked and fell forward, leaving a yawning cavity behind. Cara froze as the candle-light glittered off of something wedged behind the fallen beam. It spilled out of the opening, falling with a thud to the ground below. It was a bar of silver. She moved closer and, inside the cavity, saw stacks of bars, each marked with a single rose.

"The silver!" Cara breathed the words just as Patrick and Loralee said them almost in unison.

The walls shuddered again, and she was thrown off balance, stumbling forward, her hands out to break her fall. Her left hand slammed into the pile of gleaming metal, pain shooting up her arm. Strong hands grasped her elbows, pulling her upright.

"We've got to get out of here." Michael's voice was hard to hear over the cracking and groaning of the mine. The whole place was beginning to break up. Large chunks of rock and timber were falling everywhere. Dust swirled, filling the air.

"What about the silver?" Patrick yelled above the din.

"Leave it!" Michael's words were sharp, and he was already moving toward the main tunnel.

Cara choked on the dust, and Michael pulled her closer, protecting her from the falling debris. As they came through the opening into the main tunnel, the shoring broke and crashed to the ground behind them. Cara whirled, her eyes searching the swirling grime for Loralee.

"Patrick!" Michael yelled, his voice lost in the rumbling.

Cara waited, her heart beating out the seconds; then suddenly the pair was there, emerging from the cloud of dust. "Which way?" Patrick mouthed, and Michael motioned toward the glimmer of light at the east end of the tunnel. With a nod, the younger MacPherson ushered Loralee forward. Michael's arm tightened around Cara and they hurried forward, too, dodging and ducking as the walls crumbled around them, rushing, literally, for the light at the end of the tunnel.

They burst out into the bright afternoon light, onto a rock shelf on the cliff face high above the stream below. After the gloom of the mine, the light was almost blinding. The wooden planks inside the mine shuddered as the tremors from the collapsing tunnels rippled outward. Cara looked down at the tiny ribbon of the creek beneath them. "I don't suppose there's any other way?"

Michael squeezed her shoulder and pointed at the ore cars, like the one she'd almost died on before. "You're looking at it."

She eyed the cables with resignation. "I guess it was pre-ordained."

The platform shuddered again, the mine exit collapsing into a solid wall of timber and rock. Michael shoved her toward a car already occupied by Loralee. "There's no more time. It's now or never."

Cara looked deeply into his eyes. "I choose now." She kissed him and jumped into the already moving car. With one last shove, she and Loralee were airborne.

As Cara locked her arms around her great-grandmother's waist, Loralee's laughter filled the air. "I've always wondered what it felt like to fly," she cried out.

The landing wasn't quite as wonderful as the takeoff. The little car jerked as it hit the bottom station and ground to a halt. Michael's car skidded to a stop inches from theirs, bumping them as it landed on the platform. Behind Michael, Loralee heard Patrick swearing as his tramcar slammed down with a crunching thud.

Well, at least everybody was in one piece.

"You all right?" Loralee turned to look at Cara. Her eyes were still tightly closed. "We're on the ground."

Cara opened an eye. "You're sure?"

"Yes, indeedy, and we all made the trip just fine."

Cara opened both eyes, looking relieved when she saw the inside of the rickety building. "So how do we get out of here?" The two women laughed, giddy with relief as they worked to untangle arms and legs and climb out of the car. Finally they were each in charge of their own limbs again. Loralee stood up and took the hand Cara offered. Clutching petticoats to belly, knickers in full display, she straddled the ore bucket, one foot in, one foot out.

"Here, let me help." Michael stood by Cara, his amused gaze taking in the show.

The Promise

Despite the fact that many a man had seen her in a heck of a lot less than her knickers, Loralee felt the heat of a blush steal across her cheeks. "Thank you kindly, but I can manage." She stepped out of the bucket, quickly releasing cotton and lace, allowing her skirts to tumble back into a more ladylike position. The clatter of metal striking metal filled the tiny station as several silver bars tumbled out of her skirt and onto the platform.

Loralee froze, her eyes on the silver, purposely avoiding Michael's gaze. Patrick stepped to her side, his face the perfect picture of a little boy caught with his hand in the cookie jar. "We, ah, hated to see it all go to waste."

"It was my idea," Loralee put in hastily, trying to judge Michael's reaction.

"You could have been killed." Michael spoke softly, but there was a tremor in his voice.

"But we weren't," Patrick argued.

"Michael?" Cara stood by the ore car, looking like a cat who'd swallowed a canary. She slowly pulled two silver bars from the pockets of her own pants.

He ran a hand through his hair. "You, too?"

She smiled and shrugged. "It seemed like such a waste. And they were right there."

Michael sighed and removed a bar from the waistband of his pants. "I guess we all had the same idea."

Everybody started laughing at once, and what started as a tickle soon dissolved into hysterics. They were all suddenly hugging everybody else and chortling, until Loralee figured they were bound to have used up all the laughter they had between them.

Loralee was the first to sober, and she walked to the edge of the platform, looking up at the remains of the mine.

"You thinking of Zach?" Cara asked, coming to stand beside her.

"Yes. I know his bones are trapped up there, under all those rocks, but somehow I think his spirit is free." She sighed, her eyes still on the mine. He'd kept his promise, never broken it. She knew that now. Her hand automatically reached for her locket, surprised when she found nothing there.

"I think maybe you're looking for this," Cara said, handing her the necklace.

Loralee's hand closed around the familiar silver and a feeling of absolute serenity settled around her. Yes, indeedy, Zach Bowen was doing just fine. And now that she thought about it, so was she.

She held the locket back out to her great-granddaughter. "You keep it. I suspect you need it now more than me. It's the key to your going back."

Michael's face tightened at the words, but he didn't say anything.

Cara waved it away. "No, it's yours, Loralee. Zach gave it to you. And you in turn need to pass it along to Mary. A little piece of her father." She reached up and laid a hand against Michael's cheek. "Besides, I have everything I could ever want right here."

Loralee fastened the chain around her neck, turning once more to look at the mine perched high against the rocky cliff.

"Godspeed, Zachariah. Godspeed."

"Did you mean what you said?" Michael's voice was cracking with emotion.

"You mean about having everything I want?" Cara whispered, knowing her heart was reflected in her eyes. "Of course I did. Do you want me to say it again?"

He nodded, his jaw set, drinking her in with his blazing blue eyes.

"Everything I want is standing right in front of me, Michael Macpherson. I love you. I think maybe I always have."

"And you don't want to go back to your own time?" He looked worried.

"No, I want to be here with you. Now and for always."
She kissed him lightly on the nose. "That is, if you still
want me."

"Want you?" Michael exploded. "I want you every single moment of the day, with every breath I take." He tightened his hold on her shoulders and drew a shaky breath.
"I love you, Cara Reynolds, and I'll do everything in my
power to give you the best that life in any century has to
offer."

"Well," she smiled up into his eyes and whispered,
"there is one thing."

"Name it."

"I'd really like a shower."

His eyes sparkled as he pulled her to him, his mouth
tracing hot circles along the line of her jaw, his hand skill-
fully massaging the back of her neck. "Now *that*, my love,
is an absolutely marvelous idea."

They stood on the platform of the turning station looking
up at the ruins of the Promise. A hazy cloud of dust still
hung over what had been the entrance. Timbers hung at
crazy angles, leaning drunkenly against each other. One
shifted and fell end over end, crashing against the hard
rock of the cliff, a last tumbling testament to man's insig-
nificant attempt to conquer the mountain.

Michael stared at the remains, his mother's tomb, and
wondered if it had all been worth it. Cara stirred in the
circle of his arms, her golden head lifted up to the cliff.
The sun came out from behind a cloud, its rays catching
particles of dust that glittered and twinkled in the light;
then with a last flash the rays were gone, leaving only the
magnificence of the sun-washed mountain.

He tightened his arms around Cara, the day suddenly
seeming bright with promise.

Chapter Thirty-three

Silverthread, one month later

The railroad station was busy, the small frame building teeming with people. They were mostly miners—the wide-eyed hopefuls in search of their fortune, and the weary-eyed wounded heading home with empty pockets.

And Loralee was leaving it all behind.

She watched as Patrick tipped an elderly porter. The old man hoisted her brand-new trunk, settling it on his shoulder with the ease of long practice. She clasped her gloved hands together and wondered for the hundredth time if she was doing the right thing.

Patrick started back toward her, his green eyes narrowed against the noontime sun. "All taken care of." He took her hand in his. "You're sure this is what you want?" His voice was low, and held in tight control.

She nodded. "I need to be with Mary. She's got a right to know her ma."

"But you could do that here."

She sighed, tipping her head back to meet his solemn gaze. "Folks here know who I am, what I was, and no one

The Promise

is likely to ever let me forget it. I want more than that, Patrick. For her, if not for me."

He drew in a deep breath, his mouth settling into a thin line, but he didn't say anything.

She licked her lips nervously, reaching out to cover his hand with hers. "You could come with me." She wasn't sure why she asked; there wasn't anything between them—only the promise of things that would never be.

He released his breath with a sigh. "You know I can't do that."

She nodded, the plume of her hat bobbing in front of her face. "I suppose I do."

"Loralee, my brother has spent all of his life trying to make a home for our family. And now I'm the only one he has left."

"He's got Cara." She heard the pleading in her voice and she was ashamed. The right thing to do was to let him go. She'd always known there was no chance for them. It was silly to wish for things she couldn't have.

"It's not the same, and you know it. He built Clune for *me*, Loralee. I can't just run off and leave him here on his own. We're partners. Hell, it's more than that. We're brothers. And I never appreciated it before. I belong here, with him."

"And I belong with my Mary." Which left them right where they'd started. She bit her bottom lip, trying to prevent the threatening tears. Her sadness was interrupted.

"Thank God you're still here! I was afraid we'd missed you." Cara rushed up the platform steps, taking them two at a time.

Loralee smiled. Her great-granddaughter wasn't fond of nineteenth-century clothing. At the moment she was wearing men's jeans with one of Michael's flannel shirts, the tails knotted carelessly at her waist. The only concession she'd made to this time period was her boots, and she constantly complained about that, saying that there simply wasn't anything that could compare with a good pair of

Dee Davis

Nikes—whatever the heck those were. "I'm glad you came."

Cara swept her into an exuberant hug. "We would have been here sooner, but Pete wanted Michael to take a look at one of the horses. Something with his foot, I think. Anyway, Michael said the trains always run late."

"And I was right." Arriving behind them, Michael draped an arm around his bride of three weeks, pulling her close to his side.

Cara laughed. "Listen to me running on. Have you got everything you need?"

"More than that. I can't get over all this frippery." She gestured to the blue satin morning dress and matching hat. In all her born days she'd never worn such beautiful clothes.

"You have to look your best when you get to Richmond." Cara reached out to tuck a strand of hair back into the new chignon Loralee wore. They'd copied it out of the Sears catalog.

"It's more like I'm playacting."

"You look beautiful." The tenderness in Patrick's voice made Loralee's knees feel like taffy on a hot summer day.

"There's the conductor," Michael said.

"I guess it's time." Loralee smiled at the three people who'd come to mean so much to her, but she couldn't quite make herself meet Patrick's gaze.

Cara hugged her again, pressing a small white envelope into her hand. "This is for you and Mary."

Loralee could feel the bills inside. "I can't, I mean—"

"It's not much, just our share of the money from the silver. We want you to have it."

Loralee felt the tears threatening again. "Thank you," she whispered, kissing Cara's cheek.

Cara pulled back, her cheeks wet with tears. "That's what family is for."

Loralee looked at Michael. "Thanks for all of this. The clothes, the luggage, all of it."

"I think Zach more than earned it, Loralee." He gave her a quick hug and then stepped back, pulling Cara with him. "You know you have a home here anytime you want it."

She nodded, afraid to try to say anything else. They meant so much to her. She'd never had a real family before. Except for Mary. Everything always came back to her daughter.

She turned to face Patrick. His look was guarded, as if he had already put distance between them. She tried not to feel hurt. After all, they were just friends. It was best if they got on with their own lives and forgot about each other. She just hadn't expected it to happen like this.

"It's time." He held out his arm, and she placed a hand on his elbow—just like a real lady, a respectable lady.

They stopped at the train steps and stood for a moment simply looking at each other. She tried to memorize each little detail of his face. The way his hair fell forward into his eyes. The way his mouth curled a little higher on one side than the other.

The whistle blew a warning, and Patrick lifted her up to the bottom step of the train. This was it, then. Time for good-bye. Without saying anything or asking, he kissed her once—hard—then turned away, walking back to Cara and Michael. Back to where he belonged.

She sighed and stepped into the train. A new life awaited her in Virginia. A better life. It was best to close doors and move on. She'd managed just fine without Patrick Macpherson. And she'd just have to keep right on doing it. Squaring her shoulders, she settled into the high-backed velvet seat.

But, lordy, it was going to be hard.

Patrick stood stone-faced watching a few last-minute passengers scurry to board the train. This was it. She was really going. Up until this moment, he'd kept the hope that she'd change her mind. He should have told her how he felt. Should have stood up for himself and his feelings.

"You okay?"

He looked over into the worried eyes of his sister-in-law. "Yes. No. Hell, I don't know. I guess I thought maybe she'd stay."

"She can't, Patrick."

"Why the hell not?" His eyes went back to the train.

"Because here she'd never be anything but a whore. And she deserves a whole lot more than that."

"I know." He said the words with conviction. It was the one thing of which he was certain. Loralee deserved the world. It was just that somewhere deep inside, he'd hoped he'd be the one to give it to her. But that was impossible. She belonged in Virginia and he belonged here—at Clune.

In a way he envied Loralee. She was getting a clean slate—a chance to start over. The events of the past few days had changed him forever, forced him to face himself, to grow up. He stared at the train. It taunted him. Just a few short steps and he could find his own way, be whoever he wanted to be, but that would mean turning his back on his responsibilities, and he couldn't—*wouldn't*—do that anymore.

"You've got to live your own life, Patrick." Michael's words were uncannily accurate—as if he'd read his mind. They stood shoulder to shoulder, watching the train.

"But my life is here . . . with you."

"Only if you want it to be. Patrick, you'll always belong here. But that doesn't mean you have to stay."

"But I . . ." He trailed off, still looking at the train. He wanted to go, needed to go, but he also needed his brother. Or did he? Maybe he was falling right back into the same old patterns, Michael taking the lead. He turned to look at his brother. Their eyes met and held, a lifetime of emotions reflected there.

"Go." There was finality in his brother's voice—and freedom.

The train began to inch forward.

The Promise

"Hurry." Cara's soft plea roused him to action.

Patrick ran across the platform toward the moving cars and leaped for the steps, grabbing the handrail, swinging up onto the train. Balanced precariously on the top step, he turned for a last look. They stood together, waving, arms looped around each other. Michael and Cara. Patrick smiled. His brother would be all right. Owen was dead. The evil that had been a part of their lives for so long was gone. Vanquished.

It was a time for new beginnings. His own, too.

He raised his hand in final farewell, and then turned to go into the railcar. One life was behind him; another was about to begin.

Cara stepped back, looking at the painting with a critical eye. *Not bad. Maybe a little more gray in the mountains.* She bit her bottom lip, looking from subject to easel, then back again. The ranch lay spread out below her, the bright summer sun outlining each building with streaks of white. Wildflowers ran rampant up here on the bluff and down in the meadow below. Monet would have had a field day.

She smiled, tucking an impudent strand of hair behind her ear, her mind focusing once again on the painting. A wooden cross provided a focal point for it. The monument occupied the left corner of the canvas, looking as if it, too, were viewing the valley below: Duncan Macpherson surveying his kingdom.

Her gaze moved to the real marker, trying to gauge her accuracy. *Perhaps a little darker shadow, or more red . . .*

Behind her, Jack's bridle jingled as he munched wildflowers. He was worse than a goat. If they ever needed anything mowed, he was certainly the horse for the job. She looked at him. As if aware of her thoughts, he raised his shaggy head, ears twitching, listening to a sound only he could hear. Cara followed the line of his sight. A lone rider appeared, making his way across the bluff.

Cara reached for her rifle, but stopped when the old

horse whinnied a welcome. A second later she recognized the silhouette.

Michael.

Shading her eyes with one hand, she watched her husband approach. He sat easily in the saddle, his dark hair blowing in the breeze. They'd been married almost a month now, and still just the sight of him sent her heart pounding. She'd never have been happy anywhere but with him.

"I thought I'd find you here." He reached her and brought his horse to a stop. His warm smile made her knees turn to jelly. "Can I see?" He swung down from the saddle and walked toward the painting.

"It isn't finished yet." She followed him, her critical eye already finding fault with her work.

Michael stood back, arms crossed, studying the canvas. She held her breath, staring at the crimson roses climbing the weather-worn cross, hoping he would like what he saw, understand what she was trying to portray.

"The roses." He pointed to the flowers twining around the pine. "They're my mother, aren't they? She's found him again. In death, if not in life, she's finally come home."

Cara slipped her arms around his waist and leaned her head against the broad expanse of his shoulder. "I'm the one who's finally come home."

"No regrets?" His eyes held both the question and something more.

She smiled up at him. "None at all. I belong here, Michael, with you. Nothing makes me happier."

"Not even painting?" He nodded at the canvas.

She turned to face him, her gaze locking on his. "Not even that."

He smiled slowly, then bent his head, his lips taking possession of hers, his hands stroking the contours of her hips and back. The painting was forgotten as he lifted her into his arms and laid her carefully on a bed of wildflowers, his need etched across his face.

With skillful hands he stroked her body, buttons yielding to a masterful touch. Quickly naked, she smiled and opened herself to him. It was easy, knowing she already belonged to him body and soul.

Braced on his arms, their bodies joined, he looked down at her, his heart reflected in the cobalt of his eyes. "I love you, Cara Macpherson."

"No more than I love you," she whispered in answer. "Forever."

And there on the mountain, among flowers and grasses, rocks and pines, they made love. The only witnesses were a white wooden cross and a wild red rose.

Epilogue

Silverthread, Colorado, present day

"This is amazing." Margaret Wagner stood in front of the painting, her eyes riveted on the canvas in front of her. "Is it for sale?" She pulled away from the powerful brushstrokes to focus her attention on the vivacious blond who ran the gallery.

"No." Carrie Macpherson came to stand beside her. "That one belongs to me. My great-great-grandmother painted it."

"You're kidding." Margaret frowned, her gaze returning to the haunting imagery of the dilapidated mine, stark against the wild beauty of the mountains. "When?"

"In 1891. The mine belonged to her father-in-law—my great-great-*great*-grandfather." Carrie smiled, her green eyes lighting with the gesture. "The money they made was used to build up my family's ranch."

"Well it's fabulous. If it were for sale, I'd buy it in an instant."

"You're not the first one to say that, but I'm afraid I could never part with it. It's a legacy of sorts."

Margaret nodded, fighting disappointment. "There's just something about it that calls to me. It's almost as if there's a secret there—a story embedded somehow in paint and brushwork."

"There's always a story, isn't there?" Carrie's gaze met hers, her face inscrutable, and Margaret had the distinct feeling that the gallery owner was talking about more than just the painting.

"Do you have more of her work?"

"Some. Not nearly as much as I'd like."

"I'm only asking because I saw a similar painting in New York once. It was the most marvelous thing I'd ever seen. And this"—she gestured to the painting—"is almost identical in style."

It was Carrie's turn to nod. "I've had other people mistake her paintings for modern work."

"Well, I can see why. There's certainly a timeless quality about them. Something almost magical." Margaret sighed. "Anyway, I guess I'm destined to see but never own. The other painting wasn't for sale either. I looked for more work by the artist, but never found any. I suppose she just stopped painting."

"Maybe," Carrie said, smiling up at her great-great-grandmother's canvas. "Or perhaps she simply had other promises to keep."

MADELINE BAKER

Chase the Lightning

Amanda can't believe her eyes when the beautiful white stallion
appears in her yard with a wounded man on its back. Dark and
ruggedly handsome, the stranger fascinates her. He has about
him an aura of danger and desire that excites her in a way her
law-abiding fiancé never had. But something doesn't add up:
Trey seems bewildered by the amenities of modern life; he wants
nothing to do with the police; and he has a stack of 1863 bank
notes in his saddlebags. Then one soul-stirring kiss makes it all
clear—Trey may have held up a bank and stolen through time,
but when he takes her love it will be no robbery, but a gift of the
heart.

___4917-1 $5.99 US/$6.99 CAN

GABRIEL'S FATE

EMMA CRAIG

Sophie Madrigal tells the fortunes of anyone curious enough to pass the velvet curtain of her makeshift parlor—and Gabriel Caine is just such a man. The black-clad bounty hunter is on the hunt for a murderer, and nothing will stop him from bagging his prize. So when the gorgeous Gabriel laughingly offers his palm, Sophie feels compelled to reveal everything . . . or almost everything. What Sophie doesn't divulge is that she, too, appears in his future. Or that she is at a loss to explain the heady scent of sweet spice that swirls around her whenever Gabriel is near. "Magic," claims her wise old aunt, and Sophie fears the woman must be right. For nothing short of magic—unless it is love—could have ensnared her so completely in Gabriel's fate.

___52429-5 $5.99 US/$6.99 CAN

STOBIE PIEL BLUE-EYED BANDIT

Darian Woodward had been a hero in the War Between the States, but somewhere he's been blown off course. Unjustly ruined by a superior officer, the handsome soldier turns to crime. His blue eyes and daring deeds earn him a name throughout the old Southwest, but bandits seek gold, and this gunfighter's interests are entirely different. Fate has blown in a sexier bounty.

Though she is swept away by it, Emily Morgan is less awed by the mystic whirlwind that carries her into the past than by the handsome desperado who greets her. Joining the man's close-knit band of outlaws, Emily learns the fun of being bad—but also its dangers. And when the Feds come to capture her Blue-Eyed Bandit, Emily will prove that Western justice has its limits, and that true love can break any laws—even those of time and space.

___52394-9 $5.50 US/$6.50 CAN

Dorchester Publishing Co., Inc.
P.O. Box 6640
Wayne, PA 19087-8640

Please add $1.75 for shipping and handling for the first book and $.50 for each book thereafter. NY, NYC, and PA residents, please add appropriate sales tax. No cash, stamps, or C.O.D.s. All orders shipped within 6 weeks via postal service book rate. Canadian orders require $2.00 extra postage and must be paid in U.S. dollars through a U.S. banking facility.

Name_____
Address_____
City_____State_____Zip_____
I have enclosed $ _____ in payment for the checked book(s).
Payment <u>must</u> accompany all orders. ❑ Please send a free catalog.
CHECK OUT OUR WEBSITE! www.dorchesterpub.com

IN THE SHADOW OF THE MOON

KAREN WHITE

A lunar eclipse. A twentieth-century comet. And suddenly, thoroughly modern Laura Truitt is swept off mysterious Moon Mountain, away from her enchanting Southern home—and over one hundred years into the past. . . .

There, dashing Confederate soldier Stuart Elliott whisks her to his eerily familiar plantation, and his powerful masculinity evokes impossible desires. But the Civil War rages, forging unspeakable danger, threatening to wrench Laura from Stuart's arms. She must await the moon's magic to come full circle. But will it carry her back to the future, heartbroken and alone? Or keep her with Stuart in this passionate, perilous past?

___52395-7 $4.99 US/$5.99 CAN

TESS MALLORY
HIGHLAND DREAM

When Jix Ferguson's dream reveals that her best friend is making a terrible mistake and marrying the wrong guy, she tricks Samantha into flying to Scotland. There the two women met the man Jix is convinced her friend should marry—Jamie MacGregor. He is handsome, smart, perfect . . . the only problem is, Jix falls for him, too. Then a slight scuffle involving the Scot's ancestral sword sends all three back to the start of the seventeenth century—where MacGregors are outlaws and hunted. All Jix has to do is marry Griffin Campbell, steal Jamie's sword back from their captor, and find a way to return herself and her friends to their own time. Oh yeah, and she has to fall in love. It isn't going to be easy, but in this matter of the heart, Jix knows she'll laugh last.

___52444-9 $5.50 US/$6.50 CAN

FRANKLY, MY DEAR...

SANDRA HILL

Selene has three great passions: men, food, and *Gone With The Wind*. But the glamorous model always finds herself starving—for both nourishment and affection. Weary of the petty world of high fashion, she heads to New Orleans. Then a voodoo spell sends her back to the days of opulent balls and vixenish belles like Scarlett O'Hara. Charmed by the Old South, Selene can't get her fill of gumbo, crayfish, beignets—or an alarmingly handsome planter. Dark and brooding, James Baptiste does not share Rhett Butler's cavalier spirit, and his bayou plantation is no Tara. But fiddle-dee-dee, Selene doesn't need her mammy to tell her the virile Creole is the only lover she gives a damn about. And with God as her witness, she vows never to go hungry or without the man she desires again.